PRAISE FOR

ZACHARY KLEIN'S
MATT JACOB SERIES

STILL AMONG THE LIVING

"Matt Jacob, a private eye from Boston, makes his debut in a novel that offers rich characterizations...if he can resist the impulse to turn Matt Jacob too straight too soon, the author can keep his singular detective on good cases for a long time."

—*The New York Times*

"I'd call it one of the best and certainly the most off-center detective novels I've read...Klein's is a terrific idea—have Jacob work on two very different mysteries at once, the deep human disorders disturbing him and the case he's called upon to solve... Klein's private eye and his prickly prose are original. Savor 'Still Among the Living' and pray this is not the last we will read of Matt Jacob."

—*Boston Globe*

"Matt Jacob is a terrific character with a lot of life in him beyond this book."

—*Globe and Mail*

TWO WAY TOLL

"Entertaining...Matt Jacob comes across as a heartfelt creation...A refreshing character in a genre rife with male posturing and two dimensional psychology."

–*The New York Times*

"[A] real payoff...The return of Matt's whole entourage guarantees pleasure for fans of Klein's first."

—*Kirkus Reviews*

"Klein returns with another compelling tale featuring private detective Matt Jacob."

—*Publishers Weekly*

NO SAVING GRACE

"Like Phillip Marlowe, Matt seems to take every case as an invitation to look deeper inside himself."

—*Kirkus Reviews*

"Jacob is a man in search of himself as much as he is in search of solutions. When the perpetrators are revealed, the surprise is real and discomfiting; as the title states, the truth offers No Saving Grace."

–*Hadassah Magazine*

TIES
THAT
BLIND

A MATT JACOB NOVEL

TIES
THAT
BLIND

A MATT JACOB NOVEL

ZACHARY
KLEIN

Copyright © 2015 by Zachary Klein
Cover and jacket design by 2Faced Design
Interior formatted by Tianne Samson with E.M. Tippetts Book Designs

ISBN 978-1-940610-26-9
eISBN 978-1-940610-49-8

First trade paperback edition March 2015 by Polis Books, LLC

1201 Hudson St.
Hoboken, NJ 07030
www.PolisBooks.com

POLIS BOOKS

The Matt Jacob series by Zachary Klein

Still Among the Living
Two Way Toll
No Saving Grace

To Susan Goodman whose faith in me has withstood the test of time. Life without you would be no life at all.

And a special dedication to my cousin Hank Ashen; his life was a reminder that refusing to risk is refusing to really live. I miss you.

Finally I'd like to acknowledge Sherri Frank whose time, help, and support were instrumental in the writing of this book. Thank you.

CHAPTER 1

Lovemaking had slammed my ass to sleep. A good sleep, deep enough that I hadn't heard the ring of Boots's cell phone, not so deep that I couldn't feel her body crawl across my own. I lifted my hands to stroke her buttocks, grew confused when she twisted out of reach, then dimly understood when she grabbed the phone. Still, I turned to hide my disappointment. A disappointment that instantly disappeared when she poked me with the cell.

"It's Lou," she said, worry flooding her hazel eyes and smooth face. "And he sounds serious."

I couldn't ignore the belly-dread. Lou was my dead wife's father, the money-half of our partnership in two attached six-flats we both called home. It was much too late for the call to be about the buildings.

"Why didn't he call my phone?"

"He knows you keep it off—now take the damn thing!"

"Lou? Are you all right?" I stared blankly as Boots swung out of bed and bent her lean, limber body to pull on a pair of thigh-high jeans while I tried to push the image of Mrs. S.'s funeral out

1

of my head.

"I'm fine," Lou wheezed. "I hate to bother you this time of night, but I need a *mitzvah*."

I closed my eyes with relief and didn't notice Boots trying to get my attention until she tugged my arm. "Is Lou okay?" she whispered. "He called me Boots, not Shoes."

I raised my eyebrows and shrugged.

"Matty," Lou continued anxiously, "Lauren's son is on the other telephone line bleeding from knife wounds. She'll keep him on the telephone until you pick him up and bring him to the hospital."

"Who are you talking about?"

"I'll explain, but please, first will you do what I asked?"

I shook my head in bewilderment. "Okay. You know where he is?"

"At a bar in The Plain. Jimmy's on Washington, near Forest Hills Station. The boy says he's standing in an old fashioned phone booth, one with a door."

I hadn't thought any of those were left in our new digital age. "Lou, an ambulance makes more sense."

"Sense doesn't matter here, the kid won't deal with anyone in a uniform. You can understand that. And you'll have to bring him to Beth Israel. He won't go anywhere else."

"Why doesn't his mother pick him up?"

"We're at Lauren's house on the North Shore. It will take too long to get there."

"He'll come with me?" I took one of the lit cigarettes Boots was holding and dragged deeply, my initial fear and Forest Hills's cemetery receding into nervous apprehension.

"Lauren promises by the time you get there she'll have him ready and willing." He paused then added proudly, "She's not wrong about much, *boychick*, she won't be wrong about this. Anyway, you look shaggy enough for him to trust."

His tone troubled me more than the words. "Lou, if the kid

was stabbed someone has to call the cops."

There was a momentary pause. "Matty, he did this to himself."

After a long moment I quietly asked again, "Who are these people?"

This time it was the words, not his tone, that got to me.

"He called her his '*squeeze*," I said, wrestling into my pants. "What the fuck is he talking about?"

Boots sat cross-legged on the bed, her back pressed against the modern metal headboard. By now she was wearing a beige tank top that left a strip of her flat, tan stomach exposed. "Squeeze means girlfriend. You're not that out of touch."

"I know the definition, smart-ass. Only Lou's never mentioned a girlfriend. I've never even heard of this lady."

"You keep calling her 'this lady.' She has a name, doesn't she?"

I stopped tying my sneaks and glanced up. "Lauren. Her name is Lauren. Where's the dope?"

Boots frowned, raising slight ridges on her forehead. "You've been pretty good, Matt. Why not wait until you get back?"

"I don't know if I'm coming back. I might have to take Lou home or something."

"You don't have weed at your apartment?"

I returned her smile with a quick, worried grin of my own. "Then light me another cigarette, okay?"

The ride across town was a smooth sail—no post 9/11 twenty-four, seven patrol cars, detours, or potholes..—Other than the cops, much like the past years. Boots and I met after Chana, my wife, and Rebecca, my daughter died; a period in my life when I could barely collect rent in the building Lou had bought just to keep me busy and out of trouble. Though depression wasn't Boots's vice, during those years she had her own form of protection—Hal. Old enough to be her father, vaguely married, always on time. Therapy and years had eased some of my gloom, and Boots had long since shed Hal. Now things were going so well that, for the first time in what seemed like forever, I'd been thinking our longtime, on again, off again relationship was gonna keep. Neither of us was direct, but lately conversations were sprinkled with veiled references and humorous quips about our stability.

And I'd still managed to tamp down my drug use, though it cost me a small fortune for cigarettes. Who'd a thunk I'd been able to become somewhat straight—though very somewhat. From the jump I didn't do intimate alliances all that well, and the closer they veered into "family," the further I usually leaped in the opposite direction.

No real surprise. The only fond memories from my own original family were stories about my grandfather's rabid love affair with baseball. How he'd sit in the darkened front room smoking his pipe, head cocked toward his tubed radio inning after inning, game after game.

Hell, I was even a little like him. I collected old-fashioned Bakelite radios and followed baseball. But I usually sat across from a television and filled my pipe with marijuana. Tobacco I bought pre-rolled.

Lou was the nearest thing to family since the accident. We'd always liked each other, our relationship bound by mutual love for Chana, my second wife. But our friendship hadn't blossomed until the death of his wife Martha, his move to the building from Chicago, and a serious boundary war which ended after Mrs. S.'s surprise death. She'd been Lou's closest friend in town and though almost a year had passed, I thought he was still mourning. I guess I was wrong. So here I was, hard into the night, driving to some godforsaken gin mill to fetch a failed suicide—a failed suicide who was talking on the phone with his mother. My father-in-law's secret squeeze.

4

CHAPTER 2

L ou said the bar was close to Forest Hill Station, but it wasn't close enough. When the city moved the overhead El ten blocks north into a neatly coifed, middle class trench, it promised the working people, working people who now had to trudge an extra ten blocks, they would dismantle the useless metal girders that kept Washington Street in perpetual dusk. The Pols also promised an end-to-end refurbishing of the dilapidated buildings that lined much of the boulevard. They did remove the hulking overhead, but only partially kept the rest of their rehabilitation promise; the half that gentrified in the frenzied speculation that follows any large urban development project.

I was cruising the city's unkempt half looking for Jimmy's among carwashes, warehouses, and the Transit Authority's bus barn. It took two passes before I finally spotted the hole-in-the-wall tavern nestled on a small side street. Somehow, I didn't think the bar attracted too many first-timers.

My hunch was confirmed when I opened the door, caught a couple of quick looks from the human barstools, then was immediately ignored as soon as it became apparent I wasn't a member of the tribe. I had wondered how the kid had gotten to a telephone booth without attracting attention. Now I knew; if you weren't a regular you weren't there.

It took a couple of seconds to see through the smoke filled haze, a couple more to fight a sharp urge for a double Wild Turkey when the heartwarming smell of booze and tobacco hit my nose. Then I reminded myself there wasn't a chance in hell the joint served my beast. No matter what the label promised. Whoever owned this dump was paying serious scratch to let the barstools light up wasn't gonna serve the real deal.

I don't know what I expected when I pulled on the flimsy, folding telephone door, but it wasn't the well-built long-hair wearing a blood soaked karate outfit and open-toe sandals. His age also threw me. I'd imagined Lou's "kid" as a sixteen year old. This robed Schwarzenegger was in his late twenties..

He looked at me with zonked-out eyes and tried to close the door with trembling fingers, but I kept my foot flush to the cheap slatted wood. The receiver dangled at the end of its coiled metal cord and I heard a woman's firm, controlled, "Ian, Ian, are you still there? Stay with me, Ian!"

I reached past the swaying Ian and grabbed the phone. "This is Matt Jacob. Your son is conscious, but he's in pretty bad shape. There's a lot of blood on his... his..."

"Gi, the robe he wears," the woman interrupted impatiently. "Could you see if the knife is in his stomach? He told me he threw it away, but I'm not sure he really knows what he's saying."

I carefully opened the "gi" and peered at his bloody body. Knife marks scored his muscular abdomen as if he had used his belly for a game of tic-tac-toe. Although the scratches oozed, most of the wounds appeared superficial. Two gashes didn't. They looked ugly and deep. I pulled my first-aid kit—a dishtowel from Boots's apartment—out of my back pocket and pressed it against his belly.

Then I tried to get him to hold the towel in place. Ian's grip was ineffectual so I wedged part of my body into the booth, held his hand on the towel with one of my own, and grasped the receiver with the other.

"The knife is out but a couple punctures look pretty serious. Shattuck Hospital is a lot closer than Beth Israel."

"No, please! Ian wants to go to B.I. He trusts their emergency room."

I looked at the bleeding Jesus and decided not to waste time arguing. "Beth Israel it is, lady."

"Thank you, Matthew. Ian can be volatile, and I'm afraid if you take him where he doesn't want to go..."

I looked at the swaying boy. It's tough to raise a stink if you're out on your feet, but I swallowed my caustic rejoinder. She *was* his mother. "Okay," I replied defeated, "we'll meet you at the hospital."

"Thank you. You're as kind as Lou said."

I jammed the receiver back into its cradle. Right then I wasn't feeling all that kind; I was worried the kid would die in my car.

I draped Ian's arm around my shoulders, placed mine around his muscular waist, and half dragged him through the dingy joint while its customers kept their eyes fixed on their boilermakers. They had their own empty lives to wash away, let the barkeep scour a stranger's blood.

I squeezed Ian's big bleeding body into the small back seat and laid him down as gently as possible while his tears mixed with small moans. I felt relieved he was conscious and silently cursed his mother for not calling an ambulance.

I jumped behind the wheel and glanced into the rearview mirror. My stomach lurched when I saw the entire side of my face slathered with blood. I didn't wipe it off, just hoped no cop noticed me on the way to the hospital.

I was familiar with city's medical center emergency room so was surprised by the calm wooden paneling of Beth Israel's. When the automatic doors swung open as I dragged him inside, a nurse with two orderlies pushing a gurney rushed forward as if they'd been waiting. I felt sticky, then anxious, when I noticed a security cop watching the scene from across the room. I walked to the desk and, before a beefy woman could grill me about insurance, asked where to wash.

I spent a very long time inside an oversized john equipped with a handicap stall. I stripped to the waist and scrubbed clean. Afterwards, I couldn't deal with wearing my ruined sweatshirt and settled for my less bloodied tee. I almost felt worse about the shirt than the kid; I didn't have too many comfortable, familiar companions and hated to throw one away.

Which probably accounted for the scowl on my face when I strode out of the bathroom and saw Lou and a woman talking to the thick receptionist and the security guards. I automatically slowed at the sight and stared. Lou's "squeeze" looked young, supple, and her skin sparkled like a diamond. As I tentatively crept forward I realized how artfully she dressed. About five foot six, Lauren wore no makeup, loose fitting jeans, a thin black blouse, and a baggy, bleached denim jacket. Her hair was covered with a black satin scarf tied gypsy style. She probably drove a Volvo. The closer I edged, the older she looked, though appeared considerably younger than my father-in-law. Whatever her age, this was one *very* attractive woman.

"There you are, Matty." Lou's loud whisper echoed through the almost empty room. He sounded relieved as he lumbered toward me.

"There was no trouble at the desk, was there? Lauren called ahead to pave the way," he said, a tense smile crossing his face. "You see why it made more sense for you to pick him up than an ambulance, *boychick*?"

I leaned down and kissed his cheek. "Not really."

"You won't walk next to a hospital security guards. Imagine

the kid's reaction to a carload of uniforms."

It hadn't been the guards who'd brought me up short. "This "kid" was no "kid". Anyway, the deal only works if he doesn't drop dead from blood loss." Even as I spoke I caught myself staring over Lou's shoulder watching Lauren finish her conversation at the desk.

"I don't think he'll die. God, I hope not," Lou added anxiously, the relief of our meeting melting away. I knew both of us were thinking about Mrs. Sullivan.

Once Lauren moved in our direction I stopped paying attention to Lou's anxiety and started noticing my own. Whatever her concerns, she carried herself with an easy grace and confidence, though neither calmed me down. Lauren stopped next to Lou and took his hand. "They're working on him now," she said. "They probably have to operate."

"*Gutenu!*"

"It's a good sign he remained conscious," she added.

Lou dropped Lauren's hand and put his arm around her shoulder. I stared at my sneakers, saw new red Rorschach's, and felt a twinge of anger.

Lauren noticed. "You have Ian's blood all over you. I'm terribly sorry."

"Not to worry," I said, suddenly embarrassed by my attitude.

She looked me over carefully. "Aren't you cold?"

I shook my head. I didn't want to tell her about the ruined sweatshirt. I didn't want to speak to her at all.

Lauren emerged from Lou's protective cover and I spotted thick strands of black hair peeking out from under her scarf. I couldn't tell if they were dyed. Her coal black eyes punctuated a strong jaw and full lips. Still, there were a few tells: creases lining her neck, a small droop to the corners of her mouth, furrows across her brow. Of course, the worry lines were probably fears about her son. But if they were, the rest of her anxiety was well hidden.

Lauren rolled up the baggy sleeves of her jacket and stuck out her hand. "We haven't formally met. I'm Lauren Rowe. The boy you retrieved is Ian Brown, my son. Thank you."

I noted the name shift as well as her long tapered fingers. I also noticed her strong, sure grip. "I'm Matt Jacob," I said, forcing myself to speak. "I hope everything works out okay."

"It's too late for that," Lauren replied. Then, spotting Lou's alarm added, "I don't mean the operation, sweetheart. Ian will be okay." She smiled sourly. "There are some things a mother knows. Even a lousy one."

Lou grimaced, "You aren't a lousy mother."

"Look at where we are," Lauren waved her hand around the emergency room. "And think about why we're here."

Lou shook his head stubbornly. "Don't be foolish. I saw the way you reacted when the boy called. The way you spoke to him, settled him down. You never lost your composure."

I stepped forward. "Maybe we can find a more comfortable place to wait. Did they give you a time frame?"

Lauren appeared grateful for the interruption and flashed a warm smile which, though weary, added to her appeal. "You don't have to wait around, Matthew. You've already been more than helpful."

"Don't be silly," Lou cut in. "Of course he'll stay."

I didn't know whether to feel angry at Lou's presumption or pleased by the undercurrent of pride in his voice. I shoved the former on hold and conceded to the latter. "I wouldn't feel comfortable leaving without knowing whether Ian, uh..."

"Survives," she finished grimly.

I glanced away, "Yeah."

Just then, the large glass doors to the emergency room swiveled open and a tall, athletic, silver-haired man wearing a black sport coat, checkered sport shirt, and jeans barreled through. The man paused, then walked rapidly to our small circle. Lauren raised her tweezed eyebrows, glanced at Lou's wristwatch, then nodded her greeting.

"How is he?" the man asked Lauren but glaring at Lou.

"They won't know anything for a while. I think he'll be all right."

"That's reassuring," he snapped, turning his attention back to her.

Lauren's mouth tightened. "Don't get nasty with me. *I'm* the one he called. Where the hell have you been?"

Before silver-hair answered, Lauren leaned toward Lou and me. "Paul, you already know Lou. This is his son-in-law, Matt Jacob. He picked Ian up and brought him to the hospital. Matthew, this is Paul, my former husband."

CHAPTER 3

I should have split when Lauren had given me the chance. Even Lou shifted from foot to foot. But before anyone broke the tense silence, a gown flapping doctor with a clipboard rushed up.

"I'm Dr. Schneider and I'll be doing the surgery on..." he glanced at his papers, "Ian. They're prepping him now." The doc kept his eyes on the clipboard while he gave us a moment to register his announcement.

Lauren twisted toward Paul, stared coldly, then returned her attention to the White Coat. Me? I was real sorry I'd listened to Boots about the dope and doubly sorry I'd talked myself out of Jimmy's bourbon, whatever the fucking brand.

"We'll have to go in," Dr. Schneider said somberly. "He's lost a great deal of blood, but we don't know where it's from." He added curtly, "It makes a difference..."

I barely heard the rest of his words.

"...Stomach, liver, vital organs... young, strong, in and out of consciousness... I'm sorry to say there are no guarantees," Dr. Schneider warned.

The surprise of learning about Lauren's existence, rushing Ian to the hospital, the night's thick, pungent blood, the doctor's "we just don't know, no guarantees" pushed past my guard, shoving me back to the countless hours I'd spent glued to an uncomfortable hospital couch. Stuck helplessly, hopelessly for Chana and Rebecca.

"We just don't know, Mr. Jacob." I could still hear the doctor's words after all these years. *"We have nothing in the way of guarantees in situations like these."*

They claimed not to know, but it was a lie. Those doctors said everything was a "maybe." And *that* was a lie. Everything was a when, and I'd known it the moment I saw them lying in the Intensive Care Unit. I knew what I was waiting for during those interminable days and nights. I was waiting for them to die. Strapped onto beds, invaded by plastic tubes, obscenely scoped through cold scraps of metal machinery, and monitor screens. Their deaths had been the unspoken guarantee.

My memories triggered the same bitter rage and I felt it trickle through my veins. Soon after Chana and Becky died, that rage had me booked for assault and battery charges brought by a bartender who'd refused me a drink. But I was lucky. My longtime friend and high-powered attorney, Simon Roth, called in the outstanding paper and made it disappear. When I couldn't face returning to social work, Simon pulled another ace and bought me a new career as a private investigator. My part of the deal was therapy. Four long years of it, I reminded myself, biting back the growing bile.

"Are you okay, Matty?" Lou asked quietly.

"Yeah," I lied, relieved to be dragged back into the room. "I'm just tired of standing." I wanted armrests for my clenched fists.

The doctor pointed toward a hallway. "There's a waiting room a couple of doors down on your left. Don't bother asking for information," he said to no one in particular. "I'll tell you as soon as I know something."

I started down the hall while the Gown walked briskly in

the opposite direction. I wasn't sure if the rest of the group was following, but I knew my ghosts weren't far behind.

The next few hours were a bone tired crawl. Lauren sat on the floor, straight-backed, hugging her knees on a tired braided rug right in front of a brown, Scotch-guarded couch. Most of the time she kept her eyes closed.

Paul slouched on the sofa behind Lauren, his long legs stretched alongside her rigid body. Lou sat in a chair, a respectful distance from the two. I sprawled across another hard settee on the other side of the room. Paul's legs constantly jiggled though he wore a bored expression occasionally interrupted by a hostile glance toward Lou or me. Once in a while he'd brush against Lauren and she would purposely shift her body out of reach. When the general tension and Lauren and Paul's dance became too much to take, I slipped out of the building for a cigarette.

It wasn't much better. Chain smoking next to a hospital's emergency room in this day and age, even on a quiet night, wasn't a relax. Despite the cool, deep-night air, anxious sweat feathered my body. I crushed my second cigarette under heel and reluctantly returned to the waiting room.

Something had gone down during my absence. Paul was pacing, angrily pushing empty chairs out of his way and glaring back and forth from Lauren to Lou. He continued his tantrum until he reached the coffee machine, shoved some coins into its slot, and slapped the plexi with his palm. "If you teach these bastards respect, they don't steal your money."

"Damn," he cursed, as a tilted cardboard cup slid through the chute. I watched as Paul futilely tried to right the cup before he lost all the coffee. His hand was lucky machines kept everything lukewarm.

Lauren now sat in the corner of my couch, long fingers covering her face. If she was aware of her ex-'s act, she kept it to herself. Lou seemed torn between joining Lauren and remaining where he was.

"Have you heard something from the doctor?" My throat felt tight but I sounded okay.

Lauren moved her hands, met my eyes, and shook her head.

"Nothing from the doctor," Paul said pointedly. He looked as if he would continue talking if I pressed, but the only press was my silence. So he stood there, empty wet cup in hand, seeing me, really, for the first time.

"You picked Ian up from the bar?" he asked.

"Yeah."

"He give you shit?"

"He was out on his feet."

"Lucky you."

"Paul!" Lauren jerked upright in one harsh, powerful motion.

Paul quickly swung his attention toward her. "Ian isn't easy to be with, and you know it. If I picked him up he would have raised hell. Out on his feet or not." When he turned back after a long pause, his eyes looked genuinely unhappy.

Lauren wasn't buying. "You just can't stop complaining about the children, can you?"

"The boys, Lauren, just the boys." Paul's remorse scurried behind his sarcasm.

Lou finally made up his mind, sat down next to Lauren, and took her hand.

"I don't know why I'm holding onto this," Paul said nodding toward the wet cardboard, ignoring Lou's place change. He threw the sog into the trash can, wiped his palm on the back of a chair, then rummaged through his pockets. "Damn, I'm out of change."

I failed to fish enough coins for two. I despised vending machine coffee, only I hated having nothing to do even more. Lauren leaned into Lou's bulk, resting her head on his shoulder. Every so often he'd run his fingers across her cheek. Watching them, I suddenly felt a disquieting kinship with Paul and amazed by Lauren's connection to Lou.

"I think there's a bill changer," I said walking over to the machines.

Paul slapped his pants. "I ran out of the house so fast I forgot my wallet."

"And if you'd brought it," Lauren muttered audibly, "you'd only have a twenty."

"I have plenty of singles," I said quickly. The damn night was threatening to dredge up *both* my marriages. But before I had time to feed the machine, Dr. Schneider strode through the door.

"He's okay," Schneider announced. He still wore his gown, but now it was blood splattered. Ian's no doubt. I wondered if that made me and the doctor blood brothers once removed.

"But just okay," he added before any of us could relax. "The wound almost hit an artery."

"Where was he bleeding from?" Lauren asked calmly, her row with Paul forgotten.

"Stomach." Schneider looked around the room. "I'd like to speak with the parents privately if you don't mind."

"Of course," Lou spoke for the two of us. "We'll be in the hall." He patted Lauren's shoulder then started for the door. I began to follow but the doctor grabbed my arm. "You brought Ian in, didn't you?"

"Yes." After poking around someone's insides he didn't need his papers to remember the name.

"Where did you come from?"

"The Plain."

"There are plenty of good hospitals over there. Why did you drive all the way here?"

"I made that decision, Doctor," Lauren said succinctly, taking me off the hook.

"Well, you were extremely lucky," Dr. Schneider remonstrated, still looking at me. "Ian lost quite a bit of blood."

I kept my mouth shut, walked into the hallway, and joined

Lou.

Out of someone else's fire, into my own. Lou leaned against the wall, a wary look on his tired, pale face. "Nu?" he asked.

"I need a cigarette."

"You can't light up in here."

"I'm going outside."

He pushed himself off the wall. "I'll keep you company."

"You look pretty wiped out. It's okay if you want to wait here."

"I said I'll go with you," he answered testily.

I didn't know why he was annoyed at me. This was his gig, after all.

Lou followed me to my secluded outdoor corner and wheezed while I lit up. "I'm doing the smoking, how come you're breathing like a bull?" I asked.

He ignored my question. "You shouldn't smoke. So what do you think?"

"I think I'm exhausted and want a big fat joint and a bottle of bourbon."

He tiredly rubbed his hand across his face.

"I'm sorry, Lou. This has been rough on you."

His face relaxed as he misread my meaning. "*Boychick*, you can't imagine how difficult it's been to tell you about Lauren."

"I meant the stabbing," I said, instantly uncomfortable.

Lou shrugged. "I'm old enough to know situations like this are part of any package."

I dropped the cigarette onto the ground and carefully toed it out. "This package ain't exactly tied with a ribbon, Louie."

He shook his head. "You keep talking about tonight. I mean my, uh, my..."

"Squeeze," I supplied.

Lou looked sheepish. "I just heard the expression and it popped into my head when we were on the phone."

"What else are you popping?" I snapped before thinking.

17

"From here it looks like you're in *above* your head."

Lou stepped out of the circle of light. "This doesn't happen all the time, Matty."

"The woman looks half your age, for Christ sake."

"That young?" Lou asked, his pleasure evident.

"No, but plenty younger than you."

"Is that a sin?"

No sin, maybe a blessing. I clamped a bit onto my attitude. "I don't know," I said, fighting off another wave of fatigue. "She is beautiful," I admitted.

"What's so wrong?" Lou asked stepping into the light. "I didn't run out looking after Martha died. I didn't look at all. Lauren and I met, we had a pleasant conversation, and one thing led to another."

"Where did you meet?" I asked.

"Charley's."

Charley's was a breakfast joint owned by Phil, both a friend and an ex-cop who was my conduit to our local police. A break for me since I stayed as far away from cops as I could. A legacy from the seventies, and eighties,, and nineties. I knew why Lou ate there, "great *traif*," but Lauren didn't look like 'grease and grill.' Course, I didn't know what Lauren really was—just that I felt uncomfortable about and around her. But before I could wriggle away from Lou's hopeful gaze, the doors swung open and she and Paul walked into the night.

"There you are. We looked all through the building." Lauren was visibly relieved by the doctor's prognosis and her smile gleamed bright through the darkness. "I'm glad you didn't leave."

Paul didn't appear nearly as happy.

"Don't be silly," Lou replied. "I would never leave without you."

His words hung in the air before Paul, visibly tense, broke the silence. "Look, I didn't thank you back there," he said to me. "I appreciate what you did tonight."

"Enough to replace his shirt?" Lauren bit, her smile gone. "He's not wearing a bloodstained undershirt for fashion."

"No problem, Lauren," I hastily intervened. "It was just an old sweatshirt."

"That's not the point."

He didn't look pleased but Paul nodded. "Send me the bill. Look, I have to get some sleep. You heard the doctor, it's senseless to wait around."

He stepped closer to Lauren. "I'll take you home. We can pick your car up tomorrow."

Lauren shook her head and took Lou's arm. "I'm going to Lou's house if it's okay with him."

Paul didn't wait for Lou's answer. He shook his head, shrugged, swiveled, and walked into the night.

Lou just stood beaming. It was better than okay, much better.

CHAPTER 4

More okay by him than by me, I grumbled to myself late the next morning, contorting my body into a car cleaning position. A tough fit. The lingering late summer, early autumn sun scattered through my alley, working its magic on my faint but persistent headache. Faint because I hadn't allowed the return from Beth Israel to become open season for my Holy Trinity of television, alcohol, and pot. Persistent because we weren't talking abstinence either. Actually, the real head-banger was about my discomfort with the surprising, unexpected turn in Lou's life.

"His life, his life," I reminded Mr. Clean. I rubbed my father-in-law's proud face from my eyes and stared at the blood on the back seat. My long time campanero and mechanic, Manuel, scored an impeccably restored, black '2002ti after my old car caught a slew of bullets. He swore the ancient Bimmer had my name on it, insisting I needed a car to *drive*, not ride, if I planned to remain a P.I. And Manny said it in English. When we first met we'd agreed to help each other learn the other's native tongue, but only one of us made it.

I'd come to like the lively little square, but always felt a twinge of class guilt about driving a B.M.W., regardless of its age. Well, no relationship is perfect, I thought, which unfortunately brought me right back to Lou. I twisted onto the rear floor and worked the seat while pecking away at my reaction. Lauren wasn't *that* much younger than Lou despite her good looks. Somewhere in her middle fifties, I guessed. We weren't talking much more than twenty-some years here. Probably sported Spandex at a yoga class a few times a week.

I tasted my disdain and tried to swallow. I felt protective of Lou; but my reaction was more complicated than that, shaded with hints of stronger hurts and fears—stuff to avoid. So I scrubbed up a sweat—better success at something than nothing at all. Eventually, I uncorked my body back into the fresh air, reached into the glove compartment, and retrieved a joint. Before I sat down I took a last look at the damage. Manny was sure to shoot me a soulful look. The rear of the car, while acceptable, was no longer pristine.

Well, neither was I. I sat on the gravel, leaned against the oversized front tire, and welcomed the sun's rays—another twenty-first century cancer monger but I wasn't counting. I kept my eyes closed while I toked, letting myself fall into a pleasant swirl until, with a start, I realized I was high.

My eyes snapped open, the dead joint in my hand framed by a jean covered pelvis. I raised my head, my eyes meeting Lauren's amused face. A strong face that now wore a light shade of lipstick and a hint of rouge. I quickly stood up, caught the whirlies, and carefully slid my ass onto the fender.

"Smells like good dope," Lauren smiled.

"Pretty good." My foot had fallen asleep so I pushed further back onto the hood to take off the weight. Somehow I wasn't surprised by her familiarity with marijuana. "You look pretty good."

"Thanks, but you don't have to move away, I don't bite."

I grinned, but stayed where I was. "Who you kidding? I watched you nibble last night."

Lauren returned the smile. "Extenuating circumstance. Paul and I are usually pretty good friends."

I ignored her casual description of Ian's suicide attempt. "Isn't that a little unusual?

"Not really." Lauren seemed no more eager to pursue last night than I was. "Over the last twenty five years or so there have been more rearrangements than total breakups among our old friends."

"Rearrangements?" I took my flattened cigarette pack from my pant pocket, tilted them toward Lauren, then lit one for myself after she shook me off.

"Call it what you want. Paul's been living with Anne Heywood for a long, long time. We were all close friends before the breakups and we still see a lot of each other. I don't believe in throwing away whole chunks of your life."

I grunted noncommittally. The idea of a friendship with my first wife, Megan, left me scratching my head. The same feeling I'd had when she fucked her way out of my life.

"Look," Lauren continued, noting my distrust. "We laughed together, played together, argued together, and raised our children together. There was, is, no reason to reject your entire world because marriages don't always work." She moved a couple of steps closer to the Bimmer. "I've been happy for Paul and Anne and glad they're part of my life."

"You don't have to explain," I said, growing uneasily aware of Lauren's attractiveness and my response. I immediately wanted to talk about anything—including Ian—rather than her personal life. But Lauren was quick to remind me I was part of that life.

"I'm not trying to explain, I'd like you to know who I am." She held her palms upward, "You don't seem thrilled about Lou and me. But I want you to know what you're judging."

I flipped the cigarette away from the car. "I'm not judging

anything." Disarmed by her directness, for that moment, I wasn't. But when I thought of the previous night's bitter interchanges with her ex-husband, today's "we're all friends," and my response to her charisma, my ambivalence rushed right back.

"You're being polite. Your karma is easy enough to read."

I wondered about Lou's notions of karma; he wasn't exactly an old New Ager. "Lou means a lot to me."

"It goes both ways. You mean an enormous amount to him. He's pretty clear about that."

"Lou's usually clear about everything."

Lauren nodded. "When he says something you can actually count on it. You can rely on him." She grinned but there was sadness in her eyes. "It's not something I'm used to."

"Lou's a good man."

"Better than good." Lauren paused then added quietly, "That's why I want you to give me a chance. I want him in my life and if you and I don't get along, well..."

I was embarrassed. "I'd never interfere with Lou's friendships."

"We're more than friends, Matthew," Lauren said gently.

Someone pushed a shopping cart into the chain-link fence that separated the grocery store's parking lot and my back alley. The scraping rekindled my headache. I appreciated Lauren's straightforwardness, her caring toward Lou, apparently her good looks, but right then there was no shaking my distance.

"Lou makes his own decisions, Lauren."

She frowned and placed a hand on her cocked hip. "A touch disingenuous, don't you think? You're practically his entire life."

I was spared from responding by the crunch of footsteps on gravel. Lou appeared around a corner of the building and walked alongside Lauren. "I didn't realize you were back," he said. "How is the boy?"

Lauren smiled, but the troubled look never left her eyes. "Ian's doing great. I can bring him home in a few days."

"That's terrific! He must be strong."

"Lou," I blurted, "the *boy* tried to kill himself!"

Maybe it was the leftover stain on the car seat, maybe it was seeing them together, or maybe the ease with which they talked about bringing Ian home, but my criticism was harsh, and it stung. I saw Lou frown and Lauren's hand pull off the scarf. Her thick, black hair dropped almost to her shoulders, youthful, despite wide streaks of natural gray. No more suspicions about dye.

"Don't sound so damn sanctimonious," Lauren said mildly. "I've already been in contact with a therapist. He'll see Ian as soon as possible."

I slid off the fender onto my wide awake feet. "I'm sorry, Lauren, I was out of line."

She reached up and placed her hand on my shoulder. "That's okay. You did me a huge favor and got rewarded for it with a ruined shirt, bloody car seat, and an ugly scene between me and Paul. I owe *you* the apology."

I willed myself to leave my shoulder where it was. "How about no apologies, period? Ian's okay, the car's okay."

"That sounds good to me," Lou said, relieved. He nudged Lauren, "Did you tell him?"

Lauren removed her hand, "No, Lou. I told you it's probably my imagination."

"What if it is? It can't hurt to talk."

"Tell me what?" I lit a cigarette and eyed them warily through wisps of smoke.

"It feels as if someone has been stalking me," Lauren reluctantly admitted. "I know it's absurd, but I can't get rid of the sensation."

Lou chimed in, "This is no one or two day thing, Matty. It's been going on for a while. I'm pretty sure I felt it too when we've been out together."

I wanted to tell him paranoia was contagious but instead groped for something polite. "How long has it been happening? Is it regular?" I sounded like a fucking doctor.

Lauren gave no sign of noticing my skepticism. "Maybe six months. I can't date it exactly."

"But you've never actually seen anyone?"

"I told you it sounded foolish," Lauren said with a quick toss of her head.

"Matt's not saying you're foolish," Lou disagreed. "He's asking for information. That's how he does his job."

I glanced toward Lou and confirmed my fear. He wanted to deal me in. "Let's slow down a little. Have you *seen* anybody following you?" Right then I didn't want to be dragged into Lauren's life through any door.

Lauren shook her head. "No," she grimaced, "but I'm not prone to delusions."

I didn't care *what* she was prone to. My game plan was "in again, out again, Finnegan." "Does anyone have reason to stalk you?"

She paused. "Not that I can think of."

"But you feel it all the time?"

"Not all the time. Sometimes."

"Is there a pattern?"

She tilted her head appreciatively. "I've never thought about that."

I plotted my escape. "Well," I said, all business, "keep track of the situation. See if there is any rhythm or pattern."

"That's all?" Lou asked, dissatisfied. "I thought you would look into this, Matty."

"First things first," I replied.

"He's right, Lou. Who knows? Maybe it will be like a toothache, hurts until you get to the dentist, then goes away."

I wasn't thrilled with Lauren's metaphor, but at least she wasn't forcing me to sign on.

Lauren stuck her hand in my direction. "I have to change

clothes before I can walk into that hospital again. It's been nice talking to you, Matthew, and I'll take your advice."

She let go of my hand and hugged Lou. "You don't have to go back with me tonight."

"You're going to drive back and forth and again tomorrow?" he asked.

"Maybe I'll just stay at the hospital."

"Don't be silly. You'll come here after your visit. We'll have tea."

"It may be late."

"It's never too late to boil water."

Lauren smiled appreciatively then kissed Lou on the lips. I was okay until he kissed back. I turned away and heard Lauren chuckle, "I think we're embarrassing Matt."

I watched them walk toward the front of the buildings before turning my attention back to the car. I had finished gathering the cleaning materials when I heard Lou approach.

"You had time to talk?" he asked.

"You knew she was back here?"

He nodded. "I want you to get to know each other. It doesn't help to have me hovering around."

"It's been a long time since you hovered over anything."

"Oh, I don't know about that." A wide smile lit his grizzled face and he winked.

"You're a dirty old man," I said grinning in spite of myself.

"So *nu*? There's a problem with that?"

"What do you want from me?"

"I want you to tell me what you think of Lauren," he replied obstinately.

I chose my words carefully. "She's charming, forceful, a real looker, and direct. How's that?"

"You don't like her?"

"Her family situation makes me uncomfortable."

"What do you mean?"

"She has a grown kid who tried to kill himself then called her on the phone when he changed his mind. That's trouble, don't you think? And last night's scene between her and Paul was right out of *Who's Afraid of Virginia Wolf.* Today she tells me they're close friends. You need this?"

Lou sagged against the car. "You line it up one way and that's all you see. I can't say anything about the boy, I barely know him. The couple of times we met, he didn't talk much, just wandered around the house. Anyhow, Lauren's doing right by setting up the therapist. What else can she do?"

Lou caught his breath then continued. "As far as her friendship with Paul, since when are you Mr. Conventional? They got married young and lived together for a long time. Why shouldn't they be friends? You know better than most the changes there were in the seventies."

"Seventies?"

"Their marriage ended sometime in the early eighties."

"For a couple who haven't been together for this long they seem pretty attached."

"You make them sound like our buildings. So they're friends, big deal. Last night brought out the worst, that's all."

"And you accuse me of seeing things one way?"

"You don't know the rest of it. Since we've been together I feel alive. Not because Lauren's younger than me, but because she is enthusiastic about life. She's lived through hard times without forgetting how to enjoy, how to look ahead." Lou stopped speaking as another wide smile covered his face. "I sound like a teenage romantic, but I can't knock it. It's been a long time since I've gotten to know someone new, a long time since someone has been interested in me."

Lou was singing in the rain and I was freezing in the sunshine. Something old, something blue, something bitter was brewing. Something I still didn't want to think about. I was growing very tired and my mind kept circling the living room couch. I had plenty of Fritos, Diet Coke, and the last half of my joint.

I must have yawned because Lou, cheered by all his good fortune said, "You're tired, Matty. Why not take a little nap? Last night was rough on everyone." He started heading toward the house, stopped, and about faced. "One last thing. You didn't just tell Lauren to watch for a pattern because you wanted to put her off, did you?"

My words sounded like they came from a distant canyon. "Of course not, Bwahna."

CHAPTER 5

"It took you long enough to get here," Boots complained.

Though there wasn't much tooth to her bitch—when Boots was really angry she didn't have to speak—I grew defensive. Actually, the defensiveness I'd been carrying since Lou's late night telephone call just sprang to life. "I had some catching up to do."

"With what, NCIS repeats?"

I smiled, determined to keep the evening light. Boots was leaving on business the next morning, and I didn't want a lousy conversation to ruin our night. I took my traveling stash from my pocket, then removed my pants. "Of course. You think I can get by without my comforters?"

"I thought that was my job."

"Certainly." I reached under the elastic of my boxers, "Just ask Mr. Johnson."

"Put it away," Boots said unable to squash a smile. "I'm serious. It's been a long time since your phone's been turned off when we're not together."

I climbed on top of the covers and sat with my back against the headboard. "It's getting close to fall sweeps."

Boots didn't answer until she'd stripped down to her string bikini, a bright white exclamation to her naturally dark, tanned body. She walked to the doorway, her faintly muscled cheeks burying the scanty white, switched off the overhead light, and tied her auburn hair with a black top-knot. "I've been thinking of buying a television."

I felt my face flush, then hoped she couldn't spot it in the dusky room. Boots hated television. Never owned one. Never would own one except for me. This was her strongest signal yet about our relationship. Unfortunately, it came at a bad time. A real bad time.

"How do you tan your entire chest?" I asked inanely. Well, inane was better than running home in my underwear.

"I roll onto my back." Boots returned to the bed, and flopped beside me. "Light me a cigarette?" she asked.

Rotten timing or not, this just wasn't going to be a no talk night. I glumly reached over to the night table and lit two. I wanted to raid my stash, but hung in with the nicotine.

"Why aren't you saying anything about the TV?" she asked, studying her smoke.

"Where would you put it?" I finally asked, inanity still intact.

Boots pulled her eyes away from the orange glow of the cigarette tip long enough to flash me a searching look. "In here. I'd get the kind with earphones." She paused, then disguised her hesitancy. "What's happening, Matt? Did you go over the top with buds and booze?"

The image of sitting hooked to an earphone transformed into a picture of a plastic bag wrapped around my head. Suffocating me. "Not really. I've been okay," I answered, my eyes drawn to the dope. I rushed to change the subject. Both subjects. "I told you at dinner. Dealing with Lou and Lauren fucks with my head."

"You keep saying that, but you don't say why." Boots seemed relieved to drop the television talk too.

"I don't trust her. However young she looks, the lady is too damn old for her karma crap. This is a woman who married too soon, stayed too long, and seems lost without her old life. I'm afraid she's using Lou."

"For what?"

"I don't know, maybe she's scared to end up alone. Her ex is apparently living with one of their 'good old friends,' and if Ian is representative of their brood..."

"You don't know that."

"I don't. But I'm not talking about what I know. I'm talking about what I feel." I also felt I was dodging a bullet, without knowing where it was coming from, or what it could hit.

"I don't understand your problem," Boots countered. "Lauren sounds like a straight shooter. So what if she's old for New Age? That sort of thing helped lots of women take some important steps. It isn't easy to regroup after a shitty marriage. You know that."

I thought about Boots's long term affair with Hal and wondered whether she was talking about Lauren or herself. But before I could feel too self-righteous she leaned onto her side and looked up at me. "Lauren wasn't the only person who married young; you had your Megan."

"I didn't stay friends with her."

"You didn't have a choice."

"Low blow."

"Low blow," Boots agreed. "Listen honey, Lauren has kids, that makes a clean break impossible."

I was still rubbing my kidney. "I've basically let go of Chana and Rebecca and that seems a lot harder."

"It is and you have. That's why we're talking instead of me getting an earful of silence. I'm not saying you're off the wall, just jumping to conclusions."

"Lou didn't mention Lauren for more than six months. I'd say he has his own doubts."

"Or he didn't want to hurt your feelings."

"Hurt my feelings?"

"Matt, you, Mrs. S, and the buildings have been his entire life since he moved here from Chicago. Now Mrs. Sullivan is dead and all he had was you and supervising Charles. He needs more than that to have a life."

"You forgot Julius."

"Lou avoids Julius."

"But likes him."

"I'd call it respect mixed with intimidation."

"Same as me."

"Stop joking," Boots shook her head. "You've been Lou's world since Martha died and the man needs more. It's not Lauren's New Age talk or her ex-husband that's bothering you, your feelings are hurt."

They were, though I wasn't sure why. "Maybe you're right," I said, twisting toward the table, finally giving in to the weed. My nerves thanked me for the first-toke rush. "I guess I have to let it play out," I said after slowly releasing my breath.

Boots rolled over, reached down next to her side of the king-size, and came up with a sweating gin and tonic. "Live and let live," she toasted. "It's always been your motto."

"Right," I replied before taking another large lung-full.

Boots took a long swallow. "Doesn't it make you happy for him, even a little?"

I treated the joint like we were down to strikes instead of innings and chopped off its orange head with my fingernails. After a long pause I exhaled, satisfied to see very little smoke. "It should, but I smell trouble. And guilty for feeling this way." I suddenly felt embarrassed and vulnerable.

My admission satisfied her because in one of Boots's patented one-eighties, she leaned her head back exposing her long neck and smooth breast. "Do I smell like trouble?"

Her invitation didn't make everything else disappear, but did push it farther back. I aided and abetted by relighting the bone and taking another two quick tokes. "You are trouble," I answered, shrugging when I realized I meant it. Only right then I didn't know what kind; and right then didn't want to know.

If Boots noticed my shrug she ignored it. Instead, she wedged her head under my outstretched arm and reached down to my fly. "Enough talk, it's time to get that thing back out into the open."

I shook everything out of my mind as Boots turned and followed her hand with her head. She pulled on my cock and placed her lips around the top, her mouth overcoming any lingering thoughts. I grew hard, pushing past the cotton, startled by my degree of desire. I held myself in check but when Boots's teeth scraped lightly across my crown, I reached down, lifting and shifting her body. When her legs faced my head I opened her knees, and lightly rubbed my palm over her cloth covered mound.

I stroked skimpy material while she pulled off my shorts. We stayed that way for a time, gently touching each other, letting our heat build, catching a hint of something special. Boots was running her tongue up the underside of my hard when I tugged lightly on her panties. She shuddered, lifted her head, and looked back in my direction. "Put your tongue inside."

I grasped her sides, shifted her onto her knees, and slipped off her damp underwear. Her buttocks curved in front of me and I explored her feet, legs, and ass with my hands. Boots turned her head and leaned forward on her elbows, her mouth open, tongue touching her lips. I licked my hand to add to her moisture and reached between her thighs.

Moments passed before I lifted her up while I slid onto my back, lowering her knees to each side of my head.

I stayed mouth to moist for a long time, gently exploring both lips with my teeth, occasionally slipping my tongue inside. Each time, Boots would flatten her entire body, blacking out everything but her taste and smell and her excited mouth between my legs.

Boots moaned and slid her body lower, away from my lips. She nipped and sucked and scraped her teeth against me while I cupped her ass with both hands. She motioned for me to raise my knees and, when I did, she wriggled lower.

As I leaned forward and licked between her cheeks, Boots squirmed toward my ass. She was shuddering, both holes open, and I could feel her darting tongue replicate my motion. This was something new between us, and I could feel our passion overwhelm everything else.

In unspoken synchronization, we twisted to provide easier access. The room shattered and disappeared as we joined through the forbidden—a surrender to each other. All that existed was another abandoned barrier and the discovery of the unexplored.

Maybe it was the evening's earlier anxious vulnerability, or perhaps the vulnerability of newly crossed boundaries, but I clung to her, losing myself in our Mobius strip across the king size bed. Clinging until the fire in my mouth finally demanded thirst quenching lips. I broke our kinetic weave and reversed direction. Eyes open, our mouths melded as I entered her, both of us moving in hungry harmony until our bodies exploded.

Later that night, much later, long after Boots fell asleep, I retreated to the living room. Her spectacular living room. I quietly turned the lone low easy chair toward the glass wall and sat staring down at the Charles.

The first time Boots invited me up, the view took my breath away. Despite believing, wrongly, that Hal had paid for it. The slow, handsome river, tree-lined park, bustling Storrow Drive, the sparkling nighttime city lights. The illusion of presiding over undulating motion or eerie quiet still delivered a jolt. From my perch in Boots's living room, I could watch a soundless urban mambo as distinct as New England's four seasons. This wasn't the Big Apple where the core of the city might slow but never sleep. Boston kept hours.

And now Boston was asleep. Now there was nothing twinkling except my nerves and the city's iconic CITGO sign, so I smoked more dope, sipped a small 'Turkey neat, and unsuccessfully tried to sync my insides with the calm before my eyes.

Boots's talk of television hadn't washed away. Hell, I hadn't felt like running from her apartment since dirt. At the same time, our lovemaking had blown a hole in the plastic bag I'd pictured covering my head. Now I had no idea what I felt.

"You look bummed."

Boots's voice surprised me and I turned to see her in the doorway wearing a gray silk robe. Her hair, free of the top-knot, covered one of her sleepy eyes but there was no mistaking the worry. She looked frightened and frail. I had no desire to talk about my fears, hopefully enough heart to assuage hers.

Boots walked behind my chair and stood looking over my head, her hands on my shoulders. "It's very quiet out there, isn't it?" she asked. "Even The Big Dig."

I kept my eyes on all that quiet.

"When I woke up I got scared you went home."

"Without my pants?"

"I wasn't looking for your pants, I was reaching for you."

"Well, you found me. My running days are over." The second I said it my skin felt like tightly stretched tarp. "Especially when all I'm wearing is underwear," I forced.

Boots sat down on the floor and leaned her head on my thigh. She started to speak, changed her mind, and wrapped an arm around my leg. I couldn't tap my toe, much less run. I leaned over the low coffee table and lit two cigarettes. We sat silently smoking, the only noise in the sparse, Japanese accented room was the rustle when I'd pass the ashtray or run my free hand through her disheveled hair.

Maybe it was the time, the stillness, or the warmth of Boots's tight fingers on my calf, but my nerves slowly quieted. I wanted to wipe the worry from her face, lessen the fear from her grip. "The problem with Lou is more than hurt feelings, Boots. If I'm wrong about Lauren it changes things between him and me. If I'm right, then I'm gonna watch him take a beating."

A little of the tightness left her hand and Boots sighed as if making up her mind to say more about us. But I relaxed when she followed my lead.

"It doesn't have to change anything between the two of you."

"How am I supposed to act if he's serious about her?"

"The way you always act. Like family."

"I don't want more family."

"Does that include me?"

"You're different." I groped for words. "We're different."

"Maybe, maybe not, eh?"

I wasn't going to allow her to leave town, even for a couple of days, worrying about whether I'd be here when she returned. "No maybes about it, Boots," I said, hoping it was true. "Whatever is going on with Lou has nothing to do with us."

CHAPTER 6

I didn't know if it was true when I said it and, a couple of days into Boots's troubleshooting trip for Verizon, it was still too close to call. Boots's television talk had raised the stakes and our lovemaking called and doubled. When I got depressed, I generally stayed home, stayed stoned. This time I did stay home, but mostly straight, though my goddamn confusion drowned more than one good line from the movies I kept watching. The continual chitching almost seemed worse than completely surrendering. Still, I managed to nail a little luck during my mini-shutdown; Julius didn't deliver any new treats.

It would have been difficult to juggle consumption with appetite if he had. Julie had come with the buildings and years ago, after feeling me out, offered to pay his rent with dope. He'd made it clear that dealing was not his main bag, though I'd never been able to pin down exactly what his "main bag" was. Then or now. No matter, at the time and throughout the succeeding years, I believed his offer one of my few gifts from the gods. These days, I was a little less certain the gift came from heaven—but not all that much.

By the time Lou called I was actually feeling better. I figured the tension in his tone reflected annoyance with my less than enthusiastic response toward Lauren. But once he pounded into my apartment, jacket in hand, I knew better.

"There's no time for sitting," he grunted at my gesture toward the enamel top kitchen table.

"What's the matter?"

"I need a ride to pick up Lauren," he replied curtly.

"No sweat." I started to gather my carry-ons but he grabbed my arm.

"More *tsouris*," he said taking a deep breath.

I shot him a sharp look.

"Nothing like the other night. Lauren's car was broken into and she can't drive it."

"Where is she?"

"Here, in the city."

I pocketed my cigarettes and grabbed my keys.

"Better wear a raincoat," Lou said. "It's pouring and supposed to get worse."

Once he pointed it out, I heard the rain drumming against the house. I hadn't noticed it earlier. I suppose I'd been more shut down than 'mini.'

I pulled on my black and red baseball jacket, Boston cap, and led us out the alley door. We b-lined through the heavy rain to the B.M.W. and onto the street before I asked where we were headed. When he told me, I almost hit the brakes.

"What the fuck is she doing there this time of night?" There was a warehouse/gay nightclub/loft neighborhood, a short bridge from downtown. Although the area was "city" safe, non-cruising suburbanites usually stayed on the downtown side of the span.

"I didn't ask," Lou's voice a mixture of anxiety and anger. "I was never convinced that just looking for 'patterns' made any sense," he snapped.

"What are you talking about?" The rain was burgeoning into a late summer version of a Nor'easter, forcing me to keep my eyes on the road.

"What you told her to do about the stalking, dammit."

"Whoa, Lou, Lauren said she felt watched. What makes you think this has any connection?"

"The woman feels followed then someone breaks into her car. What should I think?"

For a second I shared some of his fear then tossed it aside. "Attempted auto theft?"

Lou used his annoyance toward me as a carry for his anxiety. "What else would you say? You didn't want to be bothered so you found an easy way to put her off."

I resisted an impulse to jam the accelerator to the floor. "You're overreacting. I've been less than gracious about Lauren and you're right to be angry, but don't let it affect your judgment. You've been to this neighborhood. We're not talking a straight white man's world." I had my own questions about what Lauren was doing in that section of town, but wasn't willing to add to his wrath.

My comment cooled him down and he squirmed into a more comfortable position. The wind rocked the car; the small wipers no match for the gusting rainfall. Magnificent lightning bolts streaked across the sky illuminating Boston's storybook skyline as thunder crashed overhead.

I detoured twice to avoid street floods caused by overflowing sewers—the price paid for ancient systems held together with insufficient funds. Very few of our "no new taxers" lived in threatened neighborhoods.

Lou's impatience jumped as we approached the bridge. "Lauren said it's a couple blocks past The Wharf."

"I know the place." During my social work days I'd counseled a guy who desperately wanted to cross-dress. He could sing and dance so I hustled hard and scored an audition with a local act.

39

Turned out he was terrific and landed a steady gig at The Wharf, a transvestite nightclub. My man assured me the absolute high point of his life was stripping off construction clothes and lip-synching Sinatra's *My Way* until he got to his bra and panties. The Wharf was happy, the act went national, and I got real alcohol instead of tan water. Might have been the salad days of my social work career.

I turned onto A Street and spotted Lauren's car. Couldn't miss it. Hers was the one severely beaten about the head and legs. I heard Lou stifle a groan and saw Lauren emerge from a dark double doorway as I splashed toward the rear of her wreck. She was dressed in a pair of pleated chinos, blue work shirt, and a light khaki blazer. Her clothes were no protection against the hard wind and driving rain.

Lou squeezed out of the Bimmer before it rolled to a stop. He ran to Lauren's side and pulled her toward my car. She resisted, shaking her head emphatically. I took my cigarettes and lighter from my pocket, placed them on the dash, and waded over. "How about the doorway?" I asked ending their disagreement.

The three of us leaned into the wet wind and sloshed to the semi-protected enclosure. Though the lightning and thunder had stopped, the storm continued to howl down the deserted street.

"I came for it and this is what I found," Lauren said pointing at her car and shivering. Her full hair was reduced to sopping, twisted strings. Her face was shiny wet, streaks of makeup blotching her cheeks. And she *still* looked pretty.

I pushed the rain dripping from my cap away from my eyes, turned, and stared. So much for my guess about a Volvo. The ancient Toyota's glass was shattered, the doors and fenders dented as if someone had used a metal baseball bat or lead pipe. The tires had been slashed so the car rested on its ankles. It looked like an interrupted torching, only torching had been out of fashion for a long, long while. These days destructors preferred bullets. As much I wanted to hold onto my skepticism, what I saw disturbed me.

"Wait here," I commanded. I ran to the Toyota and dragged open the door. The seats had also been slashed and the dashboard ripped apart leaving the wire harness exposed. The cheap am/fm dangled close to the floor hanging by a fistful of colored tangled wires. I opened the glove compartment, saw it had been left undisturbed, and stood thinking, momentarily oblivious to the pelting rain.

I stood there too long because when I looked up Lou and Lauren were next to me.

"What is it, Matty?" Lou asked.

"It's rain," I smart-assed. "Let's get into my car. This box isn't going anywhere."

While they both trotted toward the Bimmer I reached back inside Lauren's wreck and grabbed everything from the glove compartment.

"Here," I said. Lauren and Lou were crammed into the back seat and the inside of the B.M.W. felt humid and close. I cracked a window and lit a smoke from the pack on the dash.

"I've messed up your car again, haven't I?" Lauren said. "This has been a hell of a way to get to know one and other."

I turned to look at them and shrugged. "I hope you have insurance."

Lauren waved it off. "It's not worth the trouble. They'll give me enough money to buy a roller skate."

"Why didn't you wait from where you called?" Lou asked, still trying to shake excess water.

"I couldn't let the car sit there all by itself." She smiled wryly, "Sounds nuts, doesn't it?"

"Of course not," Lou reassured.

"Well, it wasn't on order, I said. "Nobody wanted it for parts."

"Just what I said on the way over," Lou scowled. "Maybe now you'll take Lauren seriously about being followed."

"I said it wasn't done for a chop-shop, Lou. It looks like the start of an old fashioned torching. Or the work of bashers who thought the owner was gay." But underneath my blasé` I was bothered by the viciousness of the beating.

"Matty, the radio is still there," Lou said, "and I saw you empty the glove compartment."

Lauren watched me carefully as I stubbornly shook my head. "Someone might have interrupted the party."

"Take it easy, honey," Lauren said, turning to Lou. "This is Matt's line of work. If he thinks it was gay bashers, it probably was. Anyway, since we talked about feeling followed, the feeling hasn't returned. It *was* like going to the dentist." Lauren's laugh sounded natural, but her eyes were opaque.

Which goosed my professional conscience. "Maybe Lou's right, Lauren. It doesn't make sense to take chances. When we call the cops about the car we might as well tell them about what's been going on."

"No!" Lauren shook her head vehemently. "We're not talking to the police about any of this."

I leaned against the door and lit another cigarette. "Why not? You'll need them for whatever couple of dollars you have coming."

"To hell with the insurance. The car was dying on its own, and I need a new one anyway," she sidetracked.

"*Shainele*, this may not be the best time for you to buy a new car," Lou said surprised by her outburst.

"I'll find the money, Lou."

"Whatever you do about the car, Lauren," I said, "why not tell the cops what you've been feeling?"

"Because it's gone away," Lauren retorted sharply. "There's no reason to embarrass myself in front of people who will just think I'm crazy."

There was something more to her refusal to speak with the police, but I nodded my willingness to leave.

Only Lou wouldn't let me. "Hold the phone," he ordered. "If

we're not reporting this, what are *you* going to do about it?"

The question hung in the air until Lauren snatched it. "Don't put Matthew on the spot, Lou. He's done enough."

Lou's large wet body turned in the tiny back seat. "If you don't want the police then Matty has to track this down."

"Listen to me Lou, I don't want Matthew to track anything."

Before their argument continued I jumped in. "I can check if anyone reported the incident."

"You mean check with the police and I don't want them involved," Lauren said adamantly. "I want to forget the whole damn thing, okay?"

I turned around, stared out the window, jumped out of my car, rushed to the back, and took out a wrench. Ran back to her Toyota, removed the plates, returned to the bimmer and turned the key. "The police will get in touch with you anyway if they bother to trace the VIN number."

"I'll deal with it then," she said. "Let's just leave."

Lou began to argue but Lauren shook her head and he pressed his lips together.

I took a deep breath and pulled away from the curb. "Where are we going?" I asked.

"To my house," Lauren directed. "I don't want to leave Ian alone. But first let's stop so Lou can change his clothes. You too," she added.

"Matty..." Lou growled, unable to leave the argument behind.

"Lou, listen," I said, feeling my stomach knot. "If Lauren feels like she's being followed again I'll be on it. I promise."

CHAPTER 7

Promises, promises. If the first don't get you, the second one will.

"They didn't bother to catch their breath before Lou called," I grumbled into the telephone. "I don't understand it. They have no car, they're home tending for a recovering suicide, the weather's lousy, but Lauren's being watched. Again. Where the hell could anyone follow her?"

Boots tried to humor me out of my grouch. "Maybe there's enough room in the house for someone to sneak around inside. That part of the North Shore is rich as hell."

"The house is big but no mansion." I paused then added sarcastically, "They call it the Hacienda. Wrong part of the fucking country for a name like that."

"What did it look like?"

"I only saw the outside," I replied. "It was a dark and stormy night…"Auditioning to host a P.B.S program? ?"

"Better that than this."

"Right, Matt Jacob in a tuxedo on G.T.N., Gonzo Television

44

Network."

I smiled through gritted teeth. "*Anything* but this."

"Why? You'll find out soon enough if Lauren's fears are real. Do it and be done."

"You never say that about sex."

Boots laughed, "Maybe I don't have to."

"Wise guy." It was good to hear her voice. The storm had screwed with the airline schedule, and Boots had piggybacked a few more work days onto the delay.

"I'm serious, Matt, what's the big deal? It's just a job."

The busman's holiday wasn't a big deal. Lauren was. She cast a powerful undertow, a pull I found disturbing—though unsure of exactly why. "They keep coming after me, and I don't want to be drawn into their orbit. Let her go to the cops."

"You said she won't."

"Yeah, but why not? Though she's probably right about their usefulness," I conceded, my own distrust of Blues bouncing to attention. "But this is different than just anyone asking me to take a case."

"It's different, all right," Boots said sharply. "This is your father-in-law and the woman he's involved with. Lauren is bright enough to see the way Lou loves you. Hell, you've even begun to make me nervous about using the "L" word."

"I make *you* nervous about saying "love?""

Boots caught her breath and my mind's eye watched her bite her tongue. "Let's save this particular conversation until we're together," she finally said. "Right now I'm having trouble with your attitude. You're chewing glass about Lou and Lauren. You're always Mr. Tolerant, but when it comes to Lauren there's no saving grace. You attack her clothes, her kids, her age for crying out loud. The truth is, you sound like a jealous little boy."

"It's not jealousy," I replied with more certainty than I felt. "Something else is going on, but I don't know what it is."

"Then find out. Find out, because what you're doing now isn't working."

Boots was absolutely right; something wasn't working and part of it was me. "Okay, lady, you got it. Your intrepid sleuth will gird his loins and mount his white steed to make certain his father-in-law's *squeeze* is safe."

"Well, don't gird them too tight and make damn sure you only mount a horse."

"You understand I'll be expecting my reward when you return. Which is when, by the way?"

"It's nice to know you still think of me as a reward," Boots answered, somber slipping into in her tone. "I'll be home late Friday night. Meet at the condo?"

I didn't like our goodbye, but then, there had been a lot of the conversation I didn't like. I hung the heavy black Bakelite receiver on its squat base, watched my wall hanging cat clock wag its tail, and brought a Bass back to the kitchen table. Substance substitution. Most other times I'd have gone directly to dope. Might still, I realized, after two long pulls failed to relieve my tension.

I played with the tightly packed joint for a long time before lighting. I was angry about chasing my own tail around weed and alcohol. Mad at myself for allowing Lou and Lauren's relationship to rock my life. Truth was, I was feeling hostile toward everyone. Boots's complaint and her quasi-tell pissed me off. Lou's proprietary, paternal proclamations pissed me off too.

But mostly I was angry at Lauren. For no real reason and, unfortunately, I knew it.

I also knew there had been something creepy about the damage done to Lauren's car, and her refusal to report it. Which meant strapping on my holster and crawling closer to someone I wanted farther away.

Still, the thought of my holster had me reaching under the bed for the '.38. I could never entirely shake a sheepish sense of absurdity every time I seriously thought about the way I made my living. Something I considered whenever I found myself on my knees groping under the bed—which fortunately wasn't too often. Most of my work for Barrister Simon took place in libraries or Government agencies. Even did a stint as a mall-man.

But once in a while I stumbled into something different, usually reeling out in worse shape than when I began. Those cases blew off any smile. When I thought about them, I became grimly conscious of the weight that the custom Bakelite grip placed in my left hand. And conscious of a sick sort of pleasure.

But Lauren's undertow was not going to lead me toward any abyss. This was going to be an exercise in futility, a harmless waste of time.

Still, I spent most of the day smoking cigarettes and drinking beer while mindlessly cleaning my gun.

CHAPTER 8

"**Y**ou asked me to ring you up," I said, trying to sound as friendly as possible. It had been a longer night than afternoon with more dope than I'd really wanted, but I was determined not to let it slow me down. "He told me you're feeling watched again."

"Oh, Matthew. I expected your call yesterday so you've caught me by surprise."

I automatically listened for reproach, but all I found was my drug-over. "If this is a bad time I can always call back."

"No, it's fine. Just give me a minute to switch phones."

Lauren shouted over an MTV promo, asking someone to hang up the receiver when she got upstairs. I cradled the black Bakelite between my shoulder and ear and vainly fought the aspirin bottle's child proof lid.

A bored, sullen, voice mumbled into my ear. "My ma said you were the dude who picked me up at the bar."

"If you're Ian, I'm the dude," I concurred.

"Yeah, I'm Ian. Well, thanks for the help."

"You're welcome."

48

There was an uncomfortable silence, then Lauren's loud, "I've got it now, Ian."

"See you around, I suppose," he added before closing down the line.

"Did he thank you?" Lauren asked. "I don't think he remembers too much about that night." She paused momentarily then said, "He won't talk about it with me."

"He thanked me." I gave up struggling with the aspirin, lit a cigarette, and pulled the receiver from my cramped neck.

"I feel pretty uncomfortable asking for more help," Lauren began. "I probably wouldn't..."

I expected her to dump it on Lou.

"Except I really don't know who else to ask," she finished, taking the weight.

"I don't imagine Lou would be too happy if you hired a different P.I."

Lauren chuckled briefly, "I know better than to try. I also know you think I'm overreacting." Again she spoke without condemnation.

"I'm honestly not sure what I think, Lauren. I'm surprised that you haven't spotted someone following you. Six months is a long time," I said, pushing the image of her car from my mind.

"Yes it is," she agreed. "But common sense doesn't erase the chill. I've only spoken to Lou about feeling followed, but it's more than that. It's like a laser beam of hatred trying to bore into me.

"It's incredibly strange. During a part of my life in the seventies I became involved with different spiritual movements, searching for something I thought was missing. Most of the different groups were benign, people like myself looking outside for answers that really come from within. But I ran into a few situations that weren't quite so harmless. People who really just wanted to play with your head behind their gentle smiles. People who wanted power for the sake of it."

Her voice became distant as she traveled back in time. "It's virtually a mental rape."

"This is happening now?" I asked, struggling with images of Charley Manson and his 'family.' "It's been a real long time since any of that world actually exists."

"Tell me. But I can tell *you* it's not succeeding and it won't. No one can make me feel anything that's not truly coming from me. I've worked too hard and paid too high a price for that to ever happen again. But trust me, someone is trying to get into my head."

I was glad she couldn't see my face. I sucked in a deep breath and tried Boots' advice. Make this a regular job. After all, Lauren was completely serious. "So when you feel followed, it's not actually a physical stalk?"

Despite my effort Lauren caught my doubt. "You're humoring me, aren't you?"

"No, but I'm not big on feelings that really seem ethereal," I admitted.

"I don't blame you for your skepticism. But someone *is* physically out there and watching me. I'm certain of it."

"Are there people in your life who were involved with your spiritual searchings way back then?"

There was a small pause. "I was really only talking about one individual." There was another, longer pause. "Why do you ask?"

"Could this person be stalking you?"

"Absolutely not."

"How can you be sure?"

"He's been dead for more than a decade. Someone tried to rob him on the street and he resisted. Stabbed to death."

So much for spiritual power. I'll stick with a good pair of sneakers. "And you still can't think of anyone else who might want to hurt you?"

"I can't imagine anyone disliking me to the degree I've experienced. I have no idea who'd spend the time and energy to traipse after me. But I'm telling you, this is *absolutely* real. And really quite frightening."

Her fear was communicable. For a moment, my cynicism vanished, the image of her tortured car once again bubbling to the surface. "Okay, Lauren," I said shaking my head but keeping the resignation from my voice. "I'll find out if anyone is really out there."

"That's very encouraging, but there's another problem. I can't afford to pay you. Of course I'll eventually…"

"Don't be ridiculous, I'm not going to charge," I interrupted. "Couldn't even if I wanted. Lou would kill me."

"We won't tell him. I don't like charity."

"I'm not talking charity. I prefer to do this as…" I groped for words, "a friend."

"That's very sweet, but we're not friends. And I've already asked you for too many favors."

"Then think of it as a favor to Lou. There's just no way I'll take your money."

There was enough silence to give me time to work on the aspirin container.

"You know, Matthew," Lauren began regretfully. "I feel terrible about the timing of all this. I keep wishing we met under different circumstances."

And right then I wished we'd never met at all. "Me too," I lied. "What finally happened to your car?" I asked, changing the subject.

"Junked."

"How are you getting around?"

"I've been using my oldest son Stephen's car. He lent it to me until I get a cheap rental."

"What does it look like?"

"One of those truck things. A silver and black Cherokee."

"Well, tell me a couple of places you'll be going today and roughly when you'll be there. Same for tomorrow and the day after."

It took Lauren a couple of minutes to organize and relay the information. "There may be other stops but these are the ones I'm sure about. Do you want to meet somewhere?"

"No. I want you to go about your business and leave the rest to me."

"You're familiar with the North Shore?"

"Enough." Throughout the years I lived in The Hub I'd come to appreciate New England's craggy coastline. Before the car accident, Chana and I frequented a jazz club in Beverly. We usually managed to get lost, often exploring the surrounding affluent towns under moonlit, marijuana cover. The last I'd heard the club had burned down. Seemed appropriate, somehow.

"I'll pick you up today and if I do it right you won't know I'm around. In fact, try to forget I'm doing this at all. I don't want you to inadvertently scare anyone off."

"You really don't mind?"

"Not at all." It began as a lie but came out true. Despite my mixed feelings about Lauren and Lou's relationship there were worse things to do than keeping an eye on a beautiful woman. Also, I often forgot how much I liked to work. The smell of a hunt never failed to sneak behind my usual lethargy. Or, in this case, my discomfort.

After we hung up I finally pried the lid off the aspirin and spilled the pills all over the floor.

The glare of the sun didn't hurt. In fact, the cool sea breeze hit like a first day furlough. I drove to Manuel's, switched cars, then rode the sedan back to a sub shop where I bought enough bad food to fry my arteries.

I returned to my apartment and studied my notes along with a detailed map of the North Shore. Lauren's town, hamlet, really, hugged the ocean. If I rushed I could pick her up at home, the Hacienda, but now the distant echo of seventies spiritual yearnings subverted my hunt head. I heard the couch call and felt a channel surfer's finger-itch. For a moment I rationalized that if I left the house before the itch subsided I might accidentally shoot someone. Hell, I *felt* like shooting someone. It just wasn't easy getting right with my father-in-law's Big Romance.

But I'd promised. Lauren planned to pick up Lou from the commuter station in Magnolia later that afternoon. Plenty of time to amble my way up the coast and find her, them, there. But it wasn't until I offered myself that languid, stoned amble, that I pulled together a cooler of beer, a small stash, binoculars, smokes, and an old Ross Macdonald mystery.

My mood lightened when I passed the thirty-five foot Madonna blessing the stretch of highway that led to the abandoned horse track. The church always knew who lived where. Here, it was working class and Hispanics—the same for the connecting towns beyond. One of them used to have an oceanfront amusement park, but it was replaced by condos built for urban dwellers ready to have kids. Sadly, the town forgot to throw in a decent school system. They also forgot that the sky overhead was wall-to-wall aircraft stacked to land at Logan. Now, the burg's oceanfront view translated into available storefronts and rooming houses for the itinerant elderly. An unfortunate example of "location" being nowhere at all.

I lit my joint when I passed Mary Baker Eddy's birthplace. And felt its kick by the time I drove by her adult home. This was one of the very few times I regretted not having my cell phone on. I'd heard Mary was buried with a telephone and I wondered if she'd take my call. But, by the time I reached the outskirts of Magnolia, I realized Mary probably had an unlisted number.

I had plenty of time before Lou's train and used it to search for an artful lookout. I picked a spot up the hill, lucking into an exiting sleek, green Jag. Though we were on the summer's downside peering into very early fall, the town, like so many in the area, bustled with visiting pink and green clad boaters. Very different from the snowy winter when the population shrunk to a fraction of its summer size—which was exactly how the ritzy year 'rounders liked it.

With five to go before the train's arrival, a silver and black Cherokee double parked in the station's lot. My eyes combed the slow moving traffic, but no one stopped or even looked for a parking place. I reached into the back seat, grabbed the binoculars, and checked for anyone staked or suspiciously loitering. Nothing caught my eye. Manny's heavily tinted car windows kept me well hidden so, when the train pulled in, I focused the glasses toward the platform.

Lou bounded out of the last car wearing pleated linens and a white windbreaker. When he turned in my direction I saw the bright multi-colored shirt and dark suspenders—a long reach from his typically tired threads. My stocky father-in-law looked downright sporty. He also looked as if he had lost weight.

Lou paused at the edge of the platform. For a brief instant I grew paranoid about my tinted glass protection and slumped in my seat. By the time I lifted my head Lauren had joined him. I raised my glasses and watched up close as Lou unzipped his overnight bag and pulled out something white and cylindrical. He unrolled and shaped it into a large brimmed Panama which he handed to Lauren who clapped her hands, kissed his cheek, and plopped it on. The two appeared oblivious to the surrounding foot traffic. When I saw Lou reach back down into his nylon bag, I once again scanned the entire area and, once again, came up empty. Lou didn't; when I turned back to the station a plum beret perched jauntily on his head.

CHAPTER 9

Pleats, thinner, a lilt to his step, and a fucking beret. I huffed and puffed on my cigarette until they left the quaint station. Then I started my engine and concentrated on my job. I knew where they were going, but wanted to see if anyone else was curious.

No one was. I looked around again to make sure no one had their eyes on me before pulling out onto the street. The Hats were on their way to Rockport, an artsy/fartsy town on the tip of Cape Ann, Cod's smaller sister. If Magnolia was busy, Rockport was going to be tourist hell. There'd be no way to use the car as a blind so I'd have to pick them up on foot.

By the time I passed the fishing wharfs in Gloucester, all trace of my buzz was gone. The day remained bright and beautiful, but my mood was darkening. The shock at seeing Lou decked out in colors had evaporated. Now I just felt tired, torn, and an odd, forlorn sadness.

I pulled into a parking space about eight blocks from Rockport center, retrieved a beer from the cooler in the trunk, and retreated inside the dark interior. The town was dry and I didn't want to flaunt the law. Or carry a brown paper bag. I finished the Bass, smoked the roach and, finally, unable to stall any longer, kicked myself out the door.

My pace quickened as I approached the pedestrian swamped town center. The crowd was even larger than I'd anticipated and, for a moment, I worried about locating the lovers. An irrelevant concern since my eyes locked onto Lou's plum beret and Lauren's Panama the moment they bobbed out of a two hundred year old doorway. I controlled my claustrophobia and plunged deeper into the moving mass, one eye on the hats, the other on the surrounding crowd.

Lou and Lauren rambled up the narrow winding street. The painted colonials housed art galleries, pseudo-scrimshaw shops, t-shirt concessions, and salt water taffy "factories." Our country's forefathers couldn't have built a better outdoor shopping mall if they'd had blueprints. How wonderful it was that we lived in the age of recycling.

Store after store was jam packed with Bermuda shorts. The air overhead reeked thick and tangy with an odor war between the salty ocean and a mélange of perfume, pizza, and fried dough. I stayed far behind the strolling couple, continually monitoring the flow for anything the least bit unusual.

But the only thing extraordinary was the old clapboard buildings' ability to absorb the crush of shop-'til-you-droppers.' Lou and Lauren sauntered in and out of different stores, her stylish leather sack swelling after each stop. More than once I saw Lou fiddle with his wallet. Eventually, they broke free of the swarming crowd and walked hand-in-hand toward the public benches overlooking the ocean. I ducked into a tight doorway and kept watch until I was sure no one followed.

There was no reason to hang around, but oddly, the unending mass shopping bags had triggered my own acquisitiveness. After a few long, madness induced minutes resisting the lust to consume, buy, steal, something, *anything*, I slowly trucked back to Manny's car.

Nothing occurred on my guard, unless you counted the last second decision to bypass their exit and scoot to Bill & Bob's Roast Beef in Beverly. Lauren ran in and brought out a large bag of what I presumed was cooked cow. But once she drove to her house, my evening, night, and early morning were spent reading Macdonald and a backlog of sports pages.

By the time I returned to my apartment I was stiff, stuffed, and drained. And felt even worse after the telephone rang early the next morning.

"Where the hell were you last night?"

"Oh, Christ," I groaned. "I forgot to leave a message." I unscrewed my body from the couch where I'd fallen asleep and groped for a cigarette. "I've been stalking Lauren—shit, somebody has to. Got home about four."

"Why didn't you come here?"

"I didn't want to disturb you," I lied. I'd forgotten more than the message; I'd forgotten she was home.

"So we're not going to see each other until you're finished?" Boots' voice was strained.

"No, I'll come by tonight."

"Why will this night be different?"

"I won't be spending most of it in Manuel's car."

"What happened to the B.M.W.?"

"Too easy to recognize."

"So you decided to take Lauren seriously." Boots sounded satisfied despite herself.

"I did what I said I'd do."

"Well, that's a start," she said.

I crushed the cigarette, glanced at the time, and realized I wanted off. "Boots, I overslept and I'm running late. I've got to hit the street."

"Hit it once for me," she said, feigning humor. "What time will you be here?"

"Between eight and nine. Don't wait to eat."

"I'm waiting to talk, not eat."

"What does that mean?"

"You'll find out when you get here," she warned before hanging up the phone.

I thought about calling her back. Then thought about having forgotten her return and my immediate relief when the phone went dead. I didn't understand what was happening between us, but I didn't like it.

The conversation with Boots later that night did little to clear up my confusion.

"This last week reminds me of the way we used to be and I hate it," she said, her wide eyes drawn into slits.

"C'mon, Boots, I haven't been that much of a fuck-up. I followed your advice, that's all."

I had spent another day and much of the evening driving and hiking up north. Lou, wearing different pleats and suspenders—mercifully sans chapeau—and Lauren, in a hip-hugging short skirt and a fully filled late summer sweater, had romanced their way through another shopping spree, this time in a newly rehabilitated section of Gloucester. I followed them to a small state park where they walked, held hands, picnicked, and kissed. Since I couldn't enjoy Lou's happiness, I focused hard on making certain Lauren's fears were in her head. Unfortunately, I spotted nothing to alleviate the persistent picture of the two of them frolicking and necking. A picture that hadn't left me in great shape for talking.

"Forgetting to call doesn't bother me as much as you crawling into a shell, shutting me out again—like the old days."

"This *isn't* the "old days," Boots. Maybe it's BWS—bourbon

withdrawal syndrome." Better to discuss that than the way I used to be.

Boots smiled, "You're being clean?"

"Careful not clean. I'm doing all right. marijuana and beer, no coke and the occasional Turkey."

"Maybe there is something to your syndrome idea."

I stood, readying myself for a move to the bedroom, hoping to end all talk. But Boots remained where she was so I sat back down, surprised by a relief rush.

"I don't think drug withdrawal has much to do with any 'shell,'" I said quickly. "I'm not exactly marching to 'just say no.' Hell, I'm not even sure 'shell' is the right word." I paused hunting, "'Distracted' is more like it."

Boots shook her head emphatically. "When I brought up buying a television you turned green."

"It surprised me. I know what you think of the tube."

"Don't play dumb," she snapped. "The conversation was about us, not about televisions."

"And my distraction is about Lou and Lauren and her imaginary fears, *not* us. Anyway, if the television was about our relationship, you weren't exactly Ms. Direct."

"You're not the only one who gets the willies about living together."

Though Boots spoke the words softly, they reverberated inside my head. Loudly.

"It's time for a real drink," I said rising. "Do you want anything?"

I half expected shit for scoring whiskey but all I got was, "A glass of white, please."

I walked into the postage stamp kitchen, poured the Turkey and wine, and started back into the living room. I thought of a funny remark, but kept it to myself. It wasn't time for funnies. No matter how uptight I was.

I handed Boots her wine, retreated to the glass wall, and stared.

Traffic moved slowly due to a concert on the Esplanade.

"Why are you standing there, Matt?" Boots asked.

"Just looking."

"You don't have anything to say?"

"Not a heck of a lot. This is coming at me pretty fast."

"How many months do we have to quibble about interior decorating before it's apparent we're really talking about living together?"

I kept my eyes on the trail of headlights. One of our running debates concerned my thirties, forties, fifties taste, versus Boots' minimalism. "I thought we were discussing aesthetics, not decisions."

I heard her chair scrape the floor, then felt her hand on my shoulder. "I'm worried, Matt. Everything has been so good between us."

"*Is* good between us." I swung my arm over Boots' shoulder, pulling her close. "I don't know how I'd react to living together in the best of times. This stuff with Lou makes it worse."

"I thought it would help if you got involved."

"I know you did. I was off the wall about Lauren's age and kids, but now I've had conversations with her about spiritual searchings. She's even got me spooked, though I haven't seen anything suspicious. Nothing at all."

"She's into spiritualism?"

"Was, not anymore."

"When?"

"The seventies."

"So were a lot of people back then."

"Maybe people you knew. Mine were into sex, drugs, and rock and roll."

She wiggled out from under my arm. "Two sides of the same damn coin."

"Lauren still talks the talk. Unseen people pumping her with

60

feelings that aren't hers. Old New Age gibberish. Next thing you know Lou will be buying free range chickens."

Boots smiled. "It might help his cholesterol."

I walked back to the chair and plucked a cigarette from my pack. "I don't find it funny. The woman says she's doesn't have much money, goes on shopping sprees that Lou is likely financing, and you can piss into the Atlantic from her house. The situation stinks, and you wonder why I'm distracted?"

Boots walked over to me, relief flooding her face. "So you're not getting ready to go AWOL?"

I fought my doubts. "I wouldn't be here if this was the Army. I'm no fool, Boots, I know a good thing." Or did I?

Boots smiled though worry flickered in her hazel. "It's taken both of us a lot of years to recognize a good thing. I just don't want anything to screw it up."

"I'm telling you, it's Lou I'm worried about. I'm watching a guy whose prick is stiffer than it's been for decades. New clothes, losing weight, smooching in parks, copping feels while they're walking down the street. He's wearing a fucking beret."

Boots tried to hide her pleasure about my description but her laughter lit the room. At least the worry was gone.

"Don't laugh. After Ian's suicide attempt I thought Lauren was leading Lou into quicksand. Now I think she's taking him for a ride."

"Come on," Boots said, pulling my arm. "I want to take you for a ride."

Though I was relieved to stop talking, part of me didn't want to follow when she silently turned out the living room lamp.

CHAPTER 10

Either I misunderstood Boots's ride, or she changed directions by the time we sat naked on her bed. Despite the humid night, a teal Egyptian cotton sheet loosely covered the lower half of our bodies. "I think the anger about Lou and Lauren has to do with your own pulling away," Boots suggested.

"I don't understand."

"You weren't even aware that Lou was dating."

"He kept it secret," I objected.

Boots placed her fingers on my shoulder. "I'm not trying to give you a hard time, but you didn't notice because of us. Let's face it, for the last year we've spent virtually all our free time together." She took her hand from my shoulder and ran it past my forehead, pushing my thinning hair from my eyes.

"I'm not complaining," Boots said smiling. "Believe me, I love it."

I reached toward the table next to my side of the bed, clicked on the lamp, and rolled a joint while the twenty-first century fluorescent bulb slowly brightened. "What's your point?" I asked.

Boots shrugged, "During the time we've grown closer, relationships between us and other people have changed. Like yours with Lou."

"So I'm feeling guilty? Painting it over with stupid suspicions and anxiety?"

Boots ignored my defensiveness. "Not that linear, honey. But we've been spending all our time with each other and talking about living together."

She might not be linear... "We talked about it for a second, five minutes ago. Twice, if you count the television."

"What you're saying just isn't true. "We have been talking about living together, just indirectly."

I fought the only way I knew. I ducked. "There's a difference between tiptoe and stomp."

"We do a lot of tiptoeing."

"So now it's time to trample?"

Boots hesitated. "No, I don't want to trample anything. It scares the hell out of me when it doesn't go good between us. I keep thinking we'll slide back to where we used to be," she said.

Boots didn't want to stomp and, in my gut, I didn't want to backslide. It had been a long struggle to get past the years, fears, fights, and reconciliations. I wasn't an easy do.

I flicked off the lamp. "Maybe there's something to what you say about me and Lou. Maybe I do feel lousy about my role in all these changes. I know it's been rocky lately, but lately isn't always and it's certainly not forever. It's true I screwed up last night, but think about the night before you went away. Did you feel any shell then?" To make certain she knew what I was talking about, I slipped my hand under the sheet.

"Some of my feelings have to do with the other night," Boots answered as her hand found mine. "We ventured into something different than I'd ever experienced." She saw me raise my eyebrows, relaxed, and playfully punched my shoulder. "Don't leer, goddamn you. I don't mean the sex. We went someplace special and I think it frightened me."

The tension was seeping out of the air and I stroked her hair while lighting another smoke. But out of the air didn't mean out of me; I felt a withdrawal calling. I eyed the joint but instead forced myself to speak.

"I liked where we went, but it probably frightened me too." I admitted. "Right now I just have to get past this situation with Lou and Lauren."

"What's left?" she asked, resting her head on my shoulder.

"Tomorrow."

"And that's all?"

"Boy, I hope so. I haven't seen anyone tailing her and don't think I will." But despite my certainty, I couldn't completely wash the battered car from my mind. Maybe Lou wasn't the only one catching Lauren's paranoia.

Boots shook her head. "If Lauren is making this up she wouldn't involve you. Why ask for trouble?"

"In with me helps her with Lou."

"You're incredibly cynical. I can't imagine her creating all this just to get you involved. I have this uneasy feeling that something peculiar is happening. Doesn't her car seem too coincidental?"

I didn't want to tell her about my own unease; didn't want to think about anything. "Freud said nothing is coincidence but he was wrong about a lot of things." I nuzzled her neck slipping my body lower on the bed, ending our conversation.

No new ground, but we didn't lose any. Our lovemaking felt full of the private, personal touches that come with comfortable familiarity. Sensuous and slow, I kissed my way out of nervous. Growing calm through the comfort of knowing what pleased. Taking time to turn the disquieting conversation into a small gray cloud well hidden behind the swell of desire, pleasure, and excitement.

Hidden 'til morning, anyhow. Some of my wakeup bleak had to do with the clock. Early on a Sunday morning, alarms grated worse than usual. But I knew my annoyance was just icing on a fierce desire to be far from the romance I was witnessing between Lou and Lauren, away from my relationship with Boots. I'd lost too many loved ones to be easy with love.

I dressed quietly, hoping to leave a note. But before I made it out the door, Boots stirred and lifted a groggy head. "What time is it? Why are you dressed?"

I sat down on the edge of the bed. "Another day and night of tail-chasing."

She grabbed the pillow and placed it over her head. "Don't talk to me about chasing tail, Jacob."

I leaned over, lifted the pillow, and kissed the back of her neck. "Not to worry, I'll call you at work tomorrow."

The pillow was gone in a flash. "What do you mean tomorrow? Why aren't you coming back tonight?"

"I have a hot date with the interior of Manny's sedan," I lied.

"All night? You said there was no reason."

I stood and finished gathering my things. "Most of the night," I lied again. "I want to finish the job right."

Boots rolled onto her back, pushing the sheet to the side of the bed. With breasts lying flat, the sleepy look, and the tiny black birthmark next to her right eye, she looked like a petulant teenager. "Isn't there something I can do to slow you down?" Boots offered.

"Plenty, but don't."

"Okay, okay," she said covering herself. "But lock the damn door. I'm going back to sleep."

The ride to my apartment was a wrestle between relief and guilt. I had no intention of spending the night in any car, but the thought of more intimacy raised a sweat. I didn't regret clearing space, just my inability to clear it honestly.

By the time I roused myself off the couch I'd already blown any possibility of picking up Lou and Lauren at the Hacienda. If I offed the shower I could catch them at the end of their pre-planned brunch. It was nip and tuck, but nip won. If it hadn't, I'da been tucked on my *tuchas* all day long.

As it was, I got to the restaurant just in time to see Lou at the cash register. This time they drove through a number of small towns stopping along the way at different parks and ocean views. I hung in the distance though there were times when the Cherokee's erratic town-hopping had me playing catch-up. When late in the afternoon they finally wound up at the Magnolia train station, I was exhausted.

This had to be one of my perverse days because there was no other reason to watch their farewell. Oblivious again to any passersby, their talk was punctuated with hugs and kisses. I knew the scene was supposed to leave me soft and mushy, but, but, but.

I should have scrammed when the train approached, but all I did was toss the binocs onto the back seat. Maybe I was trying to justify my lie to Boots, or maybe I was reluctant to return to the couch. Either way, I decided to see where Lauren went after Lou boarded the train.

A part of me hoped she would dash into another man's arms.

Lauren didn't dash anywhere. Instead, she drove slowly through the coastal towns as if reviewing her weekend. When she turned toward home I kept following, surprised to see her pull off onto Shore Road, park, and leave the Cherokee. I pulled the bulky sedan into a small rest area and watched Lauren hop a fence and stroll down a dirt path through the thick woods toward the ocean.

Maybe she was meeting someone. I waited a good three before following. I hung the binoculars around my neck, carefully hauled my aging body over the same fence, and followed the same path. At first I couldn't find her. Then I saw a dark form crawling on the scabrous face of a steep cliff which dropped straight down to the raging ocean.

Once I recovered my breath and focused my view of the harsh, ragged rocks and crashing waves, I watched Lauren grapple her way to a narrow ridge that jutted over the roiling water. When I aimed the glasses she was sitting on the ledge, her light windbreaker pulled tight against the ocean's splatter. As if on cue she turned her head and stared in my direction. I was too well hidden to be seen but I stepped deeper into the woods anyway. The next I looked, Lauren had turned east, knees up, chin on hand, staring into the darkening horizon.

The two of us held our positions for about twenty minutes before Lauren headed back toward her car. At the same moment my neck hairs prickled and I suddenly felt watched. I quickly scoured the cliffs then retreated into the woods, gun drawn, tense and ready for a confrontation. I quietly pushed my way through a number of bushes until I wound up at a small, protected clearing with trampled sticks and grass. Right in the middle of the area it looked as if someone had rolled a rotted tree trunk to use as a seat.

CHAPTER 11

I rummaged for clues on my hands and knees until my back stiffened and I realized I wouldn't know a clue if I saw one. A downside of buying my license, city living, or both. So instead of playing in the dirt, I carefully toured the woods hoping to surprise anyone who might be in the vicinity.

I found no one but couldn't shake the hair stand. I returned to the sedan, drove relatively close to the Hacienda, staked, and betrayed my morning lie to Boots.

Though the feeling never returned, for the first time, I actually began worrying that Lauren was onto something. Worried again that the trashed car hadn't occurred in a vacuum. But hard as I tried, I couldn't just figure her refusal to speak to the police or her inability to notice anything unusual.

By 4am I was home blearily staring at more reruns. Not much choice—nothing new is *ever* on at that time. . The coffee table in front of the couch held an overflowing ashtray, empty beer bottles, and my dope pipe. Sleep was coming, but I wasn't exactly getting there on my own.

Unfortunately, the next day began no better than the last one ended. Worse. Instead of worry and depression, I awoke with a brain-banging mad, dragged from a dreamless, dry-mouth sleep by the relentless shrill of the landline. In self-defense I grabbed the receiver, ready to curse.

An unfamiliar voice spoke quickly, impatiently. "Mr. Jacobs? Mr. Jacobs?"

"Hold on," I growled, swallowing my swear. I swung my legs off the bed and lit a cigarette. Nothing like a brushfire in a desert, but I needed help restraining my temper.

"It's Jacob, without an 's,'" I finally said, eyeing leftover water in a smudged drinking glass. I couldn't remember if it was last night's or from the night before. "Who's this?"

"Ted Biancho. I was wondering if we might meet?"

"How did you get my number?" I lifted the glass and killed the water. As soon as he told me his title, I surveyed the room, irrationally worrying about hiding all my dope. Ted Biancho was the Police Chief of Lauren Rowe's town.

"Is this a formal invitation?"

Biancho chuckled. "You've lived in the city too long. We're more easygoing up here."

Easygoing or not, there clearly was no room for refusal. "And what time am I expected?"

"Whenever is convenient. Let me give you directions or you'll miss it."

"That would be a shame, huh?"

"Not a shame, a mistake."

I stubbed out my smoke. "I'll get a pencil."

No more sleep for this head hurting weary. No comfortable breakfast of caffeine, nicotine, and newspapers. No sit-ups, pushups, or long loping laps around Roberto Clemente` Field. What the hell, the older I'd become the less I liked to run. But nor was I thrilled to be on the receiving end of an invitation from a town's top cop.

Although the morning was ruined, I stubbornly refused to rush. Shower, smokes, and caffeine after all. It was past twelve when I picked up my car from Manny's, long past one when I drove into Lauren's tiny town. Hopefully the office closed early.

If I hadn't taken the Chief's directions I might have made the mistake he warned me about. It was difficult to imagine a more unlikely looking police station. The rambling New England farmhouse had been added to—clumsily—at least twice during its lifetime. One addition was tacked to the back, the other stretched at a right angle from the middle of the main structure. All the connected buildings were painted a pleasant pale yellow, effectively masking its bulk. The only indication that it was headquarters was a small wooden plaque hanging on a hook next to the front door.

I stood on the wooden porch, finished my smoke, and tossed it onto the sidewalk. Uniforms never failed to strum my anxiety and an invite from a heavy Blue had me checking pockets, making certain I wasn't accidentally holding.

I took a deep breath, walked through the screen door and found myself in a huge white room, completely empty save a large desk and chair butting up to an arch on the far side. Someone had taken decorating lessons from Mussolini.

I was halfway across the oak floor when a slim, medium height, dark-complected figure with close cropped brown hair appeared from the back and leaned against the arch's frame. I stopped as he took a bite of an apple, chewed, swallowed, and pitched the core into a pail.

"You're Jacobs?" he asked in a soft, polite voice. He was in his late thirties—an age I hadn't seen in quite a while. No uniform, although his pleated green chinos and yellow Izod were close to an official something.

"Jacob," I reminded. "You're Chief Biancho?" I walked close enough to see his sharp features. Despite the languid pose, his intense dark eyes scraped my face and scratched my nerves.

"Thanks for stopping by."

"Thanks for the directions. You get hit during the night?" With me, banjo nerves usually came loaded with an open mouth.

Razor thin lines crossed Biancho's smooth forehead. "What?"

I waved my arm around the empty room. "Some terrorist steal all your stuff?"

He smiled briefly. "I told you we're a small operation."

"Small is different than empty."

"Just a 'mom and pop' office with more pops than moms," Biancho said, a touch less pleasantly. "We don't use this room. People generally come through the side door."

"At least you don't have to rent a hall for the Police Ball."

Biancho smiled tightly, pushed himself off the frame, and turned his back. His alligatored knit back.

I followed it through the rest of the great hall into a long corridor that led to the additions. The Chief waited until I caught up before heading toward a plain, but large and comfortable, office.

"You usually man the fort alone?" I asked before sitting on a small leather loveseat across from a floral upholstered wing chair. On the other side of the room there was a neatly kept mahogany desk with a framed photograph of a beautiful redhead. Dum dums to silver bullets, we were talking wife.

Biancho shook his head as he sat down in the pretty chair. "Deborah called in sick. I was planning to send her on errands when you arrived, anyway."

I tried to ignore my sudden shot of panic. "It's good to be Chief."

"Pretty good. Got me pegged as a regular small town shit-kicker, don't you?"

I couldn't stop wagging my tongue. "Not yet."

Biancho's mouth moved but I couldn't tell if it was a smile or swear. "This morning you asked where I got your number.""After you told me who you were I figured the phone company."

"I went through your car yesterday when it was parked near Shore Road and ran across your ticket. Bad habit to leave your wallet in the trunk. Trunks get popped all the time." Biancho eyes bore into mine.

I hoped he didn't see how fucking stupid I felt. I'd spent half the goddamn night in a car worrying about nothing. While Biancho's b&e didn't explain the trampled grass in the woods, it probably did explain the "feeling." Still, something about that campsite continued to disturb me.

I raised my brows. "This time it was the good guys who did the popping." Now that I knew he'd been in my car, I felt a mixture of anger and alarm; I couldn't remember whether I had finished all my weed before I'd followed Lauren out to the rocks.

"There's no reason to worry, Mr. Jacob. We're on the same side. When I called your police department to check on you, an interesting thing happened."

"Everybody cheered?"

"No cheers, but your name caught their attention. It took a couple of hand-offs but I finally spoke to a mutual acquaintance. Washington Clifford. They called him your "babysitter.""

Whatever wind left in my sail escaped. Washington Clifford was a vicious son of a bitch who more than once Buddy Rich'd my body.

"I'm sure he gave you a balanced report," I said sarcastically. Clifford lived a sanctioned life between the official cracks of Boston's Police Department. My dislike was matched only by fear. Clifford's dislike was undiluted, despite situations where we had helped each other out.

"You leap to conclusions awfully fast, Mr. Jacob."

"Why don't you just call me Matt? Mister makes me feel even older than I am."

"Sure. Clifford was complimentary."

"Why not? I make him feel like Mohammed Ali during his prime." I angrily reached into my pocket and pulled out a cigarette. "You own an ashtray?"

Biancho sprung to his feet, walked over to a cabinet, and returned with a fancy glass bowl.

"Okay," I said. "So you talked to Clifford. Let's stop dicking around. What is it you want?"

"Information." He saw my puzzled look. "Let me explain. This is a small town. We only get large in the summer. The residents like it that way."

"You mean the rich folks like it that way, don't you?"

"That just about covers everyone."

"I hope they pay you well for protecting all that wealth."

"I do all right," he said tersely, "but here's the rub. While there is concern for safety and security, the town doesn't want to feel like an armed camp."

"Don't worry, they'll spring for crime lights when the. Jihadists show up. "

Biancho frowned. "Clifford told me about your mouth."

I raised my hand in front of my face. "That my cue to shut up?"

"Just the opposite. You see, people talk and I listen. That's how I keep a handle on security."

"Well, I'm not from up here and I don't like serious talk."

Biancho ignored me. "People have been gossiping about Lauren Rowe and her new boyfriend. When rumors start, I keep my eyes open."

"And I rolled right in front of them?"

"You're pretty good. I've never seen anyone stay as far away from a subject as you and still do a decent job."

I didn't know what he knew or whether he'd spoken to Lauren. Stonewall time.

"What subject is that, Chief?"

"Please, Jacob, I keep hoping we can work together. I know

73

your father has been seeing Ms. Rowe so I understand your interest. But I won't have you tailing any of my town's residents. I just can't allow it."

In Biancho's head, one and one added up to three. It gave me some wriggle room and I decided to squirm. "Father-in-law, Chief. I'm impressed, you give good security. I can back off, but it would help if you gave me some idea who he's dealing with."

"I thought you might ask," he said, nodding his short-haired head. "Now you see why I wanted us to meet alone? Chatter flies around this town."

The telephone interrupted and Biancho walked to his desk. "Yes. Of course I will. No bother at all. Thanks for calling."

After he replaced the receiver, Biancho leaned his tight body against the desk. "Quality of life, Matt. That's what we worry about up here. Apparently some teenagers broke a few bottles on our public tennis courts."

"Easily remedied," I replied. "Find the bastards and shoot 'em."

Biancho chuckled. "Not my style. Excuse me for a moment. I'm going to send someone to clean up the mess. Tonight I'll talk to the boys and their parents." Biancho stretched and took a few steps toward the door.

"If you find out who they are," I said to his back.

He took a few more steps then looked over his shoulder. "This isn't the big city, Jacob. I already know."

CHAPTER 12

I smoked while Biancho raised the quality of life in his corner of the world. His comment about my interest in Lauren Rowe and his contact with Washington Clifford fueled my curiosity, so, when the young, good-looking Chief returned, I planned to prod. He couldn't bust me for pushing, I'd already cleaned my pockets. If I had to, I could always tell him I was working for the person he was trying to protect. The Chief seemed a whole lot more amenable to listening than Washington Clifford.

Biancho strode back into the room.

I stayed silent until he was seated. "Look, Chief, I don't want to hoof after your flock. It's my time and dime. But it would go a long way if you told me something about the Rowe's."

Biancho studied me as a small smile softened his intense face. "Your father-in-law and Lauren Rowe have been seeing each other for a while. A little late off the mark, aren't you?"

"Part of my charm," I paused, "late or not, I'm not comfortable letting him walk into something ice cold."

Biancho wasn't buying altruism so I tried avarice. "He and I are partners in a couple of buildings."

The Chief's eyes bore into me again. "Washington Clifford told me you're stubborn. I'll talk with you now so that stubbornness doesn't get you in trouble later, understand?"

I nodded, though I'd already begun considering a talk with Clifford myself.

"This has always been a wealthy, right-wing town. In the seventies, Lauren and Paul Brown moved into the old Fuller house. Let's say they didn't exactly fit into the community."

"Too liberal? Not rich enough?"

"Everything must have gone into the house and this was long before the boom. The family had trouble making ends meet. Around here people buy from local stores and run tabs. Paul and Lauren fell behind to everybody."

"That's a credit card society for you."

He ignored me. "Their house became a quick cure center for anything from war to herpes. For a while the place functioned as a commune."

"Sex and drugs?"

His lips tightened. "Rumors."

"Rumors about both Paul and Lauren?"

"Most people didn't think Paul had much choice. Look, in this village, if you aren't rich or don't service 'em, no one understands why you're here."

He noticed his own bitter undertone and quickly corrected. "Lauren Rowe has changed over the years," Biancho said impassively, "but around here she's still an outsider."

"And her husband?"

"He never had her reputation."

"And Lauren still makes people uncomfortable?"

Biancho shook his short hair while I lit another cigarette. "She's had problems with her sons and that hasn't helped," he said flatly.

"You like the lady, don't you, Chief?"

"My job is to protect everyone who lives here, Jacob," his voice neutral.

"And you take your job seriously."

"Part of my charm. It also keeps me employed. Lauren Rowe could live to be a hundred but people will still think of her as a misfit," he added testily.

"Sounds personal."

His thin features were pinched, but his voice calm. "I don't like private detectives who put words in my mouth."

I understood the warning. "Where are you from, Chief?"

"Here, California for college, then eventually back home. I worked on the force until I became Chief."

Another grim look washed his features. "What I'm telling you is actually quite simple. Whatever you may hear, Lauren Rowe's reputation exceeds any present reality. Whatever relationship your father-in-law has with her, there's no reason to be tagging along. Am I clear?" he asked, rising.

Clear, and clear that our conversation was over. I considered confiding Lauren's concerns, but remained reluctant to betray a client's confidentiality. Even hers. Especially to a Top Cop.

"Thanks," I said following him down the corridor to the side door. "I appreciate what you've told me."

"I don't remember telling you anything," he warned. "I'm simply asking you to stop trailing after our residents." He showed teeth, but there was no warmth in his smile as he ushered me out the door.

I passed a couple of paunchy middle-aged Blues on the path alongside the station. Both took hard looks, waiting until I was at my car before continuing toward the door. I guess the Chief was more tolerant of funk than his force. And given the age difference between him and his troops, much more ambitious.

I wasted no time telephoning. Biancho wanted me gone and so did I. I pulled the Bimmer onto Lauren's block and parked oceanside, across the narrow street from the Hacienda. But before leaving the car I sat staring at Lauren's large, rundown house. Chipped paint and tired clapboard, the far side perched on two thick, brick stilts lifting it over a small rock mountain. Extending over the top of the columns was a huge deck. If the stilts held, the deck offered a hell of a view.

Lauren opened the door while I was still climbing the wobbly stairs. "I didn't know whether you wanted to come inside."

"I was finishing my cigarette."

She waved me inside and pointed to a cluttered sitting room directly on the right. "Good timing," Lauren said. "I just got back from taking Ian to his apartment."

Lauren pointed toward an oversized easy chair alongside large bay windows. "Please. Can I get you anything?" she asked waiting in her fashionably wrinkled linen palazzo pants and matching coffee silk tee. It was easy to understand Lou's attraction. Real easy.

"Just an ashtray," I said sitting, her stylish manner magnetic.

Lauren placed a glass ashtray on the tired table next to my chair and I immediately fired up. She made me nervous.

"You smoke a lot, don't you?"

"Too much."

"I gave it up when I left Paul," she said making herself comfortable on a worn velveteen couch. "These days it seems like nobody smokes."

"I grew up in the wrong time and place to function without 'em."

Though the room wasn't large and the furnishings dark, the open bay windows allowed a warm afternoon light. "I guess good things can come from bad situations," I said absently, listening to the ocean in the background.

Lauren shrugged. "I suppose. Have you tried to quit?"

"No," I said fidgeting. "Other habits are in front of the line. Ian has recovered enough to return home?"

"He thinks so," Lauren said.

"You don't?" Better to talk about him than me.

"He insisted. It's probably for the best since we haven't been getting along." Lauren's fingers picked at the large gold hoop in her ear.

We remained silent until I got down to business. Or lack of it. "I don't have much to tell, Lauren. I covered you the whole weekend and came up empty. Did you get any of those negative feelings?"

"After Lou left I climbed out to a cliff by the ocean. I like to sit there and think. I sensed I was being watched, but it wasn't the same."

"That was probably me," I said. "It was the only time I got close." And perhaps Biancho, but I didn't want to admit to being caught. Nor did I want to share any of my leftover unease. "I don't think you really have too much to worry about."

Lauren tossed her head. "You follow me for one weekend and decide that?" she asked. "Someone is frightening me!"

The upshift in her voice drove me to my feet. "Lauren, when we first spoke about the situation even *you* weren't taking it this seriously."

"Don't you realize what it would do to Lou if he knew I was this scared?" she snapped.

Lauren stood up, placing her hand on her hip. "I've lived through plenty and, frankly, I don't scare easily. But this has me freaked. Do you realize how difficult it is to even ask for help?"

What I realized was I wanted out. "I don't know what to say. There was no one following you."

"I already knew that. I can tell when I'm being stalked."

"But you won't go to the police."

Lauren marched to a lacquered black liquor cabinet in the corner of the room. "Do you want anything to drink?" she asked disgustedly.

I wanted to empty the fucking cabinet. "No thanks," I heard

myself answer. "Hard liquor is one of the things in front of the line. But I'll take a beer if you have one," I said sitting back down.

There was a sheepish smile when she returned with a Miller. "Ian's attitude and leaving has definitely put me on edge. I know you've gone out of your way and I'm sorry about my temper."

"And I'm sorry if I sound callous. I just don't have anything to report." I stupidly tried to reassure her. "I met with your Police Chief before I came here..."

"You what?"

"Not by choice," I said, pitching my embarrassment. "Biancho called and suggested it."

"What did he want?"

"Someone noticed me and he wanted to make sure I wasn't harassing you."

"What did you tell him?"

"I was checking up on my father-in-law's relationship."

"And Ted believed you?"

"Why not? He seemed okay."

"You like him?"

"I wouldn't call it like, he's a cop."

"You're wondering why I won't talk to him?"

"It crossed my mind," I said, watching as she seated herself back on a couch.

"I'm not well thought of in this town," Lauren said bluntly. "Anyone who doesn't fit is a pariah. Especially me. There have been incidents involving my kids."

I waited for more about those incidents, but all I got was an earful of tense silence. "Why not move?" I finally asked.

"And give up the Hacienda?" Lauren shook her head vehemently. "I love this house too much to ever leave. I've learned to live with my red letter, and I'll be dammed if I'll give the pricks around here the satisfaction of driving me out."

"Biancho didn't sound as if he dislikes you."

"Teddy Biancho is something of an exception. It changes the way you think about people when you're a dirt poor townie in a wealthy community. He was in school with my daughter who was one of his few friends. Maybe his only friend and their friendship has given me breathing room. At least with him. But if he starts poking around, everyone in town will hear about it.

sust what I need," Lauren added sarcastically. "Another round of ugly assumptions about that strange woman. Believe me, there's already plenty of talk about me and Lou. Everybody wonders about the difference in our ages—just like you."

Lou targeted by gossip amped both my annoyance and guilt. He wasn't going to be happy when he heard about this conversation and I wasn't going to make it worse so I slid past the age thing. "The police up here are one thing, but you refused to report what happened to your car in the city. *That* I find really hard to understand."

A sad, hurt look flashed across her face but instantly disappeared. "I want nothing to do with authorities, Matthew. For too many years I felt hounded and harassed every time someone disliked my politics or lifestyle. Do you want to guess what it cost for zoning fights once people discovered we were something of a commune?" Lauren asked. "After a while treatment like that sours you toward officials, no matter where they're from. If the car had been worth anything I might have reported it, but it wasn't, so why put up with crap?"

There was more in her closet about the car, but I had no stomach to bang on the door.

"You have a strange look on your face, Matthew."

"I'm trying to figure out what to do. I don't like this hanging over your head."

"You mean Lou's head, don't you?" Lauren said without rancor. "I know you think we're a bad match. You don't hide your feelings all that well."

I edged out of the room toward the front door. "Lou comes from a different place than you, Lauren. I'd hate to see him make a fool of himself."

"You mean you'd hate to see me make a fool of him."

"I'm afraid of Lou getting hurt."

A smile broke through her stormy face. "I feel exactly the same way, but I don't think you believe that."

I started to lie but she interrupted. "Maybe we can meet halfway. I'm throwing our annual summer's end party next Saturday. I was undecided whether to go ahead because of Ian's accident, but I don't want anyone to think I'm ashamed of him. My whole family, Paul's, and other people, will be here. Come and see us in a normal circumstance. Of course, Lou will love it."

There was that word "accident" again. "Paul's family?"

"Anne and Heather Heywood. I think I told you that Paul lives with Anne, and Heather is her daughter."

"A strange mix," I said dubiously. I was just getting used to the idea of more surveillance and now I was listening to this tired New Age shit again.

A broad grin lit Lauren's remaining shadows and she grabbed my arm which immediately grew warm. "You can't be that old-fashioned. Lou tells me you're on the cutting edge."

I returned her smile and tried to retrieve my arm. "The only thing that gets cut when I'm on the edge is me. I'm not sure about the party, but I'll continue to watch your back. That seem okay?"

Lauren nodded gratefully. "Except for the party, it's more than I could hope for."

CHAPTER 13

Halfway home I realized I hadn't asked whether Lauren's invite included Boots. Halfway through the week it didn't matter; Boots was off on another unexpected business trip. During the nights we spent together I'd been locked hand-to-hand with desire for distance, while she ping-ponged between quiet anxiety and false cheer. Didn't make for fun times overlooking the old, shimmering town.

Back home, Lou left little doubt that the only way out of his crapper was to obliterate Lauren's fears. That I had no power to discover the unknown meant nothing. Lou also expected me at the party and had a hard time accepting my noncommittal response.

The more he pushed, the more I wanted to disappear. From Lauren, from Lou, from Boots, though I wasn't certain why. I definitely wanted to ditch my drug and alcohol moderation.

Despite my promise to check up on Lauren, by Thursday I was bunkered, unwilling to spend time with anyone, barely able to tolerate myself.

Which changed late that night when Julius picked his way

through my front door. As many times as I'd switched locks in our endless game of 'keep out,' Julie always made it through. Of course, I never latched the chain and he never broke the frame. We had our rules.

When I heard the door open the only light in the apartment was the glow of my television. The only sound was Bob Mitchum ripping into Kirk Douglas.

Julie leaned against the inside wall, his brown hands and face fading into the darkness. "Can't find something in color? Afraid it might perk you up?"

"*Out of the Past*," I said nodding toward the tube. "A classic."

"Slumlord, every time I catch you on the couch you're watching a classic. They call 'em classics because there's only a few."

I was uncomfortable talking to a disembodied conscience so I sat up and pulled on the lamp chain.

Julie cocked his head raising his low-riding eyelids toward his short, salt and pepper hair. Lucky I hit the light; this way I could see the bloodshot whites of his eyes.

"You're looking at me like I just fucked your mother," I said. I guess I was still feeling hostile.

Julius let my nasty slide off his broad back. "Not *my* mother, Slumlord. That lady had taste." He walked over to the television, turned down the sound, but left the machine running.

"You can shut it off."

"And drag you from the tit?" Julie helped himself to my Newport's.

"You don't sound happy to see me."

"I do find it rewarding to discover you still talk."

"Able but unwilling." No matter how many times it happened, I was always caught napping when someone noticed my withdrawals.

"Haven't beat on my door for new medicine either. Bummed and clean. You on a twelve- step?"

"A tap dance. Doing, but doing less."

"You gonna want bread for rent?"

"Don't be ridiculous. I'm not going to cut off my nose or my lungs."

"Then you ain't gonna slam me into a smoking section if I get right?"

"Only if you bogart."

Julie reached into his charcoal gray vest, pulled out a joint, lit it off the end of his cigarette, and handed it over. I took a deep drag, another, then passed the joint back.

He waved the stick toward the cluttered coffee table. "The only thing missing from this pile of shit is your Turkey bottle. Maybe you're on a half-step program."

I leaned into the couch. "It'll be a back step if you keep this up. What are you doing here? Out of coffee?"

"Your vibes been knocking at my door. Charles be pestering me to find out how long you plan on living under a rock."

"Vibes," I groaned. "I gotta deal with more vibes?"

Julie bent forward, pushed his cigarette into the ashtray, and ever so slightly raised his brows. "Shadow is more like it. I can ignore your ugly, but Charles' clucking is another matter entirely."

Charles was our wildly attired building manager, the flamboyant half of the Richard and Charles couple who lived in the building. Richard was the architect who had renovated and attached the two six-flats when Lou expanded our empire. Charles supered the buildings since I became a working P.I. The image of his batting mascara'd eyes pleading for Julie to chop through my no trespass almost made me smile.

I willed myself unstuck and took the smoldering roach from Julius's fingers. I'd grown tired of neurotic channel surfing. I wanted to drag myself from the body carve in the couch. Or be dragged.

"I've been worried about Lou," I hesitantly offered. "He's involved with someone I don't trust."

"You have a fucked up way of worrying. You been avoiding

everybody, including the Bwahna."

I tried to explain. Told him what had been happening, my take on Lauren and her family scene, her fears, my work, even my disquieting experience in the woods.

The fumes from Lou and Lauren's relationship tumbled out. "A family rope around my neck. An extended community of reorganized relationships. A fucking bunch of middle-aged, middle class refugees from the communal counter culture. Only no one told them that the counter culture disappeared about thirty years ago." I paused to catch my breath, "Which is a long fucking time ago. Maybe the way they play it is to save postage—just hand each other the alimony checks during Sunday morning brunch."

I shrugged resignedly, "And I'm supposed to find the ghost who's stalking Lou's young old lady. Find out who's been casting *hate projections* into her head, despite being warned off by the fucking Police Chief."

Julius slow-mo'd another cigarette from my pack. "You sound like a jealous kid."

"And you sound like Boots," I retorted, stung by his words.

"Doesn't matter how I sound. What matters is the Bwahna. His woman calls it vibes, you call it ghosts. I call it trouble. I don't know squat about his old lady, don't really care, but if there *is* trouble you might want to change your attitude."

I tried to ignore his warning, couldn't, and lapsed into a sullen silence.

Julius crushed his smoke in the ashtray and rose to his feet. The corners of his mouth turned upward in what passed for a sleepy smile. "If Charles don't stay off my back I'm going to drag him down here and feed him to the lion."

"Some fucking lion."

Julie walked to the edge of the room and let himself out. "Got to get off your ass to roar, Matthew," he added before closing the door.

Leaving me drained, drugged, and depressed.

CHAPTER 14

Remarkably, the next morning I awoke refreshed, invigorated, with no trace of a headache. I perc'd a pot of coffee and sat down for a long read of the sports section. And kept right on reading until I finally began to think. Unfortunately, sometimes to think is to do.

I was off my ass but I sure wasn't gonna roar. Squeak was about all I could muster; still, squeak was better than mute. I called my favorite short-order cook and cop conduit, Phil, and asked whether he could set up a meet between me and Washington Clifford. It bothered me that Biancho had found his way to my "babysitter." I hoped a preemptive chat might keep Washington from finding his usual way to me. On the other hand, I wasn't particularly pleased when Phil called back and rushed me over for a late breakfast.

One delicious plus about eating at Charley's was the decor. My kind of taste: wooden counter, enamel topped tables, faceted glass sugar dispensers with silver peaked tops. The chi-chi cafes stole his business, but everything in Charley's was original down to the thick, chipped china. Got me wondering what Lauren was doing eating here.

"Where's Red?" I asked walking through the door into the empty diner. Charley's used to be a place where social workers and cops mingled without much hostility. But the city, with its infinite wisdom and outstretched hands, had cleaned up the neighborhood and homophobia scared both groups away.

Phil hung tough. Didn't have many customers, but apparently socked enough away during the boom years to stay afloat and attract a waitress who strolled into the new century right out of the fifties. Red was the entire package—white uniform, pointed bras, bright vermilion lipstick, an ageless figure and face. Phil and Red lived together in a small apartment above the restaurant. Maybe Red was afraid of Clifford too.

"Visiting her folks."

"Somebody sick?" I asked sympathetically, though butterflies were already fluttering about my impending face-to-face with Clifford.

Phil turned his back from the grill and looked across the counter. "Went to tell them she's through living in sin."

"You're breaking up?" Despite their constant bickering I'd always believed Phil and Red were fused at the hip.

"Nah. I'm not getting any better looking so I figure it's time to settle down. Gonna pull the trigger, get married."

Everywhere I fucking looked. And it was almost autumn, not spring. All I needed was Julius to break in wearing a tux. "Congratulations. Church?"

"Government Center. They can flatten the place with as many plazas as they like, it's still Scully Square. And City Hall is still the biggest brothel in town. Seems right for us. You eating?"

"No. I learned to stay away from Clifford when I have a full stomach. Wouldn't want to mess your floor."

Phil shook his head. "He's not gonna slap you around."

"I'll believe that after he's gone."

"What's your worry? You're bigger than him."

"Taller isn't bigger plus he's twice as tough."

Phil lost his smile the moment the door creaked behind me.

"You wanna use the upstairs?" he asked as Clifford's shoes jackhammered toward my back.

"Hell no. And don't you disappear on me either."

Phil rolled his eyes and turned back to his grill as I spun my stool to face the Black Brick Shithouse. He hadn't lost any muscle since our last rendezvous. He had, however, shaved his head.

"Styling?" I cracked, unable to quiet my anxiety.

Clifford stood very still before answering. "Nothing worse than a half bald nigger unless you include a leftover stoner playing shamus. Ain't that right, Jacobs?" he asked setting his rock hard butt down on the stool next to mine.

"Without the 's,'" I said spinning back toward the counter.

Clifford ignored me and spoke to Phil. "Eggs over easy and I want extra ham. Skip the home fries but throw in a large glass of iced coffee, no sugar, no milk, no wait. Jacobs here works for himself so everything goes on his bill."

Phil looked at me. I nodded and said, "Just water." I glanced at Clifford. "I do a lot of pro bono."

"Beats working the malls, don't it? Nice you got those buildings to fall back on."

Right, Tycoon Matt. The room grew silent except for the sizzle on the grill and the tinkling of the coffee's ice-cubes. And stayed that way until Phil placed a mountain of thick ham capped with a couple of eggs in front of Clifford and retreated to the sink at the far end of the counter. I wondered if Washington was going to use a fork.

He did, stabbing the eggs, and we both watched the yolk slowly slide down the mountain. What the fuck had I been thinking when I called Phil?

"Order your own," Clifford said, misreading my stare.

"Don't worry, I'm not hungry."

"You look hungry," he said after a couple of large forkfuls. "Why do you want to see me, Jacobs?"

Good question. "Just to talk."

"Then talk," Clifford commanded after razing more of the mountain.

"I was surprised when Chief Biancho said Downtown had passed me off to you. Something about "babysitting.""

Clifford stopped chewing long enough to flash a dirty smile. "Cops have a way with words, don't they?"

I watched Washington's large hand circle the heavy glass of iced coffee. "When they use 'em."

Clifford signaled for more coffee. "You understand this guy, Phil?" he asked while Phil was pouring. "A private dick who hates cops. The rest of those scumbags spend their lives swearing we're in this together, but this one runs the other way. You get it?"

"Maybe he's just more honest. Or maybe it's a Commie thing." Phil smiled before moving out of earshot.

Clifford's laughter filled the room. "Scared, Phil. He's more scared than the rest of 'em. Ain't that it, Jacobs?" His laughter was gone, nasty taking its place.

"Maybe so Boss, but all that extra attention surprised me."

"Don't flatter yourself. Keeping an eye on you is like watching a three-toed sloth. Anyway, people appreciate how much I like to know what you're doing." Clifford pointedly polished off the rest of his meal in silence, but I knew he wasn't waiting for me to speak.

I sipped at my water trying to wet my parched mouth. I knew he wasn't going to hit me here, but just his mere presence recalled prior beatings. Unfortunately, the water didn't work so I gave up and lit a cigarette.

"Can't you see I'm still eating?" Clifford suddenly snarled. "And you're not supposed to smoke in restaurants. Can't you do *anything* right?"

"Sorry," I said, stubbing the cigarette into the ashtray.

"Well, too late now, asshole. I can't eat with that shit in the air." He pushed his empty plate away, rubbed his bald head, then shook a smoke out of my pack. "Can't fight 'em, join 'em," he said lighting up. "Something you never seem to learn."

I held my temper, reminding myself I'd asked for this meet as I lit a fresh cigarette. "So what are they paying babysitters these days, Washington?" I just couldn't help it.

Clifford shot me a humorless grin. "I like you so much I do it for free. You've been useful every once in a while. But useful stops at the city's limits. You're straying a little far from your dope dealer these days, aren't you?"

Clifford despised Julius. Never busted him, though. Maybe Wash was waiting for the day he could use him.

"Family business, that's all. Checking out my father-in-law's new girlfriend. Just wanted you to know so there'd be no misunderstanding. I figure better tell you myself."

Clifford dropped his cigarette into the ashtray without putting it out and spun off stool. "I appreciate your attitude, Jacobs. I spoke to Biancho and he wants you to make yourself scarce. I like him better than I like you. You understand me?"

I nodded.

"Then I don't expect we need any more talk, do we?"

"No, I guess not."

Clifford nodded and gracefully marched his thick, muscular body toward the door. "Stay out of burbs, shamus. As you now know, I have some friends there."

"Don't worry," I said to his broad back. "And by the way, bald is beautiful."

If he heard me he didn't show it, just walked out the door letting it slam behind. I breathed a sigh of liberated relief, cursed at myself for my last remark, and suddenly felt ravenous. "Phil, I'm fucking starving. Could you make mine the same as his?"

CHAPTER 15

I stood fiddling with my tie in front of the full length mirror. The Boots and Julie Show had finally caught hold, their combined words worming past my defensiveness, forcing me to reconsider my hostility. I told myself I was going to Lauren's party because I wanted to make amends. Told myself it would be interesting to observe Lauren's extended family and friends.

I told myself a lot of things, but eyeballing the mirror invited the truth. I wanted to boogie. To stop my twisted thinking, apologize to Lou, and lose myself. Wanted to get right with one entangling alliance and momentarily forget the other. And right then I wanted my tie straight.

But only the tie; it had been a while since hard liquor trailed flaming traces toward my bloodstream. I sat on the edge of the bed and cross-ruffed small shots of bourbon with little hits of the pipe. It wouldn't help with the alliance I wanted to untangle if I wasn't coherent.

Still, it was a long way to the Hacienda and plenty of time to worry off any excess. I added more to my glass, topped the pipe, and took another run at the closet. I stripped off my gray slacks, white shirt, and noose in favor of a comfortable pair of Levi's with a familiar black tee, black cross trainers, and a dark green, unstructured jacket. The look wasn't going to break me into GQ, but at least I could walk and breathe.

When I turned onto Lauren's street, muted multi colored paper lamps snatched my eyes and strains of a marimba filled the hot, humid air. I hadn't been to a real party with live music in a millennium. I instantly contemplated a retreat, but tail turning meant slamming my ass back on the couch.

So I drove past the decorated deck until I spotted a small break in the rows of expensive, spotless, off-roaders. I wedged in the old B.M.W., stared into the rearview mirror, then toked off a tightly rolled city slicker.

The refreshed high renewed my party head. People were talking and dancing on the Hacienda's upper deck and I could hear Lauren's throaty laugh rise above the syncopated Latin rhythms.

I hesitated when I reached the front steps and saw a good looking couple taking a desultory time out. My nerves squawked so I lit a cigarette. But the tinkling of glass and ice cubes seduced me, and I flipped the smoke nodding my way into Lauren's spacious front hall.

Where I found myself alone in a sudden pocket of quiet. The marimba had stopped its Caribbean and, for a split second, the party chatter vanished. Just as suddenly, I heard Lou's grunt from a room at the rear of the dimly lighted hallway. I rode my resolve into the kitchen where he was wiping sweat from his face with a towel as he leaned against the sink. Lou was wearing one of the sporty, suspender outfits I'd spotted the weekend before. No beret.

As soon as he saw me his flushed face broke into a pleased grin. "*Boychick*, I'd given up. Let me run upstairs and get Lauren."

"'Oh ye of little faith.' But don't run anywhere, I need a minute to chill."

"Where is Shoes? You knew she was invited, didn't you?" Lou asked anxiously.

"We're not Siamese Twins, Lou." I heard the way it sounded and added hastily, "Actually, she's away on business."

Lou's face relaxed and he took a short swig of Sam Adams.

"Just tell me where to get one of those," I pointed to his bottle.

"We can step onto the back porch," he said, immediately bending into the open refrigerator, "if you want a cigarette before we go up."

He noticed my look when he handed me a Bud. "Everything good is upstairs: food, a bar, music. I just came down for a little less commotion."

Lou raised his voice against a fresh burst of melody. I tapped his shoulder and pointed to the back porch. The music, laughter, and voices were louder outside, but at least I could eat my shit with a cigarette.

"I've been acting like a shmuck," I said into his ear, catching a strong whiff of cologne.

He placed his hand on my shoulder, "There's no need to apologize."

"Yes there is. I've been anxious about all the changes and it's spun my head." I covered my embarrassment with a fast slug of Bud and a slow drag on the smoke. "But there's no excuse for my rotten attitude."

"Attitude isn't everything," he said dropping his arm. "You've been there when we needed you. That's the important thing."

"Yeah, it hasn't been entirely black or white but..."

Lou interrupted with a smile, "Not black or white? What's come over you?"

"Middle age."

"But not too old to party, I hope?" He clapped me on my

shoulder, "Stop *shtupping* yourself, Matty. What's done is done, and no harm has come from it. My only real concern is this stalking business, but tonight isn't the time."

Lou pulled my arm. "Come, we'll take the rear stairs. I want to tell Lauren you're here."

I forced my suddenly resistant body to follow by promising myself a real drink. When we arrived I saw that Lou hadn't been kidding. A makeshift bar with a uniformed bartender stood next to the marimba along one side of the huge deck. Next was a long table lined with chafing dishes and rows of overflowing trays. The colored lamps hung from the corner poles; up here they shed just enough light to see people's features, but not their sweat.

Which meant no one could see mine. Though we were a spit away from the ocean, the air hung like a heavy woolen shawl. My throat was dry, the beer can empty, but I didn't know whether my parch was due to thirst or jitters.

Both called for the same solution. While Lou went searching for his woman, I slipped to the marimba corner of the bar and waved to the bartender. As soon as I thought double, I felt guilty and asked for a beer. At least here they had the Sam Adams. Lou was right, there was good stuff and a lot of it. Lauren couldn't afford me but could pay for this? We definitely weren't talking potluck.

I drowned my quick rush of suspicious anger with a serious swallow and stared stonily into the crowd. Despite the music, food, and alcohol, there was only one center of attention—Lauren Rowe.

She slid from group to group, stopping just long enough to laugh, hug, or introduce Lou who stood comfortably by her side. Occasionally Lauren would grab someone's hand and talk intensely into their ear. Perhaps a pariah to the townsfolk, Lauren was the cat's meow to her guests—her approach invariably treated with open arms.

And watched by most everyone else, just like I was watching.

I turned my back and slowly finished the bottle. But before I could call for another, a hand clasped my shoulder.

"Thanks for coming, Matthew. You keep surprising me," Lauren said in a low voice that sliced through the racket. "Let's go to the other side," she suggested, pointing to a small secluded spot where Lou stood. "He won't hear a thing this close to the music."

I nodded, signaled the bartender for a fresh, and took a deep breath. Lauren looked glowing, her eyes brilliant and glittering as if lit from within. Center of attention became her. She wore a sleek, dark burgundy dress with a long slit up the back which I followed as we haltingly made our way across the vibrating floor boards. Haltingly because we couldn't move more than a couple of feet before someone would rush up. Lauren was unfailingly good spirited, making certain to always introduce me. *I* never caught a name.

Halting turned into a full stop as Paul Brown popped up out of nowhere just as the marimbist flipped his sticks and shouted "Meringue`."

"Dance, darling?" Paul asked, an inviting smile on his face before glancing at me with cold eyes.

"Do you mind, Matthew?" Lauren asked.

"Of course not," I started, but before I could finish Lauren and Paul had already begun a series of intricate steps.

The two moved with elegant familiarity, Paul's lean body and silver hair a perfect foil for Lauren's full figured grace. Classic ballroom partners, the two unerringly anticipated each other's moves, their polished dance captivating.

And I wasn't the only one who thought so. The rest of the couples split apart forming an enthusiastic circle around Paul and Lauren who fed on the energy. The marimbist screamed "Tango" over the noise, changed the beat, and the couple effortlessly slipped into a new set of backbreaking bends and whirling spins.

The party went wild with whistles and foot stomping as the old deck trembled under the excitement. I even caught myself clapping, though I was careful not to spill the beer.

But, like everything else in life, good things come to an end. Lauren, with an exaggerated pantomime of wiping sweat from her brow, placed a hand on her heaving chest, and bowed toward Paul. Paul bowed deeply in return, though he wrapped his arm around her waist and whispered in her ear. I stayed where I was as Lauren wriggled free, leaning forward and placing a friendly peck on Paul's cheek.

"I hope that didn't upset Anne," Lauren commented breathlessly, as we finally got close to Lou's quieter corner.

"What a show!" Lou praised, wearing his wide smile. "I almost had a heart attack watching the two of you."

"We used to sneak out for lessons. We called it our "straight world" vice," Lauren explained, still breathing heavily. "It's fun but I don't have the same stamina."

"Who does?" Lou asked.

"Paul," Lauren replied, scanning the deck. "He would have danced the rest of the night."

There was a long pause before Lauren, having finally caught her breath, pointed, "I don't see the kids, but my mother, Vivian, is over there."

At first, all I saw was an enormous floppy hat. Then, as if she felt Lauren's finger, the hat turned and started over. Mama marched like a macho pigeon. Fists at her sides, she strutted her square body with short jerky movements. When she arrived, the body stopped but her mouth picked up speed.

"Aren't you the Queen of the Ball?" Vivian mocked. She angled her husky torso in my direction, banished her bite, and smiled coyly. "We haven't met."

Even in the dim light I could see the thick pancake powder and bright red splotches of rouge. But before I could nod in return, Vivian's smile vanished. "It makes me ill every time I think about the two of them," she slanted her head toward Lauren while Lou hung in the rear. "My own daughter in bed with someone old enough to be her father." Vivian's lip curled, "I don't know why I screwed hers—and he was my husband."

Lou looked shocked and helpless, but Lauren was one cool cuke. That, or she'd been assaulted by her mother too many times for one more to matter. "Mom, first of all Lou *isn't* old enough to be my father. And this is Matthew Jacob. He's Lou's son-in-law," she said as if speaking to a child.

Vivian turned on me with another seductive smile chiseled into her plaster. "Well don't misunderstand me, I have nothing against your father. What the hell, every old man wants what he's getting."

"Mom," Lauren sounded exasperated. "Stop it. You're humiliating yourself."

And me. Lauren's loose-lipped mother was voicing some of my own hostility.

"You mean I'm embarrassing *you*."

Lauren smiled grimly, "Always, Mom, always."

"You don't need *me* to make an ass out of yourself, child." Vivian reached into her baggy, brown dress and emerged with a Lucky Strike. "I don't usually smoke outside of my house, but around here ladylike doesn't matter. Light this, will you please?" she asked waving the cigarette in front of my face.

Vivian turned her attention back to Lauren. "You were a damn fool to let Paul get away. He's someone you could count on," she said, as if they had recently broken up. She took a long puff on her cigarette leaving a red stain on the filterless paper. "Not like the rest of your hit-and-runs."

Vivian swung her hat back to me. "Be a love and fetch a scotch and soda, emphasis on the former?" she winked, her mean magically gone.

"Mom, you aren't supposed to drink with your medicine."

"And you aren't supposed to sleep with old men," Vivian

snapped. "Just stay where you are, sweetie, I'll get my own."

She held out her rough hand and I shook it. "Nice meeting you Mrs..."

"You just call me Viv, honey. Now what was your name?"

Before I answered Viv dropped my hand, glanced toward Lou and Lauren, snorted, and pigeon-walked toward the bar.

CHAPTER 16

The party continued to swirl as Lou sputtered and I kept my eyes on the trembling floor. Lauren eventually shook her head, a smile tickling the corners of her mouth. "Doesn't hesitate to speak her mind, does she?" the smile growing to a grin then into peals of genuine laughter. Lou stopped his huffing and tried to join. Me? I managed to nod.

"Don't let my crazy mother ruin your fun, Matthew. I should have warned you," Lauren said, wiping tears from her eyes. "If she takes her medicine she's a shit. If she doesn't, she loses all track of reality. It's a tough call, isn't it?"

"This was the worst I've seen," Lou finally managed.

"Well, she's been drinking. We're lucky she didn't haul out the story about knocking her Navy man on his ass." Lauren stifled another round of giggles while she grabbed Lou's arm, "God, did you see her makeup?"

"Now don't be mean," Lou said with a smile.

"Speaking of drinks," I said, "this one zipped right through.

Where's the bathroom?" Vivian's explosion hadn't cheered me up, and I needed a little down time. Just me, a fresh beer, and my smokeless dope pipe in a tiled New Jerusalem.

"Take the backstairs," Lauren said pointing, "then go up and into my bedroom. There's a bathroom attached and you won't have to wait."

I sauntered a couple of feet, glanced back, and saw the two of them huddled close, Lauren fighting to keep a grin off her face. I detoured to the bar, relieved that Vivian had already waddled away. I once again talked myself out of a bourbon and traded my empty for a full. When I dragged my eyes from the beer, the bartender was talking to a jaw dropping, full breasted, tube-topped, tangled-haired blonde. I felt my mouth Sahara as everything and everyone else faded to black.

Though I stood on the far end of the long bar, the woman's screaming sensuality seemed close enough to touch. Close enough to catch myself stroking the beer bottle. I downed another long swallow desperately hoping to unglue my mouth. It didn't work nor did it matter. The blonde finished her conversation, momentarily captured my feverish eyes, then disappeared behind a clump of dancers.

It was as if a bright light snapped shut leaving behind a flickering golden afterimage. Which I toted through the crowd, into the house, and all the way to Lauren's bedroom.

I hit the overhead and was whacked with a Pier One showroom. Wicker bed, dresser, desk and couch. Even a wicker television stand where a flat screen squatted like an electronic Buddha, perhaps a modern variation of Lauren's spiritual searchings. Unfortunately, the TV reminded me of Boots so I quickly found the bathroom and locked myself inside.

To hack the rest of the night I needed "now," not "no." Sucking hard on my smoke-free pipe slowed my anxiety, finally leaving me ready to face more people. But not ready enough when I came out of the bathroom to find two of 'em hunched over the glass-topped wicker desk in Lauren's bedroom.

A lanky, olive skinned youngish man with stringy black hair chopped close around the ears and temples, swung quickly around in my direction. A dark Andy Warhol clone. Startled, he maneuvered his narrow linen ass to obscure my view. But his wiggle didn't hide the tightly rolled dollar in his neatly tapered fingers.

The string-bean, who had been hidden by his shuffle, stepped out, a worried look on her chalk white face. White accented with black. Black long sleeved skirt and black leather knee-high boots. Her hip length hair was bottle black, her mascara heavy and black, lipstick and nail polish pale white. Thick dark eye-shadow covered her round eyes. The young lady gave no truck to the sticky, hot late summer night.

"This is my mother's bedroom," the flop-top complained. "It's off limits during parties, there's a john downstairs." He leaned his baggy silk shirt toward the door suggesting I leave.

I ignored the invitation and stared at the rolled bill in his hand. "I was told to use this bathroom."

"By who?" he asked irritably. "My mother always keeps this floor to herself."

"If your mother is Lauren Rowe, she made an exception."

The tall man looked at me with a sudden flash of understanding. "You must be related to Lou. His son?"

"Son-in-law."

"Geez," the black and white anorexic said. "I don't remember hearing anything about a daughter."

"She's dead."

"I'm so sorry," the girl said.

"Yeah, me too," I replied, instantly softening. It was tough to work up a mad toward someone floundering between waif attractive and Goth.

"Son-in-law, huh?" the man asked caustically. "You don't look the part."

This twit was a different day in the park. "What part is that?"

"I heard you're a detective."

"Private."

"I thought all cops wear thick leather shoes and get haircuts." He kept trying to palm his homebrew coke tube so I decided to jerk his chain. I walked within reach and stuck out my right. "I like sneakers. Anyhow, I'm Matt Jacob, Lou's son-in-law. You must be Stephen. Pleased to meet you."

I watched his face pucker with worry before I dropped my arm. "Don't worry about the dope, I'm private, not the law."

If I thought my comment would tone him down I was mistaken.

"That's a relief," he said sarcastically. "With Lauren and Lou hanging out, it might be difficult to bust me even if you were." He did, however, shift his body from its awkward position against the desk.

"Oh, Stephen," Waif interjected. "Why are you always so hostile?" She turned to me, "Don't mind his trip. I'm Heather Heywood, and he's Stephen Brown. But I guess you already know that." Heather frowned, "Our families are sort of, sort of..."

"Overlapped," I offered.

"That's a good word," Heather said, her face brightening.

"I guess you know all the gory details?" Stephen turned toward the desk to organize his cocaine kit.

"Don't put it away," Heather exclaimed. "We were just getting started. Maybe Matt wants some. He looks cool. It's okay to call you Matt, isn't it?"

I wondered how young Heather was, asking if it was all right to use my first name. Then I turned it around; it wasn't her youth, it was my age.

"Both sound fine." I didn't want to appear too eager and blow that cool.

Stephen glanced at me then shrugged. "I shouldn't be surprised, you look freaky enough."

"Nothing like a detective," Heather earnestly concurred. "Or even someone related to Lou. You look more like a... a..."

"Dropout," Stephen supplied, chopping a chunk of ice into snow.

"You got that right, I lied." The repetitive flick of Stephen's razor blade made me happy. Looking at the cocaine wet my lips and had me thinking about Hendrix's *Foxy Lady*. A blonde foxy lady.

"Terrific, another Lauren," Stephen muttered. "Maybe she belongs with you instead of your old man."

"How did you become a cop?" Heather interrupted quickly.

"I'm not a cop," I repeated patiently, though growing impatient with the time Stephen was taking to prepare the coke. There was some satisfaction watching sweat dampen the armholes of his light green silk.

Stephen finally nudged Heather. "Here, do a couple lines."

"Let Matt go first, Stephen. He's the new family member."

I shelved the second half of her remark as he reluctantly passed me the tightly rolled dollar. When I came up for air I saw a sardonic smile on Stephen's face. "No virgin."

"Is it me, or are you always like this?" I asked, feeling the coke drain down the back of my throat.

"Always, always, always," Heather answered, lifting her head. "Don't take it personally, Stephen has a big chip on his shoulder."

Her remark drew a smile from Warhol man. "Spend enough time with my family and you'll need one too."

"I've known your family my whole life." Heather carefully placed the tooter next to the mirror and stepped aside to let Stephen take her place. She made a sour face. "Twenty-seven and back living with my mother. Sheesh."

"Worse," Stephen lifted his nose. "Living with my father."

"Lose your job?" I asked Heather sympathetically.

"Not really. I broke up with my boyfriend."

"Living with him *was* a job, Heather," Stephen said supportively, low-riding the desk. "A lousy one."

Heather smiled. "Well, he was no prize. Trouble is, now I'll have to get a real one."

"It's better than allowing that asshole to shit all over you. And better than hanging around the house having my father hound you. Trust me, Heather, Paul is big on other people's Protestant Ethic."

"I've lived with him before, Stephen. I'm more worried about a job. Where will I get the time to paint?" Heather smiled at me, "My ex-boyfriend runs a small gallery and I helped out. It left plenty of time for my art."

I tried polite but Stephen interrupted with a wave of the bill. "Here, chat later. You want any more?"

I nodded gratefully. Fuck my cool. While I lingered over the drugs, the two of them continued on about Stephen's family and Heather's money problems, their words melding with the noise outside. I hesitated before taking seconds, fourths, if I was counting nostrils. But a quick review of my night's raging chemical intake convinced me not to count. Still, I wasn't above rubbing some flakes onto my gums.

"Stephen, I know what to expect," Heather said.

"I just hope you haven't forgotten."

"Sometimes it's better to forget," she retorted. "I think you're obsessed. You say you hate them but you keep coming around."

Stephen gathered his paraphernalia. "Him, not them. Anyway, I have as much right to use the Hacienda as anyone else in this damn family. Hell, if *he* can still come around I can too."

"That's not what I mean and you know it."

I'd grown bored. "I've been gone from the party for too long," I interrupted. "Don't want Lou or Lauren to think I ran off without saying goodbye. Listen, thanks for the sugar, it made my night."

And woke me up. Whatever misgivings I had about dropping off the wagon were brushed aside in the rush of coke induced, ego boosting energy.

Heather spun in my direction. "Well it's been a pleasure meeting you, Matt. I hope we see each other again."

"Let's see how long the happy couple last before you add him to your Christmas list," Stephen grunted.

I forced a smile over my numb gums. "Don't pay him any mind, Heather. You send me a card any time you want."

CHAPTER 17

The marimba player was into showboating to the crowd while I vainly tried to locate Lou. Almost unconsciously, I stopped my search and scanned the deck for the looker. But no Lady Luck. Worse, my beer was still upstairs. I started toward the watering hole and nearly shed my skin when a hand snaked out and grabbed my arm. Hard.

"This guy rescued Ian and brought him to the hospital. Might have saved his life." The trembling fingers digging deep into my biceps belonged to Paul Brown.

"Hey pal, didn't mean to startle you," Brown roared over the music, a sloppy grin on his thin, pale face. No question what he'd been doing since his fancy dance.

"That's okay, Paul. When you're on your way for a drink everything else gets pushed aside," I said, thinking about the coffee machine in the hospital as I pulled my arm away.

Paul tilted his silver head deciding whether I was taunting before introducing me to a tired looking, short-haired woman with a pinched mouth, wary eyes, and little makeup. "Anne," Paul said. "This is Matt Jacobs."

"Jacob. Without the s."

"Sorry with a capital S. Anne, this here is Matt Jacob, Ian's savior. With a small s."

Anne's mouth relaxed ever so slightly. "It's nice to meet you, Mr. Jacob," she said, her stern face softening.

"Matt, please."

"Matt. We really appreciate what you did for Ian. Paul's just had too much to drink." Anne stopped speaking and stood looking blankly around the deck. "Can we leave yet?" she asked abruptly, turning toward Paul and placing a hand on his shoulder.

Which he promptly shook off. "It's not even eleven."

"We've been for hours already, and I didn't want to come at all," she said.

"I could say 'you never come,' but I won't," he slurred.

Anne jerked her head as if slapped. "You bastard," she hissed walking away.

I expected Paul to follow but he just grunted, "Lauren's parties are always tough on her."

I shrugged and plotted an escape route, but it wasn't going to be easy. Mister Nice Guy had my arm again.

"Every year we go through the same fucking argument," he said shaking his head. "You'd think after all this time she might loosen up."

I hoped he was talking about Lauren's party and not their sex life.

"You were on your way to the bar, weren't you?" he asked his eyes suddenly opaque.

I nodded glumly.

"I'll keep you company."

"Thanks."

I caught another look, but he wasn't listening to his better instincts because he matched my steps across the weathered wood.

At least he was quiet until we were served.

"Just a beer? This is damn good scotch."

"You sound surprised," I said. And generous with your ex-wife's refreshments, I thought.

"This year Lauren outdid herself. And without putting her hand into my pocket." Paul grinned through his glare. "Your father-in-law must have some money."

"He does okay ." Maybe Paul had followed his instincts. I was forever a magnet for unhappy drunks. Had to do with growing up inside my father's tavern. No matter how many years passed, I guess whiskey was still in my sweat. I felt my mouth water while I watched him drain his drink and signal for another. "Doesn't sound like you enjoy contributing."

Paul shrugged. "What the hell, Lauren makes it her business to keep the family together. It would have been easy for everyone to go their separate ways."

"What do you do for a living?"

"Shipping manager for a plastic company. You know, *Today's Tupperware, Tomorrow's Antique.*" Wish they were worth something now. When you have children every penny flies. Not a big money job, but I have plenty of spare time."

"Your kids seem pretty old to be costing you."

An uncomfortable look crossed his face. "Kids always cost. Anne's daughter Heather recently moved in with us. Can't charge her room and board, can I?" Paul waved his hand dismissively. "I suppose it's better than having them scattered across the country."

I took a long draw from my bottle. "You do all right with this extended friends and family, don't you?"

Paul ran his hand through his tousled silver hair. "Like I said," his eyes hardening, "it's a way to keep everyone together." A sour smile wrapped around the rim of his glass. "Anyway, I'm used to it." He paused, "You find us difficult to understand, don't you?" He stopped, rocked unsteadily on his feet, then added, "That reminds me, I owe you an apology for the night at the hospital. Wasn't on my game. Lauren and I do better than that, much better." He grit his teeth and reached out to grasp the table.

"You want a chair?"

"Nah. I need to find Anne and get the fuck home before I do something stupid. Let me tell you about kids, Jacob. Trouble never ends. Heather back in the house, Ian in the hospital." Paul killed his drink and planted the glass on the bar. "The only one I count on is Alexis."

He hadn't mentioned Stephen but I kept my mouth shut. Despite his sloppy self-pity, I almost felt sorry for him. He seemed like a guy who spent his entire life trying to catch up to the next paycheck. Three kids—four, if you included the Heywoods—meant a lot of hard running to keep from riding in reverse. Besides, a lifetime sniffing plastic ought to allow for bitter.

I was about to offer to find his lady when the sky suddenly caught fire; my bare-bellied beauty was approaching our end of the bar. Paul noticed me staring over his shoulder, turned and, for the first time since we'd been together, grinned with genuine, unadulterated pleasure.

"Allie, my girl, I was just talking about you. Matt, this is my daughter Alexis."

Unable to talk, I nodded my greeting and noticed her likeness to Lauren.

"I'm surprised you can speak and stand at the same time, Dad." Her voice was husky and affectionate.

Alexis's proximity dried my mouth and wet the rest of my skin. Asian eyes, high cheekbones, and a drop dead body. Inviting. The genetic best of each parent rolled into a whole greater than the sum of its parts.

I felt like a teenager; her sensual, exotic beauty knocked my socks. For one quick moment the feeling reminded me of my first impression of Boots. A moment I instantly suppressed.

"Alexis, meet the newest member of the entourage." Paul turned to me. "He calls us an extended family but it's really Lauren and the rest of us." His daughter's arrival lent him a little less hang-dog, a little more overt aggression.

"We know what you think, Dad. Now, how about a nice, large cup of coffee?"

"You're worried about me," Paul smiled drunkenly.

"I'm worried about Annie," Alexis teased. "You're too big for her to carry home."

"Allie, you know she hates to be called Annie."

"And I'm not too fond of Allie, but that doesn't stop *you*." Alexis walked a couple of steps toward the bartender and pointed to the giant coffee urn. "Black," she ordered.

I considered making it two, but eyeballing Alexis's body called for a cold one.

"Now, who are you?" Alexis asked after handing Paul his coffee.

"Sorry." Paul lifted his nose from the Styrofoam. His hand trembled and he dribbled some of the hot liquid over his fingers. This was one unlucky guy when it came to coffee on the go. "Matt Jacob, Lou's son-in-law. The guy who rescued Ian."

"I didn't know Lou had a daughter," Alexis said.

"She's been dead for a long time," I answered for the second time that night, this time waiting for the inevitable loss of breath and jolt of anger. But a save by Paul pulled me off the cliff.

"He's also the private detective who's 's been checking on Lauren's spooky stalker," Paul chuckled.

"She doesn't quit, does she?" Alexis grimaced.

"You know your mother," Paul said, a touch of anger in his tone.

Alexis tried to change the subject. "Why don't we find Anne before you say something you'll regret."

"I'm done with regrets," Paul boasted, suggesting the opposite.

Alexis took his arm. "Then let's make sure you don't create any new ones. You stay right here," she called over her shoulder as she helped her father. "You got lost once already."

I didn't know what she meant, but wanted to. Enough to root me right where I was. Actually, just flexible enough to bellow to the bartender for a bourbon neat. Underneath my excitement was a hint of guilty discomfort—a hint I wanted to ignore.

I didn't have long to wait. Alexis returned with a brisk, hip-shifting stroll, and an emphatic shake of her thick curls. "He doesn't get drunk all that often," she said apologetically.

"No problem." I was relieved to discover the bourbon unlocked my tongue. "Would you like something yourself?"

"That would be great. Bombay Sapphire and tonic with an extra lime. Have you met everybody?"

The marimba was on hold which made listening to her purr a pleasure. "I don't know who you mean by everybody. I've met Stephen, Heather, Vivian, and Anne. Now you."

"And you've already met Ian," Alexis said directly. "I guess you know the whole cast of characters."

I nodded and we lapsed into silence until the bartender returned with our order.

"Fetching Ian must have been difficult," she said after a quick swallow.

"Nah," I smiled. "Now Vivian, *that* was difficult."

A dazzling white grin split her angular features, driving her high cheekbones up another notch. "How bad was she?"

"Well, she didn't have any trouble expressing her opinions."

"It's the price we pay. If Vivian's not on her pills she's pretty loopy. But then, everyone in our family is loopy."

"You too?"

Alexis flashed her gleaming teeth. "Of course."

I lit a cigarette.

"Does that make you nervous?" she asked.

"I was nervous before I got here."

"Why?"

"My intro to your clan has been a little 'roundabout.'" As was our conversation. If it weren't, I'd be running my fingers across her naked midriff.

"We're not a very straightforward group of people. Certainly not straight."

"That part's fine," I said, trying, but failing to push my prurient aside.

Alexis made a sour face as the marimba man returned to his instrument. "Hello south of the border, goodbye conversation. Let's get out of here."

"Leave?" I don't know what hit first: understanding, desire, or reluctance.

"Sure."

"Where do you want to go?" I stalled.

"Wherever my convertible takes us."

I drained the last of my drink. "I have my car here."

"We'll come back for it."

Alexis turned and said something to the bartender who handed her a bottle of champagne and two long stemmed plastic glasses. Without a backward glance she worked her way through the crowd toward the outside stairs while I hesitated. What the fuck was I doing sneaking off with Lauren Rowe's *daughter*?

CHAPTER 18

I didn't hesitate for long. What slowed me wasn't sneaking away, but desire. I was crawling very close to one of those cutting edges, knew it, and still followed her long legs and suede bottom.

Alexis's low slung, open air Saab, was almost as breathtaking as she. Creamy pearl-gray exterior with white trim, wire wheels, and a plush coffee interior. No kiddy carpools for this classic, updated and restored landshark.

Alexis pressed a red button on her key-ring and the fat tire'd four wheeler flashed its eyes.

"Doesn't seem like a town where you need that," I said, twisting my tingling body into the lush leather bucket.

"Every town is that sort of town," she replied. "Anyway, it's a habit, the way I try to live my life."

"Why don't I believe you?"

Alexis smiled, opened her legs under the padded steering wheel and looked me over. "I don't know, why *don't* you?" She glanced into the rearview mirror and deftly pulled onto the street. I grabbed the crash handle anticipating multiple g force.

"No need to hold on," she said smoothly shifting into second. "I don't drive as fast as I look."

"Should I be disappointed or relieved?"

Alexis laughed and aimed the car out of town. "Getting away is the relief."

"Not big on these annual get-togethers?"

"The party was fine, better than most. Lauren actually had the place looking decent."

"It's the house you don't like?"

"I love the damn house. I hate what's happening to it."

"You want to explain?"

"Have you seen the Hacienda in the daylight? Rotten clapboard, cracks in the brick pillars under the porches, mildew on soffits—and the foundation has serious problems. The main beam needs work and the furnace truly frightens me. It should have been replaced years ago. Also, someone is going to break their neck on the goddamn front stairs." Alexis's voice rose as her grip tightened on the plump steering wheel. "I haven't even mentioned the chimney and roof. My wonderful mother won't spend a dime on the place and by the time she finally sells, it will be worthless."

Alexis noticed my open mouth because she burst out laughing. "Don't look so surprised, I'm in real estate."

"Passionate about it too."

"About the Hacienda. It's a very special place and I hate to see it neglected. Watch, now that Lauren and Lou are an item, she'll manipulate you into playing handyman."

"It must be difficult for your mother to care for the Hacienda by herself."

"If that's what she's telling you, it's bullshit. My father works his ass off on the house. He spends an enormous amount of time keeping it upright. And believe me, he puts up with an earful from 'Little Orphan Annie' because of it."

We left the town behind, speeding our way through a series of curves and back loops. Alexis concentrated on the dark, winding road and I hunted the Euro dash for an ashtray. I found it, noted the empty, gleaming interior and lit up anyway. I hoped she didn't have the same low opinion of body abuse that she had about house neglect.

The longer we remained silent, the louder my anxiety. "It didn't seem like you or your father think much of Lauren's worry about being followed," I said, rolling my guilt about being with her into the one concern I was willing to contemplate.

"I can't speak for him since he won't talk about it. For me it's just another family drama, *"full of sound and fury, signifying nothing."*

"Your mother isn't an idiot, Alexis."

"My, my, a literate gumshoe."

I was torn between watching the road and her nearly naked legs. Legs won. "The only gumshoes I know are in paperbacks. Anyhow, 'literate' is too fancy to describe my taste."

"What's the line from that Brando movie?" Alexis asked.

"I coulda been a contendah." Wonder why I picked that one?

"I'm thinking of the one where the woman says..."

"I've always relied on the kindness of strangers," I said showing off.

"Well, with my mother, it doesn't stop with strangers."

"You do have a mad-on."

"Not really. From the outside, Lauren's life looks like a model of courage. The original brass-balled broad. Progressive politics, experimental lifestyles; a lot before any of it became fashionable.

"Unfortunately, living on the inside wasn't nearly so wonderful. She did the experimenting and the rest of us paid the price. Lauren dragged us through one strange trip after another, no matter the cost. Now it's this stalking bullshit."

"So you're not worried?"

"About someone stalking my mother?" Alexis kept her eyes

on the road. "Are you taking her seriously," she asked, shaking her head.

"Enough to check."

"Did you discover anything?"

The only thing discovered had been me but I wasn't gonna tell. "Not yet."

"And you're a professional."

"Thanks."

Alexis grazed my face with a sideways glance. "If you're not careful my mother will run you in circles. I'd drop the whole ridiculous thing if I were you." As if to soften her remarks Alexis added, "Tell you the truth Matt, I think my mother's relationship with Lou has unsettled the family. He's very different than anyone she's ever spent time with and she's *very* different when they're together. It has everyone unhinged—including me."

The speedometer climbed to eighty and I reached for the strap.

"Relax, I'm not going to kill us," Alexis said unconvincingly. We have a long way to go.

Before I could ask where she was taking us Alexis said, "My mother lives in her own imaginary world.. On top of which, she hands my brothers built-in reasons for their personal failures. Look at Ian's accident."

Alexis used the same euphemism all of them used. Maybe anyone would. I didn't know whether it was the sound of Ian rolling onto the Bimmer's floor, but I couldn't help asking, "Why does everyone call Ian's suicide attempt an accident?"

Alexis gave no outward indication she was bothered by my question, though her accelerator toe tilted forward. "Because no one believes he ever intended to seriously hurt himself. He just fucked up. Hence, accident."

"He didn't cut himself shaving."

"He's had plenty of practice fucking up," Alexis said in a chilly voice. "He should know better than to play with knives.

117

Ian continually finds pathetic ways to beg for attention." A less than amused grin rearranged her lush lips. "We've had some real doozies. My father had to fly down to Orlando to pick him up from Disney World. Seems my little brother ate enough acid to take center stage during a performance and tried to convince the tourists he was the reincarnation of Walt. It took seven security guards to remove him. Plus

Ian's also Bruce Lee if kicking at yourself in a mirror earns a belt."

"How's he doing?" I asked mildly, hoping to throttle back her foot. And her.

Alexis's mouth tucked into harsh, "Don't know and don't care. But if he weren't okay, my mother would be bedside holding his hand."

Ian was clearly not a topic to pursue if I wanted to pursue Alexis. And despite a continuing undercurrent of conscience, pursuit was exactly what I wanted. Bullshit, I wanted to catch. So she wasn't a warm and tender mother, brother lover; I wasn't sitting here for warm and tender.

"Well my friend, you got yourself mixed up with a real zoo." Alexis tossed her head in a way that reminded me of Lauren, but I didn't think it wise to point out the similarity.

Or wise to be where I was. Part of me wanted her to turn the car around, most just wanted to rid her of her hostility. So I kept silent and watched the Saab's sloping hood chow down the onrushing white line.

Alexis hooked a sharp right and pulled onto a secondary highway. The engine noise rose, though the front seat stayed remarkably wind free. Alexis pushed a button and all four door windows rose simultaneously. The night sky was still our roof, but big bucks also bought quiet.

We rode in silence while Alexis chewed on our discussion. Literally. Her high cheekbones and jaw shifted until she finally said, "I dislike perpetual victims. You have a problem, I say fix it. Victims don't think like that. It's always someone else's fault. Welfare is stuffed with victims and so is my family."

"Stuffed?"

"Well, Dad's different. He's a loyal guy and had the lousy luck to fall head over heels for Lauren. But as soon as he stopped taking orders she dumped him. But look at the rest. Ian, Stephen, my mother—despite her various poses."

I looked at Alexis instead. "Stephen just seemed dour."

"Just dour? He must have been high." She suddenly shook her head and grinned, her anger forgotten. "Let me guess, you were getting stoned with him when you disappeared from the party."

I nodded, "Him and Heather Heywood."

"Funny how things work. Lou seems so damn normal."

"Lou *is* normal."

"And you?"

"I usually don't fit in, that's all."

She caught my eye and winked, "Maybe you fit in better than you think. Anyway, you're doing okay with me."

"It's an unusual night."

"I hope so," Alexis grinned wickedly. "Could you believe Heather's clothes and make-up? Black and white is all she ever wears.

"Portrait of a young woman as a dead artist."

"Only she's very much alive and talented. Her work is really very good."

"You're kidding? She seemed like an air-head."

"Anything but. Heather is soft, but she's not dumb." Alexis glanced at me then shifted her eyes back to the empty highway. "If you hang around long enough you're going to discover that people in this family are not always what they seem."

CHAPTER 19

I hoped Alexis was who she seemed to be. The cocaine was starting to ebb but it didn't affect my flow. Alexis was a burning candle and I was a high flying moth. Wherever we were going, I hoped we got there soon.

As if she read my thoughts, Alexis opened her knees another inch. "P-Town," she said.

"That's really far."

"Not anymore."

Alexis did drive as fast as she looked. We'd covered a huge distance in a very short time. Eighty to a hundred rushes things along.

"I come down all the time. I have an office to handle summer rentals. Around here you can pawn off a doghouse for a grand a week," she chuckled, a satisfied look crossing her face.

"I guess you're pretty good at your job," I said.

"You too. Very good."

"How so?"

"The only thing we've talked about is my family. You haven't said a word about yourself and Lou. Somehow, I don't think it's accidental."

Well, we were off greed, though the change wasn't exactly a relief. "Lou is a helluva guy. A real character. Wheeling and dealing before Chicago slapped tomatoes on its hot dogs. Worked his way through the Democratic Party holding hands with Lord Mayor Daley The First. For a long time he had enormous political clout. He moved out here when his wife died. I was the closest thing to a living relative."

Alexis reacted impatiently. "Lou isn't the one I'm interested in." To underscore her point Alexis added ten to the dial.

I resisted an automatic impulse to grab the strap. "I'm not sure how to begin," I juked, worrying that fleshing out reality would undermine my heat-laden fantasies.

"How about the badge?"

Luck was running my way. Alexis picked an area that only occasionally bordered reality. It was a riff I could play, and did, emphasizing the lack of excitement and danger that defined this dick's day-to-day.

I told her about my old mall-man gig, filling the next portion of the trip with numerous, humorous tales of human nature unleashed by consumer madness. I bypassed anything close to important to keep reality at bay and because Alexis thoroughly enjoyed stories that presented people in an absurd light. Her cynicism bothered me until I remembered who was choosing the stories. After that I relaxed and laughed as much as she.

As we pulled onto the single road leading into the arty, Portuguese fishing town, Alexis reluctantly slowed her signature machine. Unfortunately, the change in speed brought me a little closer to earth. What the hell was I doing next to this strange and beautiful woman? With no answer other than my original hard-on. But that answer was still good enough.

Alexis drove slowly down Main Street past rows of small inns and guesthouses until we came to the first of the art galleries. Garbage under glass, though in fairness, the colony contained talented artists and honest writers. Even had legitimate galleries away from the main drag.

Alexis brushed by packs of late night pedestrians still crowding the narrow sidewalk-less street. "Damnit!" she cursed.

"What's the matter?"

Alexis shot her left thumb toward a small cedar shingled storefront. "I'd planned on the upstairs, but it's still being used."

I saw lights above the store and a long white Infinity in the driveway.

"Still?" I asked, facing front.

"I meant someone is up there."

"You don't sound surprised." Now that a piece of the real world pierced the bubble of our open air excursion, it threatened to invite the rest.

"I'm not. My real estate business has a silent partner from New York who occasionally spends time in the apartment."

"He doesn't tell you?" Some of my disappointment slipped through.

"Usually. Sometimes he doesn't know himself."

"You're sure he's not waiting for you?"

Alexis frowned, "We've done a good job avoiding these kind of subjects. You want to change that now?"

I knew better, much better. "No thanks. Just hoped to, uh, to..." I glanced beneath the steering wheel, "...stretch my legs."

Alexis smiled and cruised through the city center. Given the town's renowned tolerance, I usually felt a certain ease, a sense of homeland. But now I sat muddled, confused whether to allow my relief full run or to let my libido hope Alexis had a backup.

The confusion wasn't long lasting. We neared the eastern tip of the road and pulled into a motel parking lot. When Alexis stopped the Saab I released my seatbelt but she told me to stay where I was.

I shrugged and ogled her luscious body as she walked to the main door. Maybe she received professional courtesy. I settled back in the seat, lit a cigarette, and heard Billy Holiday moan, "I got it bad, and that ain't good." Blue Billy wasn't singing just about herself.

But the longer I smoked the less I believed. I had it bad and it was *gonna* be good.

Alexis returned from the motel holding a large plastic bag. "Grab the champagne and glasses. We only have a few minutes if we don't want to get soaked."

It didn't look like rain, but I did as told.

"Follow me." Alexis took off her shoes, broke into a trot, and led us to a long block and boulder breakwater. She ran surefootedly across the seawall toward a lighthouse at the far end. Though she toted the bag, I had to hustle to keep pace. Now I understood her rush. The tide was rapidly rising and, while we weren't in any danger, I preferred my pants dry.

"Where to?" I shouted over the ocean's roar.

"The lighthouse."

"Can we get inside?"

Alexis just kept running.

I grunted, paying attention to the tops of the uneven boulders. One thing to drown in a mad dog lust rush, another to stupidly slip into the ocean. Our race with the moon was close, but we made it across the rocks just as the water lapped at our feet.

We walked another dozen yards across the small island before Alexis pulled out an odd shaped key then climbed fire escape stairs to a metal door. "What are you waiting for?" she shouted over the ocean's noise.

Too dangerous a question. I grabbed the iron handrail and followed her inside, clanging the metal shut. The tall, silo-like building was pockmarked with tiny, square windows carved through stone walls, the hollowness amplifying the sound of waves and wind. At regular intervals light from the overhead lamp-room cast brief, strobe-like effects.

"Come on," Alexis said, her voice echoing. We climbed another set of circular metal stairs to a landing that stretched across the lighthouse's diameter. Both sides of the platform were equipped with handrails and a king-size mattress covered the middle of the floor.

When we got to the mattress Alexis took a neatly folded sheet and comforter from the oversized bag.

"The lady who has everything," I complimented when she pulled out a couple of gourmet food tins and a can opener.

"Not yet," she murmured loud enough to hear.

I placed my hand on her shoulder. Alexis backed into me, her high-riding behind rubbing against my groin. My hand slid to the strip of naked skin pulling her closer. I heard the sharp intake of both our breaths when I ran my fingers underneath the tube-top and onto her large breast.

"If we don't slow down we'll end up rutting on our feet," she said.

I didn't care where we rutted. But Alexis stepped out of my grasp and pointed to the clean, fresh sheet. She lifted one side and I grabbed the other to spread it across the foam.

Alexis removed the champagne and plastic glasses from the bag while I stripped down to my shorts. I sat next to her, watching her extract the cork with a loud pop, the liquid spilling onto her long lush thighs. I tried to quench both thirsts by licking up the spill.

Bottle in hand, Alexis bent back onto her elbows, the brief skirt riding right up to her white silk panties. I raised my head and looked into smiling eyes. "Should I spill anymore?" she asked.

"No need," I muttered, my lips against her thigh, tongue tracking a layer of invisible fuzz. She placed the soles of her feet on the mattress, and suddenly closed her legs.

"Come up here and bring the glasses," she commanded imperiously, a tone that, at least this night, added to my excitement.

While Alexis poured, I retrieved my cigarettes, lit up, and sat on the edge of the mattress.

"I forgot an ashtray," Alexis said from behind me, her fingernails digging into my naked back.

"I'll use this," I replied holding up my plastic glass, "and drink out of the bottle." Mall-man to macho-man.

I felt her body shift behind me. When I twisted around, the tube-top and underpants, were heaped in a pile at the foot of the bed, her thick blonde curls completely hidden under the silk scarf she'd been wearing around her neck.

Alexis smiled past her bare breasts without a hint of shy.

But her smile did little to lessen my shock. With her hair tightly covered Alexis was the spitting image of her mother. Now the night consisted of three people, not two—and it wasn't the idea of a simple menage a` trois that disturbed me. Suddenly I was cheating on Boots *and* Lou.

CHAPTER 20

"Let's hope there's more bite than bark," Alexis teased, noting the bulldogs on my boxers. At the same time she ran the palm of her hand between my legs.

"No false advertising with you," I whispered, avoiding her face and staring at her full breasts with their half dollar aureoles and erect nipples.

"You ain't seen nothing yet." Alexis's hand suddenly hardened around my stiff cock. For an instant I feared her hold would trigger an embarrassingly early reaction, but as soon as I felt her fingers dig in I knew I was packing an all-night hard.

"This way, you," she growled, pulling me toward her. Not exactly cruel, but we weren't talking delicate either. I was still shaken by Alexis's resemblance to Lauren, so I shut my lids and licked the sweat from the top of her upper lip, trying to fuse the two through blind taste. When I finally looked, Alexis's long legs were spread and her clipped trim glistened. I started to slide down the mattress.

But she choked my cock with her hand and snatched my

lower lip between her teeth, eyes hard and unblinking. A dull light flickered in unison with the lamp-room as I finally caught on to her game.

And didn't care. I fucking deserved it. Alexis's heavy breasts swung near my hand and I reached out.

"No!" she snapped, letting go and squirming away from my hand. "You don't touch until I tell you. Do you understand?"

I backed off and, after another long gulp on the champagne, lit a smoke. Alexis snapped her fingers and I passed the bottle. She swigged, then rubbed some of the liquid on her jutting nipples and between her legs.

"I want you all eyes," Alexis commanded.

I returned the bottle to the floor, swiveled, and stared. She was lying on her side, one knee in the air, the suede mini rolled around her waist. I smoked and watched as Alexis squeezed her nipples then moved her hand between her thighs. All the while she held my eyes in an unwavering gaze.

Though still disturbing, Alexis's likeness to her mother actually added to my excitement, so I fixed my sight on her motions; the only sign of my internal heat the outpouring of sweat across my chest and back.

Alexis reveled in her exhibition. Mouth stretched in a tight smile, her fingers tugged on the short brown hair between her legs. Widening, Alexis used both hands to open her lower lips, then used one hand to stroke between them.

I snuffed the cigarette and edged closer. When I leaned forward, Alexis slapped me across the face. Hard.

"Not yet!" she snarled, her eyes flashing. "Right now you just watch."

Every inch of my skin urged me to ignore her warning and force my way on top. But instead, I yanked off my shorts and kept my eyes focused on her self-centered fondling. Alexis's hips squirmed faster, excited by my silent obedience.

"I want you on your back," she ordered hoarsely.

I rolled over, hot but wary as she climbed over me. Only now it was my turn to tease. I let the tip of my tongue circle her nipple while my hand reached between her legs where I found her fingers.

"Suck them, goddammit, suck them," she demanded, grabbing the back of my head.

Her attitude added to my excitement but I kept my tongue light, licking then mouthing as much breast as possible. I slowly let her breast slide out, then repeated the motion. With every long mouthful Alexis pushed both our fingers deeper inside. I shifted my lips to her other breast, my free hand embracing the one I left.

"Grab the rail with both hands but don't you dare move until I tell you," she ordered, her voice beginning to tremble.

I raised my arms behind my head as she paused to remove the mini. Alexis took the soft leather and rubbed it harshly against my cock and balls. It brought tears to my eyes, but I forced myself to lie there, to surrender, allowing the pain to reduce my guilt.

Alexis finally tossed the skirt and squatted over my raging dick. "I don't have a rubber," I blurted, all the queasiness about my entire night's behavior suddenly bursting though my frantic desire.

"Too late for safe, Matt," Alexis mocked. "I want it all."

I white-knuckled the metal, and caught one of her nipples with my mouth. Now *I* played rough, biting and feeling her drench my cock. She was half moaning, half crying, pressing wildly, driving me in as deep as she could.

I released the handrail and grabbed her ass as she slid forward. I dug my fingers into her firm flesh and, on her down-strokes, dragged her down even farther. Eventually she placed her palms on my chest and leaned forward, rubbing against my groin until she burst into a shrieking, echoing explosion.

At the very moment of Alexis's/Lauren's shuddering orgasm, I knew I wasn't going to come. I wasn't going to ejaculate then, or throughout the night. We could fuck like bunnies but I wasn't coming with either one of her.

My eyes snapped opened to the rhythmic spin from the lamp-room. Now its stroboscopic effect only added to my champagne headache. I rolled over, surprised to find an empty mattress and tried to regain my bearings. Not easy. It felt like I'd barely survived a plane crash.

I forced my trembling hands to light a cigarette just as Alexis called from somewhere over my head. "You're up?"

Her voice had me up in full goddamn glory. It was as if my dick was Pavlov's pooch and Alexis the bell. Only this time my erection wasn't followed by a blitzkrieg of mind-bending lust, but a big-time bellyache—like I'd been kicked in the nuts with a steel-toed boot. Well, in some ways I had.

I doubled over, fighting nausea and the first full wave of guilt. I hadn't been awake long enough to defend against my night's submissive, sexual, incestuous cheat.

"Are you okay?" Alexis's voice reverberated in the cavernous structure as she climbed down the circular stairs and returned to the scene of the crime. "You fell asleep."

"You put my ass to sleep." I flashed on the last time that happened and shoved everything out of mind. Everything but my aching nuts—never thought I'd see the day when I appreciated blueballs.

"Well," Alexis said, dragging the tube down over her breasts, "it's time we started home."

My stubborn cock protested, but now my head was running the show. I nodded and without speaking we picked up, packing everything into the large plastic bag. Still silent, we climbed down the platform and back outside.

The sky, still dark, looked less black than when I'd last seen it. The wind had quieted and the ocean was dead calm. So calm, I heard nothing but the clang of the lock and the sound of our shoes as we crossed the seawall. Our pace was slower in this direction.

Alexis opened the car's trunk and pulled out a large towel. "Will you dry the seats while I run inside? I want to return the bag and key."

"Sure," I said, using the towel to dry my pant cuffs, socks, and sneakers.

I watched her stroll through the motel doors before I tended to the car. Leaving the top down next to the ocean hadn't made much sense, but then neither had the past couple hours. But I wasn't ready to think, so I leaned into my task.

I turned around, once more jacked by the sight of the long tangled, curly-haired, blonde. The scarf was back around her neck. Despite my guilt, my aching stomach, my plugged-up prick, I still wanted her.

The thought of home straightened my head. We had a long ride and I dreaded spending it in agonizing self-loathing. That could wait 'til I made it back to my apartment. I jumped inside while the convertible top was magically closing. A couple of latches later we were on our way without a backward glance.

And without words. In fact, it wasn't until we were well onto the highway that Alexis broke the silence. "Are you all right?" she asked, pointedly ignoring the speed limit.

"I'm fine," I answered with what I hoped approximated a smile.

"You look sick."

"Just achy."

"You're blueballed, aren't you?"

"A little," I admitted, relieved to have something on which to hang my hang-dog.

"We'll have to fix that," she suggested. Then, glancing in my direction, Alexis burst out laughing. "Don't climb out the window. I'm not *that* good a driver and I have a long work day staring me in the face."

Her beautiful face. Despite the intense hours and frantic sex, her almond eyes sparkled and her fresh skin shone. It made me feel old and ugly to look at her.

Maybe Alexis had the same opinion because she suggested I sleep. Her idea somehow granted me permission to shut down. Of course, I'd been following orders all night so maybe I just didn't want to stop.

Between napping and pretending, we were almost back to the Hacienda before there was any more conversation. Even then, we didn't say much. Not uncomfortable, just two people preparing to deal with the day.

But the closer we got to the Hacienda, the harder it was to clamp the chorus in my head. I'd just spent half the night cheating with Lauren's daughter—hell, it might have been Lauren herself, they looked so much alike. And there was a good chance Lou and Lauren knew it. At least some of it. Part of me didn't care what they knew and that worried me even more.

But Boots, blueballs, and the blonde blew into oblivion when we approached the Hacienda and I saw the last car in the dawn's police convoy pull away.

CHAPTER 21

The instant Alexis's Saab scraped the curb, I was out and running. Lauren's front door was wide open, and I was so intent on getting inside I almost knocked Anne Heywood onto the foyer floor. The room was a wreck, gouges in the walls, wood and plaster strewn about, the free standing mirror shattered.

"Matty, where the hell have you been?" Lou's voice was calm, but his breathing labored.

"I went for a long ride with Alexis," I answered numbly, staring at the chaotic hall. Too long.

Lauren, her lips drawn, stood in a quilted housecoat right in the middle of the mess. Anne moved to the corner looking very tired and very resigned.

I heard Alexis walk up the porch stairs, turned and saw a line of horizontal bullet holes straight across the middle of the front door.

"It was a gorgeous night for the convertible," Alexis said on entering. "Jesus!" she exclaimed. When she noticed Anne fretting in the corner, her voice swelled with alarm. "Where's Dad? Where

132

the hell is Dad?

"Coming, Allie," Paul called emerging from the kitchen shadows. "Nothing to get upset about, we weren't here. No one was touched. But where the fuck have you been?" he added. "It's the morning!"

"Riding around with Matt," she replied. "But what difference does that make?"

"No one knew where you were," he said, shifting wary eyes between me and Lou.

Every synapse felt trapped inside a pinball machine leaning dangerously close to TILT. "Will someone tell me *something*?"

Lauren's exhausted voice cut through the tension. "Some assholes sprayed the door with bullets. Real bullets. A few hours either way and someone might have been killed!"

A tear rolled down her trembling cheek. "You could have been killed," she choked, staring directly at Lou. She took a few deep breaths in an attempt to hold it

together. Paul stepped between them then backed away. Anne remained frozen in the corner, her eyes riveted to the back of Paul's silver head. Alexis rubbed her forehead and stared at the door.

Lou took Lauren's hand and reeled her in. Eventually she made it to shore sobbing quietly.

"Listen," Paul snapped at Lou, "no one got hurt. That's the bottom line."

His words offered little comfort, but Paul stubbornly refused to leave bad enough alone. "I'm sure if they'd seen lights, nothing would have happened. You weren't in any real danger."

Despite my earlier sympathy toward him at the party—now just a dim memory—I railed, "How the hell do you know if anyone was in danger?"

I sensed Alexis's head spin so I tried to cool off. Beating up on Paul Brown was no guarantee I'd wind up feeling any better. Maybe worse.

"I don't know what you've been smoking," Paul said grimly hostile. "It was a bunch of stupid punks."

"These days it's easier for kids to buy guns than fucking cigarettes," Alexis added.

Maybe she was trying to soothe her mother. Maybe Paul was doing the same. But if they were, it wasn't working. Wasn't working for me either.

"Alexis," Lauren retorted, "if your father said the sky was falling, you'd look for the pieces. In my life a shooting is a big deal."

"Lauren, back off! The kid didn't mean it that way." Paul stepped between them. "You heard Biancho."

"Ted Biancho is a snot-nose kid with a know-it-all attitude."

"Ma," Alexis said, "Teddy is a terrific cop. He'll catch whoever did this, and I'm sure he'll have people guarding the house."

Lauren reluctantly nodded her agreement.

I'd begun to drift, but the Chief's name yanked me back. "What exactly did the cops say?" I asked, my anxiety snapping to.

"Chief Biancho told us there had been similar incidents in nearby towns," Lou wheezed.

"How recent? Which towns?"

"He didn't go into the details..." Lou began.

"Paul, I want to go home," Anne interrupted querulously. "How many times do we have to listen to the same story?" Anne glanced around the room and added lamely, "I'm sure everyone could use a little sleep."

Paul started to object but thought better. "There's nothing we can do about the door until later in the day," he said, shutting and testing the two locks.

Lauren gathered herself. "You're absolutely right, Anne. I'm sorry for dragging the two of you out of bed."

Anne ushered Paul out in front of her. "I didn't mean to sound cranky," she apologized. "It's been a long, long night."

"It sure has," Lauren agreed, shutting the door.

As the four of us stood in another awkward silence with *my* long night kicking my gut. I couldn't control a quick glimpse toward Alexis, but was met a sardonic smile and challenging eyes. Lauren noticed, though she hid any reaction with a large sigh as she leaned back into Lou.

"Anne was right," she said. "We really ought to sleep."

"Annie is a bitch, pure and simple," Alexis retorted angrily. "She couldn't stand seeing Dad worry about you."

Dad has a strange way of worrying, I thought, my own anger looking for a bone.

"Well, bitch or not, I'm taking her advice," Alexis announced. "I'm scheduled all day long and need to freshen up."

Alexis turned to me, "Teenage carnage aside, thanks for the company, Matt. There aren't too many more nights left for a top down drive. It's been a while since I last lost track of time. You have a fine son-in-law, Lou. If he didn't have strings, I'd snatch him right up."

I felt like a shocked monkey while everyone waited for a human response. "It's been a hell of a night," I finally said. "I don't think I've ridden in a convertible since"...Chana and Becky died in her Volkswagon rag-top, I painfully realized. "...not for a very long time." This had become a homecoming from hell.

"Let me walk you to your car," I said, trying desperately to finish on a coherent note.

"No need."

"I plan to look around the house anyway." I was barely treading water, but there was one mystery I had to solve.

Alexis hugged Lou, kissed Lauren on the cheek, and followed me out the door. "What are you looking for?" she asked.

"I don't know. I'm sure the police covered everything, but there's no harm in taking another pass. Maybe they missed something."

Alexis stopped our slow walk. "I meant what I said inside. Ted Biancho is an excellent Police Chief. Smart, tough, and very up-to-date."

"I'm sure he is, but I gotta make sure."

Alexis restarted her slow pace. "If Teddy thought that anyone was in the slightest danger he'd have had them stay somewhere else."

"Maybe they *ought* to get out of here." Possible stalking, a trashed car, and now someone had shot at the fucking house.

Alexis interrupted my thinking. "You won't be able to drag my mother anywhere. She'd sooner hire an army. Anyhow, Teddy and Dad won't let anything happen. You ought to stay out of it and let the police do their job."

Alexis leaned her head forward to kiss my cheek, adding a sharp nip with her teeth before stepping away. I rubbed the side of my face as she hopped into the car. The engine roared to life so I pushed myself off the fender and rapped on the passenger window.

When it opened, I poked my head inside. "Alexis, why the remark about strings? Were you trying to put their minds at ease?"

Alexis tilted her head, staring right into my eyes. "Are you kidding? They aren't chains, but you got them, sweetheart. And I knew it the moment I laid eyes on you."

She smiled and winked, "Give me a call."

I pulled my head out of the car and stared at the Saab's rear end as Alexis wheeled around the corner. My hard-on was back and the couch was calling. It was almost time for dope and depression.

But when I turned and saw the bullet-ridden door, the angry detective dumped the guilt-ridden depressive. I'd lost too many people and damn sure didn't want to lose any one else.

So many shots hit the mark that the splintered area resembled a cutout for an oversized mail slot. I walked the width of the house, carefully hunting for stray bullets without any luck. I scoured the door, its frame, and the wall along the inside of the porch, finding nothing but the ugly slash.

I was on my hands and knees fruitlessly searching under the

flimsy porch furniture when the door swung open and I heard Lou shout, "His car is still here."

"We didn't know where you went," Lauren said in a soft voice, walking onto the porch. "Out here, Lou," she called. "Did you find anything?"

"No," I said standing, noticing my soreness. Now that the adrenaline had subsided, my body felt battered. I also felt the onslaught of a hangover, the perfect way to cap a wonderful early morning.

"The police were thorough, Matty." Lou had joined us on the porch. Puffy bags hung beneath his kind bloodshot eyes. "They searched the property and picked into all the walls."

Something else I should have thought of but hadn't. I'd been acting like a dumb dick, not a detective. And not very successful at that either. "Let's go inside and I'll check the plaster one more time."

Lauren groaned, "Please don't. Believe it or not, my fatigue is greater than my fear. All I can think about is sleep. I can't even clean up the mess."

"I'll do it," I offered. "I'm planning to hang here for a while anyway."

A smile lifted Lou's bags. "That's generous of you, *Boychick*..."

"But totally unnecessary," Lauren interrupted. "I'm sure Teddy is taking care of everything. I was just panicked before."

"Why not be extra cautious?" I asked. Something about the physical scene nagged at me but I couldn't quite catch it. "If you add the drive-by to your car and your feelings about being stalked, Biancho's theory loses some juice. Also, be pretty easy to break in with the door in that shape."

"Please Matthew, no more. I've had enough for one night," Lauren pleaded. "Nobody is going to break in especially since Teddy promised to patrol."

"Look," she said pointing, "there's a police car now."

As if on cue, a blue-and-white rushed to the front of the house. Lauren signaled her okay and the car slowly pulled away.

"I don't particularly like Ted Biancho," Lauren added, "but he's careful and efficient. I need the Hacienda to myself, to ourselves," she corrected. "Do you understand?"

I recalled the other times throughout the night I'd been asked that same question. Remembered the different tone in which it had been asked, and felt my tension grow. "Why run any risk?"

"Lou," Lauren said, "make him listen. I don't care if he moves in, just not today."

Lou was torn, but looked at me and made a face. "We'll be fine, Matty. If anything unusual catches my attention, I'll ring you right up."

"A telephone call can't get me here fast enough."

"*Boychick*, I'll call you later today."

He wasn't gonna give, so I did. Didn't like it, did it anyway. Lauren looked dizzy with exhaustion and Lou wasn't far behind. We didn't make with a long goodbye, but his last question boxed me around the ears. "Are you going home or to Shoes?"

CHAPTER 22

As soon as the Bimmer rolled its four, I started hard-nosing the highway. I quickly fired up a smoke then stuffed it into the ashtray, lighting a roach instead. If I didn't ratchet down, my mind was gonna spiral right out of my head. No way around the upcoming teeth grit, but I wanted to grind slowly. Very slowly.

Which gave me room to slam myself for leaving the Hacienda. Only it was too late to return and set a stakeout. The cruiser we'd seen from the porch hadn't been the first, nor had the blue-and-whites been the only police in the vicinity. There was no doubt that I'd be seen, rousted, and caught. I wanted another meet with the Chief, but not this morning. Or that way. And dragging Lou and Lauren out of bed to vouch wouldn't go over real big with anyone.

By the time I let myself into the apartment I knew I had to do something, anything to pull it together. For lack of better, I ate a couple bowls of corn flakes soaked in borderline milk. All I needed was hot orange juice and burnt toast. Only I didn't have any orange juice or bread. .

So I did what I always do when the roof caved. Sooner or

later the wolves were gonna chomp, but I played for later by going straight for the Valium. The only remaining problem was filling the time 'til the dose kicked in. The only remaining solution—shots of 'Turkey and a mantra of the dread' has already occurred. But I fell asleep knowing the mantra was a lie.

A restless sleep. Broken several times by sweats and feverish dehydration. If I hadn't known better I'd have thought flu. I knew better—this was my feel-bad talking.

But the insistent ring had nothing to do with sweat or sleep. And Lou's hoarse voice chopped through my haze. "What's the matter," I mumbled, instinctively grabbing a cigarette. Sometimes I really wondered whether I was trying to lessen the wrong addictions.

"Relax, Matty," he quickly reassured. "Everything is fine. Not a speck of trouble and the police are covering the entire area." Lou paused then wheezed, "I waited to call until after we cleaned the hall, but I guess I woke you?"

"I never should have let you talk me into leaving."

"For my part you could have stayed. But truthfully, it would have been too much for Lauren. These parties are difficult to begin with, to say nothing about the scare—though you couldn't tell it by looking at her, could you *Boychick*?"

Clearly Lou had slept better than me, though he kept coming up short on oxygen. "Christ, Lou, your wheeze is on overdrive."

There was a moment's hesitation. "Between the asthma and the sugar, I'm starting to fall apart," Lou said in a soft voice.

I figured a couple of other things were contributing, but I was smart enough to keep my figuring to myself. "Do you have your medicines?"

"Of course. My head isn't broken."

Another marked difference between us. "Just asking in case

you need anything from civilization," I said. "I thought I'd camp in the boonies. You can tell Lauren I'm not moving in, just going to stay until we're certain there won't be a repeat."

"It's a nice offer Matty, but not necessary. Lauren thinks we should spend the night somewhere else so we're going to a small local inn. The dirt from the party and the scare is responsible for the breathing."

He called it "the scare." I called it a drive-by shooting. "Why not stay in the buildings?" Whatever my attitude about Lou and Lauren's Big Relationship, I'd feel better having them nearby.

"Lauren doesn't want to be far from the Hacienda. She's concerned about the kids, especially since Ian never showed up for the party." Lou stifled a cough.

It was senseless to draw a line in the sand if they weren't going to be in the desert. "Maybe I should bunk at the Hacienda anyway. Keep an eye on things while you're gone." Couldn't help toeing a few granules; besides, I was nervous about staying here.

"No need. Lauren already told Chief Biancho our plans and he promised to keep a close cover on the house. Trust me, leave it be. It would upset Lauren to have you here."

I didn't want to leave it be since I felt anxious about their safety, but there was no bulling through Lou's resolve. "You're not making this inn thing up, are you?"

"Shame on you."

"Okay, but I want you to call when you get back to the Hacienda."

"I'm a big boy, Matty," he replied, though not entirely displeased.

"Maybe a little too big. If you lost a couple pounds, you might breath better."

"Enough already. If you cut back on your smoking you'd breath better too."

Well, I wasn't quitting today. I replaced the receiver, last-dragged on my smoke, and gulped the rest of the previous night's water. I'd crashed before crawling into the bedroom and still felt exhausted. But most of my fatigue had to do with me not wanting to think about everything that had happened with Alexis and my growing concern about Lou and Lauren. I lit a joint and stretched back down on the couch—with very little hope I would wake refreshed.

I hadn't counted on an anxiety attack the next time I grabbed the receiver.

"Hey, babe, how was the party?" Boots crooned in my ear.

"How did you know I went?" I managed after lighting a cigarette. I was wide awake and my heart was pounding.

"I knew you'd come to your senses," Boots chuckled. "Why do you sound wasted? It's 9pm."

I squinted at the clock and confirmed her ability to tell time. "It wasn't from a rock and roll night. Someone blasted Lauren's front door with gunshots. Left the hallway in shambles."

"Was anybody hurt? Is Lou okay?" The calm was gone from her voice.

"No one hurt and other than his asthma, Lou is fine. You don't sound like you spent the day flying cross country."

"I feel it, though. C'mon, tell me what happened."

I did the best I could, starting with a story about the convertible ride. Made it sound like Alexis was concerned about her mother's relationship with Lou and wanted to talk to someone outside the family. I told Boots one conversation led to another and I'd gotten stuck driving around most of the night.

"I buzzed out, but it was impossible to stop her. I guess she found talking a release."

"You have a way with women, lover," Boots innocently teased.

"Once a social worker, always a social worker," I joked, not nearly as innocent.

"When your head isn't stuck up your ass you can be easy to talk to."

"Thanks, maybe I was giving myself a breather." I felt ashamed and added to my lies. "I need a minute to dig up a cigarette, Boots." I placed the phone on the table and noticed a new gym bag. Julius had slipped in while I was asleep and paid his rent. I pushed the dope out of sight, stood, and stretched my sore back. I took a deep breath, lifted the receiver then reviewed the drive-by details and everyone's reactions, relieved to be on the safest part of the night—the safest, that is, for me.

"I'm surprised you came home," Boots commented when I finally finished.

"It was stupid decision. I didn't get much sleep until Lou called this afternoon."

I was thrilled to have a hair shirt and embellished my mea culpa until Boots finally interrupted. "Matt, the police are keeping close check and everybody is okay, right?"

Given my night with Alexis, not quite everybody. "I guess."

"So knock it off. You did what they wanted."

"Sure, Boss," I said, blanching at my choice of words as I remembered Alexsis's commands.

"Since you're so agreeable, do you mind if we skipped tonight? I know you can't wait to get here, but I feel like you sound."

"No problem, I'll call you tomorrow when I get back from the Hacienda."

"Do you want me to go with you?"

"I'd like it," I lied again, "but Lauren is still overwhelmed so it's probably not a good idea."

Boots made her goodbye sweet. "I missed you, Matt. It's nice to be home."

I made mine guilty. "I missed you too."

If I thought my luck about a night off was going to stick when I hung up the telephone, I thought wrong. Next to Boots, the last person I wanted to spend time with was me. I considered using the nearby park to work the aches out of my contorted body, but quickly reconsidered. Instead, I walked slowly through my rooms, hoping the quiet familiarity might give me something I couldn't give myself. The space to think about what I had done, the way I had done it, who I had done it with. The willingness to confront my actions, understand what they meant.

But this time, good on paper meant good on paper. Julie's rent kept staring me in the face and I was unable to stop from rifling through. To my mixed relief only fresh and pot and pills. No coke. To my greater relief, the reefer worked, my madness lessened, and I fell asleep watching Homer choke Bart.

CHAPTER 23

I woke up early Monday morning surprisingly well rested. Either the damned occasionally pull a long shot, or eighteen hours of sleep, however fitful, add up. I plodded to the bathroom and took a hot shower. It was too late for the cold one. One lighthouse late.

By the time the medicine mirror fogged, I'd stepped a couple of feet further from my submissive cheat. Able to steer clear of the throat tightening guilt that had hand-delivered yesterday's bender.

I climbed out of the lion-clawed porcelain, swiped at the mirror, stared at the permanent bags under my eyes, and left the face stubble alone. Nervous humor wasn't an invite to play with razors.

Especially since I was unwilling to peer any deeper into my reflection. Boots' fond farewell probably meant I'd successfully lied past my ride with Alexis; now *I* was the only accuser. If I kept looking it would make for a drawn out prosecution. And today was gonna be a hear-no-evil-about-Matt day.

I scurried back to the bedroom and perseverated in front of

the closet. Running on repressed always walloped my go-get-'em. I finally grabbed a fresh pair of jeans and a clean tee. This wasn't a day to dawdle. A tough decision, but I left my stash at home.

And seriously regretted it when I was bombarded by a series of surprises. The first was the Hacienda's new front door.

"Alexis sent the door and someone to hang it," Lou explained, breathing much better than the day before. "I could have done the job, but it was probably better this way. She and Lauren are out having lunch."

The second surprise. Despite my internal hell, fire, and brimstone, I heated at the mention of Alexis's name.

After we inspected the new oak, Lou led me into the comfortable kitchen while I body-blocked the image of the blonde flame. I wasn't going to let a long distance hard-on sink my mood.

Lou was in the middle of a Bill and Bob's roast beef, so we sat at the kitchen counter. He glanced at me but I shook my head.

"You're sure you don't want a bite? It's a little early in the day, but I've gotten hooked."

"I have better ways to clog my arteries."

"You can't find decent Chinese up here, but these guys make a good sandwich. Very lean." He bit into the bun, some of the barbecue sauce squeezing out the sides.

"That can't be good for your sugar."

"Please, you'll ruin my appetite." Lou stuck the sandwich back down on its plastic wrapper. "Sometimes you make me feel too old to wipe my ass."

"I'm trying warn you about junk food and you're giving me shit."

"Thank you. But not for your culinary recommendations. I know what you eat. Otherwise, you've been a real *mensch*."

I caught him peeking at the sandwich. "Eat the damn thing," I ordered.

"Are you sure you won't have a taste? I zapped it in the

microwave so it's nice and warm." Lou swallowed another large bite. "I tried something new last night," he said, an amused, sly look crossing his face.

I reined in my frustration. "I don't want to hear about your sex life."

He grinned broadly, the sinkholes on his highway ignored. "Don't worry, I don't plan on giving away my secrets. I ate sushi."

"Sushi?"

"It's raw fish."

"I know what sushi is, I just can't believe you ate it."

"When you think about it, it's not much different than herring."

"Pickled is different than raw," I said, momentarily diverted.

"That's right, the *alta cocker* tried something different. Is that so terrible?"

"That's not what I mean." I knew better than to continue, only I could never leave a fresh scab alone. "It's just..." I waved at the plastic on the counter, "since you started coming up here, things are different. You're... you're eating raw food," I finished, flummoxed.

"You miss the whole point, Matty. Lauren once played a record by a Black preacher with a tune about how you do different things because of love. You drive home early or you don't come home at all, things like that."

Lou's struggle to quote Al Green would normally bring a smile. But today, Preacher Al's song ran right up my guilty gut. I spun on the kitchen stool, "Do you have a beer?"

"You hock me about a sandwich, but it's not too early to drink?" he ribbed, oblivious to my discomfort.

I hoped it wasn't too late.

Lou handed me an opened bottle and picked up right where he'd left off. "My time with Lauren is teaching me I don't have to live the rest of my life following old habits. I'm learning age is an attitude. And I'll tell you something *Boychick*, love shapes attitude."

The song said love shapes *different* attitudes. I felt something jar underneath my tight repression. Lou was running full bore toward something I might be fleeing. The realization rearranged pieces of my troubles with Boots and my night with Alexis, but now wasn't the time to finish the puzzle.

Lou took a deep breath. "So I've asked Lauren to marry me."

I looked at his happy face and felt my insides chill. "What did she say?" I asked, grinding into freeze.

"She thinks we should wait."

I expected relief but didn't find it. Didn't find anything. "Wait for what?" The facts, goddammit, the facts. Maybe I did feel something, after all.

"She has to finalize her divorce."

"Divorce? They haven't been together for decades."

"It's just a formality. A lot of people wait until they need it."

"And now Lauren needs it."

"I hope so." Lou actually blushed.

"This makes you happy, doesn't it?"

"I feel things I haven't felt in ages."

"Any other reasons for this wait?"

"We want to put all these events behind us—Ian's accident, the car, the door. But to tell you the truth, I think the waiting will be over when the divorce becomes final."

"What about your apartment, the buildings?"

"What about them?"

"I don't see Lauren leaving the Hacienda, do you?"

"I'll keep the apartment and we'll use it for a place in the city. Lauren calls it something French..."

"Pied a terre," I supplied, increasingly annoyed with Lou's constant references to his personal Guru. Christ, now I was thinking like a leftover from the seventies. Well, maybe I was.

"The real question, Matty, is what will happen with the buildings when you live with Shoes."

"*When*, not *if*?" Took the hit and counterpunched with my

chin.

"The way you lovebirds have been together during the past year makes it look like *when* to me."

This wasn't why I'd come north. "I'm really happy for you, Lou, but I'm not here for an engagement party." I saw his surprised hurt and added hastily, "I'm still worried about the shooting. Afraid you and Lauren are in danger."

Conflict crossed his face but he rubbed it away with his hand. "I appreciate your concern, Matty, I really do."

"But?"

"The Police Chief is working on identifying the gang. He tells us this sort of prank has never been repeated at the same location."

"A drive-by is a hell of a "prank." What about the stalking, the car?"

Lou shook his head helplessly. "If it were up to me I'd have you involved, looking into it."

"Who is it up to?"

Before he could answer the brand new front door opened then slammed shut. "Goddamn that child," Lauren steamed, her energy rocking the kitchen. "Goddamn all children." Then, noticing me, "Sons-in-law don't count. I'll be right back, I want to hang up my jacket. No, I really want to hang Alexis, I'm settling for the jacket." She turned on her heels and stomped out of the kitchen leaving a palpable void.

"Matty, don't say anything about the proposal, please," Lou whispered. "No one is supposed to know." He seemed relieved to be out from under my drive-by questions.

Lou had nothing to worry about; I had no interest in playing Hallmark.

"So, Alexis stuck you with the check?" Lou teased when Lauren returned to the kitchen.

"The girl makes me furious!" Lauren exclaimed, clapping her hands. "She had the cheek to turn the shooting into another pitch for the Hacienda. All the same old arguments then, "Ma, why take unnecessary chances? Sure Teddy knows what he's doing, but combine the shooting with the place falling apart, well, face it, it's the right time to make a move."

Lauren's impersonation was remarkable. Slap on some long blonde curls, or maybe just take her clothes off and Mom would be her daughter. I flashed on the lighthouse, curled my toes, and felt the devil's breath on my neck.

"She's just trying to look out for you, Lauren," Lou suggested.

"Like a fox looks out for a chicken." Lauren grimaced, "Alexis looks out for herself. And for Paul."

"Why is she so persistent?" I asked, forcing myself back into the room.

Lauren eyed me suspiciously. "What? You didn't hear about the heartbreak poor Alexis goes through every time she sets foot in the Hacienda? How her childhood home is crumbling before her very eyes? The lawsuits that are right around the corner? What exactly *did* you talk about on your ride?"

"She mentioned a few things needed fixing," I sidestepped. Me and my fucking mouth.

"Nothing we won't take care of," Lou assured me.

"It's not the repairs," Lauren said glumly, forgetting, I fervently hoped, the ride.

"I don't even think it's about money, though Lord knows, money is something Alexis is particularly fond of," she added.

She hesitated. "Lou and I talk about this a lot," Lauren said looking at me, her decision made. "I think Alexis wants to wrangle a deal to get the house for Paul and Anne. I also believe she wants me out of town.

"Could she pull it off?" Despite all my last rites, the moth kept fluttering.

"Alexis can pull a rabbit out of a hat. When the floor dropped out of the housing market I thought her real estate business was dead and buried. Somehow she survived and brought it back stronger than ever. There's not too much that girl can't do when she puts her mind to it."

"Why would she want you out of town?"

"I embarrass her. I've always embarrassed her." Then Lauren nodded toward Lou. "I think our relationship is the last straw. I also know living here keeps Paul wrapped up and Alexis believes it hurts his marriage."

"This is where Lauren and I disagree," Lou interjected. "Perhaps Alexis wants the house for her father, I don't know. Kids get funny ideas when they come from broken homes. But Alexis has always been friendly toward me and very supportive of us," he said, glancing at Lauren. "She didn't have to fix the door."

"Resale value," Lauren instantly rebutted.

"*Shainele*," Lou gently remonstrated, "Alexis might be mistaken, but she really believes it's in your interest to sell."

"Alexis knows I'll never sell the Hacienda."

"So the girl is stubborn, like other people we know."

"You're talking about me," Lauren grumbled, losing some steam. "Maybe I see too much of myself in her."

"It wouldn't hurt to treat both you and Alexis with a little more charity," Lou said.

"Maybe," Lauren said, a smile softening her features, "but everyone isn't as forgiving as you."

Lauren turned to me, "Anyhow, I want to thank you for yesterday's offer to guard the house. You really are going above and beyond."

"Tell you the truth, I want to stay here for a little while."

"Don't be silly, we don't expect any more trouble," Lauren said tossing her head.

I pushed my stomach shudder aside and tried soft. "You seem pretty relaxed about having your front door blown away." Something about that old door still picked at me but I couldn't make it.

Lauren shrugged. "You don't have to exaggerate, it was bad enough as it was. Ted will keep a tight watch until he's absolutely sure about our safety. Believe me Matthew, Teddy Biancho is not going to let anything happen. The boy has his reputation to protect, and he's a bear about protecting it. Anyway, he's certain it was drunken joyriders."

I tried hard. "But I'm not. Especially when I add it to your car and your uncomfortable feelings. It might be exactly what Biancho thinks it is, but I've begun to distrust all these coincidences."

CHAPTER 24

Lou frowned, but Lauren shook her shoulders in a mock shiver. "You can be scary, you know?"

"I'm not trying to frighten you, I'm just being careful."

"I really haven't been feeling stalked. And you yourself said my car was destroyed by gay bashers. Right now we want a little peace and quiet. I think we deserve that much, don't you?"

I looked toward Lou for assistance. "I think the worst is over, Matty," he said, shrugging his shoulders.

So much for help. "I don't see any harm in keeping my eyes open."

"That's Teddy's job and I'm confident he'll do it," Lauren said.

"But not confident enough to talk to him about feeling stalked?"

Lauren tossed her thick hair again. "That was something he could say was in my head. It was something you said, remember?"

"I'm not saying it now."

"Thank you," she replied sarcastically. Then, as quickly as her sarcasm surfaced, it slipped into weariness. "I can't deal with another argument today. You mean well and I'm sure you'd make a fine houseguest, but not now. Too much has happened in too short a time. Anyway, the police are protecting us."

"For how long, Lauren?"

"How long could you stay? I'm sorry Matthew, I appreciate the offer, but the only person I want with me now is your father-in-law."

"I understand your need for privacy, but how about giving me the names and addresses of people at the party?"

"What for, Matty?" Lou asked.

"Shake some trees, see what falls."

"That's outrageous," Lauren snapped.

"Take it easy," Lou intervened. "Matt only wants to make sure we're not in danger."

"I'm sorry Lou, but I won't allow him to do anything of the sort. There's been enough "tree shaking" to last a lifetime. The police are positive the shooting was the work of a gang and there's no reason to doubt them."

Lauren glared at me. "I'm not dragging anyone else into this and that's final. Don't make me do some rattling of my own, Matthew."

I knew who she expected to fall. I looked at Lou but he refused to meet my gaze. Whatever his inclination, Lou was marching to Lauren's drum. Whatever my misgivings, I was headed home. "I didn't mean it the way it sounded, Lauren."

"Please don't think I'm ungrateful but Lou and I need time together. Time to give everything a chance to return to normal."

Not what I wanted for myself, but liked having my pants pulled about Alexis even less. "I'll back off, but I want your word on something."

"What is that?"

"If your discomfort returns, or *any* other kind of trouble for that matter, you call. And you call immediately. I'm even keeping the cell phone on and charged, I said staring at Lou.

"I promise." A wry smile replaced her frown. "This is what's meant by role reversal."

But just outside town I postponed the ride back into my life. I was annoyed at letting myself be blackmailed by Lauren's Alexis threat. Well, fuck her. If Biancho was in charge of Lou and Lauren's safety, I was going to lock and load about his competence. And I was going to give him everything I had.

The Chief immediately made time. "I expected your call yesterday." He wore an amused expression but his eyes were cold.

"Yesterday was Sunday and you never gave me your home number."

"It's listed."

If he intended to make me feel foolish, he succeeded. "I had a lot to think about."

"Now you're here to tell me about it."

"What's eating you?" I asked, trying to hide my embarrassment. "Does it really surprise you I'm concerned about the drive-by?"

Biancho frowned. "No, it doesn't surprise me. It makes me uncomfortable when people look over my shoulder. Let me tell you what I've told Lauren and, uh..."

"Lou. I know what you told them."

"So what's the beef?"

"No beef. I have information for you."

He nodded, so I took it from the top. Explained the real reason for tailing Lauren and told him about the car trashing. Even threw in Ian's suicide attempt, but the only time I got a response was when I mentioned Alexis' desire to market the Hacienda. And that only a brief twist of his body.

By the time I finished, Biancho looked disinterested. Worse, I understood why. There were no concrete connects between *any* of the events.

"Fascinating Jacob, but it doesn't change a damn thing. We've seen these drive-bys in other towns, all with the same M.O. All with the same weapons and ammunition, all in the same early hours. Police departments up here believe it's an initiation ritual."

"A strange sort of initiation."

"Stranger than killing for sneakers? Let me assure you, I won't allow this to happen again in my town." The Chief's eyes were blazing, his lips drawn tight.

This was more than a reputation protect; Biancho took the shooting as a personal affront. Still, I was reluctant to stop my pitch. "I appreciate your confidence and dedication but..."

"But what? Vibrations and trampled grass in the woods? You know how ridiculous you sound? Nobody was following her."

"I said nobody was following her when I was there. That doesn't exactly..."

"Spare me, Jacob. The car was a typical example of city life, and frankly, Lauren Rowe's intuition doesn't make for fact. Especially when I'm looking at something that's happened before."

I hadn't the conviction to shake him. Or the logic. "Well," I conceded, "let me help with the gang angle."

He barely restrained his contempt. "What makes you think I'd let a private cop work a police case? They do that in Boston?" Impatience piggybacked onto Biancho's scorn. "It's time to drop this. I'll see that Lauren and your father-in-law are safe."

"You told me there are people in town who would be happy to see Lauren move," I tried weakly, struck with the irony of the situation. I'd spent my entire life crossing the street to avoid a cop. Here I was pleading to work with them only to be unceremoniously rejected.

Before I could mourn my loss, Biancho turned nasty. "Don't even think about it, Jacob. If I see you here for any reason other than a family visit, you're going to have a problem. A big problem."

"Chief," I asked in a very respectful tone once he finished, "there's only one thing that still bothers me."

"You're getting on my nerves."

"There was something odd about the drive-by itself. Why not shoot the windows or the walls? Why just the door?"

Biancho rolled his eyes, "I'll make sure to ask when we track them down. Consider it lucky nobody was hurt and there was as little damage as there was." He paused and pointed outside. "Go home, Jacob, go home and count your lucky stars."

No way to delay; it was time to mind my business. I had a bad taste in my mouth and I expected worse. But halfway to the city I heard Al Green's song play in my head and it sent me back to my personal puzzle. Had me wondering whether my lousy attitude toward Lauren and Lou's relationship, my freak at Boots' TV talk, my passive cheat with Alexis all came from fears of a permanent relationship.

I hoped not. Hoped so hard I made myself look forward to seeing Boots.

Until I drove down my alley and saw her talking to Washington Clifford on the small half-court tucked between the buildings—a sweet throw-in when Richard designed our renovation.

I stalled as long as possible before approaching with a pleasant smile. "Did I miss something?" I asked, forcing myself to wink at Boots who seemed relieved. "Day off?"

"Travel comp," Boots replied. "I got here a few minutes ago."

"I got here earlier," Clifford said. "Helped myself to your ball."

Which had been inside my apartment, something he failed to mention. As would I. Clifford's short muscular arm circling the basketball looked menacing. Or maybe it was the gun in his back holster. His forty-four short hung on the chain-link fence that separated my alley from the grocery store's parking lot.

"Looks like you've been shooting around," I observed. Clifford's light blue shirt was damp, perspiration ringing his thick neck."

"You got a soft rim. Helps with the shot. Nice friend too, though I don't understand what she sees in you."

"Boots appreciates my hidden qualities."

"Boots's feet are tired and she wants down." Boots glanced at me, "I'll let myself in. Anyway, I have a feeling you boys want to be alone. I've heard a lot about you Officer Washington."

"That's Clifford, Ma'am. Washington Clifford. Best not believe everything your friend tells you. Oh," he added casually, "you won't need a key. I left the door open." His teeth gleamed against his ebony skin. He was the only man who could grin and grind his molars at the same time. You never knew whether he was getting ready to laugh—or bite.

And I wasn't talking breakfast.

"Thoughtful of you to pave the way, Officer," Boots commented walking away.

Both Washington Clifford and I stood silently until she passed through the alley door.

"Good looking lady, Jacobs," Clifford growled. "Play any of this?" he asked, bouncing the ball.

"When I get a chance." Why did each bounce sound like a warning?

"Big guy's game, right?"

"Spud Webb did all right."

"Yes he did," Clifford agreed, his lips tightening at the comparison. "Care for a little one-on-one?"

It wasn't a request. I flipped my denim jacket onto the fence next to his double knit. "Losers out."

"Winners," he corrected.

I nodded.

"Take it back?" This time I asked.

"Hell no, we're talking playground here." He showed more teeth. "You know how that works, don't you, shamus? Damn near anything goes."

His "damn near" was a relief. Meant I'd live to tell Boots about the game.

"I'll take it out," Clifford demanded. "It's your court."

My court, his game. Clifford slammed his shoulder into my chest before I leaned into position. I staggered backwards while he went for an uncontested lay-up.

"Better 'd-up,' Jacobs."

"I'll give it the old college try, Wash, but I barely graduated." I stiffened, expecting another shoulder but this time he turned 180 and backed into me with his granite ass. I held my ground until I felt his holster rubbing against my belt. When I stepped away, Clifford spun unmolested for another easy bucket.

"C'mon, Wash, you packing an empty?"

"What's the worry? You enjoy playing with danger."

"Sorry, Officer, I want to see your face when your gun goes off."

"Pussy," he said, unbuckling the leather and placing it alongside my building. "Try not to trip. Wouldn't want a relentless detective to shoot his own foot."

"I'll be careful."

Damn careful, though not about the gun. Clifford wasn't interested in finesse, preferring brute strength to push, hip, and force his way to the hoop. The longer we played, the more he used the game as an excuse to pummel my body. A knee here, chop there, following me even when I backed away. I was too busy protecting myself to notice whether he traveled.

I was also careful not to hit back. Beating on a cop, no matter what the guise, wasn't smart. Beating on Clifford was suicidal. Instead, I shot my jumper and kept the game close. Not too close, though there were a few times when I couldn't resist using my height to snatch a rebound off his fingertips. In fact, I'd just made my best put-back, feet never hitting the court after his miss, when the powder keg stopped the contest with a sharp elbow to my face.

I kept my teeth, but he'd added a bleeding mouth to go with

the sore body.

"Did I foul you?" Clifford asked innocently.

"See why I asked you to put the gun away?"

"What about *your* gun? Chief Biancho told you to stay away from his fucking turf."

Clifford's remark surprised me but I tried to cover. "I came directly home, Wash. Didn't pass Go, didn't collect two hundred. Just a bleeding mouth."

"Something to shut you up. Biancho warned you off before, didn't he?"

"If you know he talked to me today, you know why I was there." The real question was why Biancho had bothered with Clifford at all. I wasn't going to ask. I wanted the blood to stop trickling.

"If all you'd done was inquire about that situation, you'd be inside playing with that pretty girl instead of being out here with me." Clifford's eyes were slits in his broad face and his quiet words underscored by two-handed explosions on the blacktop.

"I went there to tell him what I knew, that's all."

"Matt Jacobs, Mister Citizen. Who you trying to fuck?"

"I'd have to see you in a skirt, sweetheart."

"Just can't keep it zipped, can you?" The next slam bounced off my groin.

I dropped to my knees and tried to keep from vomiting.

Clifford talked while I stared at his heavy rubber ripple soles. "Biancho is a good cop. Had him as a student once upon a time. He don't need a pigheaded P.I. offering help. I'd take him at his word."

I braced myself for another blow but his feet stepped toward the fence. "Don't move, asshole," Clifford commanded, throwing my smokes and lighter in front of my unhappy face.

I lit one with shaking hands.

"Only reason I'm not laying on a real hurt is Biancho asked me to talk to you. You leave the police up there alone, you hear?"

"You're being modest about the licking, Wash," I quipped,

unable to keep quiet.

Clifford shook his head regretfully. "You know me Jacobs, if I don't plant a nice kick, it don't really count."

His ripple sole'd toe found my belly and I pitched forward, my struggle to keep from vomiting a lost cause.

CHAPTER 25

"Are you conscious, Matt?" Boots was on her knees anxiously tugging my shoulder.

"Just resting my eyes," I placed my hands on either side of the puddle and pushed onto my knees. "We need a couple pairs of oversized shoes so we can do a Spike Jones."

"A who?" Boots couldn't erase her look of horror.

"Vaudeville. He used to slap a pair of clown shoes on his knees and prance around the stage. He had a TV show during the fifties.."

"I don't understand."

"You had to be there."

"The hell with there. I'm sick about here! There's blood dripping from your mouth. It might be internal bleeding."

"The inside of my cheek is cut, that's all."

"Hardly all, you idiot," but her panic was beginning to recede. "When I fell asleep on the couch, the last thing I heard was grunting. When I woke up you were moaning." Boots speed-rapped, talking off her anxiety. "I looked out the window and saw you on the ground. Then I saw something wet by your head and thought it was blood."

"Better blood than puke," I said. My mouth throbbed and my entire body ached. I rose slowly from my knees to a catcher's squat.

"What the hell happened?" Now that the anxiety had dissipated, I heard the start of her anger.

"Clifford slapped me around. The game was a cover to beat the shit out of me," I grunted, trying to clean the side of my head with the towel Boots brought.

"Did you vomit from a concussion?" A fresh look of alarm spread across her face.

"No such luck," I reassured. "Clifford hit me in the 'nads with the ball, then kicked me in the belly. A mean duet."

"We're going to report that son of a bitch, you hear? He has no right doing this to you. We'll see they fire that fat fuck!"

I smiled through my raw mouth. "Wash ain't fat, honey."

"I don't give a shit, I want his ass fried and fired!"

I stumbled to my feet and Boots hopped up to right me. "Thanks, I needed that," I said quoting an old television commercial before remembering it referred to a face slap.

"I don't understand why you call him Wash, like he's a friend or something. How the hell can you joke about it? It's criminal."

"It's cops, Boots, not criminal. Buying a private investigator's license is criminal."

Understanding crossed her face. "So you can't do anything because he might find out?"

"I'm sure he already knows." My words melted into a serious yearn for a double.

"So he can abuse you, but you can't fight back?"

"That's about it." I shrugged.

Boots began to reply but abruptly changed her mind.

I tried a small step for mankind. "Save your energy, woman. You'll need it to get me into the bathroom."

"Wait here a minute," she said loping to the fence for my jacket.

But I tentatively started toward the door and kept on walking as she rejoined me. Boots skipped in front, about to grab the handle when Charles, my flaky building manager, rushed out the other rear exit.

"Good lord, what's happened?" He was wearing a long ponytail pulled through the back of a Sox cap. "I just came home and happened to peek out my window."

"Washington Clifford came calling, I wound up crawling."

Charles grimaced with distaste. "I absolutely detest that violent, horrible man."

"Join the crowd."

I glanced at Boots. "We're going inside. As soon as I clean up I'll hose the court. Wouldn't want someone to blame the drunks."

"I'll take care of the court, Matt." Charles smiled and winked seductively, "You go inside and let lucky Bootsie take care of you."

"Thanks Charles, I appreciate it."

The lucky lady took me by the hand, carefully leading me to the bathroom while I forced my aching body to follow. The bleeding from my mouth stopped, but I grunted in pain when I pulled my cheek away from my teeth to get a better look. It looked worse, not better.

"Why don't I take a shower and meet you in the kitchen," I suggested. The kitchen was further from the liquor cabinet than the living room.

"In a minute." Boots stood behind me and we stared at each other's reflection in the mirror.

"I want to know why you turn this war with Clifford into a game. You sound almost lighthearted when you talk about it."

I shrugged. "What else can I do? You know why I can't retaliate and I'm still too young to retire."

"There you go again."

"Look, he has something on me and I have something on him from the Simon case. His is usable, mine really isn't," I said sharply.

"But it's enough to keep me from getting killed. Play in shit, you get some on your hands. Clifford makes sure I eat my share as well."

"I can't stand it when you talk this way."

She wasn't angry at me. I cracked wise when anxious, Boots blew off steam. If it were reversed, Boots wouldn't be Boots and I'd be in jail.

"What gets me is Clifford generally doesn't whomp without a reason. But I can't figure the reason. I went to see Lauren's Police Chief about the drive-by, that's all."

"I don't understand."

"Neither do I." Catching Boots' flashing eyes and taut lips through the mirror, I was suddenly bothered by more than Clifford's visit. My already tense skin was tightening. Time to be alone.

"We'll talk about this after my shower. Help yourself to anything that's out there."

"Where are your damn cigarettes?"

"Take a fresh pack from the carton on the dresser. Light one and bring it here?"

"I thought you were taking a shower?"

"Trust me, Boots, I can do both." When she walked out the door my words clipped me from behind. Truth was, I couldn't. And I wasn't thinking shower and smoke. I was thinking Boots and Alexis.

I blasted the water and waited for Boots to return. When she handed me the cigarette I climbed into the tub and leaned the top of my body out over the toilet. If I wasn't lucky enough to wash down the drain, I could always flush myself away.

I flicked the ashes into the bowl, repression broken, my head swarming with questions. Had the torrid night with Alexis been a last fling of kinky freedom before accepting my feelings toward Boots? Or, was it really impossible for me to commit to one person, however deep my feelings?

And why the hell *did* I always mouth off to Clifford?

I pitched my cigarette and turned toward the hot, stinging spray. I didn't want to answer any of those questions. If I did, I'd have to face things about myself I wasn't ready to face. Meant learning whether the part of me that existed during my brief second marriage died along with Chana and Becky; those few short years no match for the rest of my alienated life.

I inspected my bruises and tried to stretch my muscles. The movements, coupled with hot water, helped my body, did nothing for my head. Tucked between the guilt, recrimination, and slivers of hope, lurked a continuing hard-on for Alexis. Talk about being fucked.

"What the hell are you doing in there?" Boots called through the door. "Do you want another cigarette?"

"When I come out."

"Well hurry. I'm not finished with our conversation."

A couple of nights ago I'd been thankful for blue-balls, now, knock-on-wood for black-and-blues.

By the time I came out of the bathroom, Boots had picked up my apartment, opening windows to get rid of the stuffiness. The refrigerator was also open and I listened to the thud of old Chinese food cartons hitting the garbage bag.

"You do floors?" I asked.

Boots stood up from behind the door. "It's about time. Any longer I'd have called 911." She closed the refrigerator. "Not much left in there."

"You threw away all the good stuff."

"If mold is good."

I was thirsting for Wild Turkey. A lot of it. Instead, I walked to the fridge and pulled out a Bass. "Want one?"

"Sure."

I opened the bottles and sat down at the enamel top table. I noticed three lipsticked butts lying in the otherwise empty ashtray.

I'd been schizing longer than I'd realized.

Boots sat across from me. "Now please tell me exactly what's happening and why Clifford hurt you."

"It's easier to explain the meaning of life." I reviewed the entire series of events much like I had for Biancho, hoping to catch something I'd missed the first time around. But it only got worse. Biancho's decision to immediately call Clifford just added to my confusion and concern.

"It has to mean they're hiding something," I concluded, suddenly surprised by how easy it was to talk. I'd expected to be defensive and monosyllabic.

"What would they be hiding?"

"I don't know. That's what bothers me."

"So you *do* think all the stuff is related."

"I don't know that either. I sure can't tie anything together. And won't have an opportunity to try."

"Why not?"

"Lauren doesn't want me around. And we know where Biancho stands. Doesn't leave much room to operate."

Boots shook her head and reached for a cigarette.

"Where did you put the pot?" I asked, getting to my feet.

"I left it on the coffee table."

I returned to the kitchen just as Boots exhaled a mouthful of smoke. "I'm not thrilled about you operating at all," she said, keeping her eyes averted. "You walked into the living room like an old man." She inhaled her Newport. "You think what you have on Clifford will keep him from killing you, but I'm not so sure."

I smiled through my sore mouth, touched by her concern. "Clifford enjoys himself too much to finish me off."

Boots didn't see the humor. "I'm sick of your jokes and I'm starving. How about pizza?"

"Don't want to be seen with me in a fancy joint?"

"I don't want to lug you around on my back. Let's order in. You have wine and beer, maybe we could watch a movie."

"Sounds about my speed. What do you have in mind?"

"Before I arrived, anything with sex. But the way you're moving around, a good comedy seems like a better choice."

CHAPTER 26

Our time together was more than nice, though we never did get around to the movie or that conversation she'd been hinting about. I think Boots felt Clifford's beating was enough for one day. She seemed content just to be with me, and I was actually pleased she was here.

As the late afternoon faded into evening, we splurged. Ordered garlic pies from Santarpio's and hired a cab to haul them to my doorstep. Boots pulled her executive number, promising a fat tip if the pizza was delivered hot.

It was, and the two of us relaxed into comfortable domesticity. We spent a long time talking about the Verizon troubleshooting—a trip made extremely unpleasant by an obnoxious middle manager unable to accept her expertise or rank. Boots had spent her work life climbing hand over hand up the corporate ladder; from operator to national vice president of operations, so catching male hostility was hardly an isolated phenomena. This, however had been worse than usual.

"What kills me is I go back to the hotel and obsess over my

part in it. An outright misogynist acts like it's the Middle Ages and I end up feeling guilty. As if I never left the fifties."

"You weren't alive in the fifties."

"You know what I mean. It's the Lenny Bruce routine about the kid raised by wolves, then found by humans."

"I told you that story."

"No, you played the record... the boy graduates college cum laud..."

"And gets killed chasing a car after the party," I finished.

Boots leaned across the couch resting her head on my shoulder. "It's been a long time since we spent a night like this," she murmured.

"Well, Lou's situation has really thrown a curve. Clifford just threw beanball."

"I'm not criticizing, just enjoying."

Despite my kneejerk reaction, so was I. So much so that when the topic inevitably returned to Lou, Lauren, and Lauren's extended family, I was able to talk without much tension. But as many times as we reviewed the situation, I kept coming up short. No new ideas about any of it.

"I don't know, Matt. I certainly don't want you to annoy that fascist Gestapo, or even this small town police Chief, but what if Lauren, or even Lou are actually in danger?"

"I agree—though for all intents and purposes, I've been fired."

"That's a problem," Boots admitted with a small chuckle. "Hey," she raised her eyebrows, "you never rolled that joint, how about doing it now?"

A surprise. Two, actually, since I suddenly realized I hadn't been pining away for a drink. Our time together had quieted my jones. Raised a question I hadn't considered in the shower—maybe I was just a goddamn fool.

I rolled the joint while Boots massaged the back of my neck with her strong fingers. "Let's pretend we don't know anyone involved," she suggested, her mind stuck on Lou and Lauren. "What would you think then?"

"Less worry, but not much different than what I think now. After all, the cops are guarding the house. But I'd still be pretty suspicious about Biancho's decision to sic Wash on me."

"Not 'Wash,' goddammit." Boots yanked her hand away from my neck so I lit the joint. "Call him Clifford or call him an asshole, but don't call him 'Wash!'"

"We weren't supposed to know these people," I replied, my mind still working her question. "If I didn't want to mess with the law but stayed on the case, I'd work the other side of the street. Investigate Lauren's life, drag a net through the people she knows. Long odds, but better than no odds at all."

Boots inhaled on the joint before handing it back. I toked a couple times then began to drift. The feeling reminded me of when I was around twenty—the days when I believed in a world without war. Reminded me of the times I'd flop down on the floor, head between two cheap loudspeakers, letting Dylan, Motown, and Aretha carry me through strawberry fields.

I pulled myself upright, offered Boots the joint, and placed it in the ashtray when she shook her head.

"Are you planning to do that?" she asked.

Somehow I thought she was talking about the music. I'm too old for the floor. Hurts my back. Dope's different these days, more like feeling normal."

"What are you talking about?" Boots asked, a lopsided grin underneath fuzzy eyes.

"Getting high," I answered realizing Julie's rent was a winner.

"Well, you're there," Boots said, her jaw losing some of its customary jut. "This stuff is very strong, isn't it?"

I lit a cigarette. "I was floating."

Boots sipped her wine, "Are we going to work that side of the street?"

I shook some of the float out of my head. "Not *we*, not easy, not safe. Lauren won't cooperate and if word gets back to Biancho..." Clifford's beating was still too fresh to leap at another. But even before Boots' comment, I knew what *I* had to do. Fired or not.

"Does Lauren have to find out? You made friends with her daughter, maybe start there. Let her provide you with the basics and ask her not to tell."

More helpful suggestions like that and our great night was gonna disappear. Very fast.

"You're awfully quiet, Matt."

"It will get back to Lauren if I start questioning her family." Taking Boots' suggestion felt like I'd be admitting my desire to see Alexis.

"Don't interrogate. Frame it in a way her children will appreciate. Tell them the truth. You're making certain of Lou and Lauren's safety. Even if that got back, how angry could Lauren get?"

I guess Boots knew me well enough to realize I wasn't going to quit. "Plenty. She told me to leave everyone alone."

"I'm a little confused, doll," Boots replied, the high sliding from her eyes. "You complain about being locked out, but you're not showing much enthusiasm for sneaking back in."

What could I tell her? I was frightened to see Alexis?

Boots caught a distorted glimpse of my thought. "I'm telling you Matt, the daughter is the place to start. She owes you after spending all that time talking about her problems."

I wanted to pass on her comment, but decided it might seem suspicious. "Alexis doesn't strike me as the grateful type."

"What type is she?" Boots asked after a long inhale on her cigarette.

"Pushy, ambitious, hungry for success." I focused on Lauren's criticisms, "She has a real thing for her father."

"How old is she?"

"Somewhere in her thirties?"

"Well, you better be careful," Boots smiled suspiciously. "You're almost old enough to pull her daddy trigger."

"Boots, the way my body feels, I couldn't pull a trigger on a gun. Come back to earth, okay? I agree it makes sense for me to keep working," I said, hauling us back to safer ground.

"I don't know how much sense it *really* makes, but I know you. You're not going to quit. I'm just afraid you'll do something stupid and confront this Police Chief, or even Clifford."

I found it easier to listen to her fears about Clifford than her suggestions about Alexis. "You're not worried I'll deliberately light a fire under Lauren?"

Boots smiled and rearranged herself on the long couch, her head on the armrest, her calves across my lap. "Didn't enter my mind. You've made peace with Lou and Lauren's relationship. I can easily imagine you pulling a bonehead macho man with the cops, but at the same time I know how accepting you can be."

"What's worse, doll, being a schizophrenic or loving one?" I asked running my finger down her smooth, tan calf. Now that we'd gotten past Alexis, I felt a resurgence of my high and a whole lot of relief.

"I can always count on a joke at a moment like this."

"You gotta have something to rely on, Boots."

Boots shook her head, "You're hopeless."

I lifted her legs, slowly slid out from under, and stood. "You want another slice?" I asked.

"You mean there's something left? You snarfed those pizzas like an animal."

"Receiving end of an old fashioned whopping does that to me. I stood in place and carefully bent over until my palms were close to the floor.

"Your body is killing you, isn't it?"

"Uh-huh," I grunted straightening. I walked stiffly into the kitchen and chased four Ibuprofens with a shot of Turkey and the last slice.

"Well, honey, we won't add to the damage," Boots called.

"Hmm," I said returning to the living room, standing over her horizontal body, certain I never looked as good on the couch. "How are we going to do that?"

"Gently," Boots whispered taking my hand. "Very gently."

She kept her promise. Boots's warmth and tenderness elicited a nervous pleasure. Pleasure in the knowledge we actually had about each other. Nervous because I couldn't stop flashing on those psychedelic hours in the lighthouse where sex existed free of baggage and replaced by perverse.

We took our time. Time to know moments when Boots's gentleness pierced me with guilty distaste for my confused hypocrisy.

As our excitement grew, my interior felt torn between her caring and my shame. For an added treat, I came to the image of a naked, snarling Alexis.

CHAPTER 27

It wasn't supposed to be like this. I had expected to jump out of bed, kiss Boots on the cheek, then Bimmer my way north. But I awoke so far south, the john looked like the arctic. In Boots's place, a note on my dresser apologized for having left so early.

I felt a pang of loss when I realized she was gone. But then, my relief at finding myself alone quickly flew its flag. And the moment it unfurled, I knew my restless slumber had delivered me to Trouble City. I tried to motivate myself into clothes, but the closet seemed too far away.

The day threatened to plunge into serious bleak. A day to drug myself to oblivion. My only regret: I hadn't saved any pizza for breakfast.

Actually, there was more regret than the pizza. Much more, but I couldn't acknowledge it. Not until I self-medicated and crawled into a cocoon. That's how days like this worked. I lit a cigarette, found a bag of Fritos, and grabbed my stash.

But the Bakelite rang before I tumbled horizontal and I forced myself to hoist the receiver. I figured Boots and figured if I didn't get the phone before the couch got me, it might be a long time before we spoke. After yesterday and last night, that just didn't seem right.

Only all my figures were wrong and my dick knew it at her first silky note. "Remember me?"

Disgusted by my instantaneous reaction, I threw the cigarette into the ashtray. "You're impossible to forget, Alexis."

For the first time since awakening I felt the pain from Clifford's beating. I suppose that meant I was coming alive. Terrific. I dragged the phone along with my body to the kitchen table, sat, and lit another smoke. I left the stash in the living room but didn't go back to get it. I wasn't that alive.

"It was good between us, wasn't it?"

"A helluva night," I slid, caught on the line like a deer in headlights. "How did you get my number?"

"Lou gave it to me."

"Lou?"

"Don't fret, darling," Alexis chuckled, "I told him I wanted to thank you again for our wonderful evening, that's all. It might be difficult for them to appreciate us sleeping together. You know, semi-incestuous."

"Tactful," I managed.

"It would be difficult for you as well, if our night wasn't kept undercover, wouldn't it?"

I exhaled a lungful of smoke, "It's already difficult."

"Learning new things about yourself always is."

I felt myself grow embarrassed, "I wasn't thinking of, of..."

"Our dance," Alexis finished with another easy laugh. "You were thinking about your girlfriend."

"I guess."

"Well," she said in a teasing tone, "if the time we spent together is so troublesome, let's chat about your detective work."

"My what?"

"That look-see you gave the Hacienda when I left the other morning. You know, both of us have family staying there."

Surprise, surprise. Concern for Lou's safety hadn't been completely trumped by my depression. Or maybe anything was better than talking about the lighthouse. No matter; Alexis opened the door and I eagerly followed which somehow seemed too familiar. "Living there is more accurate."

"Lauren makes that crystal clear," Alexis snorted angrily.

"What's with you and that house, anyway?" I asked. "Your mother thinks you want it for your father."

"Of course she thinks that. My mother can't stand my relationship with Dad. It drives Lauren crazy to play second fiddle. To anyone, but especially her daughter."

"You're forgetting about Anne."

Alexis paused, "Anne's not much competition to anyone."

Her answer sparked my curiosity, but I remained silent as she continued talking.

"It's exactly what I told you the other night. I despise watching the house decay. If I could afford it, I'd fix it myself. But I can't. What I *can* do is find a buyer. Believe it or not, I'll be able to set up both my dad and Lauren with money in the bank and a little left over for me."

Mother and daughter had decidedly different views of the same situation. Of course, I didn't know how much Alexis meant by 'little.' "Lauren really doesn't want to sell."

"Sooner or later she'll have to," Alexis said grimly. Then, in an abrupt change of pace, her voice became light and teasing. "You're slick, Matt Jacob. I'm doing the talking even though I asked about your job."

"I don't have a job, Alexis," I answered carefully. "I didn't find anything the other morning and now the police are guarding the Hacienda. What's *your* interest?"

"Concern. I know you were looking for my mother's mythical

stalker and wondered if you made any headway with the people who did the drive-by."

"I'm not involved," I lied. "Chief Biancho doesn't want me mixing in."

"I spoke to Teddy and he says the shooting was a gang initiation."

"That's what he told me too." Part of me wanted to get off the phone as fast as possible, but I'd become interested in Alexis's 'concern.' "Teddy say anything else?"

"Just that the two of you talked."

"Yeah, we had a pleasant conversation," I said, rubbing one of my many aches. I'd begun to think of Biancho and Clifford as one. Time for more Ibi's.

"He wanted to know how long I'd known you, that sort of thing." Alexis paused then added, "Don't worry, I didn't tell him about the lighthouse either." Alexis laughed into the phone, "You did it again! I'm doing the talking." She paused then added, "You are a tricky bastard."

"Just my personality."

"Your multifaceted personality," she whispered seductively before reverting to matter-of-fact. "Anyway, Teddy is serious. He doesn't want anything screwing up this investigation."

"He doesn't have to worry about me," I said, wondering about their relationship and whether Biancho enlisted Alexis as well as Clifford in his mission to keep me from nosing around. "I know better than to cross a cop." Had the scars to prove it.

"Good, because Ted was really intense. I don't want anything to happen to you that I don't do myself."

Too late for that. "Listen, Alexis, before you hang up..."

"Clairvoyant?"

"That's your mother's specialty."

The mutual laughter covered an awkward moment before I asked for her address and telephone number. I told myself it was for work and hoped to hell I meant it. Alexis acted flattered and gave me the information for both her home and office. I pressed my luck and asked for the rest of the family's. Explained that I wanted to leave Lou and Lauren alone, but felt weird not knowing where people lived.

"That's the least of your weirdness," she jabbed, but gave them to me anyway.

Any hesitation I'd had about getting out of the house was gone. Rather than hurtling me deeper down the sinkhole, Alexis' call reignited my worry about Lauren and Lou as well as my angry questions about Clifford's visit.

I downed the Ibi's with bourbon, retrieved my stash and rolled a good sized joint. I was never too angry to do my head. Boots hadn't been rash with her concerns. I did want to confront Biancho. Demand to know why he felt it necessary to contact Washington Clifford and possibly send another message through Alexis. I wanted to lean on the son of a bitch until I got some answers. Hammer him because I had no answers of my own.

Armed with Boots's warning, the smarter me prevailed. Instead of writing my own invite to the slammer or more slaps, I grabbed all my old taxi street guides and began to place the Browns and Rowes where they belonged. I didn't have, and didn't want, a computer. Hell, my flip-top cell phone still annoyed me.

Except for Stephen, they all belonged on the North Shore. Stephen lived in town.

I sat back in my chair leafing through the Boston guide until the hair on my neck bristled. I quickly found my building-by-building city map and forgot about my growling stomach. Stephen's home was catty-corner from Lauren's car trash.

CHAPTER 28

Why hadn't Lauren simply waited inside her son's apartment instead of the street?

I'd asked a ton of questions since I'd learned about Lou and Lauren's relationship—mostly about myself. But this one wasn't and I wanted an answer. It pulled me away from the couch, but not toward Alexis; for some of us, any port in a storm—though apparently not so for Lauren Rowe.

Once I parked across from Stephen's address, my little question mushroomed. It appeared impossible for anyone living in his building to have missed the car party.

I stubbed the cigarette into the overflowing ashtray and walked to the converted brick warehouse. Climbed a couple of steps, leaned against an oversized gray door, and stepped into a medium-sized, refinished oak anteroom with a corridor leading toward the back. Each side of the hallway had a tinted gray glass door and a gallery name. Both large rooms were dark and empty.

I walked the corridor to a freight elevator where I found a buzzer and intercom built into the opposite wall. There were also two wooden boxes stuffed with junk mail and art catalogues.

It took me a moment to push the button, steeling myself for Stephen's whiny, sardonic greeting. But what I heard was just a weak hello.

"I'm Matt Jacob, and I'm looking for Stephen Rowe," I shouted into the small speaker.

"No reason to yell, Mr. Jacob," the voice whispered. "My hearing is fine. What's your business?"

I thought for a moment. "We met at his mother's party and I wanted to speak with him."

"About what?" If possible, his voice was weaker. "We don't receive many people here."

"I'm doing work for his mom, looking into the drive-by shooting that took place the night of the party. Is this Stephen?"

"No, it isn't."

I'd been so intent on getting out of my house I hadn't thought about getting into his.

"Stephen returned home long before the shooting," said the tired voice, "but he's not here now. If you leave your telephone number, I'll tell him you dropped by."

"Thanks, but there's no need." I'd wait in the car. I wanted to stay on the job,

and the B.M.W. was too small to use as a couch and it didn't have a built-in TV.

I didn't end up waiting anywhere because Stephen and I almost rammed into each other on my way out of the building.

"What the hell are you doing here?" he demanded.

"Looking for you." I followed his back to the freight elevator.

"Well, I guess you found me."

He turned toward me with a pointed look. "Have you been harassing JB?"

"I asked someone upstairs if you were home."

Stephen looked so annoyed I expected him to order me out.

But all he did was shake his head and grumble, "Stay here. If Jayson can handle it, I'll bring you up."

Stephen stuck a key into the elevator lock and the door immediately opened. "Wait here," he repeated disappearing behind the sliding gun metal gray.

The elevator sscreaked up the old building while I weathered a bad premonition.

Sadly, my hunch wasn't wrong. Stephen brought me up, the old elevator opening right inside their loft. The huge L-shaped room was sectioned through careful placement of sculpture and hanging canvases. Though the walls and tables exhibited enough beautiful art to be a gallery, there was nothing stifling or formal. With comfortable furniture casually arranged on the gleaming white oak, uniquely shaped skylights, the converted space felt warm, light, and lived in.

A lot had to do with the paintings. Their styles ranged from Pollack-like dots and splashes to super-realism, but running through all was a powerful exaltation of life. Even the darker, more somber imagery contained deep brooding energy.

But what finally drew my eyes was an emaciated man wearing a heavy cotton robe. He sat connected to an oxygen producing machine with a long plastic tube that fed into two inhalers held in his nostrils by an elastic band around his head. I'd initially missed him because the pale green of his robe and machine melted into the color on the walls. But as soon as he caught my attention, everything else disappeared.

Stephen dragged me over by my elbow while I tried to hide my shallow breath. I'd been up close and personal with different kinds of death, but never what I believed to be emphysema. And it threw me. Threw me enough that I had to force my hand to lightly clasp his fleshless fingers.

"Matt Jacobs, isn't it? This is Jayson Brook," Stephen announced proudly.

"Without the s," I stalled, trying regain my equilibrium. I glanced toward one of the paintings and the name registered. A few years earlier Jayson Brook had been white hot in big time art circles that Boots knew about before he vanished. I guess I just discovered why.

"You recognize my name, Mr. Jacob?"

I nodded, still unwilling to trust my voice. The contradiction between the canvases and the barely breathing cadaver brought on a rush of run and irrational rage.

"You see, JB? People still know you and they always will," Stephen said fiercely.

"He has a good memory," Jayson whispered.

Stephen pointed to a couple of nearby upholstered chairs. "Why don't we sit down and talk about what you're doing here. You understand you can't stay long."

My anxious anger was replaced with relief at moving away from Brook, then embarrassment at my relief.

"First time near stage four emphysema?" Stephen asked, not unkindly.

"Yeah, look, I'm sorry for barging in." I was sorry I was there at all. But when I glanced at the sickly figure, he smiled and I began to steady. Compared to Jayson I was lucky to be anywhere.

Stephen scratched his flop of sandy brown hair. "If you had called I'd never have allowed you to visit," he said. "But you're here so what do you want?"

A fucking cigarette, I thought. But instead, "I'd like to talk to you about the shooting at the Hacienda."

"Worried about your uncle?"

"Father-in-law."

Stephen's natural snide was already slipping through. "What's to worry?"

"Aren't you concerned about your mother?" I asked. Something got twisted for Stephen and Alexis whenever Lauren

183

was mentioned. "A drive-by shooting isn't chopped liver."

"Why should I be worried when she's not. You'd better get used to the idea that my mother takes care of herself. No openings for Good Samaritans. Certainly not since Lou. Anyway, I've been told that it was a gang thing," he dismissed.

Stephen's disposition reduced my desire to flee.

"The Police Chief's been telling that to everyone. I have no reason to doubt him, but theory doesn't necessarily mean true. Also, I don't really know Ted Biancho."

"I lived in the same town with Ted for most of my life and *I* don't know him," Stephen said. "He was a townie but not a jock so he wasn't popular. With anyone. The other townies thought he looked down on them. Tough titty for Teddy. No one liked me either."

Stephen turned his lanky body toward Brook. Jayson glanced toward me, grimaced, and looked at his feet.

Stephen appeared pleased to have someone new to tell. "In the movies that would have thrown us together and we would have become good friends, but of course nothing like that happened. I've always been surprised he became a cop. I would have guessed lawyer or something more ambitious."

He frowned, "I don't really think he likes any of our family except Alexis."

The air went out of his tire and he scowled before adding, "Actually, if you want to find out about Biancho, she's the person to talk to."

I should have registered the change in his attitude and shifted gears. Should have but didn't. "Why her?" I prodded.

"They were tight." Stephen shook his head. "I think they still see each other, but don't know for certain. Biancho's married, and it's been a long time since high school."

Jayson turned his head and coughed. "Not long enough," he whispered, and he and Stephen laughed sardonically.

I found it tough to enjoy Jayson's joke. "You don't particularly like Biancho, but you aren't the least bit worried about your mother's safety?" I asked sharply. Too sharply.

Stephen stared at me and Jayson fiddled with a setting on the machine. I was taking oxygen out of the room.

"You ought to listen more carefully. I didn't say I distrusted him," Stephen corrected nastily. "Teddy Biancho can't stand the thought of fucking up. Never could. Lauren says he's completely embarrassed about the drive-by so I'm sure you have nothing to worry about. Anyway, the whole incident sounds like kid stuff, the stupid shit Ian might pull."

"Are you serious?" I asked, immediately recalling the Karate Kid's absence at the party.

Stephen looked disdainful. "Don't be an idiot. Ian's an asshole, but he wouldn't shoot the Hacienda." Stephen shook his head. "He's already pulled his stunt of the month."

I was beginning to blow the interview but stubbornly plowed on. "You don't sound crazy about Ian either."

Stephen didn't give me a chance to kill the question. "What does that have to do with anything? But if you want to know, Ian's constant bitching bores me. Growing up when he did was a cupcake compared to what Alexis and I went through."

I couldn't stop pushing. "He was old enough to be affected by your parents breakup."

"Ian had it easy." Stephen raised his hands in mock surrender, "Maybe somewhere in my father's genes there's something useful but I wouldn't swear on it."

He shrugged, ignoring his own connection to the pool. "I suppose it takes a certain amount of strength to be so fucking self-destructive."

Jayson and I kept our eyes fixed on Stephen as he stood up and began to pace. "When I grew the only thing that provided any stability was the Hacienda."

He stopped and stared at a deep green and blue Rothko like canvas. "The house was my anchor and the ocean kept me sane. Even when Lauren disappeared to search for her so-called lost identity and left us with the royal asshole, the Hacienda gave me something to count on."

CHAPTER 29

"You just called your father an asshole, Stephen," I said.

"I don't want to talk about him," he snapped through taut lips. "If you're interested in Paul, speak to Alexis or my mother."

I wandered toward the windows behind the seating arrangement. "The downstairs galleries looked closed," I said, buying time.

"We only open them occasionally," Jayson said. "I own the building outright, so we're free to use it as we want."

"Are all the paintings here yours?" I asked fighting another round of sudden discomfort.

"Almost," Stephen answered for Jayson. "Heather's are mixed in."

Alexis said Heather had talent and Alexis was right. There wasn't a clunker in the bunch. I walked behind the sofa and looked down onto the roof of my car.

I stared out the window and casually asked, "You know what throws me? I just don't see how your mother's auto could have been destroyed without anyone up here knowing it."

The moment Stephen tensed up behind me I knew I'd set the table badly and burned the meal. Didn't even have to turn around. I felt angry and incompetent, thrown by how much Jayson Brook's ravaged body knocked me off-stride.

"I thought you came here about the damn drive-by?" Stephen asked, his voice strained and defensive.

"I did. But when you look down at the street it's hard not to wonder about the car."

"Jayson can't tolerate heat so we use air conditioning and keep the windows closed. No one heard a thing," he said.

I turned away from the window. Stephen stood alongside Brook, holding his hand, glaring in my direction. Jayson's eyes were closed, his chest barely moving.

"I still don't understand how you missed it. I mean we're talking demolition derby." I didn't have the chops to get in his face even though I knew he was lying.

"It doesn't much matter what you understand, does it?" Stephen released Jayson's hand and walked briskly to the elevator door. "I'm tired of your questions. Uncle Lou and my mother are completely safe so you can stop acting like a detective. Frankly, I have more important things on my mind."

Stephen twisted the key and the elevator door slid open with a growl. I nodded to Jayson, stepped forward to enter the lift, then gave a final shot. "The car looked like it had been battered with a lead pipe. Hard not to hear—even with an air conditioner."

Stephen shook his head impatiently, "There was a storm that night."

My voice was loud enough to reach Jayson. "I know—so why did your mother wait outside?"

Stephen pushed my fingers off the sliding door and turned the key. "You'll have to ask her."

I sat in the car smoking, sorting through Stephen's lies and my mishandling of the conversation. Maybe I did belong working malls. The only thing I kept discovering was more about the sad sludge of the Rowe/Brown family. Better to cut and run than sink any deeper into their lives. But then I reconsidered. If I quit now, I'd be burdened about Lou and buried by Boots.

I glanced toward the loft and spotted Stephen staring down toward the street. The macabre image of him throwing dirt on Jayson's coffin flashed through my mind and mingled with my own memories. In my haste to depart, I flooded the engine.

It was shit-list time at the not-so-okay-corral.

"You were supposed to leave things be," Lauren churned. We were standing in the kitchen but no one offered me a seat. Her eyes glittered, the clipped pronunciation a match for her rigid demeanor.

Lou sat stubbornly silent on one of the tall stools. He was uncomfortable with this scene, but was going to let it play. Maybe he hadn't been given a choice.

"We don't know each other very well, Lauren, but Lou and I are family. You're important to him and that makes yours and his safety critical," I tried, trotting out Boots' line.

Her fist clenched, "I understand all about your relationship with Lou. What I don't understand is why you bullied my son. I gave you explicit instructions to leave my family and friends alone but you turned right around and ignored me."

Something Lauren apparently wasn't used to. "I'm trying to make absolutely certain that no one connected to your life is behind any of this. I thought asking Stephen for help was a good idea. It wasn't." If I thought my admission would reduce her rage, I thought wrong. Though Lauren's body didn't move, her intensity threatened to blow the roof.

"I told you the reason I didn't want you to interfere. Instead, you snuck behind my back. Did you think I wouldn't learn about it?"

"Not much of a sneak," I countered. "As soon as I realized how angry Stephen had become, I drove here to tell you myself. It wasn't my intention to bother anyone."

"Barging unannounced into their home isn't bothering anyone? As if they don't have enough to worry about!" she hissed. "The man is dying."

"I didn't realize..."

"That's just my point! You intrude in people's lives without knowing the first damn thing about them. And why did you start with Stephen? You seem to be great friends with my daughter, why didn't you go to her?"

I felt my insides squirm, but forced myself to remain calm. "Stephen lives in town."

"Bullshit, Matthew! You accused him of lying about my car; something else I asked you not to pursue. Don't you have your own life?"

I tried holding my ground. "Once I saw his building I was surprised no one heard your car being destroyed."

"Their windows were closed and it was thundering. You know what the weather was like. I don't see what's so fucking hard to believe."

My life and body might be breaking down, but my shit detector still functioned. Lauren was lying. Something had happened in Stephen's loft that she wanted kept secret. But I wasn't going to get it by bulldozing. Certainly not with Lou sitting there.

"Stephen told me you even hounded him about my waiting in the rain."

"Hounded is much too strong." I felt like a matador dodging a bull; so much for holding my ground.

"Calling someone a liar sounds like hounding to me."

"I'm sorry he felt that way," I apologized. "I certainly didn't want him to. He has enough to worry about." I felt oily using Jayson, but I wanted to survive her charge and get in a shot or two of my own. "But why *did* you wait outside?"

"You won't quit until you rip me apart, will you?" Lauren pulled at her hair, her anger mercurially transforming into sadness. "I didn't go back upstairs because it kills me to see what's become of Jayson, and what I expect will happen to my son when he dies. Once I left their apartment, I wasn't going back. It wouldn't have mattered if it had been a hurricane," she asserted, tears in her eyes.

Lauren was good, real good, and now both of us had used Jayson Brook. Unfortunately, it didn't feel any better to have company. And didn't change the fact that she was still lying.

Lou cleared his throat and finally intervened. "Matty, It's a difficult circumstance, the emphysema and everything. Lauren told me all about it.

Lauren jumped onto his words. "I would have told you too, only Stephen and Jayson keep their relationship private. It's complicated enough without everybody knowing where they live. Jayson still attracts attention."

I wasn't an art groupie or a recruiter for hospice. "Look, maybe I went about it the wrong way, but it's impossible to close my eyes given your situation. It's damn near impossible to accept the car, the stalking, and the drive-by as simple coincidence."

"Then offer your services to Ted Biancho. Find the gang that did the shooting." Lauren's tears were gone.

"The police don't let civilians help, Lauren."

"You're a detective."

"Matt works on his own," Lou explained, "not for the police."

"Then let him work on his own to find the goddamn gang. He doesn't have to browbeat my family!"

"I'm not trying to beat on anyone, Lauren. Lou's *my* family."

"Then try to understand why I'm so angry. I'm working to calm

191

things down, but I can't if you rile everyone up. This has become a terrible time for my kids. They're having trouble adjusting to the idea that I want to be with your father-in-law."

"They're just not used to Lauren having a partner, Matty," Lou chimed in. "It's been difficult."

"I've hit them with another big change," Lauren said. "I'm sure that's why Ian did what he did."

"There's no reason to feel guilty, Lauren," Lou insisted. "The kids are old enough to deal with our relationship."

Lauren shrugged. "I don't know what anyone can deal with, anymore. But I know this. I want you to return to your own life," Lauren warned, looking me in the eye. "Lou says you have a fiancée, spend some time with her."

It was the gut shot and I felt a clammy sweat cover my body. Lauren was holding Alexis in her hand, and I couldn't let her flip the card.

CHAPTER 30

Once again I'd been instructed to turn tail. Only I was a detective, not a fucking dog. If I wasn't going to let Lauren's dismal family dynamics stop me, I sure wasn't going to bend over for her temper. Stephen and Lauren were lying about her car, Biancho was hiding something behind Clifford's fists, and I was bumbling. But fuck it, I was going to keep on, bumbling or not. Boots knew me well.

I toyed with visiting Alexis but quickly nixed the notion. Whatever possible rationalization I might concoct, seeing her was just more masochism. So I decided to talk to Paul Brown and see what he'd noticed the early morning of the drive-by. Paul had arrived on the scene before me and questioning him couldn't be construed as messing with kids. Anyway, the man owed me a sweatshirt.

By the time I found his modest brick house it was late afternoon.

"I don't know when to expect Paul," Anne said at the front door. "Lately he's been dropping by Vivian's after work."

"Vivian's?"

"Lauren's mother." Anne's tight, pinched face didn't brighten at the thought.

"May I come inside?"

Anne looked flustered. "I generally don't have people in without Paul."

"How about I promise not to sell you a vacuum?"

"It's been easier now that Heather's back," she said.

"You always stay home by yourself?"

Anne hesitated then opened the door. "Come in, but if Paul does return, you just got here, okay?"

Nothing like long term trust, but who was I to woof? "Paul the jealous type?" I asked, stepping through the screen door.

"Things are complicated these days," Anne replied, leading the way to the living room. "Would you care for something to drink?"

"A beer would be great. No glass necessary. And an ashtray if it's all right to smoke."

"It's fine. Paul doesn't care for it, but that doesn't stop Heather. Or me, for that matter. Make yourself comfortable."

The room was nondescript, the only splash of color a tilted oil painting on one of its walls. Though smaller than the canvasses I'd seen at Stephen's, the picture was just as good.

Anne returned with a Miller, a glass of water, and a large curved sea shell blotted with old yellow stains.

"Let me take those." I put the beer and shell on a dark coffee table and pointed toward the picture before sitting at one end of the tired couch. "Original?"

"Heather gave it to us as a gift when she moved back in."

"I met her at Lauren's party. She seems like a real nice kid."

"Everybody thinks so—except the man she lived with. Like mother, like daughter," Anne murmured under her breath sitting down on the other corner of the sofa.

I lit a cigarette and waited for her to continue.

"May I have one?" she asked.

"Of course."

"Truth is, Paul gets furious when he catches me smoking," Anne said. "I usually mooch off Heather."

"No big deal."

Anne inhaled gratefully. "You haven't lived with Paul Brown. Anything can be a big deal."

Her not so between the lines was beginning to bum me out. "Actually, I'm here to talk about the shooting after Lauren's party."

Anne shrugged, "The police think it was a gang thing."

"I want to make sure."

A fresh look of recognition crept into her eyes. "I knew we'd met at the party but I completely forgot about seeing you that morning. I'd taken a couple of sleeping pills and was pretty woozy. You came in with Alexis, right?"

"Right."

"Paul was pissed you kept her out for that many hours."

"He gets angry a lot."

Anne sighed. "He usually keeps it to himself or at me when he's around."

"Was he upset at being dragged out of bed?"

"Don't be silly, it was Lauren who called." Anne stubbed her cigarette into the shell that I'd placed between us. "Do you mind if I take another? I don't get many opportunities to smoke when Heather's not home."

I handed her the pack, "Take as many as you like."

Anne took three and slipped two into the breast pocket of her short-sleeved blouse. "Do you remember the song "*Whatever Lola Wants*"?"

"Lauren gets?"

Anne nodded.

"Did it surprise you that she called? Paul was in his cups when he left the party."

"The surprise was that she called the police. Lauren always calls here when there's a problem."

"You sound annoyed."

Anne coughed and stubbed out her cigarette. "I am." Her tight, thin lips began to quiver and almost immediately a few tears rolled down her cheeks. I automatically moved the makeshift ashtray, slid next to her, and awkwardly patted her shoulder.

"I never thought things would work out this way," she gulped. "I keep waiting for it to change but..."

"You don't have to talk," I said removing my hand as her eyes dried.

But my questioning uncorked Anne's pent up unhappiness. "It's all so crazy. Paul spends more time and money taking care of Lauren and Alexis than he does us. We barely scrape by. Look around, you see us living high off the hog?"

Anne didn't wait for an answer. "Everything up here costs three times as much as anywhere else. Of course, it's a privilege to live near the ocean," she finished sarcastically.

"Can't you move?" I asked edging back to my corner where I lit two more cigarettes and handed her one.

"I'd leave in an instant," Anne said. "Paul says it's the kids, but it's really just Lauren and Alexis. And these days it's probably Vivian as well. We'd do okay if he didn't keep forking over half his check."

Anne puffed nervously. "I can't believe I'm talking like this. I don't even know you."

"I can appreciate what you're saying. I've watched my father-in-law grow incredibly absorbed with Lauren and her family."

A small smile tickled the corners of her lips. "Lou seems like a very good man. It just adds to the shock."

"Of the shooting?"

"No, no," she waved her hand. "No one ever imagined Lauren would get serious about anyone, especially a man so traditional.

I'm no shrink, but I'm sure Ian's suicide attempt had something to do with their relationship."

No shrink, but honest enough to call Ian's "accident" what it was. And the same as Stephan's analysis. I tried to make her feel better. "Well, the divorce ought to help with your money problems," I said, finishing off my beer. "I don't think Lauren will need Paul's money."

"What divorce? What are you talking about?" Anne appeared dumbfounded.

It took a moment to realize that no one had told her about Lauren's decision. "Lauren's going to finalize the divorce."

Anne's jaw clamped shut, her eyes blinked, and the hand that jammed the cigarette into the shell trembled. I reached for my pack to offer her another but she shook me off.

"I've smoked too many already," she said, her voice frozen steel. "I've talked too much as well," she added, rising to her feet.

"And I overstayed my welcome," I apologized, joining her in a rapid walk to the front door.

"I want to keep this conversation between us." She looked at me, "The entire visit, if it's not too much to ask."

"No problem. Any particular reason?"

"If Paul finds out that I was crying about our relationship to a stranger I'll never hear the end of it."

CHAPTER 31

By the time I returned to my car, the afternoon was dreary and gray. Matched my mood. Worse, the weather gave promise to an early fall. I told myself the North Shore caught cold before Boston, but it did nothing to sweeten my sour. The vapid emptiness of a lifeless relationship squeezed me like a juicer. Worse, there was something about Paul's attachment to the Hacienda that just seemed odd. I got his connection with Alexis, even his distance from his sons—but the house and Lauren?

And I didn't bounce back when I got to my apartment. Didn't bother with the lights, either. Just rounded up the usuals. I sat at the table rolling a joint and pouring a double before admitting I was operating on auto. It was one thing to get high for a party, another to shut down my personal demons; but what did it say when I lined up inebriates to prepare for a night with my old lady?

I slapped the loaded shot-glass on its side. My mouth watered at the smell, but that just made me angrier. I watched the whiskey drip off the edge of the enamel and puddle onto the waterproofed fir. This was all one sick joke; I was the dick who didn't do domestic.

It took time and more hair shirt before I pulled myself together. Anne's loveless life with Paul, coupled with my cheat then fuck-up with Stephen, had produced another funk—but I told myself I didn't have the luxury to wallow. Those had been real bullets in the Hacienda's door, real hurt behind Biancho's warning, and real love in Lou's proposal.

Boots mixed herself a gin and tonic then asked if I wanted one. The question shoved my nose right back into the earlier spill. But I calmed my beating heart with a nod. And found myself able to hide the rest of my down behind Boots' talkative nervousness. I knew enough to let her keep talking until she was ready to tell me what was *really* on her mind.

Supper was spicy shrimp served with Boots' non-stop chatter. I learned more about fiber optics and the competition between Internet providers than I ever wanted to know. I hated technology.

Finally finished with corporate America, we talked about Stephen and Jayson, stage four emphysema, art, Lou's proposal, Lauren's demand to leave things be, and my decision to ignore her.

"You're just looking for dirt to throw in their faces," Boots said harshly.

"Twenty-four hours ago you told me to hang in there."

"I said I expected you to. There's a difference. And now it's not just *Wash* and Lauren warning you off. Lou wants you to leave things alone as well. What are you trying to prove?"

"B'wahna's talking hitch, Boots. Damned if I'm gonna play best man without knowing what this woman's about, without understanding what's actually happening."

"So it's back to 'this woman' again?"

"I'm not sure it was ever anything but. That was your take. Anyway, our conversation ain't about Lauren, or about me, sweetheart. Something is going on with you." Either my question reflected an honest attempt to talk, or more self-destruction. We had us here a 'pick 'em.'

There was a long pause. "I'm nervous about you staying over tonight," Boots finally said.

"Why?"

"The other night scared me."

"Clifford does that to people."

"I'm not talking about Washington Clifford. It was us, our lovemaking."

"I couldn't move around too much, but I'm feeling a lot better," I smiled.

Boots slapped her hand on the low glass table. "Don't start with your fucking jokes."

I lost the smile and took a deep drag on my cigarette. "Sorry, maybe you better say a little more."

Boots took a cigarette out of my pack. "You kept fading in and out. Half the time you weren't there. It was almost the same as the night I suggested buying a television. When I woke up, you were gone."

"I was out here."

"You weren't with me."

I shook my head. "It's not that convoluted, Boots. You know how wired I've been, and you know why. How many times do we have to talk about this?"

"As many times as you hide." Boots rubbed out her cigarette and took a deep breath. "The other night you were plenty comfortable about Lauren and Lou, so please spare me that one. What you haven't been comfortable about is Lauren's daughter," she said, a brittle tone to her voice.

"What?" I asked, my stomach plummeting.

"That's right, Alexis, and you know exactly what I mean. We've lived through these situations before."

"Lived through what situations?"

"You and other women," Boots blurted, the brittle vanishing, its place taken by round eyes and a voice full of history and hurt. "I haven't forgotten what you were like when you fucked Melanie," she said, recalling a difficult period in our relationship. Now, like then, Boots neglected to add Hal, her own ex-lover to that particular mix. But unlike then, I wasn't gonna either.

"I'm supposed to believe you spent half the night with her in a goddamn car? If all you did was talk, why do you change the subject every time I bring her up? Or act like she doesn't exist? You should have seen your face when I suggested you question her. Tonight, you didn't mention her once. Are you sleeping with Alexis, Matt? Was that your ride?"

Nut-cracking time—divulge or dance. Tell the truth, explain, apologize, get tossed. Say goodnight, gather my shit, and walk out on my own. Only Boots was my life, and I wasn't ready to lose her. "There's nothing going on between me and Alexis Brown."

Boots began to tremble so I stepped forward. "There's nothing going on between me and Alexis," I said again. "She's a very hot ticket so I steer clear of her. I just don't want anything to screw us up. My drifting is about you and me. About us. We're at some kind of crossroads and there are times when it freaks me out. But not all the time. I ain't missing now, am I?"

Her tears were falling. "No, you're here now."

Babba Ram Matt. And, despite my lie, it was true. Maybe because of the lie, I didn't know. But I did know that Boots' painful vulnerability sliced and diced the alligator skin I'd lugged into her condo for protection.

I slowly knelt by her side. Maybe I should have said more. Reassure her, reassure myself that despite the cheat, I was where I wanted to be. But right then I needed no assurance, no whip to keep me on my knees. All I needed was to let Boots cry herself out before I stood and pulled her to her feet where she leaned into me, her arms wrapping tightly around my body.

I tried to show her how I felt. Tried to show her with my hands and lips everything that I couldn't say. Make her understand how much she meant to me and how afraid I was of losing her.

I also tried to avoid any more questions.

CHAPTER 32

If I hadn't woken up alone I might have bagged the whole idea. Stayed in bed and convinced Boots to stay there with me. But it was morning and Boots had already left for work. The choice was clear; self-destruct, or stick with my plan.

No trek home for the guilty. I stopped for a couple of coffee rolls and two large containers of watery black before pulling into an alley to watch Jayson's doorway. I had no idea when, or even whether, Stephen would leave; my only option was to kick back and hope.

I'd eaten a meatball sub for lunch and was contemplating some mid-afternoon tokes when the converted warehouse door finally swung open and I saw Stephen jump into his Cherokee and pull away.

It was time to shake my slouch, slap my face, and go to work. For the first time since I'd left Boots's apartment, all my anxious reservations returned, so I lit a last cigarette and stalled. And stalled, until I sucked it up to do the dirty.

I was surprised at how readily Brook okayed my visit. When I arrived inside the loft he was standing in front of the elevator with the help of a walker but still attached to his breathing machine.

"If you don't mind I'd like to sit," Jayson said softly, ignoring my sharp, deep inhale.

"Whatever is easy," I managed.

"Nothing is easy these days," he said with an ironic smile. "But sitting helps."

I followed him to the comfortable conversation area, torn between staring at his skeletal frame and losing myself in the surrounding beauty. As usual, negative compulsion won.

He grunted as he sat down in his straight backed chair next to the machine. "I might have to stop talking once in a while," he apologized.

I shrugged, sat, and wondered if he'd let me take a hit to loosen my own constricted chest. Just what he needed. Smoke in the house. Fuck me, he was dying and I was struggling with fears about *my* mortality.

"Stephen's not here, but I expect you already know that."

Surprise replaced some of my angry self-hatred.

"Stevie actually thought he had you convinced."

"He doesn't seem like a 'Stevie.'"

"That's only because you don't know him. There's a lot of little boy left inside."

"Too old to act like one, don't you think?"

"Everything is relative, I'm too young to die."

I felt myself pale.

I guess he noticed. "Sorry, sometimes my humor makes people uncomfortable."

"Listen, with what you're leaving behind you'll never be dead," I said impulsively, waving at the walls.

A pleased expression crossed his gaunt face, "That's quite kind of you."

"No kindness intended."

"Are you interested in art?"

I shrugged. "If a know-nothing like me is blown away, we're talking good."

"I think you know more than you let on about a lot of things."

Jayson gave me the opening to steer our conversation, but I wasn't ready to turn the wheel. "Can you still work?" I asked, somehow less afraid of real contact.

"Occasionally. I'm doing a self-portrait, and I'm committed to staying alive until I finish it. Most of my stuff is light, but this one is serious."

"From where I sit, it's all serious, even the funny ones. Makes you look twice at what we take for granted."

Jayson seemed pleased and proud. "Would you like to see the self-portrait?" he asked shyly. "It's almost done."

"I'd feel privileged."

Jayson struggled to his feet and, without thinking, I walked over to give a helping hand. "Do you need me to move the machine?" I asked.

"No, I'll be all right. It's set up so I can get around the entire apartment. Just don't trip on the plastic tube." He looked at me and smiled. "You don't seem as uncomfortable today."

"I'm not."

"Because of my work?" he asked, grabbing onto the metal walker.

"That's some of it."

"And the rest?" he prodded.

"I'm not sure. Probably has to do with the way you handle yourself. I'm not a complete stranger to death," I added.

Jayson glanced at my sagging face before pushing his way to the back of the loft. "Could you get those?" he asked, nodding toward a curtained set of French doors.

I opened the doors and stepped into a messy room with huge windows and oversized skylights. Tables overflowed with tubes of paint, cans of paint thinner, brushes of all sizes and shapes. Canvasses leaned against the walls, vibrating with color and amazing images.

"Do you mind?" I asked kneeling next to a pile of paintings. "You are a prolific son of a bitch," I said, quickly looking through the large stack. I said it without thinking and when I heard the sound coming from his bird-like throat, I thought he was choking.

It took a second to realize it was laughter.

"It's a pleasure to be called 'a son of a bitch,'" Jayson almost crowed. "Other than Stephen and Heather, I haven't had a natural response in a very long time."

I looked up at him. "You represent some scary shit. And you don't look so hot either." I really liked him, and my like was letting loose.

"Thanks," he smiled.

"Don't keep thanking me or I'll just get uptight. These are terrific," I said, shaking my head.

"They're not all mine. Heather Heywood uses the studio."

I was still poking through the canvasses and noticed a couple with her signature scratched into a corner. She was good. Jayson was great.

While I was pawing, he moved to a large easel in the corner of the room and yanked off a thin burlap cover. I stood and rocked back onto my heels. Painted in different shades of gray, stages of life were superimposed one on top of another. The closer you looked, the more faces and bodies could be seen. The portrait reminded me of Picasso. With one significant difference—Jayson's images stopped at a much younger age than *The Old Guitarist* in Chicago.

I felt my eyes moisten as memories of Chana and Rebecca sprang to mind.

"You like it?" Jayson asked.

When I didn't respond he slowly turned toward me. "You said you were familiar with death."

I nodded, my eyes stuck to the painting.

He swung back and for the next couple of minutes we stood silently—me facing ghosts, Jayson staring at his life.

"Let's get out of here," he eventually murmured. "I can only deal with the smell in here a little at a time and I want to save the time.

"Do you want me to put the cover back on?"

Jayson shook his head. "I don't think so. It might be a good day to work."

When I was a kid, a group of us climbed on an abandoned train trestle that ran high over a creek. There was no water in the creek, just sharp jagged rocks and ankle deep shards of broken bottles and rusted cans. The trestle was rotted but we paid no mind. My older cousin crawled onto the highest point and it shattered under his weight. He grabbed onto another weather-beaten plank and dangled until the rest of us pulled him to safety. There was total silence on the way back to his house where we sat on the porch awed by our near miss.

I felt that way now.

And Jayson knew it. "How close were the people who died?" he asked once we were back in our chairs.

"Very. Wife and young child. A major car accident. They were running an errand I didn't want to do." I'd never told the last part to anyone. Not Boots, Lou, not Simon, not even Gloria my ex-shrink.

"Do you blame yourself?"

I shrugged, "Not as much as I used to."

"Nobody gets out of here alive, you know."

"How do you control the bitter?" I asked.

"I know how lucky I've been. I had some talent and an opportunity to use it. Even caught my fifteen minutes.

"Anyway, Stephen has more than enough bitter for both of us," Jayson said with regret.

The name jerked me back to the reason I was there. "You like him a lot, don't you?"

"I've loved him for years. I was the person Stephen finally came out with."

"How did you meet?"

"Through Lauren. She wanted posters for a Gay Pride parade."

"Lauren knew that Stephen was gay?"

"No, but she was extremely political and gay was a front-burner. I got involved with her family and one thing led to another." He paused. "I never did the posters though. Peter Max was well before my time and not an influence."

I shrugged, "You'd still be on tee shirts."

"Thanks. Just what I always hoped for. Actually, Stephen's home life was a disaster. What he said about the Hacienda was absolutely true. The house and ocean were his only stability until I came along. Ironic, isn't it?"

"I know Lauren was intensely self-involved, but what about his father? Didn't he have anything for Stephen?"

"It wasn't simply self-involvement that motivated Lauren. She always had an honest commitment to her causes. It just didn't leave her time for kids. By the time I came along Paul was out of the house. Just as well since he was pretty rough. I think he suspected that Stephen was in the closet and hated him for it. He probably thought it reflected on his own manhood."

"How old was Stephen when you met?"

"Mid-twenties. We've been together a long time."

"And the only one who caught Paul's shit?"

"Ian eventually came in for his share. Paul uses his sons to take out his anger."

And Anne. "Alexis gets off free?"

"She's had her problems with Lauren, but the relationship with Paul has always been," Jayson groped for a word, "close. Their closeness is something he never got from Lauren."

"Sexual?" I asked bluntly.

"Nothing actual," Jayson replied, unfazed by the question. "But what isn't sexual? The entire family has a truckload of worms." Jayson ran out of breath and fingered the dial on the machine.

I hadn't asked about the car night, but I was afraid I'd taken too much of his life. "Do you want me to leave?"

He shook his head so I sat quietly and waited.

Jayson spent the next couple of minutes regaining his breath then said, "I like you and that doesn't happen much anymore. I'm sorry we won't have time to become friends. But I don't think you came to find out how Stephen and I met, and I know you're not a social worker."

He was tiring rapidly so I spoke straight. "Something went on up here the night Lauren's car was trashed. I know Stephen lied about it and I hoped you wouldn't."

"I won't lie," he smiled weakly, "but I won't talk about it either. If Stevie wants to tell you he will. Why do you want to know?"

I told him I was worried about Lou's safety and his relationship with Lauren. Then I found myself talking about Lou's acceptance of my marriage with his daughter Chana, despite discomfort with my background and prior marriage. I told Jayson all about Lou's support before the deaths, his commitment to me after. I recounted my four years of therapy and the way Lou stood by me, making sure I had a roof over my head and the building to keep me from killing myself, or anyone else. Told him about the trouble Lou and I had after his wife died and he wanted to move here from Chicago.

I told him how much Lou meant to me.

When I finished, I caught myself wiping tears off my rough, lined face. And suddenly felt better than I had in a real long time.

CHAPTER 33

My feel good didn't last long. I'd missed the elevator's rumble so, when the door slid open, Stephen and Heather suddenly appeared as if Scotty had beamed them up.

"What are you doing here?" Stephen demanded, pushing the mop from his eyes with a brusque gesture.

"I invited him in, Stephen," Jayson said.

"Why?"

Jayson shrugged, "I wanted to."

Stephen looked incredulous.

One glance at Stephen's sneer, one note of his hostile voice, and my inside open clamped closed like solid steel shutters on a ghetto jewelry store. Contact with Jayson notwithstanding, I'd come to the loft for a reason. It wasn't going to play the way I'd planned, but now, there was no leaving without learning what happened to Lauren's car. Or maybe I was just pissed at the interruption.

"See, I'm not such a bad guy," I smiled, plotting a way to pop him.

"You were instructed not to bother us," Stephen said scowling.

"He wasn't bothering me," Jayson said.

"Did you tell him anything, JB?"

Jayson rose to his feet and gripped the walker. "I told him to talk to you. I'm going to the studio while I still can breathe with its smell. It's been nice visiting with you, Matt. I'm glad you liked the portrait."

"You showed him the painting?" Heather and Stephen asked simultaneously.

Jayson grunted and scraped toward the French doors.

"I'll get it," Heather said walking quickly to his side.

Stephen stood shaking his head.

"Why don't we sit down?" I asked, helping myself to a seat.

"You aren't going to be here long enough to bother."

I felt my temper kick, thought about pulling a Washington Clifford, but the remnants of my conversation with Jayson held me in check. "You can't be a total asshole," I started quietly. "Jayson likes you too much."

"Fuck you," he said.

"You talk the talk but there's nothing behind it. Must be afraid to drop your attitude."

"What should I be frightened about?" he asked arrogantly, though he sat down on the couch.

"If you strip it down, you'll discover there's nothing underneath."

"Don't you need a license to shrink?" he said smirking.

"Not to see through you and your lies."

"What lies?"

"'Did you tell him anything, JB?'" I mimicked. "Actually, I'm glad we have a moment alone. It's a chance to stop the act." If I wasn't going to whack the truth out of him, I had to push past Stephen's tenuous stability.

"I don't know what you mean," he said.

"Of course you do. You lied when I asked about your mother's car, then ran right behind her skirt. Now the two of you are playing possum."

"Who do you think you are, calling me a liar?"

"Almost part of the family, Stevie," I snapped, honing in. "And a helluva family it is. One parent ignored you, the other crapped on your parade. Neglect and abuse. But can't let go, can you?"

His face looked like a gathering storm.

"Both of us know the pathology, 'Love thy oppressor.' Let's not kid ourselves, your mom grabbed the testosterone and your old man used what was left to beat on you. And what did Stephen have? A rundown house. Looking for love from sticks, stones, and salt water."

"Blow it out your ass," he sputtered, his eyes darting around the room.

"There you go again," I shook my head. "All bluster, no balls. Story of your life. Your parents turn you into a sniveling snot; still, you run to Mommy the minute you're in trouble."

"What trouble?" Stephen asked. He tried to feign confidence, but couldn't keep his hand away from his hair. As much as he wanted me gone, he wasn't doing much to make it happen. He suddenly slumped forward, helpless, maybe weakened by all the truths I'd pitched at him.

"Me. And you know it."

Before he answered Heather returned to the room and flopped her black clad skinny next to Stephen, oblivious to the tension and Stephen's defeated posture. "Jayson had a terrific time with you, Matt."

"See, Stevie? I told you I'm okay. So no reason to keep lying." I felt bad using Jayson's term of endearment, but not enough to stop.

"Mother Theresa could have slept with you for all I care," he said. "I want you out of my life," he said without any bite.

"That's why you ran to Mommy."

"What's going on here?" Heather demanded.

"The pig was about to leave," Stephen said with a resurgence of anger.

"Sweetheart, I ain't going anywhere until you tell me the truth," I said, a hard edge to my voice. The more he resisted, the greater my need to know.

"It was gay bashing, that's all."

I ignored him. "Get real, Stevie, you'll hide behind your mama's skirt but you don't really like her. Hell, why should you? Says something when you play second best to bra burnings."

"Why aren't you out of here, asshole! I don't even know what you're talking about."

Between his helplessness and rage he was an explosion waiting to happen and I was gonna light the fuse. "Sure you do, Stevie, or you wouldn't be yanking out your hair."

"What are you two fighting about?" Heather asked.

"Something seriously violent happened twice around this family, and that's two times more than I'll accept. Lou is *my* family and if he's going to be involved with Lauren, I'm going to find out what happened to her car."

"Stephen doesn't know what happened," Heather said.

"So he lies to you too. No surprise, it's what he does best. I'm sure you've been lying to Jayson as well. One of your jealous fucks take out the car?"

I shook my head, stood, and strolled behind the couch. "That's the ticket, isn't it, Stevie?" I said, clamping my hand on his shoulder. "You've been two-timing."

"Take your hand off me!"

"What are you doing Matt?" Heather asked, twisting in her seat.

"Getting to the truth."

Stephen tried to squirrel free but I forced him to stay still. "I don't know anything," he said, breathing heavily.

"Stop it, Stevie," I warned, tightening my grip. "We're working with new rules and the first is no more lies."

"You're going to hurt him!" Heather yelped, jumping to her feet.

Stephen struggled to stand so I loosened my grip then shoved him back down.

"Matt!" Heather said angrily.

"So Stevie, who did it? A jealous boyfriend? Someone tired of blow-jobs in the bushes?" I ripped off the questions in rapid fire, then lifted my hand as if to slap his face.

"You don't know what you're talking about!" he hissed, leaping to his feet.

He faced me from in front of the couch, so I leaned across and chucked him under the chin. "You little turd. Cheating on a dead man!" Words instead of fists but they were landing.

"Leave Jayson alone, you bastard."

"There's no need for this," Heather warned. "You're acting like you're going to hit him!"

I circled to their side of the couch. "What's he gonna do? Tell his mommy? Maybe I'll just give him a spanking. Shoulda happened a long time ago."

"Get out of my fucking house!"

"Some secret boy-toy takes a lead pipe to Mommy's car and you weasel her into covering it up."

Heather squeezed her stringbean body between us. "Leave him alone! He doesn't have to take this!"

"He's gonna take worse." I reached over Heather and disparagingly tapped Stephen on the top of his head with an open hand. I didn't want to hurt him. "Leeching off a dying man. You plan to move your new friend in when Jayson dies?"

"Fuck you!" Stephen said, pushing Heather out of the way.

"I got you pegged, don't I?" I goaded. "Takes a tough leech to live off someone else's talent. Is your cheat rich, Stevie? Gonna suck him dry too?"

Stephen came flying at my face but I stood my ground while he furiously swung his fists. This wasn't going to help me heal from my last beating, but I'd wanted him over the top. Stephen flailed away while I played rope-a-dope without a boxing ring. The more ineffectual his punches, the wilder he became until he was lost in an open-mouthed frenzy.

Heather tried to pull him off, but too many years of hatred were tearing loose, and neither he nor I was in a rush to close it down. In fact, I continued to bait him. Out of the corner of my eye I saw Jayson emerge from the studio, an angry expression on his face.

Eventually I reached out and smothered Stephen in a vice-like grip. Entirely out of control, he hysterically made one attempt after another to escape until his energy slowly ground down. "I'm not your parents, Stephen," I whispered, throwing him roughly onto the couch where he completely broke.

Heather started toward him but Jayson called from the other side of the room, "Let him be, Heather!"

Stephen sobbed as the rest of us silently watched. I rubbed my stinging arms. There had been enormous fury behind his attack. I was gonna have more black and blues.

"Why did you do this?" Heather whispered, stunned.

I paused and stared at Stephen who had his eyes all over me. His tears had slowed but the rage hadn't returned.

"He didn't leave me any choice."

"Are you going to torture him more?" Heather asked, her shock quickly turning into anger. "He doesn't know what happened!"

"Just tell him, Steve, Jayson said, pushing the walker back to his chair. There's no reason not to."

"But I promised," Stephen wailed.

"Promised who?" I pounced.

"My mother, goddammit!"

Once he tanked, the rest came out in a moan. "Ahh shit, *I* did

215

the fucking car."

"What did you say, Stephen?" Heather asked incredulously.

"I did it," he repeated. "I trashed the goddamn car."

Heather threw herself into a chair. "What the hell is going on?"

"You were out of control?" I asked quietly.

"No, no, you don't understand, I was trying to keep control," he groaned. "If I hadn't run and smashed the car I might have hurt her. Lauren understood, she didn't even try to stop me."

"What were you fighting about?"

He looked toward Jayson, who nodded.

"Lauren has been giving us money to live on. I need to be home with Jayson, so we have no income. That night she told us she was tapped out. She had nothing left. My father apparently cut her off when he realized she was really serious about Lou. He'd stopped giving her money months ago, but she'd been using her savings to keep us going."

Something about his tell bothered me but I couldn't put it together. "Why not go directly to him?"

"That asshole wouldn't give me shit. Paul refuses to acknowledge Jayson's existence. He won't even admit I'm gay. My mother walked in that night with a scheme to sell Jayson's work," he panted, shaking his head. "The idea drove me crazy."

"It was your mother's car, Stephen, not your father's."

"Logic in moments of madness?" Jayson whispered with a small smile.

"I wish it had been madness, JB," Stephen said hoarsely, "but I knew what I was doing. I hated her that night as much as I've always hated him. The thought of everyone knowing we had to sell the paintings..."

Now that Stephen started, the words streamed out. "I blamed my mother for letting it happen."

Stephen covered his face with his long hands. "It always seemed like a victory when she gave us the bastard's money."

Stephen dragged his hands from his eyes and stared into space. "I spent a whole year lining up the museum tour," he said. "We were going to take Jayson's work across the entire country. Lauren knew the deal was dead if we sold the paintings in order to live."

"She gave you all her savings, Stephen," Heather said softly.

"I saw all my work shot to hell, Jayson's tribute down the drain. I had to do something. I felt so fucking impotent."

Heather moved next to him, cradling his lean, trembling body.

I looked at Jayson. "Lauren followed him downstairs?"

Jayson shook his head. "She watched from the window, called Lou, then left when Stephen returned. She really was afraid he might hurt her."

"Why didn't you just tell me this the first time, Stephen?"

"My mother didn't want me to. She made me promise and I owed her that much. It wasn't her fault she ran out of money, but I didn't feel that way at the time."

I'd gotten everything I came for. More. My arms ached and I desperately needed a cigarette. "I'm sorry, Jayson," I said standing, acutely aware of the damage I was leaving behind.

Jayson made no attempt to respond.

I turned and trudged to the elevator but before I got there Heather called. "Wait a minute, you fucking prick."

I turned around and looked at the black chopstick.

"I'm not done with you!" She let go of Stephen and stood. "Everywhere you go you leave people a wreck."

"What are you talking about?"

"Here, my mom, you're the goddamn Grim fucking Reaper."

"Your mom?"

"You show up, then off you go leaving behind nothing but pain!"

Heather's eyes were streaming and her black makeup was smeared. I started back in her direction.

"Don't come near me!"

"Okay, okay," I said, holding up my hands. "But I really don't understand what you mean about your mom."

"Don't lie to me, I was upstairs when you came by."

"We didn't fight. If you were there, you know that."

"I didn't say you fought. But later that night she and Paul had a vicious argument. You told her about the divorce, didn't you?" she asked, rubbing her eyes. "At least here you stuck around when the shit hit the fan."

"I thought she knew," I answered helplessly.

"You thought. Well, you thought wrong. Maybe people in this family aren't the most together people in the world, but they're the only family I have, so stay away. Stay the fuck away from all of us!"

CHAPTER 34

It was a short ride home but the first hill on another relational rollercoaster. The intimate talk with Jayson had reinforced my commitment to Boots, but another ugly window into Lauren's family had slammed me deeper into my disconnected self. I felt split in opposite directions.

I left a message on Boots' machine. Told her I was exhausted, promising to show the next night. Problem was, exhaustion didn't equal sleep and the more I thought about Lauren and her fucked up family, the worse I felt. More disturbing, I kept thinking about my strange, exciting night with Alexis, wondering whether I wanted another. Maybe that's why I was stupid enough to pick up the phone.

"Why didn't you just shoot him?" Lauren snapped.

Fire with fire. "Don't come down on me," I warned. "This didn't have to happen."

"You left my son an emotional wreck, Matthew. Jayson called a few minutes ago. It took all day to calm Stephen down. He's finally fallen asleep."

"You didn't wait very long to yell at me."

"I don't hear myself yelling. Do you have a guilty conscience?"

"I always have a guilty conscience."

"For good goddamn reason!"

"If you had told me the truth about your car nothing like this would have occurred."

"I didn't want you to know the truth. I didn't want Lou to know it."

I was too ticked to tame my tongue. "It? Which *it*? The cover-up about the car or your family's emotional instability?"

My aggressiveness brought her up short. "What are you saying?"

"I've known you about a month, during which one of your sons tried to kill himself and the other beat the living shit out of your car. You call one an accident and try to hide the other—that's what I'm saying. And I haven't even mentioned the door."

I steeled myself for a shot about Alexis, but the blow never came.

"Jayson thinks your confrontation will force Stephen to see a psychologist," Lauren said, a note of hopefulness momentarily cutting through her anger.

"The issue isn't Stephen, Lauren, it's you."

"So that's why you did what you did? To get at me through my children?"

"You know better. I wanted to know what happened to the car."

"Why was it so damn important?"

She was slipping away, but I wasn't gonna let go. "How many times do I have to tell you? There have been too damn many coincidences."

"Well, this puts a crimp in coincidence, doesn't it? So now you'll leave us alone, right?" The fractiousness was back in her voice.

"No promises, Lauren. There's still the drive-by and the

stalking."

"I wasn't expecting a promise. You don't keep them anyway."

"Has Biancho given you any new information about the shooting?"

"Stop playing games, Matthew. Absolutely nothing out of the ordinary has been happening except your behavior. Now will you answer my question?"

I kept silent.

"Why don't you come right out and say it?" she said tightly. "It's not the stalking, it's not the drive-by, it's us. You don't want Lou involved with me or my family. Tell the fucking truth, you don't want him with me!"

She was yelling now, but her words bounced off without inflicting damage. It surprised me until I yawned and remembered I'd eaten a Halcion.

"Am I boring you?"

"No, I'm tired."

"Well, before you fall asleep I'd suggest you pay attention. Lou asked me to marry him and I'm saying yes. I'd put him off because I wanted to give everything a chance to settle. Well, as soon as I calm down, everything will be settled. You're not going to break us up!

"Lou knows everything there is to know about me and my kids. He knows about their problems and he knows about their strengths—which they *do* have whatever you may think. Lou's eyes are wide open and he wants us to be together. You just better get used to it, Matthew!"

The slam of the phone stung my ear and I rushed to roll a joint. But despite the dope, the onset of my sleeping pill, and a quick retreat to bed, Lauren's family crawled under my skin. Especially one of them.

And they were all still there when I was lying alongside Boots at my apartment.

We'd made it through the evening without trouble. No spats, no seriousness but, when we went to a local club, no slow dancing. Then, in my bed, yesterday's news became the night's conversation.

"She's not all wrong. You've been fighting their relationship ever since you heard about it."

"Well, I'm back where I started, Boots. In spades. The more I learn about Lauren and her family, the harder they are to take."

Boots draped her leg over mine. "Honey, that's the way you feel about all families."

"Maybe, but this one is a snake pit."

"It seems to be the boys. Maybe their father is more responsible than you think."

"They're not boys. Anyway, Lauren drives the bus. And she's the one who covered up the trashed car."

"What do you expect? She knows you don't approve of them so she hid an ugly scene. I bet Lou knew about it."

"What's the difference? He still winds up in the middle of a mess."

"Matt, Lou *wants* to be there. Incidentally, he's not marrying the family."

"It doesn't look that way from here. All of them act like they're Crazy Glue'd."

"Maybe, or maybe you and Lauren are just in the middle of a great big fight. You did tear her kid apart. Like it or not, Lou and Lauren are going to be together. She's right, you'll have to get used to it."

There was nothing left for me to say.

"So when will I get a chance to meet her?" Boots asked, continuing to push, but with a lighter tone. "After hearing about this woman for so long, I'd like to see what the She-Devil looks like."

"Always with the jokes, huh?" I teased, easing up. But Boots' question jolted my cheat and, for a quick moment, I considered coming clean. A very quick moment. My ambivalence was tough enough to handle without another train wreck.

So I changed the subject and horsed around until we grew tired and fell sleep with our bodies cuddled next to each other. For another night anyhow, both of us were willing to leave our relationship alone.

It didn't stay that way for long. When I felt Boots shake me I opened my eyes to a look of terror.

"What's the matter?" I asked groggily. "We oversleep?"

"Here, it's Lauren," she said shoving my bedroom phone at me. "Something happened to Lou!"

I bolted upright, sick to my stomach and automatically shy'd away from the heavy plastic.

"Take the damn phone!"

I took a deep, wide awake breath. "Lauren, this is Matt. What's going on?"

Lauren was out of control. Hysterical, breaking in and out of gut wrenching sobs. Something about the temperature falling, an ailing furnace, and fumes while they were asleep. Lauren woke up sick but by then it was too late. Lou's asthma had kicked in and he'd "been taken" by an attack.

When she used that phrase, dread hit every muscle in my body. I grew dizzy and almost dropped the phone. Boots saw my fade because she quickly lit a cigarette and shoved it in my mouth.

"He's dead?" I forced.

"No, no, that's not what I meant. He's in the intensive care unit," Lauren cried.

I shook my head to reassure Boots who was puffing madly on her own smoke. She exhaled loudly.

"Is he going to make it? What's the doctor saying?"

Between the tears I finally understood that she simply didn't know. "Doesn't know," I said out loud. "You've got to pull yourself together enough to give me directions."

"I'm sorry, Matthew," she sobbed. "I'm sorry we had that fight. If I thought something like this could happen I'd never have acted like such a bitch. I don't want us to be enemies, Matthew, I really don't."

"Lauren, none of that matters. Give me the name and address of the fucking hospital."

"What if he doesn't make it? What if..."

"No 'what ifs,' just give me the damn directions!"

After I hung up, my hand trembled so badly that I didn't even hassle myself about the bourbon I slugged straight from the bottle. It stopped the shakes but when I got back to the bedroom, I saw Boots pulling on her clothes. Another kind of tremor hit.

"What are you doing?" I asked, rushing to get dressed.

"I'm coming with you. I love that old man and you can't drive in this condition."

"Bullshit. I've got to do this alone."

Boots looked like she'd been slapped across the face.

"If you come with me I'll only have more person to worry about."

"Are you crazy, Matt? This is what relationships are for."

I finished pulling on my clothes, "Now ain't the time for Relationships 101. Believe me, if Lou doesn't make it you'll have your hands full."

"Don't "honey," me!" She hated my words. Maybe hated me. She was angry, but knew that if she continued to insist it would provoke a blowout. "I don't like this, Matt," she said, struggling to keep her voice steady, "but I won't stop you."

I leaned forward to kiss her goodbye but she jerked away. "Look, Boots," I started.

"Not now. I'm going home. Get the hell up there and call with good news."

CHAPTER 35

I phoned Boots even though there was nothing new. Lou was hooked to a respirator and receiving fluids through an IV. The doctors were reluctant to test if he could breathe on his own. A good thing I'd grabbed Boots's Valium before I'd left the condo and ate one while I charged north. If I hadn't, I might have decked the attendant when he refused me entry into the ICU.

Not so good, Boots had discovered the missing pills and used it as a horse for her anger.

"I just took the bottle on my way out the door. Sort of an afterthought."

"Drugs are never an afterthought with you," she said crossly. "Didn't it occur to you that I might need one?"

"You don't have any tucked away?"

"Well, I found some at the bottom of a purse," she confessed.

"At least something worked out okay." The moment I heard myself I felt my stomach shift.

Boots had heard me too and swiftly dropped her mad. "Now don't get depressed while you're waiting, Matt. It will work out. I can feel it."

"*Vibes*?"

"Faith. Lou's tough."

"A tough who's overweight with breathing problems and a diabetic condition."

"Have you found out exactly what happened?"

"A wire rigging that holds the flue pipe broke and fumes spread through the house."

"The smell didn't wake them?"

"Eventually. Lauren woke up to puke and saw Lou gasping for air." The image freaked me out and I surreptitiously dry-mouthed another V. "At least she was smart enough to call a fucking ambulance," I said after forcing the pill down my throat.

"You're angry at her, aren't you?"

"Damn right."

"It wasn't Lauren's fault, Matt."

"Right this second everything is her fault." I looked up from the phone and saw Lauren at the other end of the hall. "Honey, she's waving. I'll call back if I get any information."

"I'll stay home as long as I can, but call me at work if you hear anything at all!"

My gut was near my feet by the time I reached Lauren and the attending physician. And nothing the doctor said raised it. Lou was going to be in the ICU for a minimum of six to eight hours before they removed the respirator. He was sedated and they planned to keep him on the tube. Essentially nothing had changed. Still, I called Boots and gave her the skimpy details.

I returned to the open waiting room and told Lauren I was going outside for a cigarette. At first she just nodded but when I pushed the door open she was right behind.

"Mind if I tag along?"

I took my first real look at her and she looked lousy. No makeup, hair pulled back into a ragged ponytail with lots of loose gray. Red wet eyes. For the first time since we'd met, Lauren looked her age. Older.

"You have a jacket?" I asked in the chilly dawn air.

"This shirt is warm enough. I just didn't expect it to get cold so damn soon," she said despondently. "I never even thought about it. The oil company checks on the furnace every year, but I didn't have them out. I had no idea the wire was broken."

"Blaming yourself isn't going to help. Are you sure you don't want my jacket?"

"No thank you." Lauren tried to smile before bursting into tears.

I shifted awkwardly, dragging on my cigarette. "How did you find out it was the wire?" I finally asked.

"I telephoned the fire department as well as the ambulance," she said regaining control. "I thought it might be an electrical fire. I'm sorry, Matthew, I really am. About all of it," she said choking back more tears. "I shouldn't have called yesterday and said what I did. You're Lou's only relative and I understand my family worries you."

I didn't know what to say. I was angry with her, angry she was part of Lou's life, angry it was her house that caused Lou's attack. Full of anger but still found it impossible to ignore her feelings.

"When I realized he couldn't breathe, I thought it was a heart attack." Lauren shook her head as her eyes filled again. "He was so helpless and I imagined he was going to die and we'd had less than a year with each other. I wanted to die right along with him."

Lauren paused, "Waiting for the ambulance was pure hell."

Lauren wrapped her arms around herself so I flipped the cigarette. "Let's go back inside, it's cold out here."

Lauren followed me back into the hospital where I asked the dredlock'd receptionist for a secluded spot in which we could wait. I listened impatiently to a Jamaican accented suggestion that we go home. When he finished I demanded a guarantee that Lou wouldn't die while we were away. Lauren saw the receptionist glance toward the security guard and immediately took charge, securing a private waiting room in the process. I behaved myself and followed them down a flight of stairs into a small lounge replete with the ever ubiquitous vending machines.

"No ashtrays?" I asked, still tasting my anger.

The Jamaican pointed toward a red exit sign. "Step outside if you have to smoke, *mon*. And try to relax. Nobody is going to do any better because you're all worked up and out of control."

I kept my tongue planted and wriggled into a small chair.

"You're very angry, aren't you?" Lauren asked, once the nurse had left the room.

"Nothing new."

"I know you blame me for this."

"Right now I'm just angry."

We lapsed into a long, tense silence, the only movement my regular excursions outside. At some point the tension and Valium floored me and I fell asleep. When I lifted my heavy lids, Lauren was weeping softly.

"Did you hear something?" I asked, using the chair's arms to push my ass free.

"No, no, nothing yet."

"Then why are you crying?"

"I'm frightened, that's all."

Her words cut through my cotton head and I started to pace.

"Matthew, please stop walking around. You're reminding me of Paul. Next you'll be pounding on the damn vending machine."

I retreated to my seat. "We've spent a lot of time in hospitals, haven't we?" I said, shaking my head. The nap had dissolved my anger.

"Too much time." She shook her head. "I'm so very sorry."

"Stop apologizing, this isn't your fault."

"It feels like it. There are moments when I wish we'd never

gotten involved. That way Lou wouldn't have been hurt. But when I think that, the life slips out of me. I love him, Matthew. I feel like a whole person when we're together, like I found a missing piece of me I never knew existed. And this is what comes of it," she added. "Something always goes wrong when I touch it."

"Lou's had asthma for a long time, Lauren."

"But how much did the crises with Ian and Stephen, and the drive-by take out of him?"

I had no answer other than my temper dregs. "I gotta have a smoke."

The rest of the day ran around the same track. I kept dozing, waking, and smoking. Lauren kept sniffling, fighting back her tears. Every once in a while, one or the other of us would trudge upstairs only to return without news. I wanted to hold her responsible but that day was done.

The more we talked the easier it became.

"So explain your feelings toward Lou," I finally asked. "This is not a man who presses the envelope."

"No, but Lou doesn't judge other people's lives and that might be more progressive than anything I've ever done. And it's more than that. I've always felt isolated, despite all the causes, friends, marriage, and even the kids. As if I had to be the one to make every decision. I had to be the one to take care of everybody. When I'm with Lou, all that disappears. I don't have to keep protecting myself and it frees me. Lou knows who he is and that's incredibly reassuring—and very special. Plus, he's the kindest person I've ever known."

Her eyes raked my face.

"Don't look at me like that, Lauren. My question wasn't a knock."

Lauren smiled, "I didn't take it that way. I was thinking that

Lou talks about your friend Boots all the time, but I've never heard you mention her."

"I'm pretty good at keeping things compartmentalized."

"That's a big word, Matthew. Does it mean scared?"

"Scared?"

"Afraid if you talk about her the relationship will become more real?"

"I don't know," I answered uncomfortably.

"I was surprised she didn't come with you tonight."

"I'm used to flying solo during emergencies." The hollowness of my answer rattled in my head. "Maybe compartmentalized does mean scared," I added, smiling glumly.

"Much of my life I've felt too raw to let anyone near," Lauren said gently. "Including my family, though I hate to admit it. In a way, that's what I meant earlier about wanting to die. All those empty years had finally disappeared and for an instant they came rushing back."

"Lou's not going to die."

"I don't think I could live the rest of my life the way I'd lived before. It's taken me more than half a century to learn when something is healthy and good. If your relationship with Boots is good—and you're the only one who can know—you might think about the time I've wasted."

Before I found a way to switch subjects the door suddenly burst open and last night's doctor stood in front of us.

Both of us jumped to our feet.

"Relax," she said, her voice tinged with exhaustion. "That man is built like an ox. He'll outlive us all if he watches what he eats. We're going to continue keeping him under observation after we remove the respirator. I'm going to keep him in the ICU until tomorrow, then move him to a private room."

"Can we see him?" I asked.

The doctor shook her head. "He's asleep and won't wake up

for a good long time. The more sleep the better. You can visit him sometime tomorrow. Go home, there's no reason to wait here."

"Are you certain he's okay? Reallycertain?" I asked, wary of our luck.

"He's going to be fine." She nodded toward Lauren, "Getting him here quickly made a huge difference. Now, if you don't mind..."

Lauren and I stared at each other with silent relief as the doctor backed out the door.

CHAPTER 36

"Would you like to use the Hacienda as a home base?" Lauren asked tentatively, breaking a suddenly uncomfortable tension. "It's a long ride to Boston and back."

Her offer was tempting, but I shook my head. "I think I'll take your advice and go home to Boots. Is the Hacienda even safe? If the temperature drops and the furnace switches on..."

"One of the firemen shut down the auto start. Anyway, while you were asleep I called the oil company and they promised to fix everything today. As usual, I'm late locking the barn door." She glanced at her watch. "God, time seems endless then all of a sudden huge pieces are gone. It's really warped."

"It sure is," I agreed, wondering how much of my life had been spent inside those same strange distortions.

Lauren left our names and telephone numbers with the hospital while I left a message on Boots' private line, disappointed by my inability to connect. When we strolled into the warm afternoon sun, I breathed a sigh of relief. "Lauren, I heard what the doctor said about your quick response and I want you to know..."

"Stop, Matt. Instead of thanks and apologies maybe we could just agree to start over?"

Lauren stuck out her hand and, after a momentary hesitation, I took it. A near miss can change things in a hurry.

Halfway home, my relief faded and I was suddenly dope slapped with more suspicions. Either Lauren was living under a really bad sign, or someone might be trying to hurt or actually kill Lauren *and* Lou.

I skidded to a stop and headed back to the Hacienda in record time. Lauren must have heard me park because she was waiting at the door as I rushed up the steps.

"I thought you wanted to go back to Boots," she asked, looking at me with tired eyes.

"I will but I want to inspect the boiler first."

"I told you the firemen turned off the auto-start so there's really no need for you to worry."

"It's not the auto-start I care about. I want to look at the broken wire if it's still there. Remember, I superintended my buildings for a long time."

"You don't think it was an accident, do you?"

"Honestly, I don't know what I think. That's why I want to check."

"Well, I don't think you'll find anything, but you're welcome to go downstairs. But alone. I can't stand the thought of seeing another one of my mistakes."

We were in the house and Lauren pointed to a door. "That leads to the basement. The boiler is by the left wall but one of the firemen accidently broke the light down there. At least I think I remember someone telling me that. Everything was just crazy."

"Do you have a flashlight I can use?"

"Yes. I'll get it."

Lauren returned with one of those metallic lights they used on C.S.I. It was small but when I checked to see if it worked it flashed a nice, bright l.e.d. white.

"This will be fine," I said over my shoulder as I opened the door and went down the rickety stairs. Alexis wasn't wrong about the house needing repairs, but I shook the thought from my head and walked past piles of stuff to the furnace.

Where I caught a break. The firemen had left the wire dangling. I shone the light and looked carefully at it and where it should have been connected. Neither showed any signs of rust or even much wear and tear. I grabbed the skinny metal strip and ran the light over the entire piece, spending a lot of time at the place where it had broken. But hard as I looked, both the piece in my hand and the point where it attached were in good shape. Which left me wondering why it had come apart. Or if it had simply been sliced, though I saw no tool marks.

I swung the light around the entire cellar and caught another break. Two, actually. A tool chest sat on an old table. And I noticed bulkhead doors on the other side of the room. I guess firemen were different up here. In the city they'd have axed the goddamn thing to pieces in order to get inside.

But first things first. I walked over to the tool chest, breathed a sigh of relief to find it unlocked, rummaged through, and came up with an old wire cutter. I returned to the furnace and snipped off as much of the wire as possible. Shaking my head I returned the cutter, closed the chest, and walked over to the bulkhead. I pushed up against the two wooden doors but they were locked together from the outside. I returned to the stairs and carefully climbed my way back into the house. Where I found Lauren waiting.

"Why do you have that wire in your hand," she asked.

"I want to take it home with me and really study it. No way to do that down there. Not to worry, the oil company is going to replace it anyway."

Lauren shook her head. "Your father-in-law was right. You really are one tenacious son of a bitch when you sink your teeth in.

You still think someone is trying to hurt me."

"Maybe both of you."

"Lou? Why would anyone want to hurt *him*?"

"Why would anyone want to hurt *you*? I don't have answers, Lauren, just questions. And you're right. Until my questions are answered I don't plan on letting go."

I started toward the front door, then stopped. "Since all we have are questions, it would be smart if you came with me and stayed at Lou's place.

"Absolutely not! I appreciate the offer but if the hospital calls I want to be nearby.

I felt a momentary pang of guilt about my own return to Boston, then decided to trust the doctor. "Look, the doc was very clear about Lou pulling through and for us to wait until tomorrow afternoon to see him."

Lauren smiled. "It's a sweet invitation, but I'll pass."

"Okay," I replied, nodding as I walked down the stairs. But when I began to walk toward the back of the house Lauren called from the doorway.

"Where are you going? Your car is right out front."

"I know, but I want to look at the bulkhead doors."

Lauren just shook her head and said, "See you tomorrow," as she gently closed the front door.

When I got to the bulkhead I knelt down and stared intently at the doors. They were held together by an old rust pitted padlock. But as hard as I looked I saw no scratches or any other evidence of a pick so I headed back to my car and began the drive home.

My ride was a tussle between relief and a grinding worry about dangers that might or might not exist. As I drove into town I thought about waiting for Boots at her condo, but decided on my apartment. It was time to talk to Julius.

I grabbed a quick peanut butter sandwich on on a couple of large stale crackers, a short shower, left more messages on all Boots's machines, and walked upstairs to Julie's.

When his apartment door slipped open, I was hit with an almost visible wave of heat. "Christ, Julius, open a fucking window. A little light won't blind you either."

"I want it dark, hot and sticky, Slumlord. Like my women."

I shook my head, "Better enjoy the thermostat 'cause you ain't gonna get the women. If I spent my life in skivvies I wouldn't mind 110 degrees either," I added, noting his boxers and ribbed cotton undershirt.

"You gonna stand out here and jive or slide inside? The glare from the goddamn hall is killing me."

I followed him into his simple neat flat and immediately opened a window in the dark, shuttered living room. "If I don't get a little air, I'll fall asleep the moment I hit a chair."

"You don't look too good," he said, flicking on sixty watts.

I filled him in on the past twenty-four, speaking quickly to choke back the tears. I'd held it together throughout the day but now, at home with a friend, my boogie men were marching.

"The B'wahna be all right?"

"That's what the doctor said."

"Which you believe?"

"If I didn't, I wouldn't be here. I need help, Julie. The entire situation with Lauren and her family has me unhinged."

"You must really be fucked up to talk to me about interpersonal shit." Julius lit a couple of Camels and passed me one. "Not my bag, brother. Best you take it up with Lady Shrink?"

I couldn't stop myself from smiling.

"You laughing? It take smarts for a man to know his limitations. Something you never learn."

"Want to fire the pipe?"

Julius appeared relieved by my request. "Sweet thinking. You

ZACHARY KLEIN

want a Turkey chaser?"

"I'm still regulating, but do you have any Valium and beer? I've chewed through Boots's pills."

Julie threw a fat joint on the table. "Well, suck on this while I check the medicine chest."

I shoved the Camel into his ashtray, lit the doobie, and closed my eyes. When I opened them Julie was back in his seat. There was a plastic container of pills flanked by two cold beers on the card table between us.

"Generic, but it'll do the job."

"Thanks."

"Something besides the B'wahna got you by the shorthairs," Julius said after downing half his beer and sucking on the joint.

"I can't figure out whether I'm involved with a case or long run of lousy luck."

"Same old, same old, Matthew," Julie said, though he raised his bloodshot eyes higher than the usual half-mast.

I proceeded to tell him the whole story. I detailed the complex set of Rowe/Brown relationships and my different reactions to each. Told him about Stephen and the car, Biancho and Clifford, my concern about the furnace. Told him everything. Everything, that is, except my number with Alexis. My "number?" Maybe I should start calling Ian's suicide attempt an "accident."

Julius listened quietly until I crossed the finish line.

"Well?" I asked, impatient with his silence.

He tilted his head. "Slumlord, you don't let bad things happen to your people without patting down the circumstance. You ain't built to close your eyes once they're open."

"Trouble is, I don't know what I'm looking for."

"That's because your head is pulling on your pecker."

I felt myself grow tense. "What do you mean?"

"You been busy doing a merry-go-round on Lou's old lady. A waste of time and a sorry waste of what little juice you own. That's

237

their business."

He stopped speaking for a moment then asked, "You want to stop squeezing that joint? See," Julie said after a long toke, "all this relationship bushwa is out of place. Only thing that counts is making sure nothing nasty is going down."

"You don't have to keep blasting, Julie. I get the point."

"It's a point you keep losing."

"I can't find the fucking string. I thought I had it with Stephen's lie about Lauren's car. Finally had something to follow, but it just went in a circle."

Julie lit another Camel while I drank my beer. "I been watching a movie about a couple of reporters trying to fry Nixon," he said. "I mean they really wanted his ass. Only they weren't getting anywhere until someone told 'em to *cherchez le cash*. Seems like useful advice."

"*Cherchez le cash*." Alexis's avid interest in the Hacienda jumped to mind, but I kept it to myself.

"Look for people who might benefit if Lou's lady is hurt. And maybe the same with regard to the B'wahna."

"Until they're married, nobody is in that bag but me. And I ain't a suspect."

For the first time since I walked through his door, Julie displayed his anger about what had happened to Lou. "Right now, you don't cross nobody off no list, you hear? Not even yourself! That old man does good by us and he deserves your best."

His words hacked through my negativity. "I'm telling you to run hard with this." Julius settled back in his chair. "I'm also telling you one other thing."

"What's that?"

"Stay out of Washington Clifford's face."

I was tired to the bone and higher than a kite when I finally returned to my apartment and rang the hospital. So far so good. But the moment I hung up, my phone rang and 'so far so good' expired.

"I just spoke to the hospital and Lou's breathing on his own. Where are you?" I asked, hearing loud background noise.

"I'm at the airport," Boots hollered over the interference. "I'll be back tomorrow night."

"Are you kidding, nobody works on Saturday," I complained.

"What are you bitching about? I thought you'd want me gone."

"I wanted us to visit the hospital together."

"You are a fucking piece of work. One minute you push me away, the next you're griping about me not being there. I'll be home tomorrow night. If you still feel like it, we'll go up on Sunday.

"Of course," she added sarcastically, "it's nothing I'll bet on."

"Bet the rent. I was off the wall this morning. You should have come with me, and I'm sorry."

"That's worth something, but I'll hold on to my money," she replied.

"I mean it Boots, I screwed up royal. Can't you cancel the trip?"

"Too late, my plane's leaving and I have to run."

Boots sudden departure left a void Unfortunately, Alexis rushed to fill the space. Now my cheat was a suspect. *Cherchez le cash*. However rundown, the Hacienda was worth a hefty piece of change. As hard as I tried to dodge, my thoughts kept dancing around Alexis. Sadly, not simply with suspicion. Her pull was powerful enough that when I stretched out on the couch, I was fisting Julie's generics instead of inspecting the wire.

CHAPTER 37

woke up the next morning drugged over, but called the hospital before I crept off the couch. No more Caribbean accent, this time a bored, nasal New Englander reported that Lou was better and would be moved into his room around one o'clock. No visitors until the move. None. So I placed the wire on the table, pulled out a magnifying glass, and stared thru it. I'd done my cut on a diagonal so I'd know which end was which. I could see light rust where I'd sliced but figured that was due to the old cutter. The other end had no marks but *maybe,* maybe a slight elongation where someone *might* have pulled. I just couldn't tell.

In the dawn of a new day, Julie's admonitions rang even louder than they had the night before. Alexis grinned at the top of my list like a whip toting temptress, but I pushed the leather out of my head and manhandled the phone.

To no avail. Calls to her home, office, and even the Hacienda went unanswered. I guessed Lauren had already gone to the hospital. Frustrating, but I could use the hours before visiting Lou for a little bottom fishing. Quiet bottom fishing. Lauren and

I might have gotten friendlier, but Chief Biancho wasn't friendly at all.

I gathered my day's survival kit and hurried north. I hadn't spoken to Ian since our short exchange on the telephone, and now was as good a time as any. Nor had I forgotten Stephen's off-handed remark about the kid's crazy stunts. But hey, I just wanted to see how the boy was doing.

When Ian finally remembered who I was he reluctantly unlatched the chain to his one-bedroom.

"Come in if you really have to," he muttered, clad in a dirty, white gi and matching pants. This time, without the blood.

I stepped inside and walked to a Goodwill easy chair. Ian followed, dragging his feet along the way.

"Throw the 'zines on the floor," he grunted, unhappily offing the sound on the television.

"Thanks." I looked around the sloppy room decorated with posters of comic book heroes, Indie bands, and various martial artists. One of the pictures might have been Bruce Lee, maybe Junior. In either case, a dead actor.

"It looks like you're recovering nicely," I complimented.

Ian stretched out onto the long sofa. "'Staying alive, staying alive,'" he sang. I guess he liked John Travolta.

"That's good to hear. Mind if I smoke?"

"I'm not the only one with a death wish."

"The trail's a little longer this way."

"Might not be as pleasant. Just use the dirty plate for your cancer."

"You mother said you were in a hurry to get back home. Lucky, huh?"

Ian looked puzzled. "Lucky?"

"The drive-by and the accident."

"I heard about the drive-by. What else happened?"

He seemed sincere, but then, so did I. "The furnace broke a

couple nights ago. Made your mother sick and almost killed my father-in-law. Lauren got him to the hospital just in time."

Ian placed his head on the armrest. "Nah, haven't heard shit. Good thing you don't live up here or you'da made another hospital run."

"Made it anyway." Seeing him slumped on the couch with the silent television had me uneasy. Not hard to figure; full-bore passive-aggressive was a kissing cousin to my own half-bore. "Do you mind if I shut this off? I'm not big on Judge Judy."

Ian shrugged so I reached over and pressed the power button on the remote. "So you didn't hear anything at all about the accident?"

A scowl crossed his blank face, "I told you, man, nobody tells me anything. It's not the same anymore." He glanced in my direction. "No offense, but since my mother's been doing Big Lou, I've been out of the loop."

"Out of the loop?"

Ian raised his eyebrows. "Let me lay it out. There were the old, old days, then the old days, and now the new days. In the old, old days life sucked. During the old days, me and my mother talked all the time so I knew what was going down. We were like confidantes, you know. Stephen makes her nervous and Alexis makes her mad. I bum her out, but she used me to get things off her chest."

"And the 'new days?'"

"Call 'em Big Lou Days," he said, trying but failing to hide his annoyance.

"She talks to him instead of you."

"You got it," he pointed.

"Piss you off?"

"Sure. One day in, next day out. Something like that would piss you off too."

"Definitely." The question was how much, but I didn't want to rush. I'd already blown enough conversations to kill a career. Even a store-bought career. "How about your father? Can't you stay in contact through him?"

"Sure, if I want to hear about what kind of underachieving ingrate I am. When you're a Brown, you can't crowbar him out of your fucking face." Ian snickered, "Unless you're Stephen, but that shmuck doesn't know a good thing when he's got it. Always complaining about how the old man don't think he's alive—like Pop ought to kiss his butt or something. Shit, it's the dying fag who has the talent."

An equal opportunity asshole. Still, I wondered why he seemed so willing to jabber. Wondered, that is, until his sniffle registered. Then I understood his speed rap—though it took me a hard minute to squash my immediate lust for his drugs. "Your mom and dad are friends, aren't they?"

Ian shrugged. "Dad likes to think so, but since Lou blew into town, everything is up in the air."

"Like how?" 'Like how?' Like another couple of minutes and maybe I'd ask to borrow one of his karate uniforms.

"Like I've been telling you, my mom just doesn't relate the same way. We used to be tight, now, shit, she threw a fucking party in the mausoleum before I even recovered."

"I thought everyone loves the Hacienda."

"Not me." he said emphatically.

"Why not?"

Ian rolled his eyes toward the ceiling. "Tough to tell. Stephen and Alexis bitch and moan about the way they grew up. But for me, life was cool. Then all of a sudden wake up one morning and the world is upside down. Mom does a slash and burn. Pop tries to grow a dick. Everything got fucked up pretty fast. What else can I say?"

Anything I wanted him to. All I had to do was keep my mouth shut.

"Things were tough for a long time before it finally chilled.

That's when me and my mom started conversing. Now, Big Lou. Quiet time all over again. No offense, man."

"No offense. Doesn't sound like you have warm feelings for the Hacienda or Big Lou."

"Whoa, don't get me wrong, I have nothing against the old guy. He treats me decent. But you're right on about the Hacienda."

He propped himself up on his elbow. "You know, you ain't half bad and I owe you one. Want some sugar?"

Did Shoemaker/Levy ram Jupiter? "Thanks, but I'll pass. A little early in the day for me." Right.

Ian rolled off the couch and pulled a mirror from underneath. The small rectangle was lined with coke. I'd interrupted brunch.

"You sure you don't want a hit?" he asked again. "There's plenty more where this came from."

It was close. Close enough to feel sweat dot my forehead. But I shook my head. If I started I wouldn't stop. But I watched intently as he took two long snorts from a cut straw.

"A wild question, Ian. Between you and me. You don't hate the Hacienda enough to shoot the fuck out of the door, do you?"

"Shoot the door?"

"You were pissed about the party."

Ian giggled, "Hell no, man. I'm not saying blowing up the joint hasn't crossed my mind, but I don't mess with guns."

I believed him and felt grateful. "But you don't seem too bothered by the drive-by."

"It bothers me that Mom was in the house. Things might be different with us, but I don't want her to get hurt."

"I gotta tell you, Ian, a lot of nasty shit is going on over there. Maybe it's time for your mother to get out."

Ian nodded as if he knew what I was talking about, dropped onto the floor, and took a couple more toots. When he looked up, I regretfully shook my head. Very regretfully.

"Never happen. Mom won't leave the Hacienda no matter

what. She's gonna die in that fucking shithole."

"Your sister thinks she ought to sell."

Ian laughed, "Everybody wants the fucking house. Alexis figures she can turn a quick buck, and Stephen can't wait to move back in."

"Wait?"

"I'm guessing the three of us will split the place when my parents die. But Stephen, man, he has a hard-on for that joint. He likes it better than he likes people." Ian frowned. "Stephen thinks he's better than the rest of us, but it doesn't stop him from coming here for snow." Ian glanced in my direction and offered a sweaty smile. "I sell drugs now and then to keep me going, but he acts like I'm a fucking cartel. Begs me for dope, then rides my ass to clean up. I call him Little Daddy Paul when he gets on my case. He hates it." The thought made him smile.

"Your mom thinks Alexis wants her to sell the house so she can give it to your father."

"Man, you're up to your eyeballs in this family shit."

"Is your mom wrong?"

Ian shrugged. "It's hard to imagine Alexis giving *anything* away."

I was ready to get out of there. Ian wasn't behind the drive-by and he couldn't stalk himself in a mirror. I asked whether he knew of anyone who might have a bone to pick with his mother and got stuck listening to a cocaine delusion about the possibility that some deadbeat druggie might be after him. I did have a moment of fun when, right before I left, he asked my line of work. I told him the truth but dropped the 'private.'

Back in my car I digested Ian's information, but all I could really do was light a cigarette with a clammy hand. His snorting had me drug hungry. It hadn't been easy bottom fishing after all.

CHAPTER 38

Things didn't dry up at the hospital. Lou might be on his road to recovery, but Lauren and Alexis weren't.

I spotted them talking in a corner of the main waiting room the moment I walked through the door. More fight than talk. I stayed out of sight until the surprise at seeing Alexis settled. If I waited until it completely cooled I'd become a piece of furniture.

It was tough to tear my eyes off her. She wore a slightly flared multi-colored summer dress that ended several inches above her knees. Her legs were open and I doggedly struggled to keep from filling them with a kinky montage. Pondering baseball didn't help, but my conversation with Julie did. *Cherche le cash.* I took a deep breath and joined the fray.

Lauren hugged me. "I didn't see you come in," Lauren said, clearly relieved by the interruption. "Lou fell asleep as soon as they moved him into his room and we don't want to disturb him."

Although she looked better than she had the day before, Lauren still had bags beneath worried eyes. No sags for Alexis. A small smile tugged at the corners of her full lips and she raised her sleek brows when our eyes met.

"Nice to see you again, Alexis," I said.

"Nice to see you, Matt. I'm so sorry about Lou."

Her words alarmed me. "A relapse?"

Lauren shook her head. "No, but the doctor said it would take some time for him to fully recover."

"How much time?"

"He'll probably be here only a few more days, but he'll have trouble breathing for a while. He has to stay off his feet and he's going to need oxygen."

I quickly shook Jayson and his machine from my mind.

"I'm going to take a little walk, okay?" Lauren announced. "I want to be alone for a couple of minutes."

The moment she was out of sight Alexis and I stared at each other. "You've been a stranger, Detective Matt."

"A lot's been happening." I couldn't keep the protective gruffness from my voice.

All it did was broaden her smile. "So I hear. Lauren said you'd been to see Stephen. I've been waiting for my turn. Or did I already have it?"

Before I could say anything, I had to stop wanting her. Or fake it. *Cherchez le cash*, goddammit! "Yeah, I think we had our turn." There, the words were out of my mouth.

Alexis's almond eyes crinkled, "And I had hoped it was only the first of many."

Despite the hospital's air conditioning sweat covered my entire body. "Would you believe incest issues? Your mom and Lou are going to get married.

"No, I wouldn't."

She didn't sound bitter, and I should have been relieved. Not me; I felt guilty, embarrassed, sheepish, and much to my dismay, desire. "How about, it's too complicated?"

Alexis tossed her head, "I'm not used to men turning me

down."

"You handle it well."

"Why thank you," she said grasping the sides of her dress to curtsy.

I felt my cock harden, then worried about becoming the center of attention. "Why don't we sit over there," I pointed to a more secluded corner, "and talk about it?"

When we took our seats Alexis said, "A little old-fashioned, aren't you?"

"Old-fashioned?"

"That's right. You're actually going to talk about why we're not going to fuck."

"I thought it's the right thing to do, not old-fashioned."

"What is it, Matt? Guilt about the girlfriend? Or worry about yourself?"

"Both."

Alexis shook her head. "It wasn't as if we hood and flogged you."

"That's not what I was talking about, Alexis."

"You wouldn't," she said, smiling.

I'd successfully buried any honest thinking about my masochism since Clifford's beating and had no intention of reopening the crypt now. "Sometimes a cigar is just a cigar."

"And we're done smoking?"

"I don't think it would be good again." My first lie. "Balance isn't my strong suit. I'm having enough trouble figuring out my relationship with Boots without spending time with you," I said truthfully.

"Is that really her name?"

"Comes from a home town ball player. Anyhow, I'm trying to say you ain't a simple roll in the hay—or lighthouse. If we continued it would mess with my head."

Alexis shrugged and ran her hand through her tangled curls.

"Something you don't want."

"It's not as if I don't think about it," I admitted. "I'm usually pretty self-destructive."

"Thanks for what I *believe* is a compliment. I suppose I should be flattered you're breaking a pattern."

"More than one, sweetheart," I said. " More than one."

Alexis's laughter drew looks from a few people.

"You two seem to be getting along." Lauren's voice startled me. I started to stand but she gently placed her hand on my shoulder and pushed me back down. "Don't bother."

"He doesn't have to, but I do," Alexis said rising to her feet. "Saturday is my big day. I better get going if I want to stay in business."

I felt Lauren's eyes when I stood to face her daughter. "It was nice talking to you, Alexis."

"Good for me too, Matt," she said. "You're quite an addition to our big happy family."

Alexis shifted her body toward Lauren. "We aren't finished, Mom."

Lauren looked resigned. "Are we ever? It's the only conversation we have."

"Not the only one." Alexis gave me a short smile and switched her way out the hospital door.

Lauren sighed and glanced in my direction. "I was hoping to meet Boots today."

"She had to leave town on business. We'll visit together tomorrow."

"That girl of mine is a bombshell. Sometimes it makes things a little too easy for her. It often comes as surprise to Alexis when she doesn't get her way."

"She handled it well," I said, answering all Lauren's unasked questions.

She tossed her head, closing the subject. "Why don't we see if

Lou's awake?"

I might not have been so eager to leave the waiting room if I'd known what Lou looked like. Ghost white he lay on his back, his thick gray hair Einstein like and damp, his eyes red and puffy. He was awake when we entered and struggled to lift his head.

" Lay still," Lauren ordered with a catch in her throat as she leaned down to kiss his cheek.

I stood immobilized just inside the door.

"*Boychick*?" Lou whispered weakly before covering his face with an oxygen mask. Jayson's machine suddenly filled my mind.

When I got to the bed he took the mask off. "They say I should use it when I feel short of breath."

"No need to explain," I said, trusting my voice not to break. "We've been keeping close watch."

Lou smiled feebly.

"Especially your 'squeeze.' The doctor told us you're built like an ox, but that Lauren was a hero." I would have kept babbling but the hero interrupted.

"Don't listen to him, I just did what had to be done. Matt must have driven a hundred miles an hour after I called."

Lou took a couple of hits of oxygen then smiled a slightly stronger smile. "The two of you are doing better, I see."

Lauren and I glanced at each other, "We're doing fine," I said.

Lauren sat down near the head of the bed. Her fingers were in constant motion, fluffing Lou's pillow, stroking his hair, squeezing his hand. I stayed at the foot. Each time Lou used the mask my gut rocked. After a while I couldn't take it. "I'm going to leave the two of you alone. Now listen up, old man," I warned. "Pay attention to the Gowns. This ain't the time to get a hair up your ass."

Lou raised the mask and smiled.

"I'll stop back tonight and tomorrow I'll bring Boots."

"Not tonight, Matty. I'll be asleep. Tomorrow is soon enough. I'm glad Shoes will be with you, I want Lauren to meet her."

He was signaling me about his strength so I kissed him goodbye and almost ran out the front door to smoke a cigarette. Only once my hands got it lit, I knew nicotine wasn't gonna do, so I lit one of my joints. Right then, I didn't care if I got busted. Lou's sallow face had clobbered me as hard as Clifford's forearm. Drove home what Lauren said yesterday about vulnerability. Drove home my own.

I kept both sticks working with barely an eye for the law. Despite Lou's general health, age, and my penchant for despair, I'd never imagined him dying. But the visit to his hospital room rubbed my face in it. He was going to pull through this time, but what about the next?

I was so busy collecting my fractured nerves I didn't hear anyone approach.

"Put that out!" a harsh voice whispered. "Are you crazy? The police are in and out of here all the time!"

I almost pulled a back muscle twisting toward the voice. When I saw Lauren, I knelt down, gently rubbed the lit end of the joint on the ground, and carefully placed the rest in my wallet.

"Jesus," she exclaimed. "I knew you were going to do something stupid."

"That easy to read?" I asked.

"Ian's given me plenty of practice. You looked like you wanted to hit someone."

"It upsets me to see him like that."

"He'll be all right, Matt. The doctors expect a hundred percent recovery. It's just going to take some time."

The dope had worked its way into my bloodstream and bleached some of the fear from my anxiety. "It threw me to see all the equipment."

Lauren smiled and lightly touched my arm. "That's why they

didn't let you in the ICU. But it doesn't make sense to act stupid."

I nodded, "What can I say?"

"Tell me that Lou and I won't end up visiting you in a jail or hospital."

It was my turn to smile. "I'll do my best. Why did you come out?"

"He needs his sleep and I wanted to catch up with you."

"Thanks."

"Remember? No more thanks. Matt, we both love that man and, frankly, I'm beginning to see you as one of the family."

I wasn't sure what I thought of that so I just let it pass. "Do you want a ride to the Hacienda?"

Lauren shook her head, "I'm going to wait here. The doctors say he'll be better after each nap. What are you going to do?"

I thought about lying but didn't. "Lauren, I don't want to piss you off but..."

"You want to make certain the furnace was just an accident."

I nodded and waited for an angry outburst. But, as she had since we first met, Lauren surprised me.

"Matthew, I want just one favor."

"Sure."

She chuckled at my rapid response. "Be gentle when you talk to the kids."

CHAPTER 39

Back inside the car I gave myself grass, and nicotine to polish off my anxiety. Too much time since I visited the Chief. I weighed more than ninety-eight pounds and it was time to kick some sand.

Unfortunately, Biancho was far less interested. I cooled my heels at the station's side door and chain-smoked, suddenly aware that this visit was insane—nothing more than the anger hiding underneath my fears. Or a sick invitation for more Clifford. Unfortunately, the realization occurred as the matronly receptionist brought me into the Chief's office.

"You're as persistent as a grain moth, Jacobs," Biancho commented as soon as the door closed.

"Without the 's.'"

"A rose by any name..." he said waving dismissively.

"Aren't you going to ask me to sit down?" Seeing him calm and hostile in another form-fitting alligator shirt recharged the rage that had fueled my decision.

"Been there, done that," he answered flatly. "Just tell me why you're here so I can get back to work."

It pissed me off more to stand while he sat. But in a quiet, controlled voice I told him about the furnace incident and Lou's near miss. Biancho listened with a bland expression, but waited until I finished to take his shot.

"I know all about it, Jacob. Might surprise you to learn I've already checked with the oil company and the fire department. I'm sorry to hear about your father-in-law, but do you always run to the police when a boiler breaks down?"

I bit the inside of my cheek. The good one. "Don't you find it odd that nasty things keep happening at the Hacienda?"

"I find it odd that you're here."

"So we both have questions, don't we?" I fired back. "The Hacienda is worth a lot of green. Shit happens when money is involved. Your reassurance might mean something if you'd busted the goons who did the drive-by but, near as I can tell, the only person nailed has been me." In for a gram, in for a kilo.

"What do you mean?"

"You keep calling Washington Clifford after each of my visits. I've been trying hard to stay out of your face, but enough is enough. Why not do your own ass-kicking?"

Biancho's bland slipped a notch, replaced by a strange expression. "Clifford beat on you?"

"Should I show you the bruises?"

"I didn't expect that."

"What the fuck did you expect? We'd take tea?"

"You'd be smoking alone, but I'd guess that's nothing new," Biancho said. "Don't look so surprised, I opened your trunk, remember?"

The joints in my wallet took a serious bite out of my red meat. "That doesn't explain why you called out the dogs."

"I asked Washington to talk to you because I didn't think I was getting through. I didn't, don't, want you to screw up a tricky investigation. I didn't expect Clifford to use force."

It was as close to an apology as I was going to get. I'd placed my body on the line for this? Just another variation of my earlier dope smoking in front of the hospital.

"Now what's all this cock and bull about the Hacienda?" he asked suspiciously.

"Alexis Brown is constantly urging her mother to sell. I figure if a real estate broker is that interested, maybe other people are as well."

For a moment I thought he was willing to give some credence to my concern. A very short moment.

"Uh huh, and what happened to your story about the bashed automobile?" he asked sarcastically.

"There was no connection," I admitted, though something began itching inside my head as I wondered why he'd spoken about the car.

Biancho stood up behind his desk. "Christ, you make a living as a PI? I'm telling you this for the last, and I do mean last, time. The drive-by was a gang related incident. Gang related. You keep trying to convince me it's something else, but every time you walk in here you have less than spit. Unless you can do better, I'd appreciate it if you stopped annoying me."

Biancho scowled and added, "Even if you *can* do better, mail it in. Now, am *I* getting through today?"

Time to cut and run and hope he felt sorry enough about Clifford to ignore my visit. But the itching didn't stop as I walked to my car. I drove around the area trying to piece together my information and unsuccessfully bring the itch to life. But all I was sure about knowing was the only stitches to sew were gonna be on my body if Biancho called Wash. Once again I'd led with my chin; like a bull in a china shop, I kept knocking into breakables. And paid the price since the biggest breakable was me.

Despite Lou's request, I thought about returning to the

hospital. Then thought about calling it a day. But the image of Lou lying in bed forced me to resist the couch and I aimed the car toward Alexis's real estate business.

Not an easy do. My decision making capacity was seriously suspect. After all, I'd just finished fucking up, and questioning Alexis so soon after my sexual disentanglement felt like I'd just kicked cocaine only to buy a pipe for some crack.

Nonetheless, I squeezed the Bimmer into a tiny parking spot around the corner from her office. "*Cherchez le cash.*"

Though the office's weather-beaten cedar shingles feigned the appearance of a tiny house, it was really a storefront. Halfway across the street I stopped dead in my tracks and ran quickly behind a space age van. 'Gator had gotten here first.

Biancho and Alexis emerged from the rear of the storefront to stand behind the front plate glass windows. Biancho kept shaking his head, shrugging his shoulders, and occasionally slapping the desk. Alexis, the calmer of the two, managed her own share of finger pointing.

I resisted a powerful urge to do some up close snooping. Pretty smart on my part because Biancho was livid when he stomped out of the office. If the Chief noticed me, he might not bother calling Wash and just use his gun.

Biancho rushed up the block until he reached a nondescript late model Ford. He scored his final slam on the car door, then squealed away from the curb. Apparently, the conversation hadn't gone his way.

Hadn't left Alexis a happy camper either. She stood furiously dialing the telephone, crashing the receiver back down, then pulling it up to dial again. Either she was desperate to talk to someone specific or was suddenly terribly lonely.

I didn't plan to ask. Thanks to Mr. Law and Order, I'd seen enough for one day. Even managed to scratch the itch. Biancho had known the truth about Lauren's car before he asked. And it was pretty clear who he'd learned it from.

The ride to the city was uneventful unless fighting off depression constituted an event. In my life, that was the norm. But this depression was tinged with panic. Boots, Lou, Alexis, Biancho, and Clifford all vied for anxious attention. By the time I reached town, I was too strung out to go home. I was onto something and just couldn't afford to be blitzed, bothered, and bewildered.

I drove to Boots's swearing I wouldn't rip through her handbags searching for more pills. I'd done enough dumb. There were hours before she would arrive so I stripped down to my boxers, grabbed a beer, and stretched across the bed. I absolutely, positively had to rest my eyes.

I saw the semi stick out of the car's window, Lou and Lauren laughing as they strolled on the sidewalk oblivious to the danger. I bolted upright and reached for my gun. My hysteria exploded when neither the gun nor holster were where they were supposed to be. I started to hurl my body in front of the happy couple when I recognized Boots' scream.

"Matt! Matt! It's me! Boots! You fell asleep in my place, honey, that's all."

My heart pounded while I opened my eyes. "A bad dream," I explained, wiping sweat from my forehead.

"Well, it scared the hell out of me too. How's Lou?"

"Better, but looks like day old excrement."

"Tell me while I get out of these clothes," Boots said, throwing her travel bag onto the chair.

I talked about the day. Told her about Lou, Lauren, and my newfound acceptance, the conversations with Julius and Biancho, and made sure to add that Alexis had been at the hospital. I didn't tell her about that talk, but did describe what I'd seen in front of her office and where I believed Biancho had learned the truth about Lauren's crumpled car.

Most of our discussion took place while Boots showered. When I finished talking I suddenly felt myself crawl into a casing, sorry I'd chosen her place instead of my own. And angry at myself for feeling this way. Sharing was supposed to make you feel close.

Boots stepped out of the bathroom wet and dripping. Despite my withdrawal I responded, flashed on Alexis's amused smile in the hospital, and ditched the idea. I wasn't going to be able to fuck myself out of this head.

And didn't think I could spend the night without a television. Boots looked at me.

"Not now, hon. I'm too wiped out."

"It might help," she suggested, striking a provocative pose.

"Or kill me." I paused and made a quick decision. "If it's not too much trouble, maybe we could stay at the buildings."

Boots lowered her leg off the edge of the bed, surprised but not upset. "No problem, sweetheart."

She walked over to the dresser and began choosing clothes. "Why did you come to the condo? You could have left a message on the machine."

"I wanted to see you as soon as you got in. I meant what I said on the phone."

Boots stopped what she was doing and walked over. "I'm sorry I went away," she murmured, leaning her naked body into my chest.

I pulled her tight, closed my eyes and kissed the top of her head. I *had* wanted to see her. But right now, I wanted to go home.

CHAPTER 40

During the ride to my apartment it felt like I was watching a movie, everything distant and disconnected. The longer we chatted, the darker the theatre.

Either Boots didn't notice or just didn't care. It made her happy to know Lou looked forward to her visit, and she was pretty curious about the scene at Alexis's real estate office. Mostly, she was nervous about my discussion with the Chief. Worried that news would get back to Washington Clifford.

In some ways our conversation relieved me. If we lived together, both of us needed to get used to me feeling this way. This wasn't gonna be the last of my lousy moods.

I drove down the gravel alley and pulled up next to my second six-flat. We got out of the car and were crossing the far corner of the small basketball court—the only spot shaded from the grocery store's amber crime lights—when a large hand grabbed me by the throat.

"Let go of him you monster," Boots blazed when she realized Washington Clifford had thrust me up against the wall.

Maybe we *should* have stayed at her place.

His hand squeezed tighter when Boots pummeled his back and shoulders with clenched fists. "Cut it out, lady," Clifford growled quietly, "or I'll really hurt him."

"No you won't, you son of a bitch, I won't let you!" she spat, renewing her attack with a fresh wave of anger.

Clifford's fingers loosened slightly. "Boots, stop," I croaked. "He'll hurt you too if you don't knock it off."

"I don't care," she seethed. "I'm sick of the way this bastard thinks he can beat you up any time he fucking wants to."

Even in the dark I saw the fire in her eyes and it shred my numbness. Surprisingly, I felt ready to explode.

When Clifford shifted position to stop Boots' furious attack I spun out of his grasp and chopped at the arm that had my throat. Suddenly, it was *his* back against the building and *my* forearm across a neck.

For a moment everybody froze, amazed by the unexpected turnaround. I felt exhilarated as I slipped my hand underneath Clifford's coat and yanked his gun from its holster. When Boots saw the black metal in my hand she gasped. "No, Matt, no. Don't!"

I placed my right knee between Clifford's legs, kept my arm across his neck, and tapped the barrel on his temple.

"Matt," Boots pleaded, really frightened.

"Go inside, Boots. I have scores to settle, and I don't want you around." My submissiveness in the lighthouse was flashing like Las Vegas neon along with my perpetual masochism with this son of a bitch. What goes around comes around and I was gonna make up for lost time.

Clifford stood very still and, except for a catch in his breathing, remained calm. "I'd stay right where you are, lady, and talk some sense to your friend. He's not thinking too good right now."

"The game has changed, *Wash*," I warned, leaning more weight onto my arm. "Tonight I tell you when to talk."

"Matt, your hands are shaking," Boots said pleadingly. "The gun might go off!"

"Don't worry, hon, if the gun goes off it won't be an accident. Go wait inside."

"Hell no! We're in this together. If you shoot him, we'll be in that together. You understand me?"

Her words chipped through my fury. I loosened my grip on Clifford's throat. "Don't even think about moving," I said, rubbing the gun alongside his head. "I'll be just as satisfied to shoot you calm as angry. Maybe more."

"I thought we liked each other, shamus," Clifford said, watching me carefully.

"We're close as ever, motherfucker. Only the roles are different. And you know what, Wash, I like it better this way."

"Don't get used to it, Jacobs."

"That's Jacob, without the fucking 's,'" I erupted, my whole body burning white hot. I stepped back and aimed the gun squarely between his eyes. "Without the fucking 's.'"

"Matt, please, you're scaring me," Boots begged, lightly touching my arm.

"Stand back, Boots."

"What's eating you, Jacob? I've been rough with you, but that's not driving this train."

"How do you know?"

"You'd have pulled something like this long ago. Where's your head, shamus? You're too smart to shoot a cop in cold blood." Clifford was still cool, though beads of sweat appeared on his broad, chiseled face.

I was tempted to run my free hand over his smooth dome to see if it was wet too. "Crime of passion, asshole."

"That's why I want to know what's eating you."

Boots was still frightened, but she waited for my response.

"My family's eating me, fucker. The last one left is lying in a hospital bed too weak to wave his goddamn hand. Ever have someone in your family bite the big one? Ever see 'em look like a beaten dog?

"It don't feel good, Wash. It don't feel good at all. Especially when you watched the rest of them die in the same kind of beds. Makes this one special, you know?"

I felt a trail of tears scald my face but held the gun steady. "Lou's using an oxygen tank and I'm catching visits from the friend of a dirty cop. Gang drive-by, my ass. I don't know what Biancho's mixed up in, but it doesn't have fuck-all to do with gangs. And I won't let you stop me from finding out!"

Clifford grabbed my eyes with his own. "I don't have the time or inclination to chase after your fantasies, Jacob."

"That's what your buddy keeps saying," I snarled. "Well, you might not have time to chase anything. Ever."

"Matt!" Boots cried. "Don't!"

"He's not going to kill me, Ma'am." Clifford's voice quiet but clear.

"I guess you'll just have to ask yourself if it's your lucky day, Washington," I mocked.

"Eastwood you ain't, Jacob. Put the gun down, for Christ sake."

"And take my beating and bust like a man? I don't think so. Someone jumped us in the alley and got shot with their own weapon. Happens all the time. Sorry it had to be you." I was talking tough but my frenzy was starting to fade.

"Not going to be a beating or bust. You hear me? We go back a ways, Jacob, and I'm not going to lie to you about that. No beating, no bust."

"There's always a first, isn't there? Something we're both finding out."

Clifford's teeth flashed white in the darkness. "I guess we are. But one new thing a night is enough. Listen up, there's been rough times between us, but I don't hate you or even the way you work.

You don't go by the book, but then, neither do I. You got a feel for the job and you're stubborn. Anyone else standing here telling me Biancho was dirty, I wouldn't believe it, couldn't believe it. That white boy is so button-down, he probably strips naked to take a shit. But you're the one telling me, so I'm listening."

"Thanks for your indulgence, only I'm the one holding the gun. And you're the one who's been playing Steppin' Fetchit for Teddy. *Now* you're willing to listen? Gee, I wonder why?"

"I keep telling you, shamus, you ain't gonna shoot me. And I didn't come here tonight for Biancho."

"So why are you here?" Boots asked, her breath a little easier, though her eyes were still riveted on my hand.

"I didn't like listening to Ted Biancho bitch about the way I told your boyfriend to stop making a nuisance out of himself. I came here to remind the shamus here what goes on between us, stays between us."

"Why do you keep beating on him?"

"I learned a long time ago that Jacob isn't a real good listener until you get his attention."

"That's a helluva reason," Boots snorted.

"Did you bother to ask why Biancho wanted you to play drums on my fucking body?" I scoffed.

"See what I mean, lady? I just got done saying he was ripped that I hit you. Biancho just wanted to keep you from fucking with a police investigation. Said you were getting in his way."

I felt the brunt of my anger dissipate and briefly wondered what would take its place.

A small smile crossed Clifford's face and the last trace of my rage flared. "Don't look at me like that. You're not out of the woods yet."

"Sure I am, and so are you. We have us a deal. You're going to give me my gun, and I'm going to let you do your thing. I'll also forget this happened."

"Ain't you sweet?"

Clifford chuckled and stuck out his arm. I shrugged and handed him his gun. Boots bit her lower lip, afraid I think, of what might come next.

"Not sweet, Jacob, smart. And so are you."

"Why? Because I didn't blow your fucking head off?" Despite my harshness I had no fight left. Fatigue had taken the anger's place. High risk recreation does that.

"That has something to do with it," Clifford said, "but not all. I appreciate your attitude toward your dead wife's father. Though I got to say it surprises me. I didn't think you cared about anyone except your shyster friend Simon and your dope dealer." Clifford turned his granite body toward Boots. "Sorry, I don't know where you fit in."

"That's okay, neither do I." Boots was so relieved she seemed giddy.

"You been beating on me for years, Wash. You should know I'm all heart."

Clifford slipped the gun into his back holster. "You're all mule, Jacobs. And, if you're right about Biancho, which I seriously doubt, don't even dream I'll lift a finger to bring him down."

"Gotta be true to the Blue?"

"We all have our families," Clifford said. "I won't stop you, but you're on your own."

"All of a sudden I'm the lucky one, huh?"

"More than you realize." Clifford nodded his head toward Boots as he walked past. "Sorry about the ruckus, Ma'am."

Clifford ambled down the short end of the alley, his thickripple soled shoes crunching gravel while the two of us stood in immobilized silence. Wash never turned back to say goodbye.

"I need a drink." Boots was almost running around the

apartment. "Do you want one?"

"Hell, yeah! I have a joint in my wallet."

Boots poured herself a double, slugged down half, and continued to pace between the living room and kitchen. I sat at the table, smoked my joint, sipped my second bourbon straight, and stared at my holstered gun hanging off the back of my 'Dutch Schultz' kitchen chair—a legacy from my paternal grandfather's rum running days. The old wooden chair came right out of the Big Man's bar.

"I feel totally wired, Matt. How can you just sit there?" She walked to the refrigerator, handed me a beer chaser, and kept on trucking, her long legs eating a lot of floor.

I placed the joint on the edge of the table, careful to keep the fire away from the signature on the enamel design and lit a cigarette. "My rush is gone. Want to grab an ashtray on your next lap?"

Boots brought the ashtray from the living room, sat down on the other side of the table, and sipped her drink. "Jesus, I thought you were going to do him, I really did."

"Do him? You've been watching too many mafia movies."

"Part of me was scared shitless," Boots said, "but another part almost wanted you to shoot. I felt excited, turned on."

"You were pretty hot when you jumped his back," I said smiling at the memory.

"I wasn't turned on then, you asshole. I just wanted him to let you go."

"I'll walk the mean streets with you, doll."

"Promises, promises." Boots gulped the rest of her drink then yawned and yawned again. "What's happening to me? A minute ago I couldn't sit down, now I can't bear the thought of standing. I'm completely wiped."

That made two of us. I stubbed out the cigarette and held out my arm. Boots grabbed it and we walked hand in hand to the bedroom.

The taste of murder does things to you; I didn't need the television after all.

CHAPTER 41

I woke the next morning bellied against Boots's back, my hand cupping her breast. I felt lighter, relaxed, as if someone had loosened a knot in my gut I hadn't realized was there. For a while I didn't move, halfheartedly trying to poke holes in my weightlessness. To my surprise, it seemed like it was gonna take more than half a heart to bring me down. A nearcop kill cleansed better than a shrink.

I carefully unwrapped my arms and legs, tiptoed into the kitchen, and put up the coffee. I showered, ran the Bakelite handled straight razor across my face, and returned to the kitchen. Boots was sitting at the table wearing one of my tees.

"I tried to keep quiet."

"The bed felt empty," she said sleepily. "Did last night really happen or was I dreaming?"

"No dream," I said smiling. "We played Bonnie and Clyde. Now Clyde's gotta get some clothes."

When I returned to the kitchen, the mugs were steaming on the kitchen table. I sat down, lit a cigarette, and sipped. Boots looked like a Cheshire cat. "We really showed that son of a bitch, didn't we?"

"We almost committed homicide, woman." But I smiled too.

"How close were you to shooting him?"

"Too close."

"Matt, you were raging! Your hands were trembling and you had your knee pressed against his nuts." She didn't seem bothered that her boyfriend was a potential cop killer.

"Pretty fucking stupid."

Boots nodded, "It sure was, but it felt great to bring that fat bully to his knees."

"I keep telling you Clifford ain't fat. And he didn't exactly beg for his life."

"No, he was calm, I'll give him that."

"Better be glad it turned out the way it did. Beats crashing in a prison cell."

"We slept good, didn't we?" Boots said smiling.

"Catharsis does that." And that's exactly what it had been. I'd finally stopped feeling like everyone's doormat.

I grinned and drank from the mug. "Do you want your egg fried or fried?

We kibitzed after breakfast, made long, languid love, then drove to the North Shore. Conversation was easy—easier perhaps than it had ever been. Even when I clutched on the approach to the hospital, I was able to separate my concern for Lou's health and safety from my pleasure with Boots. It had been a long time since I'd been able to keep my anxieties in a row.

When we entered his room Lauren was shoulder to shoulder with Lou on the bed. They were huddled together looking like kids caught in the cookie jar. Or maybe, just after the jar was emptied.

"We didn't mean to interrupt," I said, dropping Boots' hand.

"No interruption, Matty," Lou smiled. His voice was strong, breathing almost normal. "Now, a half hour earlier..."

"Lou!" Lauren actually blushed. "I've never met the lady."

"That's Shoes. Shoes, this is Lauren."

"Boots," Boots said with a grin.

"So now we can get back to that half hour?" Lou joked.

It was both a relief and surprise to see how well he looked. I usually believed that sick only led to worse. Lou appeared flushed, but I wasn't sure it his health or the cookie jar.

"You look terrific," I said.

"I feel pretty good. Short of breath but no more IV." A frown creased his face. "I want to leave today but they want to keep me here for another day."

"They're right and you're wrong," Lauren said firmly. "The last thing we need is a relapse."

"But..."

"But nothing. You'll stay until the nurses can't put up with you. Now why don't you and Boots visit with each other? I want Matt to keep me company while I get a Coke."

"What's the matter?" I asked as soon as the door closed. "He looks much better."

"He is."

I felt myself relax. "Then what's the problem?"

"I finally told Lou I wanted to marry him the moment my divorce is final. " She hesitated then continued, " "I just don't want to be without him. I want to get married as soon as we can." She finished on a defiant note, as if expecting an argument.

"Lucky guy, lucky lady. Congratulations."

Her body relaxed but she kept her eyes on my face. "Do you really mean that?"

"Look, I'm not totally comfortable with the rest of your family, but I think you make Lou really happy."

Lauren seemed both pleased and put off. "You don't like the

kids?"

"Like isn't the issue. They seem troubled and your relationship with Paul makes me uncomfortable. He mostly acts like a go-fer for you. Works on the house, hangs around. That sort of shit."

I expected anger but she just shook her head. "I thought as time went on they'd all get used to us. And don't forget Paul's anger. It's been much more difficult than I imagined."

Lauren was still ignoring problems that had nothing to do with her and Lou but nobody was perfect.

Lauren tensed, watching my face. "I told you I wouldn't accept Lou's proposal until everything returned to normal but it hasn't. I'm feeling stalked again."

I hadn't thought about the 'case' since my crazed blowup with Clifford and it took a second to find the gear.

"It's really bad, Matthew, worse than before." A shiver ran through her body.

"What do you mean worse?"

"I'm afraid you'll think it's bullshit."

"Talk to me, Lauren."

"I'm starting to feel watched all the time. As if I'm surrounded."

"When did you notice it?"

"A week ago, maybe more. I don't know for sure because I didn't want to believe what I was feeling. But the last few days it's been really bad and I can't ignore it." Lauren stopped talking and took a few deep breaths. "Matthew, I'm really scared."

She looked it. "Does Lou know?"

"No. He has enough to worry about. I haven't told anyone." She chuckled grimly, "You can probably guess why I've been reluctant to tell you. Anyhow, I'd like to keep it between us."

I nodded. I wanted to reassure her but couldn't. Her feelings reinforced all my suspicions about the drive-by and the furnace.

"I'm glad you told me. You'll come home with Boots and me. I'm not going to clear anything up by tonight and I don't want you alone in the Hacienda." I also wanted time to decide whether to use her as bait.

Lauren looked grateful but shook her head. "There's no need. I'll be fine, Matthew. I'm spending the night with Lou."

"Here?"

Lauren smiled, her fear momentarily forgotten. "Yes, but don't ask how I managed it." She looked as if she had something else to say but changed her mind.

"What is it?"

"I feel guilty about the marriage with this still going on."

"I'll take care of it," I said with more confidence than I felt. "Accepting Lou's proposal is just fine."

She touched my arm. "You're taking a load off my mind."

I felt embarrassed. "Now, you're sure about staying here tonight?"

"Absolutely."

"Okay, But time to exchange cell numbers."

"Do you think that's necessary?"

"I know I'll keep mine on for a change. And it's the way we're going to work. The relationship with Lou is your turf, your safety is mine. Now tell me what you know about Ted Biancho."

"Ted?" She shrugged. "There's not much to tell. Serious, competent, and conventional. He's always been a loner."

"What about his personal life?"

She looked confused. "Why do you want to know about his personal life?"

"I'm a suspicious guy. He's married, isn't he?"

"Yes, but I don't know anything at all about his wife. I can't imagine there's much gossip about either of them. Teddy is a real straight arrow."

"What about his friendship with Alexis?"

Lauren smiled. "During high-school he used to be over the house all the time. Matthew, why are you asking about Teddy

Biancho?"

"I've never been satisfied with his instant conclusion about the drive-by. Were he and Alexis an item?"

"I wouldn't call them an 'item.' He sort of trailed after her." She glanced at me and smiled. "Alexis can do that to people." Her smile twisted into a frown. "Maybe it's something she inherited."

"You don't seem pleased about the trait."

"I don't want to feed my ego like that anymore," she said, lapsing into an unhappy silence.

There was more to her silence than her ego, but it wasn't the right time to press. "I should probably talk to Alexis about the Chief."

"She could tell you much more than I can." Lauren tossed her head, "When you talk to her, could you please ask her to leave me alone about selling the Hacienda?"

"She's still at it?" I felt the knot return to my belly.

"The girl won't take no for an answer, and I can't stop her."

"I'll see what I can do, but don't count on it.

"I don't know how to thank you, Matthew. You make me feel safe."

"Thank me by keeping your eyes wide open and taking good care of my father-in-law."

Lauren threw her arms up around my neck and kissed me on the cheek.

"We better go back inside," I said, "or they'll think we were out looking for a dealer instead of a machine."

The rest of the visit went fine. Boots and Lauren found plenty in common while Lou and I caught up on the buildings and the home stretch of the pennant race. Somewhere in the middle Lou grandly announced the marriage. His declaration triggered a round of real cheer and more excited conversation.

But back in the Bimmer during the late afternoon, the glow began to dim.

"What's the matter," Boots asked. "Toward the end of the visit you seemed distracted and now you seem withdrawn. Are you upset about their marriage?"

"No, I'm actually good with it."

"So I don't have to tell you we don't?"

"Don't what?"

"Have to get married."

"No assurance necessary." I told her about my discussion with Lauren and talked about it through our dinner at a decent bar. But we could riff 'til morning, and there would be no escape. If something sinister was happening—and something was—Alexis was my prime suspect.

CHAPTER 42

Alexis was still gnawing on my head when I woke up to an empty apartment. Boots had already gone home for fresh clothes and, truth be told, it was a relief. Despite my 'walk' talk, it was tough to have Alexis on my mind with Boots in front of my eyes. This way I could be uncomfortable all by my lonesome.

It took two cups of coffee and my morning dose of nicotine and tokes to admit that a sizable slice of yesterday's shine had already tarnished. A few good days do not constitute a personality transplant. Also, I still had a horrible hunch that my investigation would lead to more unhappiness.

I telephoned the hospital, talked to Lauren, and discovered that our proposal party had been a boon to Lou's spirits but not his health. The Stethoscopes had already decided his earliest release was at least a day away. Lauren told me she had managed to finagle another night for herself in the hospital.

Since Lauren had errands to run, I made her promise to take her cell and return directly to the hospital right after she finished. I also made her promise to call then immediately hightail it to his room if she felt even the slightest sense of stalk.

So Lauren had her marching orders, but I still needed mine. After slugging down the last of the coffee I drop-kicked myself into action. For the second time since this insanity began, I strapped on my holster. Wearing it made me feel more like a thinking detective than an unthinking dick.

To talk, or not to talk. That was the question. And not simply because of Alexis's erotic charms. What bothered me now was her connection to Teddy Biancho. If Alexis and Biancho were conspiring to drive Lauren from the Hacienda, it wouldn't take him long to learn about my visit. And if he heard about it, Teddy wouldn't be content to talk.

But I wasn't ready to make book on my suspicions. I'd been wrong about Lauren's car and, frankly, I didn't want to believe the worst. Telling Lauren that her daughter and the police Chief shot up the Hacienda and were trying to run her out of town would be difficult to say, harder to swallow. Especially if I couldn't prove it.

I stopped by my mechanic man, Manny, and borrowed another grandfather car. The new conservative me parked the loaner a few blocks from Alexis's real estate office. No need to advertise my wheels. At first I thought no one was there, the door was locked and the front office dark. But Alexis heard the handle jiggle because she stepped out from the back of the building wearing an interested, though not unpleasant, look.

"You're here bright and early," she said. "Change your mind?"

The moment I saw her angled eyes and skin tight blouse, I wanted to. "Tempting as it is, I don't think so." I managed in what I hoped was a similarly light tone. Hell, I was pleased my voice hadn't cracked.

"I didn't think so," she chuckled. "Come on inside."

I followed her to a plush seating area in the rear of the office and sat down on a black leather sofa.

"I'll stay over here," she said stepping gracefully around a marble-topped coffee table. "I wouldn't want to tempt you." She laughed, then sat directly across from the couch.

"Nothing you can do about that, Alexis."

"Thanks," she replied. "You're very gallant, but honestly, there's no need. Are you here because you're interested in relocating?"

"I'm strictly a city rat. Do you mind if I smoke?"

Alexis shrugged and I lit up. "I just want a little information."

"About what?"

"The Hacienda. The furnace situation threw me and I'm trying to get a handle on how much work the place really needs."

Alexis looked me over coolly, all her laughter gone. "Your detective is showing." She pointed toward my right shoulder, "There, under your baseball jacket. You don't believe the furnace accident was an accident at all, do you?"

"What else could it be?"

"*Nothing* else, but that's not what you think."

I gave some ground. "I just want to be sure. We're still only a short throw from the drive-by."

Alexis shook her head. "Why can't you believe Teddy? He's been very clear about the shooting."

"Crystal, but there haven't been any arrests."

"He probably doesn't have enough evidence, that's all. And nothing terrible has happened since then."

I kept silent.

"Jesus, you actually think the furnace was deliberate, don't you?"

"All I want is your opinion on the building. You know the house better than anyone. Though I suppose it makes sense to ask you about Biancho as well," I added, gently raising the stakes. "Just some assurance the man is competent." I was dancing with danger, but sometimes you got to trust your gut.

Alexis laughed but her eyes never caught the joke. "Teddy's competent, all right. He's been competent his whole damn life."

It hung there so I took it. "Well, if anyone would know about his life it would be you, right?" I plastered my face with a warm smile; the hell of it was, I felt jealous. But this was work not play and I'd better remember it. Biancho would.

She frowned, "What do you mean?"

"Just that both your mother and brother mentioned you'd been his friend for a long time."

Alexis shrugged, "Friend is an overstatement. At least since he went away to college. Before that you might say we were friends, but even then it was sticky."

"Sticky?"

Alexis looked embarrassed but the look was a lie. "He had a crush on me."

"That doesn't surprise me. You can do that to men," I said, parroting her mother.

"Some men," Alexis said too quickly.

It was starting to dawn on me that our night together had been no big deal. At least for her. "But you don't crush back?" I smiled, hoping I didn't look like I felt.

"Attachments restrict my freedom." She thought for a minute then added, "I've seen too much damage when people can't let go."

"Talking about your family?" The words slipped out without thought. Fuck it, in for an ounce, in for a pound.

Alexis's eyes grew hard. "You're a quick study, aren't you? Actually, my mother has been doing a pretty good job since your father-in-law came aboard." She didn't sound ecstatic. "Except, of course, with the Hacienda.

To put your mind completely at ease," she continued, "it's no surprise that the furnace broke. I told you there were accidents waiting to happen. My father does what he can to keep the place from disintegrating, but it isn't enough. The house needs an enormous amount of work and Lauren won't, or can't, have it done."

"Why does Paul work on the Hacienda? I mean he has his own house and family to worry about."

Her lips tightened. "He spent his happiest years at the Hacienda; also, Dad knows how much it means to me, how much I care. He can't stand seeing me this upset." The last was spoken defiantly.

Time to talk my way out of her office. During the conversation her long legs had shifted further apart, and I had a hard time keeping my eyes on her face. Worse, Alexis had dealt me enough partial truths to reinforce my suspicions. In fact, my instinct told me I'd crossed a line and now *she* had had become suspicious of *me*.

It wasn't until I was smoking in Manny's car that I realized the usefulness of that crossing. My clumsy attempt at subtlety just might flush them out. Alexis wasn't the type to let the game come to her. All I had to do was make sure Biancho didn't flush first. I didn't think I could repeat last night's performance.

So I spent the day being very, very careful, moving the sedan regularly, working the area on foot. I followed far in the distance when Alexis left her office to show listings. And spent serious time hoping Alexis and Biancho wouldn't meet. I wanted to have it wrong. Most of me wished he wouldn't show and, for the rest of the day, most of me won.

Night was falling, with it a patented North Shore fog. I was two sub sandwiches fatter before I began second-guessing my strategy. If Alexis and Biancho did meet, they weren't going to invite me into their cabal. But the only other option was running Lauren out as a mechanical rabbit. Problem was, I just didn't feel like a winning greyhound.

The thick fog gripped the darkening hills by the time I followed Alexis from the office to her condominium. A town within a town. When she pulled into her sub-division, I grew anxious about being seen. I killed the lights and white-knuckled the wheel, relieved when she finally turned onto a circular driveway in front of a tiny cottage. Cars were pock-marked throughout the wooded area making it easy to find an obscure spot. Between the fog and the tinted windows on all of Manny's sedans, it was unlikely I'd be seen.

I stretched my legs as best I could, expecting a long night of nothing. The Chief appearing at Alexis's door would be more than enough—if it happened.

As if my ruminations mattered. Two hours into my stash I fell sound asleep.

CHAPTER 43

Forty-five minutes later, I jump-started to the roar of an engine. Alexis's Saab growled toward the street, its fog lights cutting a swath of bright white through the thick brume.

But I'd have made book the engine noise had come from a different direction. Sleepy, stiff, stoned, and confused, I remained stuck behind the steering wheel, even after the convertible slowly drove out of the circular driveway.

And lucky. Another car without lights pulled from the curb about a quarter of a block away and rolled past. Despite my tinted windshield, I reflexively ducked behind the dashboard and only caught a glimpse of the driver. I wouldn't raise my right, but it sure looked like Chief Biancho.

Which added a whole new wrinkle. If Biancho and Alexis were in cahoots, why was he tailing her? I grabbed my bottle of water and splashed a handful on my face. I waited another thirty seconds then followed the second car. Carefully. The roads were dark and slightly murky and Alexis's tail still wasn't using lights. Neither was I and I'd be in deep shit if I plowed into Biancho's behind.

The procession seemed to be retracing the route Alexis took home from her business. I knew it was only a matter of time before I'd be noticed, headlights or not, so I chanced an alternate path and turned on the lights. If I didn't get lost, I could beat the other cars to the office. That is, if the other two cars were actually going there.

I found a decent spot to park and waited anxiously until the low-riding Saab swung onto the street. Alexis pulled directly in front of the office, bouncing one of her tires onto the curb. Then she sat motionless, head cupped in her hands. A minute later the second car drove past and kept right on going.

Alexis finally left the Saab and walked to the office door. Instead of unlocking, she rapped. The door cracked open just enough to let her slip inside, but the front part of the building remained dark. I wanted to hop out of the sedan and work on foot, only I kept thinking about that second car. I was trapped right where I was, curious and claustrophobic.

Not for long. Out of the corner of an eye, I saw a shadow turn the corner and storm up the street. I watched with both eyes as the solitary figure strode toward Alexis's office. As soon as he walked under a lamp my earlier guess was locked: Police Chief Teddy was now on foot patrol.

Biancho approached Alexis's office presumably to join the get-together. My assumption was correct, but not before a couple of detours. First the Chief walked past the building and stared at a long white Infinity. I flashed on a similar car in the driveway next to Alexis's other office in Provincetown which we'd seen on our way to the lighthouse. The thought brought a flurry of self-recrimination. I'd completely forgotten about Alexis's business partner.

Biancho returned to the storefront. But instead of knocking on the door or kicking it down, he slowly worked his way up the small path alongside the building until he was out of sight.

"*Something is happening here but you don't know what it is,*" ran through my head, Dylan's raspy voice and all. And as long as I was Mr. Jones I wasn't *gonna* know what it was either.

My frustration took flight when Biancho charged into view and banged on the door with an angry fist. Eventually Alexis flicked on a lamp and let Biancho enter the dimly lit area behind the plate glass. She was surprised and unhappy to see him, standing with her legs planted, her arms folded across her chest.

Despite a less than spectacular view, I could see their conversation heat up. Biancho was waving his arms excitedly. Alexis occasionally stamped her foot. She kept pointing toward the door, but the Chief was adamant. This time he won the argument since Alexis finally stepped aside, her body communicating defeat and angry displeasure.

I waited patiently for a couple minutes before I snuck up the same path alongside her office. The fog was lifting, and there wasn't much to hide behind. I made damn sure to keep quiet. When I caught a glimpse of the tete-a`-tete through a small window into the back room I was even more careful. None of the participants looked pleased; two downright mad. The same two who had just been fighting in the front of the office.

The other guy didn't look angry. He looked like a heavy from a grade B black-and-white: a slick, Caucasian businessman. Slim build, slimmer waist, shaved bowling ball head, custom uit blue suit with a slight bulge at the contoured hip, gray shoes, and four fingers full of platinum and stones. A well-dressed hammerhead shark. Maybe I should introduce him to Clifford.

Alexis and Biancho stood motionless in the spacious room, but Hammerhead kept gliding, talking to both. Satisfied with their responses, the shark slid onto the black leather couch and unceremoniously plopped his pointed shoes on the marble table. From my uncomfortable angle, all I could see were his crossed at the ankles. That was enough; this was a *schtarker* who cleaned his manicured fingernails with a switchblade.

Now it was Alexis talking. Mostly to Biancho, who wore the look of a caged animal. He clearly disliked what he was hearing, hated being there, but his deflated posture gave proof of his helplessness. Me, I couldn't hear a fucking thing, no matter how hard I pressed my thick head against the triple pane. After a couple of seconds I just watched the show.

And a helluva show it was. Alexis emptied her arsenal of smiles, smirks, and seduction, sex spinning off each gesture. Twice she leaned her full bosom against Biancho's arm while her fingers touched his hand. Squeezing it for emphasis before backing away. I got hard watching her. 'Course, nothing new in that.

Every once in a while Biancho glanced over to the couch for corroboration or to ask a question. The Hammerhead's ankles would uncross as he replied, cross when he finished. But this was Alexis's performance. Talking, touching, beguiling, she waltzed in and out of my view.

I became so mesmerized by her movements, I stopped looking at anyone else and didn't notice the shoes disappear from the table. But Biancho caught my attention when he unbuttoned his sport jacket and pointed to his gun. A moment later I heard the office door and I ducked behind a garbage can in case Hammerhead glanced up the path. But he walked directly to his car and, with a farewell hit of his horn, peeled rubber.

When I turned back to the window Biancho and Alexis had already moved on to Act III. She looked contrite as Biancho took center stage, giving Alexis a vicious tongue-lashing. His face was purple, his hands clenching and unclenching at his sides.

I was tired of being on the outside looking in. With Lou and Lauren, with Boots. Even the lighthouse tryst had been managed by Alexis. The only time I'd felt any control was when I'd rubbed my gun on the side of Clifford's face. I wanted more, and I wanted it now.

I was draped pretty far out on a limb when I knocked. There was no evidence that this get-together had anything to do with my concerns. Hell, maybe they'd been organizing a fun-loving threesome.

But when Alexis yanked open the door, her look of disaster told me all I needed to know.

"What are you doing here?" she exclaimed.

"Happy to see me?" The pro had finally wrested control from the moonstruck puppy and my voice was harsh, free of sexual ambiguity. This was business, had been since Lou almost died. I felt strong and powerful. And I enjoyed it.

"No, not really, Matt." She struggled to mask her apprehension. "I'm pretty busy right now. Why don't we set a date?"

"No dates and no blue bird on my shoulder. I've been watching you nuzzle up to Biancho, but that shit won't work with me."

Apprehension transformed into fear. "You've been watching? Tonight, here?"

I wedged my foot into the open door. "That's right, Alexis. Your building has windows and I like to watch. I would have preferred to listen, but I'm low tech."

"Have you been drinking?" she asked. The woman didn't quit easy.

"Stone sober, not high, and hardly horny." I saw Biancho slink silently into the hallway at the back of the building. I took a deep breath and pulled my gun. If I'd guessed wrong about him I was gonna be in a heap of trouble.

"That you Jacob?" Biancho called.

"Sure is, Chief. I'm tired of the fun always happening without me."

"Let him in, Al," Biancho ordered. "I planned to talk to him anyway. Jacob, if that's a fucking gun in your hand, put it away. Washington Clifford told me about last night, but some things can't be repeated, you understand?"

I'd jacked myself up to get into the office, but was sane enough to stick the .38 back into its leather. Unfortunately, Alexis was still stubbornly standing in my way.

"Just let him in," Biancho barked.

For a moment Alexis looked like she would tell Biancho where to place his order but, with a snort and a Rowe toss of her head, she moved out of my way. I stepped around her and passed Biancho on the way toward the back room.

Much to my relief he didn't shoot or slap on the cuffs. Didn't even have his gun in hand. Just nodded wearily as I strode by. I picked an easy chair and made myself comfortable. I'd finally made it to the Big Dance.

CHAPTER 44

The tension was so explosive that when I lit a cigarette I was mildly surprised the room didn't blow. Alexis motioned and I stifled an impulse to light one for her, instead, slid the pack and plastic lighter across the marble table. She leaned forward on the edge of the couch, her knees crossed, thighs uncovered. Biancho remained standing, his face downcast and surly.

"Talk to him, Al," Biancho said, fatigue replacing his earlier Commandant.

"About?" she snapped. "You want him here, you talk."

"No one invited me, Alexis, I'm crashing." The nasty in my tone cancelled any possible embarrassment, ambivalence, or confusion.

"You saw Silverstein?" Biancho asked.

"I saw somebody I'd be scared to have as a partner."

"You're scared to have anyone for a partner," she sneered.

Chagrin crossed Biancho's face when he understood Alexis's sexual innuendo.

"Why the venom? I thought we were friends,"

"Friends don't spy on me," Alexis retorted.

I let her attitude feed my hound. "*My* friends don't lead me around in circles." Lou popped into my head. "And that's the least of it."

"You really don't have any idea about what's been going on, do you Jacob?" Biancho said.

I smiled grimly, "Just one, Chief. You and Alexis are trying to drive Lauren from the Hacienda. The house is worth serious silver and you've been trying real hard to stuff it in your piggy-banks. Condos with an ocean view? *'If you lived here you'd be home now'* signs?" I chuckled. "Here's the rub, you almost killed my father-in-law."

Biancho ground his teeth and Alexis choked back a burst of angry laughter. "Talk to him? You actually thought he knew something. Teddy, you shmuck, you're the fucking Police Chief. Send him home!"

"Nice try, Al." I plowed forward. "Did you pick me up at the party to get me out of the house? I made for a great alibi while your honey did the work."

Biancho moved to the other armchair and sank down on the seat, tension escaping from his taut, wiry body. "Clifford said you thought I was dirty."

"Pillow talk Chief, or do you and Washington have a hotline? You shoot up the Hacienda then damn near kill my father-in-law with a phony furnace accident. I call that dirty. What do you call it, off-duty fun?"

"I didn't do any drive-by." Biancho sat back in his chair shaking his head. "And there's nothing to your suspicions about the furnace."

"Why are you still talking, Teddy?" Alexis asked, eyes blazing. "You don't have to say a damn thing!"

Biancho shook the tired from his face with a visible show of resolve. "He's going to find out about the shooting sooner or later. You're going to tell him now."

Alexis protested but Biancho cut her off with a sharp demand. "No more lies! I've covered for you more times than I care to remember and I'm through."

His anguished words hung in the air like a coyote cry on the Discovery Channel. Seems Biancho was still head over heels for Alexis Brown.

"Talk to him, goddammit," Biancho whispered, "Stop fucking around."

"Where should I begin, Teddy?" Her attitude was a mix of resentment and compliance.

"Start with Silverstein."

"Teddy!" she groaned.

"Don't 'Teddy' me!" Biancho wasn't gonna brook much shit.

"Maury Silverstein bailed me out when my business was going belly up," Alexis said in a resigned monotone, her aggression on hold. "When the housing market crashed his cash kept the agency alive."

"Dirty money?" I asked.

"What money isn't?" she laughed sarcastically. "Maury is connected, if that's what you mean."

"It sounds worse than it is, Jacob. There's been no laundering." Biancho didn't realize his interruption was an unconscious protect.

"Clifford said you're smart and stubborn," he continued, buying time. "He never said anything about imagination."

"My imagination was right about Silverstein. Now, are you going to talk, or is she?" One thing to give him time to shuck, another to listen to his jive.

"Go on, Al," Biancho said.

"There's nothing more to say," Alexis said with a sudden spike of temper. "Once Maury becomes a partner, he stays a partner. I asked him for a favor, okay? I knew he could hire someone to shoot the house door safely. I wanted to be absolutely certain no one would get hurt."

"It wasn't you?" I looked at Biancho who just shook his head. I turned back to Alexis. "So you convinced Maury to pull the drive-by."

"You don't convince Maury to do anything. You pay him. It cost me another piece of the business."

"You must really want the Hacienda, Alexis."

She didn't respond.

"And you?" I asked Biancho. "Just along to lend official sanction? You knew the truth and fed everyone that gang bullshit."

"I don't talk before I know what's happening. We're different that way. I thought it was done by a professional, or at least someone with experience. The bullet holes had no incline and there was no sign of rubber on the road, no report of tire squeals, so the car was probably moving when the shots were fired. Too clean for boozed up teenagers."

Biancho glanced at me, shook his head, and continued. "I thought you had it figured, but all you asked about were the windows."

I shrugged, "Something wasn't right, I just didn't know what it was."

"Don't you have any technical training?"

"The door was gone before I got a good look. Anyway, we're not talking about me."

"Yeah, well, we are," he said. "When you told me about Alexis's interest in the Hacienda everything fell into place. I've known Maury a long, long time."

Biancho sighed an old man's sigh. Silverstein was an argument he had lost more than once. "I originally thought the drive-by was a message to Alexis," he said bitterly, looking at her. "I thought she owed Silverstein more money, couldn't pay, so he left a calling card. I wasn't going to say anything to anyone about that."

"Business is fine," Alexis shrugged, her mood still swinging. "And you're an idiot to sit here and tell this man anything."

Her arrogance was returning and I didn't want to give it room to grow. "Idiots stick together."

"Don't get carried away, Jacob," Biancho warned.

"Well, I hope you like your new friend, Teddy, because you've lost an old one," Alexis said.

It didn't take a weatherman to see the rain on his parade. "Straighten out your personal life later. I'm here to find out why my father-in-law is in a hospital. And what I'm hearing is that *Al* paid Maury to blow the door away. You thought it was a love letter to your lady, but it was only *Al's* way to crowbar the house from her mother."

I paused and looked at the two of them. "That's Round One. Round Two takes place after Lauren still refuses to sell. So you poison them out."

"That was an accident!" they said at the same time.

Their spontaneous response shook me. "Sure. And Clifford tripped over me on his way to work."

"What do you mean?" Biancho asked.

"You didn't have Clifford beat on me because you're a Boy Scout."

The Chief shook his head. "How many times do I have to tell you that I asked him to *talk* to you. You may not believe this, but I wasn't happy about covering for her."

I looked at Alexis who was leaning back on the couch, a disdainful expression on her face. "The truth comes out," she said.

"Knock it off," Biancho replied. "I've spent a lifetime carrying your books."

"You always were an ass, Teddy. Back door Biancho." A harsh look crept into her eyes. Something was starting to eat at her insides.

"No, Alexis," Biancho said with a sad smile. "You like to pretend it's all about sex. You know better, you've always known better."

It was tempting to eavesdrop on their personal life but turned the conversation back. "Both of you want me to believe the furnace was an accident?"

"It *was* an accident," Alexis snapped.

She sounded disappointed. The drive-by cost another piece of her business, the 'accident' only cost Lou his health. I felt like smacking her, but kept a heavy hold on my temper and tried to punch through their denial. "You'll admit to the drive-by but won't admit to the wire since Lou almost died."

"I wondered about the furnace too," Biancho said, "but Silverstein convinced me he had nothing to do with it."

"You bastard," Alexis couldn't keep her disappointment from slipping through. "You actually thought I'd do something to hurt them."

"I didn't know what to think, Al," Biancho said. "I knew Maury was behind the drive-by. I assumed he had something to do with the furnace. It was impossible not to link the two."

"Still is," I said stubbornly despite inklings of doubt.

"No it isn't!" Alexis swung her head in my direction. "Damn right I want the Hacienda, enough to hand over another piece of my independence, but that's different than letting my mother or Lou get hurt. I feel badly about what happened to him. It's not his fault my mother let the place turn to crap!"

By the time she finished, she was wiping her angry eyes. Worse, my goddamn shit-detector wasn't ringing.

CHAPTER 45

"And Silverstein confirms all this?" I asked.

"He said if he were going to kill someone it would have cost Alexis the entire agency," Biancho grimaced. "And I believe it. Anyway, he has no reason to lie. Maury knows enough to understand I wouldn't let anything happen to *any* of the Rowes or Browns."

Everyone was finally on the same damn page and it didn't make for a good read. Biancho believed Alexis and Silverstein; I believed Biancho. Only now I'd run out of suspects.

"Even if I buy this, there are still too many questions," I pressed, scratching to hold on in the face of case interruptus. "Like toxic fumes."

Alexis shook her head. "I already told you, Matt. There are worse disasters lurking in the Hacienda. The bitch won't spend a dime."

I wanted to jump her nerves. Burrow under Biancho's skin as well. Even if I accepted the furnace "accident," I still believed Lauren was being followed. Believed it enough to dig deeper.

"Even a 'safe' drive-by is a helluva stunt to run your mother out of the house. What's that about?"

"Daddy's girl," Biancho muttered.

"You son-of-a-bitch!" Alexis snarled. He'd struck a nerve. She turned her back on me, trying—but failing—to regain her composure. "Since when have you been on top?" she challenged the Chief.

"I'm through being bottom dog, Alexis. No more evasions, no more lies, no more unanswered questions. Jacob may not need to know why you did what you did, but he ought to. The man treats his own better than we treat ours."

"Do you act like a big shot with Bunny, too?" Alexis smiled in my direction, but there was a tick in her cheek and her pupils were dilating. Biancho was calling her on something she didn't want to touch.

"Her name is Barbara, but I think of her as Princess Bunny. Teddy had to marry a prom queen." Alexis stared at me but her words were whip-cracks aimed at Biancho. "So fucking classic. The poor outsider returns home in triumph. Our town's brand new cop with his own redheaded bimbo. Just had to prove he was better than everybody who ever looked down on him. You forced your way to Chief because a Police Chief can push people around with a tin badge. Nobody who grew up with you believes any of your crap about making your hometown safe."

Alexis kept her gleaming eyes on me while she continued to slap Biancho. "You still feel like a great big nothing, but you think I'm the only one who knows it."

Alexis waved her hand encompassing both me and the Chief. "Two ass-licking ball-less wonders. If either of you had the guts to be honest, you'd spend your nights strapped up in a leather bar." Alexis's outstretched arm was shaking.

Biancho and I avoided each other's eyes while I blasted back. "The Chief called it 'Daddy love.' I call it 'hate.' Which do you think, Alexis? Or are you afraid to really look at yourself?"

She rose to her feet and I stood to meet her head-on.

"What's that supposed to mean?"

"Look at what gets you off, sweetheart. Shows what you think of men, doesn't it? Last I checked your Daddy had a dick.

"See, I don't buy this 'doing it for Dad' crap," I continued. "You don't give a shit about anyone. Either you want the Hacienda for yourself, or you've got some fucking john waiting to be fleeced."

The words clipped across her pale face. My attack pushed her deeper into herself and she answered as if speaking to a large audience from the rear of a dark stage. "I don't believe how stupid you are. You make me sound like my mother, but I'm not *her*. I did what I did for my father. She's fucked him over their entire life.

"I'm not going to let him watch Lauren and Lou play house in the Hacienda." Alexis moved upstage even as she shakily grabbed the back of her chair. "I can't stand what their relationship does to him."

"Does to *him*?" I shrugged. "He been out of your mother's world for decades. "Get real! Your father's life has very little to do with Lauren or the Hacienda. And certainly not Lou."

"Annie means less to Dad than Princess Bunny means to Teddy here," Alexis spat. "Lauren has his heart. Always will. It doesn't matter whether they're together or not." Her voice zeroed in on shrill.

I waved off Biancho's interruption before he could open his mouth. "So tell me about it," I invited. "Tell me why you tried to poison them out of the house."

"The furnace was a fucking accident. What isn't an accident is what's happening to my father. He doesn't sleep, barely eats, spends enormous amounts of time with Mom's mother. I'm really worried about him, don't you understand? If Lauren's romance lasts, the least he deserves is the one place he truly thinks of as home."

"Anne might have something to say about what's home and

what isn't," I jabbed, but my sense of foreboding was beginning to grow.

"For Christ sake, back off! Don't you see how upset she is?" Biancho snapped. He led Alexis to her seat, and gently helped her down. Alexis's heart did belong to Daddy.

"Damn right, I'm upset. His fucking father-in-law is moving in!"

Biancho placed his hand on her shoulder and began to lightly squeeze. Maybe he still thought there was a chance to salvage. Or maybe he just had to play out his role.

But I had to keep probing. Paul and Lauren's relationship was back on Red Alert. "Okay, Alexis, I got it. Daddy's having trouble dealing with Lauren and Lou so you want to make sure he gets the Hacienda."

"He's the only one who puts any effort into the place. Why should Lou prance in and reap the rewards? If Dad can't have what he really wants, I'll make sure he gets something."

"And what is it he really wants, Alexis?"

"His wife. His wife!"

"His ex-wife. And your grandmother? How does she fit into this?"

"Until I understood what Lauren did to him, Vivian was the only person who did. She knows what my mother means to him."

"You keep talking in generalities, Alexis."

"What are you after, Jacob?" Biancho protested. "Either you believe her about the wire or you don't. I can't see forcing her to talk about the family."

"It's our family, Chief. Lauren and Lou are getting married as soon as her divorce is final. I want to know what I'm getting."

"Are you sure?" Alexis asked wild-eyed.

I nodded.

Her face seemed to shatter. "You want to know what you're getting? Someone who turned her children against their father.

Someone who blames my father for Stephen's homosexuality and Ian's self-destructive behavior. If that's not enough go ask Lauren! She'll be happy to tell you what you're getting!"

Time to reel her in. "So you want your dad to have a fair shake and you figure the Hacienda is it. Does he agree with you?"

"He doesn't know anything about any of this."

I glanced at Biancho who had returned to his seat. "I don't know *what* Brown thinks," he shrugged.

"Enough already," Alexis complained wearily. "You've solved all your little mysteries."

I didn't know what I'd solved. "It's difficult to believe your father has nothing to do with your scheming, Alexis. He's the one to score." Julie's words rang in my ears: "*Cherchez le cash.*"

Her fatigue flared into instant anger. "My father wouldn't lift a finger to drive Lauren out. He's somebody who keeps everything inside. He sometimes does stupid things but..."

"What stupid things?

She was too deep into her rap to hesitate. "Annie. He didn't have to live with that bitch. But he felt bad about what happened with Jim."

"Jim?"

"Her husband."

"Aren't we stretching here, Jacob?" Biancho snorted. "You're not joining *that* family."

"No, Teddy," Alexis shook off his intervention. "I want him to know the kind of person Dad is. It was Lauren's affair with Jim Heywood that ruined both marriages. Something else you can ask her about."

I'd managed to outstay my comfort zone. Alexis had kicked open a door I wanted shut. "Your dad's living with Annie because he wants revenge for Lauren's affair with her husband?"

I felt the revulsion rise in my throat. Lauren and her "overlapped family" were the incarnation of my worst nightmares. If I didn't bring this scene to a quick close, my personal phobias would shift into overdrive, disintegrating the fragile accommodations I'd made for Lou and Lauren, for me and Boots. Whatever small corner I'd been able to turn was suddenly turning back; it was time to find my way out the door.

CHAPTER 46

But not before one last shot at the Police Chief. My close encounters of the Clifford kind still rankled me. Besides, I needed something to purge my rancid reaction to Alexis's rendition of the Rowe/Brown saga. "So I was right about your job—'serve aAnd Protect.'

"What do you want, Jacob? A letter of resignation?"

"I'll settle for an apology."

"I'm sorry about involving Washington Clifford. But I'm not going to apologize for protecting Alexis. If I had to do it again, I'd probably do the same fucking thing."

"Got you by the shorthairs, doesn't she?"

Teddy shrugged.

"Teddy can't help himself," Alexis's breathing slowed as she found her way into a familiar groove.

"Love, Alexis," Biancho said. "A word that never crosses your lips. You never use that word." The Chief shook his head. "I thought my marriage would finally free me, but I never should have returned."

Biancho's mouth twisted. "It's ironic Jacob, you got involved because you love someone, and I kept chasing you away for the same damn reason."

"I'd call what you've got a 'jones,'" I said, preparing to leave.

Biancho rose from his seat but Alexis didn't even glance up, her mind far away.

"I haven't exactly covered myself with glory," he said. "but I'm a better cop than you have reason to believe."

"I'll tell you something," I said waking toward the door as a conversation with Lou slapped me upside the head. "If love is your disease, it can make you do right or do wrong. And you've been doing wrong. Both of you."

I sat in the dark sedan and lit a cigarette and a joint. Mr. Bluebird still wasn't perched on my shoulder and nothing was particularly "satisfactual."

And hadn't changed by the time Alexis and Biancho left her office. He stepped close to her but she roughly shoved him away. The Chief shook his head despairingly and started down the block. Alexis scrambled into her Saab and gunned the car off the curb. Without returning his weak wave.

Their farewell shook me out of my stuck. Goosed about the case, but once again bummed about close relationships. One for two. Probably the wrong one.

But the right time for that conversation with Paul Brown.

It was pretty late and Anne wasn't very pleased to see me. "Paul's not here and I don't know when to expect him," she said peering over a door-chain, her eyes baggy and bloodshot, her spearmint breath a poor hide for the booze.

"I'm not here to see Paul," I said in a moment of professional, or perhaps sleazy, inspiration.

Anne's head was already shaking before I finished. "Our last little talk didn't help my home life." No slur to her words, but the cadence was off.

I nodded. "Heather told me. I didn't mean to complicate things."

Anne's face softened at the mention of her daughter, but the latch remained on the door.

"She said I cause trouble wherever I go," I admitted.

"Heather exaggerates." She unhooked the chain, but held her ground. "Why do you want to talk to me?"

I took a deep breath. "I don't know who else to turn to,"

"Let me guess, you want to talk about Paul. Well, come inside. We can't discuss him on the porch."

Anne led me to the room where we'd talked the last time. Everything but her slight stumble was the same, including the tilt to Heather's picture.

"Do you want something to drink?"

"A beer and ashtray would be great. Do you know when Paul will be home?"

"No," she called from another room, "but it will be late. It always is these days." She returned carrying a slanted tray with a couple of Sam Adams, a bottle of Jack Daniel's, a glass, and the same shell ashtray. "I have plenty of time to bum your cigarettes."

"Help yourself," I said, placing the pack and lighter between us, ripping my eyes off the whiskey.

"So you're still worried about your father-in-law and Lauren?" Anne asked after we'd lit up and settled in.

"I'm not comfortable with it," I said. "Especially when I keep hearing different pieces of her family history."

"I'm not the person to put your mind at rest."

"Well, I suppose I'll have to get used to it since they're going to be together."

"This is not the first time I've heard about it." Anne sighed, but almost looked relieved.

She took a long sip of Jack. "I'm the last to learn about anything. It's always been that way," she said without looking up. "When Jim and I moved up here, the town was even more exclusive than it is now. We were lonely and isolated. I was pregnant with Heather and the move was a real disaster until we met the Browns."

"When was this?" I asked, though I hadn't come here for history.

"Seventy something. Too long ago to remember."

"During which of Lauren's lifestyles?"

Anne chuckled. "It's hard to keep track. She's been in everything that even smelled "alternative." But our trouble didn't start until she got into open marriages." The humor left her face.

"Lauren was my hero. Fearless, powerful. But no matter how much I worshipped her, Jim always came first. For Lauren as well." Anne paused.

"There was an undercurrent of sexuality between everyone," she admitted. "At least after I gave birth to Heather," she added, averting my eyes.

"Lauren and Jim got together while you were pregnant, didn't they?" I asked softly. The faster I got through the past, the closer I'd be to the present.

Anne nodded, "Told you I was always the last to know. I didn't find *that* out until Paul and I started living together. He thought I knew." She bottomed up and drizzled another couple of fingers worth into her glass.

"What makes it worse was how kind Lauren had been during my pregnancy. It's sick, but I still don't believe it was totally bullshit." Anne shook her head. "Even sicker, I still don't hate her."

"So you understand my mixed feelings," I said.

"Of course."

Anne was talking because she was closing in on drunk.

And wanted to get there. She sipped from her glass. "After Heather was born we moved into the Hacienda. Caring for the babies together was much easier. For a long time the living arrangement was fun."

"But the air went out of the balloon?"

"Control issues. Jim and I, especially me, always did what Lauren and Paul wanted. What Lauren wanted, really."

"But it was the open marriage that blew you and Jim apart?" It had been a half open marriage that had ruined my first. My first wife Megan's half.

"Experimenting with sex masked everything. For a while it was pretty exciting. I'd never slept with anyone but Jim, and Paul seemed so experienced."

"You didn't feel threatened?" I asked, thinking about myself. "Jealous?"

"Not at first. Lauren was almost ten years older than Jim and pretty wild looking. Sunburst hairdo, weird makeup, and tied-dyed tee shirts. I thought their sex trip was an extension of friendship, like mine with Paul. I actually imagined that Lauren and I were much closer than we were with our husbands.

"It's hard to believe how long it took me to catch on. I was devastated when I finally realized they'd fallen in love."

"Sometimes it takes a while for reality to sink in," I said. Again, I couldn't help thinking about my own rationalizations about Megan.

"I thought she and I talked about everything with each other."

Anne took a deep breath, poured more bourbon into her glass, and snagged another cigarette. "As badly as it turned out, those were exciting years. And to be honest, most of the excitement was generated by Lauren."

Her voice dropped, "But so was the pain. Jim was so damn blind he didn't believe we had problems. He thought I was captive to my "bourgeois" background. For the longest time I agreed with him. The solution wasn't to stop the experiment, but to "overcome the contradictions." By the time we realized we weren't going to overcome a goddamn thing, it was too late."

Anne took a deep slug. "Too late for everything but another fucked up marriage."

"Where was Paul in all this?"

"Let me quote: 'The way to keep a butterfly on your shoulder is to let it leave. Once the butterfly realizes it's truly free, there's no need for it to depart.'"

"He was mistaken?"

"About butterflies, but not himself. Paul was the same then as he is now. Lauren never made a move to keep him, and he never left."

Anne swiped another cigarette and puffed thoughtfully, not yet ready to return to the now. "When it became clear the situation was totally out of control, my family moved out."

"But it didn't help?"

"Jim and Lauren never stopped fucking," Anne said bluntly. "Our move was supposed to give the "friendships" an opportunity to heal. Believe it or not, I wanted everything back the way it used to be."

"You didn't have any trouble breaking off your sexual relationship with Paul?"

"Not really. Paul had been a radical departure from the rest of my entire life; anyhow, sex between us was nothing terrific. I thought the trouble was me. At least that's what I thought then," she added sourly. "I was naive and stupid."

"You were inexperienced."

"And you are tactful," she smiled crookedly. Anne pulled her hands apart, then seemed confused about what to do with them. "You have to understand, we're talking years to wipe the bloom from this rose," she said, covering her sudden embarrassment.

"But you stayed with Paul." It had taken a while but we were finally where I wanted us. Wasn't sure what I was searching for, but I'd know when it showed.

"Our relationship deepened when Lauren deserted the Hacienda. She never said a word, just disappeared leaving a note that she couldn't stand living in a nuclear family. To be fair, she stayed in touch with the kids which is more than you can say about Heather's father."

"What happened to him?"

"When Lauren disappeared he hung around for a while then left the country. I haven't heard from him since. That woman breaks a lot of hearts."

"That's when you and Paul linked up again romantically?"

"Romance has never been a part of our relationship. When Lauren left, Paul wanted more than a friendship, but I was frightened I'd be abandoned the moment she returned. We didn't sleep together until Lauren came back and kicked Paul out. Sounds like a soap opera, doesn't it?"

"Sounds like a lot of people who didn't have their shit together. There are a lot of us like that."

"Some people never get it together."

I smiled, "Are you talking about Lauren or Paul?" Or me, I wondered, losing the smile.

"Mostly about myself. And Paul."

"You know which end is up."

"Knowing isn't doing. I should have left the moment I understood what makes Paul tick. I still should, but ending up on the meat market at my age is more than I can handle."

"What *does* make him tick?" I asked after a short draw on my beer.

Her eyes flashed with pain and anger. "Lauren Rowe. Always has, always will. Time hasn't changed a damn thing. The moment it became clear that Lauren's relationship with Lou was unlike any she'd had before, all hell broke loose."

I nodded my agreement. "The kids were shattered."

"And it's been even worse for Paul."

CHAPTER 47

Winning number, aching gut. I'd found what I was looking for.

"Once Paul understood how serious Lauren and Lou were, I thought he'd finally let go. Sorry, stupid me again." Anne unsuccessfully tried to bury her anger. "Paul's more withdrawn and even tighter about money. Now he's barely around."

"Where does he go?"

"I thought the bastard was putting in overtime. Turns out he's playing Mr. Fix-it at the goddamn Hacienda. The rest of the time he's with Vivian. He visits her after work, comes home for dinner, then goes back to watch television. And sometimes he just vanishes."

"Why does he spend time with Vivian?"

"He *says* he feels compelled to look after her, it's Lauren's mother, after all. But it's a load of shit. I think the two of them just sit around feeling unappreciated." Anne shook her head with disgust. "Mr. Goodguy, that's my Paul, as long as it's a female Rowe or Brown and not a Heywood."

She heard her self-pity because she reached for the bottle. "You sure you don't want any?"

"No thanks," I lied.

She took another gulp. "Did Heather tell you much about the fight after your last visit?"

"Just that it had to do with the divorce."

"When I confronted Paul he told me it was only a technicality. I asked him whether he understood that Lauren was planning to get married. Asked him if that meant he would finally spend time working on *our* house instead of the Hacienda. Fix *our* roof, clean out *our* basement, weather-strip *our* windows. Spend some goddamn time with me. If Lauren marries Lou, my significant other is out of a fucking job!"

Anne reached for another cigarette. "I have to give him credit, the son of a bitch stayed calm. I thought scaring him about Lauren's marriage would shake him."

"But it didn't?"

"He told me if Lauren married Lou nothing would change." Anne shivered as if she just felt a chill. "He backed off that one fast. Maybe he saw the look on my face."

I watched her spill more liquor into her glass and onto the table. Paul's response to the divorce, his access to the Hacienda, his unexplained absences: All of it opened a door. And a dark suspicion was walking through.

"Anne," I asked calmly, doubling back, "I know Paul stopped giving Lauren money months ago, but you say he's still tight."

She placed her glass on the table with controlled care. "Lauren's lying, or Paul's been lying to me." She took a long inhale but the cigarette had died and she halfheartedly tossed it toward the ashtray. "I don't think it's him. Paul lies to himself, not to other people."

"You still care about him, don't you?" I asked. My intensity was heating but tried to hide it. I'd just hit the curve in the road.

"I honestly don't know what I feel. I became an adult with Paul and that's impossible to write off." Anne shrugged. "Truth is, we're alike. Both of us are willing to go wherever the river leads." She paused. "For Paul the river is Lauren and for me it's Paul. I've been so angry these past months, it's hard to admit how worried I am about him. He really has been acting strange."

A bleak despair permeated the small room and it seemed right at home. The shamus in me tried to wriggle out from under the gloom. Anne wasn't the only person hauling history. If I let it, this conversation would land me back on my couch.

But I couldn't let it. I had a father-in-law to protect. If Lauren had been lying about the money and was still tied to Paul, what were her real reasons for being with Lou? Maybe Rowe and Brown weren't as separated as Lauren wanted me—and everyone else—to believe. Maybe they weren't really separated at all.

Cherchez le cash. It might be cynical, but I was wondering whether Paul and Lauren had a scheme to separate Lou from his money. A scheme using Lauren's stalking claims to create an explanation if something happened to Lou—like a furnace accident. I was suddenly angry I'd never asked Lou whether he'd added her to his frigging will.

I felt my distrust of Lauren combine with all of my own baggage about relationships and deceit. The combination was lethal and I knew it, but I'd be damned if I was going to let Lou, at this stage of *his* life, walk a possible plank.

Anne leaned toward the table so I held out the pack of smokes. But she ignored the cigarettes and reached for my hand. "You've been kind to listen to all this," she said, her fingers stroking my palm.

I tried to find a polite way to free myself. "You need more friends," I said standing and helping her to her feet. "You're locked into a very small circle. It would help having people to talk to."

She walked around the table and leaned her thin body into

mine. "Right now I don't want to talk," she whispered, the Jack Daniels washing my face. Tonight she had a different river pulling her downstream.

"You need a less incestuous world, not a new addition," I said stepping back.

Anne's mouth twisted into a sardonic smile. "You're not interested in a loser." There was no heat to her words, just drunken resignation.

"No law says you have to keep losing, Anne."

"Are you kidding? No one gets out of this. Look at Paul, me, the children, Lou. Look at yourself."

"Jim got away."

Anne reached down to the table for the cigarettes, wobbled, pulled three, and handed me the pack. "Jim doesn't even speak to his own daughter because he's unable to face an entire portion of his life. You call that getting away? We all live in one big web. And Lauren is the spider."

CHAPTER 48

auren and Paul or just Paul? There was only one way to find out—and it wasn't through confronting Lauren while she was spending the night with Lou. But I'd run out of kid gloves and all my passivity. The weeks of emotional flip-flops had come down to right now. Lauren and Paul or just Paul. I was sick of maybes.

Vivian Rowe's apartment was located in what the billboard proudly dubbed a Senior Citizen Housing Community. The project resembled any other townhouse complex, though the grounds were shabby and bathed in yellow crime lights. The sign had neglected to add "Low Income" to its proclamation.

It took two impatient drive-arounds through the sprawling low-rise community before I located Vivian's vinyl clapboard two-story. At least I'd remembered to bring my list of addresses along with the gun.

But when I pulled to a stop it looked as if I'd have no use for either. Vivian lived on the ground floor and the apartment appeared pitch black. Maybe Anne had it wrong—or maybe Paul had already left for home.

I quickly toked off a joint before I decided to wake the old lady. And was relieved to hear a gravel voiced invite when I rang her doorbell.

I stopped as soon as I entered her apartment, my eyes struggling to adjust to the strange light. Vivian lived in a studio with only a freestanding screen separating her sloppy bedroom and sloppier living area. A half dozen end tables were scattered through the larger section, all of them loaded with framed black-and-whites of the same woman. The "bedroom" had mounds of clothes strewn about, as if different ensembles had been tried and rejected. When my eyes grew accustomed to the crime light's yellow stripes filtering through the Venetian blinds, I saw that all the walls were decorated with photographs. The pictures presented Vivian from early childhood to her mid-thirties. There were none of anyone else.

Shunted off in a corner of the living area sat a tired, twelve inch TV. If, as Anne claimed, Paul came here to watch television, it wasn't for his viewing pleasure. In any event, he wasn't watching now.

"Why you're not Paulie," Vivian said without surprise or fear from the shadows next to the Formica table. "Much, much too big. Paulie doesn't take up that much space," she said, sounding delighted.

"I'm Matt Jacob, Mrs. Rowe. We met at Lauren's party a couple weeks ago. I'm Lou's son-in-law."

"Come closer, boy, so I can see how that large body moves."

The squat figure sitting just outside the small stripes of light made a noise that sounded like a throaty purr. "It's turned into quite an evening, two men calling."

Vivian paused to catch her breath. "I said come closer," she ordered. "I simply will not wear glasses when a gentleman visits."

Vivian didn't bother with too many clothes when a gentleman came calling either. She sat on a red padded kitchen chair dressed only in a gigantic black underwired bra and a frayed black half-slip. Her wrinkled stomach protruded and her button winked a greeting. Regrettably, she made no move to cover herself. Didn't matter, I found myself staring at her hair which hung halfway to the kitchen floor. Apparently, Vivian liked trying out different colors on different sections. Maybe she was trying to keep up with today's styles, an eyebrow or belly ring next on the list.

The gray-flecked table was crowded with a pack of Lucky Strikes, a deep ashtray full of bright red, lipstick stained butts, a really old table radio, an assortment of hairbrushes, and cigarette scorch marks. I also noticed a half empty gin bottle and two drinking glasses—one half full, the other dry and empty.

Vivian held a freshly lit Lucky in one hand and a long-handled mirror in the other. She was clearly torn between me and the mirror. "You're here early," she accused. "Well, there's not much I can do about it now. Pull up a chair, but don't even think about naughty before we go out. This is one lady you have to feed."

Vivian put down the mirror, stubbed out her smoke, and reached for one of the brushes. "I have to finish with my hair."

I suddenly remembered Vivian's problems with reality when she didn't eat her meds. Paul's absence and Vivian's half deck slashed any hope for a quick conclusion. Fuck it, bye and back to the car.

But before I made my excuse, she spoke in a completely different rhythm. "So you're Lou's son, are you? I've a lot to say about that scoundrel father of yours. Be a good boy and hand me that robe?"

So much for an easy out. Vivian took the aged terrycloth, though instead of slipping it on, she placed it carefully beside her and went back to brushing her wild hair. "I'm too tired to move," she complained. "Should be asleep but Paulie is going to need me." Vivian's hand fumbled as she placed a new, unlit cigarette between her painted lips.

"Light?" I asked, leaning toward her, forcing myself to look at her garish face while I lit her smoke. Tilting back in my seat I lit one of my own.

"A real gentleman you are. Too bad your father isn't more like his son."

"Actually my father-in-law is the real gentleman."

"A gentleman doesn't steal another man's wife or filch his property."

Vivian puffed hard on her filter-less smoke, every so often spitting tiny shreds of tobacco behind her hand. "At least these have some goddamn taste," she said, the earlier singsong springing back. "But they burn your tongue and force you to act unladylike. That's why I rarely smoke outside."

She finished the gin in her glass. "You might have offered to pour some more," she accused, then softened. "I suppose if you're sitting here while I'm half naked, we're past polite."

Vivian took a deep drink, staring at me as though I was out of focus. "Were we good together?" She suddenly grabbed the mirror and watched herself slowly, sensually, French inhale.

I glanced at the nearest wall. It was almost impossible to believe this bat shit crazy lady with her multi-colored hair had ever been that young, attractive child and woman.

"You never answered me," Vivian said, the cigarette out and the mirror back down on the table.

"You were telling me about Paul," I said.

"No, I was bitching about your father. Don't worry, I don't blame sins of the father on the son. Or, as I tell Paulie, sins of the daughter on her mother. I'll never understand why he hangs on so."

"Lauren and Paul are separated," I said quickly. If I peppered, maybe I could keep her eyes away from the fucking mirror.

"Paulie thinks my daughter will come to her senses."

Vivian snorted, her voice rising. "That child has never been sensible about anything! She's tormented me my entire life, cock-teased a good man into marrying her, then destroyed their lives. Destroyed their children."

Vivian frowned into her drink. "Let her blame me all she wants, I never had her advantages. I never had a father for my child, someone to work for me while I sat on my ass."

Vivian lifted the mirror and jerked it harshly as if trying to shake her ghastly reflection into a different image. "The past is the past, that's what I tell him. But he just won't listen. Well, tonight I think he'll listen."

"Tonight?" I asked, flashing on Lauren's odd mood during our last discussion about her family.

Vivian smiled sadly, "I'll be here for him to cry on. Where else can he go? Who else can he talk to? That mousy live-in will just get angry."

I was listening to the drunken ravings of a crazy old lady, but was Vivian's madness hers alone? "Do you expect Paul tonight? It's pretty late."

"Not too late for you to be here, is it?" Vivian's smile deepened her powdered and rouged wrinkles. "Paulie thinks everything will turn out the way he wants. But I know better, I always have."

Sometimes the shortest distance between two points has little to do with straight lines. "Lauren's relationship with Lou must have hit him pretty hard," I said calmly, fighting a fresh rush of concern. Lauren and Paul were rapidly turning into just Paul. Some fucking Sherlock. Watson wasn't gonna write this one up. I instinctively reached for the nearby gin bottle, caressed it with my fingers, then jerked my hand away. No need to compound my stupidity.

"Lauren brushed him aside like so much garbage." Vivian was watching herself blow thick smoke rings. "I always drove men crazy, but I was never mean. I let them down gently."

I didn't want to hear about her men. "Has Paul been spying on Lauren?"

ZACHARY KLEIN

Vivian dropped the mirror onto the table and yanked at her patchwork hair. "He's been protecting her. They're only separated, that's all. She had no business falling in love with your father. The man is so old he's half dead." Vivian was almost panting. "After everything she's done to him, Paulie still wants her back."

"Paul believes that Lauren will go back to him after all this time?"

"I've kept Lauren's father waiting a helluva lot longer," Vivian cackled, stroking then lifting the mirror. "There's been nights I almost let him return, but I'm strong. Paulie is different, a kind and forgiving man. Joe Rowe would as soon slap your face than listen to you." She stared into the chipped glass, "To love is to forgive, to hate is to remember."

"You think Paul and Lauren are meeting tonight?" I asked, my concern turning into anxious horror.

"I'm sure of it. They were planning to meet at the Hacienda. Paulie's chair was still warm when you took it."

When Vivian realized I was leaving, she said she'd be dressed in a flash and we'd party the night away. She flew to the bedroom continuing her desperate chatter as she dropped to the floor and ripped through the piles of clothes. She finally stood, holding a fifties velvet evening dress in front of her, cursing as the door slammed shut.

I didn't bother to call. Instead, I gunned the sedan toward the Hacienda. Call it *vibes*. Bad vibes.

And they got no better when I squealed to a stop in front of the big old house. Like Vivian's, the place appeared deserted. But when I ran up the front stairs serenaded by the ocean slapping against the rocky shore, I spotted a low-power lamp in the cluttered room behind the bays. I let myself inside the unlocked door, rushed into the sitting room, and felt something shatter across my head.

315

CHAPTER 49

I awoke to Elvis singing *Fools Rush In*, blood matting my hair and Paul Brown sitting cross-legged on the floor cradling Lauren Rowe's head. The rest of her inert body was on its side, stretched between us.

Paul aimed a gun—my gun—at me as soon as I sat up. His eyes were glazed, his teeth bared. No silver fox now; he looked like a mean wolf.

"What happened?" I asked, fighting to keep calm, picking bloodstained pieces of a vase from my hair.

"She won't breathe," he said as if insulted. Carefully he rolled Lauren onto her back.

"Maybe we ought to call the hospital?" I suggested, though I knew it was useless. My controlled calm plunged into a cold numbness. Strangulation marks were still visible on Lauren's white throat.

"It's too late," he whispered hoarsely, "too late for everything."

"Not to give me my gun," I said tonelessly. I'd been too stupid for too long, and it had cost Lauren her life.

He stared straight through me; gave no sign that he'd even heard me. "I came here expecting so much," he complained. "She sounded so friendly on the phone. Her voice was happy. I felt full of promise."

He kept the gun trained on my body but rested his free hand on her arm and petted her skin. "What was I supposed to think?" he asked.

"I think you ought to give me my gun. If we hurry, we might have time to get her help." Yeah, time for an autopsy. Fuck me and all my crazy about Lauren and close relationships. It cost her her life.

"You're talking about time? Our hair was black when we met, now look at us. So damn much time and you want more? For what?" he demanded. "The fat man?"

As I thought of Lou, Lauren's death, all its implications started slicing through my helpless rage.

Paul pulled Lauren's body up a little higher, onto his legs, holding her possessively. "She used to make fun of fat people, said they had no control. But there she was with this guy," he said, waving my gun.

I cringed, wondering if I'd get out of this alive. Knowing the only way that was gonna happen is if I talked my way past this stupor. "Must have been hard," I said, "waiting all these years."

Paul kept waving my gun, and I grit my teeth to keep from scrambling. "I never left," he insisted. "It didn't matter where we lived, who we were with. We were always one with each other." He looked down at her, smiled tenderly, and stroked her thick hair.

I felt my skin crawl. "Until Lou came along." I wasn't sure whether I was playing chickie or searching for a crack in *his* crazy.

"She was different with him," Paul said. "I always knew it was in her, always wanted to give her a chance to flower."

"Only she flowered with Lou, not you."

He squeezed Lauren's shoulder. Hard. "I'd be working on the

Hacienda and hear them laughing. When they left together, I'd follow. You know what got to me?"

"What?" I asked, sliding forward until my sneakers touched Lauren's shoes, hoping he was too distracted to notice

"They held hands," he said despairingly. "Whenever I tried to hold her hand she'd refuse. It feels *claustrophobic*," he mimicked, tossing his head, his hand snaking down to clasp hers.

"You didn't stop with the occasional follow, did you?" He was getting more and more upset, but his grip on the fucking gun was steady. I wanted to keep him talking while I looked for some sort of opportunity. Opportunity for what? There was no opportunity left for Lou, no opportunity for Lauren. But Lauren's cold body didn't matter to Paul—death didn't do them part.

"Sometimes, watching them was almost enjoyable. Lauren was blossoming, and I knew it was only a matter of time before we'd be back together," he said.

"You mean a matter of time until you murdered her."

He looked confused. "You never murder someone you love." He let go of her fingers and ran his hand across her breasts.

His obsessive pawing was weirding me out. "I get it, you killed her with kindness."

He glanced at me with the first hint of anger shining through his cloudy eyes. "She took him to the cliffs. Our cliffs. He couldn't make it to the ridge, so they only went out a little way. I'd sit and watch them from the woods."

"That made your blood boil, didn't it? This man sitting on *your* rocks, taking *your* place, with *your* woman while you hid in the woods."

Paul's eyes gleamed as he shook his head. "Patience."

For a moment I thought he was warning me.

"I have patience," he continued, "there was no need for anger."

He might have patience, but I was losing mine. My headache was starting to recede, my self-loathing quieting. I wanted out, and I wanted to bring this motherfucking murderer with me. "You stopped following them for a while," I said.

"You," he said pointing the gun. "When I heard that Lauren asked you to help, it worried me." Again he drew his lips across his teeth. "A blessing in disguise; it gave me time to think. When she called it "stalking" I knew I was finally having an effect."

"Scaring the shit out of her was one hell of an effect."

He bent down from his seat on the floor and gently kissed Lauren's forehead. But he lifted his head too quickly for me to do anything but prop myself up with the palms of my hand. "I was sending her all my feelings, all my love," he said with a pleased expression.

Lauren had promised to listen to me, had promised to stay with Lou. But she hadn't. Lauren never fucking listened to anyone, always did what she wanted. I heard my own 'blame the victim' and shook it out of my head. It was time to shift gears. If Paul remained in his delusions, I'd be dead without him even realizing he killed me. "You loved her so much you tried to murder her in her sleep, poison her."

He frowned, "You're talking about the furnace. Yes, I was upset about the divorce but that had nothing to do with the furnace. Alexis needed to sell the Hacienda. I'm sure she owes that Shylock of hers money. I wasn't trying to hurt anyone. I just wanted Lauren to sell the house!"

Daughter helping Daddy, Daddy helping daughter. One big, happy murder.

Paul's eyes blinked rapidly, drops of spit gathering at the corners of his mouth. When he spoke it was directed to Lauren. "Even after I stopped giving you money, I put it away for us."

Paul caressed Lauren's cheek, running his fingers lightly over her parted lips. "I love you, I'll always love you."

I pushed past my disgust and clubbed him with words. "You're one sick fuck, Paul. You've never loved anything but yourself and power. That's why you stopped giving Lauren money, why you went back to stalking. You loved the power it gave you, the power to frighten her."

"No," he protested, his calm finally starting to crumble.

"That's what floats your boat," I barked. "You want 'em scared. Or you want 'em dependent like Anne. You love the power, Paul, not the person."

Paul's hand moved to her upper arm. "You make it sound simple, but it isn't."

"Bullshit! Lauren wanted a divorce and you made her pay. Made her pay for all those wasted years you played house with Anne while you waited. Only Lauren wasn't coming home and all your waiting wasn't gonna matter."

He rubbed his forehead with the trembling gun. "No matter where I really wanted to be and who I wanted to be with, I helped Anne heal a broken heart."

"Man-Of-The-Year," I said snorting. "All that patience for nothing. All that good housekeeping for nothing. All that time for nothing. So when Lauren told you about the divorce you decided to kill her. If you couldn't have her, no one would, right!"

"I never thought about killing her, " sweat staining his madras shirt.

"Then why isn't she breathing, Paul? Why is she lying in your fucking lap branded with your fucking finger marks?" I sat completely still while he looked down and stared at Lauren's lifeless eyes.

"It just happened," he murmured, his eyes widening with rage. "It was the same our entire life. Things just happened. One after another. No matter what I did or what I tried, things just happened."

His hand—and the gun in it—started to shake.

He glared down at Lauren. "You told me the old man was moving in. You told me to stop coming by, you didn't need a handyman. What was I supposed to do, walk away? I wasn't even working on the Hacienda for you. I was doing it for Alexis."

"Alexis, Anne, Lauren, Vivian" I spat, "you were helping 'em all! What about Stephen? Or Ian? Were you helping them too?"

He acted like he'd been asked a different question, from a different person: The dead one in his lap. "You didn't mind Allie being mine as long as the boys were yours," he said. "But you never expected them to despise me. I don't blame you for that."

Paul suddenly pushed her head, dangling it over the side of his thigh, his eyes blazing. I tensed, thinking he was finally going to shoot. He glared at me but kept speaking to Lauren. "You let that old man take care of you and taking care of you was all I ever wanted!"

He paused, his hand coming to a full stop on Lauren's shoulder. "That's why I couldn't understand what you were talking about," he said, his voice cracking, a violent convulsion rocking his body. "Your words didn't make sense," he shouted, shaking his dearly departed. "But you wouldn't stop, you wouldn't listen. You just kept saying the same thing over and over again."

Before I realized it, his large hand was around Lauren's neck. "You were going to marry Lou, you were going to fucking marry Lou..."

I leapt head first over Lauren's body, heard a shot, then listened to Paul shriek as a bullet grazed his leg. I grabbed the gun and slammed him on the side of his head. Slammed him again, this time knocking him unconscious. But *still* had to pry his fingers from Lauren's throat.

CHAPTER 50

The funeral was a continuation of the nightmare. Not even called a funeral, the *"Rite of Passage,"* as Ian demanded was held on the wooden deck of the Hacienda and at the rocky edge of the ocean. Closed to the public.

The day was early fall chilly, but not nearly as frigid as the small cluster of gatherers. Heather, Stephen, and Jayson, whose ghostly attendance surprised me, hung together. Alexis stood by herself in a corner, her arms folded. Vivian and Anne didn't bother to show. One deck, one urn, and two mourners with portable oxygen tanks. One killer in prison.

Ian, sober and straight, was the only one who expressed any outward emotion. He stood next to the small wooden table and regularly burst into tears, his hand trembling as it touched the engraved silver container holding his mother's ashes.

Every once in a while, Teddy Biancho approached Alexis, but she shrugged him off. She'd meant it when she told him he was out of her life. Whatever else Alexis might have felt, she acted more interested in the rotting gutters than in the service for her mother.

Sweet kid. Made it easy to lose any guilt I still harbored. I'd seen only one split in her skin. When I arrived on the deck with Boots and Lou, Alexis's eyes glittered with deep hate. I'd done Dad.

I stood in the Lou and Boots circle, but we weren't doing much talking. At first Lou had absorbed the news of Lauren's murder stoically, with no signs of a physical relapse. But as the days passed he descended into a bottomless depression. Boots was the only person able to reach him. I wouldn't say his despair lifted when she was around, but at least he'd talk.

While Boots helped draw Lou out, her presence drove me deeper into my own version of hell. I was haunted by my incompetence. My inability and stupidity to prevent Lauren's death, my responsibility for its effect upon Lou. Each and every time I'd aimed my hostile glare in Lauren's direction I'd been wrong. But I'd kept on glaring because she and Lou had threatened a frightened, confused place in me. And now Lauren was dead and so was part of Lou. And more than likely a part of me.

Paul Brown's strangle had breathed full life into my pessimism about the fine line between love and hate. About the invisibility of that line to those who danced along its edge. Breathed life into the recognition that I was a dancer.

Lauren's murder overwhelmed me with hopelessness every time I thought about the ties between her and her husband. Until she fell in love with Lou, Lauren had held onto Paul as he had clung to her. Not as tight, and certainly without delusions. But Lauren hadn't really let go until near the end. Their neurotic interlock represented my bleakest vision of family—and its result was shredding every other image out of my system.

I even doubted my memories of Chana and my fantasies about *our* family. Skeptical that the pictures in my mind of Becky growing up, of growing old with Chana, could have developed in life as they had in my imagination. Why *should* I believe them? I'd never seen a family like the one I'd been carrying inside.

The minister urged us to leave the Hacienda's deck and head toward the water. Ian led the cortege, holding tightly to the urn. Alexis refused to walk with Biancho, Boots helped Lou, and I lent Jayson a hand. Stephen started to protest but Heather quieted him down. Eventually, the whole motley crew stood at the water's edge.

The minister talked about Lauren as a minister friend would. She talked about Lauren's confidence, path-cutting, risk-taking, assertiveness, and commitment to living a complete life. She spoke of Lauren's politics, social conscience, and her self-reliance.

The minister left out a lot, but it was probably better that way. When she asked if anyone had something to add there was only silence. A silence broken only by Ian's quiet tears. "Can I spread her ashes?" he asked plaintively.

A few nights later Lou and I still weren't doing much talking, though we spent a lot of television time in my apartment. Lou continued his intermittent use of the oxygen mask. He was also smoking my dope. Despite the threat to his health, I didn't have the heart to stop him, or the strength to stop myself. At least he hadn't blamed me for Lauren's death. He didn't have to, and I think he knew it.

Boots was in and out but unable to splinter the thick desperation. And although she and I were able to talk, our conversations were strained. But Boots being Boots knew better than to push. Wrong time, wrong place. Lou had found something he'd been looking for, lost it, and with his loss my hopes had gone missing as well. I'd thought my masochistic cheat with Alexis had been a perverse reflection of my fear to commit. A fear I thought I was close to overcoming. Now when I looked back, my inability to come seemed closer to the truth.

When the telephone rang, we were sitting in the dark watching Arthur Miller's *A View From The Bridge* with subtitles. We should have switched stations but neither of us bothered.

The telephone continued to ring until Lou finally grunted. "Aren't you going to answer that? It's probably Boots."

I wanted to, I really did. Instead, I reached for the bourbon. "I know."

About the Author

Zachary Klein is the author of *Still Among the Living* (a *New York Times* notable book), *Two Way Toll*, and *No Saving Grace*. He is a founder of the People's School in Uptown Chicago, a school for high school dropouts. He also worked at Boston's Project Place, a worker-run social service collective that provided free crisis intervention and other community services. Klein spent fifteen years as a trial and jury consultant for local and national law firms.

Visit him at www.zacharykleinonline.com
or on Twitter at @zach_klein.